"I DREAMED OF THIS."

Her voice was faint, barely above a whisper, but easily heard in the stillness of the valley.

"Not a nightmare." Michael was not surprised. She'd already proved herself susceptible to the lure of his native land.

"No."

The misty air turned thick. Somewhere in the winter-barren trees a lone bird called out; a heron rose from the reeds at the edge of Lough Caislean; a black swan landed, causing barely a ripple in the glassy surface.

"It's only a coincidence," Erin insisted.

"If it's only that, then why do I know how you feel in my arms?" Michael moved closer, but did not touch her. "How can I know your taste?"

"You can't." She let out a shaky breath. Drew in another. "*We* can't."

"Perhaps not. Perhaps it's only coincidence. Or imagination." His mouth was a mere whisper from hers, his voice rough. "Perhaps I've been too long without a woman, you too long without a man. But tell me, Erin O'Halloran, how is it that I know you want this as much as I do?"

Books by JoAnn Ross

Homeplace
Fair Haven
Far Harbor
Legends Lake
Blue Bayou

Published by POCKET BOOKS

For information regarding special discounts for bulk purchases,
please contact Simon & Schuster Special Sales at
1-800-456-6798 or business@simonandschuster.com

JoAnn Ross

Fair Haven

POCKET BOOKS

New York   London   Toronto   Sydney   Singapore

This book is a work of fiction. Names, characters, places and incidents are products of the author's imagination or are used fictitiously. Any resemblance to actual events or locales or persons, living or dead, is entirely coincidental.

An *Original* Publication of POCKET BOOKS

 POCKET BOOKS, a division of Simon & Schuster, Inc.
1230 Avenue of the Americas, New York, NY 10020

ISBN: 0-7434-6727-2

First Pocket Books printing September 2000

10 9 8 7 6 5 4 3 2 1

POCKET and colophon are registered trademarks of Simon & Schuster, Inc.

Cover art by Ben Perini

Printed in the U.S.A.

To Jay,
who first took me
to Ireland

Acknowledgments

Every book is a collaborative effort and with that in mind I'd like to thank:

Damaris Rowland, agent and friend, who believed in this book from the beginning and pushed for my best effort

The wonderful team at Pocket Books who believes in me, most particularly Caroline Tolley and Lauren McKenna who always provide brilliant editorial advice, encouragement, and take care of all the details; and Jeanne Lee, who actually listens to an author's suggestions (!) and comes up with such gloriously romantic covers

Terena Boone, who never gave up in our search for the perfect house, stuck with us through all the travails of a cross-country move and best yet, became my friend

Jody Allen, whose mystical *Celtic Dreams* CD kept me writing through the difficult times; the members of READ on-line, for their endless source of support and blond jokes; and the Smoky Mountain Romance Writers who so graciously welcomed me to Tennessee

And finally, all the journalists who put themselves in harm's way to witness and make the rest of us, comfortable in our living rooms, aware of the horrors of war; and most especially Doctors Without Borders (*Médecins Sans Frontières*), the shock troops of international aid, who often go where even the military fear to tread and whose astonishing personal risks rightfully earned them the Nobel Peace Prize while I was writing *Fair Haven*.

Fair Haven

∾ 1 ∾

A Wild Rover

Castlelough, Ireland

There were those in the village who claimed that Michael Joyce must be mad. What else, they asked, could make a man leave the green fields of Ireland to risk life and limb all over the world?

"Besides," Mrs. Sheehan, proprietor of Sheehan and Sons Victualers, had told him just last week after he'd sold her husband a dressed hog destined for bacon and chops, "if it was trouble you were seeking, Michael James Joyce, you needn't have gone farther than just across your own country's borders."

"Aye, it's a good point you're making, Mrs. Sheehan," he'd replied through his teeth.

Despite some less-than-subtle coaxing from locals—and wasn't the butcher's wife the worst of them?—Michael never talked about those risk-filled years he'd spent in places where the voices of sanity had gone first hoarse, then mute. Nor had he discussed the incident that had nearly succeeded in getting him killed. Not even with his family, and certainly not with one of the biggest gossips in all of Castlelough.

Still, there were times he was willing to admit—if only to himself—that perhaps those who questioned his mental state might have a point. He may well have been touched with a bit of madness as he'd traveled from war zone to war zone throughout the world. Given an up-close and personal view of man's inhumanity toward man through the lenses of his cameras, Michael had begun to wonder if insanity was contagious.

Despite having grown up in a large, loving family, he'd long ago decided against bringing a child into a crazed world where innocent people could be blown up by terrorists in a Derry railway station or burned out of their homes and murdered by a political policy gone amok called ethnic cleansing.

Whatever part of him had stupidly believed he could make a difference in the world had been blown out of him, and now, like the prodigal son in his grandmother Fionna's well-worn Bible, he'd returned to hearth and home, content to spend his days working his farm and his evenings sitting in front of the warm glow of a peat fire reading the epic Irish tales that had once spurred a young west Irish lad to seek adventure.

His first few months back in Ireland, he'd been haunted by ghosts who'd show up in his bedroom nightly like mist from the sea, ethereal and always so damnably needy, wailing like a band of banshees on a moonless night. No amount of Irish whiskey could silence them; deprived of a voice during life, they seemed determined to make themselves heard through even the thickest alcoholic fog. They'd succeeded. Admirably.

Their bloodcurdling screams had caused him to wake up panicky in the black of night, bathed in acrid sweat. It was then he'd grab yet another bottle of Jameson's and go walking out along this very cliff, which, given his state of inebriation on those occasions, he now realized had been as close to suicide as he'd ever want to get.

But just as he hadn't died covering wars, nor had he died reliving them. And so, as he'd always done, Michael had moved on. In his way. And while the specters from those far distant places still visited on occasion, he'd managed to convince himself that he'd given up his dangerous ways.

Now, as the wind tore at his hair and sleet pelted his face like a shower of stones, Michael realized he'd been wrong.

It was the first day of February, celebrated throughout Ireland as St. Brigid's Day. When he'd been a child, Michael had made St. Brigid crosses with the rest of his classmates. The crosses, woven from rushes, supposedly encouraged blessings on his household, something he figured he could use about now.

Elsewhere around Ireland, devout pilgrims were visiting the numerous holy wells associated with the saint. While he himself was out in a wintry gale, trying to keep his footing on a moss-slick rocky ledge high above the storm-tossed Atlantic.

The nuns at Holy Child School had claimed that the holy well in Ardagh had been created when Brigid demonstrated prowess as a miracle worker to St. Patrick by dropping a burning coal from her apron onto the ground. There were also those, including old Tom Brennan—who'd cut the hair of three generations of Castlelough men and boys—who insisted that toothaches could be cured at the well at Greaghna-farna, in County Leitrim.

"If you're listening, Brigid, old girl," Michael mut-tered, "I wouldn't be turning away any miracles you might have in mind for the moment."

Despite being the very date his Celtic ancestors would have celebrated as the first day of spring, the day had dawned a miserable one. A gale blowing in from the sea moaned like lost souls over the rolling fields; dark clouds raced overhead, bringing with them a bone-chilling cold and snow flurries. A ghostly whiteness spread over the bramble thickets, clambered up the trunks of the few oak trees on the island that had escaped the British axes, and probed the nooks and crannies of the gray flagstone cliff.

Offshore toward the west, a last valiant stuttering of setting sun broke through the low-hanging clouds for an instant, touching the Aran Islands with a fleeting finger of gold.

He'd spent the summer of his sixteenth year in back-bending toil on Inishmaan, helping out on a sec-ond cousin's farm, working his ass off in stony fields that had been reclaimed from the icy Atlantic with tons of hand-gathered seaweed mixed with manure and sand atop naked bedrock.

The elderly cousin was a typical, taciturn—at least to outsiders—islander. He rose before the sun, worked like the devil, spoke an arcane Gaelic Michael could barely comprehend, and went to bed before dark. Michael had never been more lonely.

Until he met Nell O'Brien, the widow of a fisher-man who'd perished in a squall two years earlier, and was even lonelier than Michael. Originally from County Clare, her speech was more easily understood than many on Inishmaan, yet they hadn't passed a great deal of time talking. They'd not confided ideas or hopes or dreams; rather, they'd shared a narrow feather bed and their bodies, about which Michael had learned a great deal, and after the harvest, when it was time for him to move on, neither had suggested he stay.

That youthful summer affair had set the pattern for other relationships. Lacking a driving need to take any woman to wife, he always made a point to steer clear of those seeking a future, and with the exception of one hot-tempered red-haired Belfast lass, who'd cursed him roundly with words she definitely hadn't learned in convent school, he and his lovers had parted friends.

"You realize, of course, we could easily die out here," he scolded the woolly object of all his vexation. "One slip of the boot and we're both bobbing in the water headed for Greenland or America."

The ewe's coat had been marked with a fluorescent red paint to designate her as part of his flock. Her frantic bawling baas told Michael that she wasn't any more pleased with this latest adventure than he was.

Atop the cliff, now safe in a cart attached to the rusting green tractor he'd bought used from Devlin Doyle, her lamb from last year's birthday answered with an ear-aching bleat.

"I should have just let you drown," he muttered as he wrapped the thick hemp rope which was attached to a winch on the front of the tractor around her belly. A sheep was not the most pleasant-smelling animal at the best of times. A wet sheep was a great deal worse.

"You're certainly not the only bloody goddamn ewe in Ireland." When he tugged to ensure the knot would hold, she began to teeter on her spindly black legs. He caught her just in time to keep her from tumbling off the ledge. "Only the most stupid."

Instructing her to stay put while he went to start the winch, Michael gingerly made his way back up the steep, impossibly narrow path slick with moss and sea-gull droppings, keeping one booted foot in front of the other. Far, far below, he could hear the roiling surf crashing against the cliff, carving out new curves in ancient stone.

In the distance, a bit to the south and east, Lough Caislean was draped in a silvery fog. A lough beastie was rumored to reside in the mist-shrouded glaciated lake that had given the town its name, a huge green creature with scales that allegedly gleamed like polished emeralds.

He'd never actually seen the beast himself, yet both his father and nephew claimed to have spoken with her. Having witnessed far more implausible things in his thirty-three years, Michael was not one to doubt their veracity.

The ewe's increasingly frantic bleats rode upward on the salt-tinged wind. He told himself that the fact that she was the first animal he'd bought when he'd returned home was not the reason he was out here. Only a ridiculously sentimental man would risk his life for livestock, especially a stupid, smelly sheep he was sorely tempted to turn into mutton stew.

Still lying to himself, he insisted that neither did he care that she was a good mother, which, he suspected, was how she'd landed in this fool predicament in the first place. He guessed that her equally dim-witted lamb, in search of a bit of green growing over the cliff, had been the first to fall, followed by its mother, who, amazingly, must have heard the plaintive cries over the howl of the wind and stupidly gone to its rescue.

Of course, none of this would have happened if Fail had been herding the sheep, but in a bit of bad luck, the border collie—named for Failinis, the mythical Celtic "hound of mightiest deeds"—was undergoing surgery in Galway after having been hit by a German tourist who'd come around a blind corner too fast in his rental car.

The vet had not been encouraging, but knowing that Fail had not just the name, but also the heart of the legendary mythical dog, Michael refused to give up hope.

Thirty minutes later, after a great deal more cursing, the two lamebrained smelly animals were back in the pasture where they belonged. The sight of his farmhouse eased Michael's aggravation, giving him a quick, private stab of pride, as it always did, and making him appreciate those same roots he'd wanted so to escape when he'd been younger.

A former crofter's cottage, which had first been built on this piece of Joyce land five hundred years ago, he'd enlarged it with stones dug and carried from his own land with his own hands. The old-fashioned thatched roof kept his home warm in winter and cool in summer, but he hadn't chosen it for its insulating superiority over slate. The truth was, the rounded roof appealed to his aesthetic tastes, and since he had no one but himself to answer to, he'd chosen to please himself.

Now it was a generously sized home with modern plumbing that included a horrendously hedonistic whirlpool tub he'd had shipped from a supply warehouse in Dublin, which had caused quite a buzz in the village.

There had been bets made at the Irish Rose pub regarding just how many women a man with Michael Joyce's international reputation as a lady-killer could fit in such a bathtub. More bets were laid down as to what type of women they'd be, George Early putting down five pounds on a certain Danish supermodel who'd won herself a top spot on the front page of the normally staid *Irish Times* after having been arrested for splashing "in the nip" in the cascading fountains of the Anna Livia statue while on a photo shoot in Dublin.

"I tell you," George insisted, "it'll be that blond model."

"I'll match your five pounds and double it," Hugh Browne said, slapping the bills down on the bar stained with circles from centuries of pints. "It'll be that French redheaded actress filming down Waterford way. The one with the tattoo of a flame-breathing dragon on her bum."

More women known for breast size rather than brains or depth of character were added to the list. Then betting began as to when these ideals of female pulchritude might begin arriving.

After a few weeks, when not a single woman had shown up at the Joyce farm, the talk about supermodels and actresses began to lose its appeal and people went back to discussing crops, sheep, and—always a good topic for conversation—the weather.

But still, secretly, they waited.

And still the women didn't come.

Living his solitary life, building his house, reading all the great books he'd never had time for while soaking muscles sore from rehabilitation exercises in his hedonistic bathtub, the object of all the villagers' conjecture paid scant attention to their speculation.

Last summer, after he'd given the weathered gray stone a coat of whitewash that had made it gleam like sunshine on sea foam, a rich American tourist had come to his door and offered him a staggering sum of money. Michael hadn't been the slightest bit tempted to sell off his heritage.

He left his muddy boots on the back stoop and entered by the kitchen door. The aroma of the vegetable soup he'd left simmering on the stove offered a warm and comforting welcome.

He hung his jacket on a hook beside the door and pulled his wool sweater, which had gotten wet as well in the rescue effort, over his head. He'd grabbed a linen dish towel from a ring beside the sink and begun rubbing his shaggy hair dry when he suddenly realized that he was not alone.

A knee-jerk instinct had him stiffen, on some distant level expecting shrapnel to come crashing through his flesh as it had during that hellish time in Sarajevo.

Reminding himself that he was not in a war zone but in his own kitchen, which was unlikely to harbor a sniper, he slowly turned around.

The woman seated at the wooden kitchen table was as solidly built as a keg of Murphy's stout, with a face that looked as if it had been chiseled from stone. Her hair was a great deal grayer than he remembered, but a few auburn strands wove through the tight bun like defiant flames sparking through smoke. Her eyes were as steely gray and cold as the wintry Atlantic, and her mouth was set in a grim, disapproving line he recalled all too well.

First the German who'd mistaken the narrow, hedge-bordered road for the autobahn, then the bloody fool sheep, now Deidre McDougall invading his kitchen. What next?

Although he'd stopped believing in God a very long time ago, as he faced the female who could make Lady Macbeth appear saintly by comparison, Michael found himself bracing for plague and pestilence.

Out of the Mist

"'Tis surprised I am to find you in my kitchen, Deidre McDougall." He didn't bother with a greeting they both knew would be a lie. "The storm must have kept me from hearing you knock on my door."

The way she was staring in reluctant horror at the scars crisscrossing his chest like a tangled mass of snakes almost had Michael pulling his sweater back on. Then he reminded himself that this was, after all, his home, and he certainly hadn't invited Deidre here today. Indeed, he'd be more likely to welcome Cromwell's ghost to his kitchen than this stone-hearted, hatchet-faced female.

His sarcasm rolled off her like rain off a swan's back. "You weren't at home when I arrived." She shrugged. "The door was unlocked."

"This isn't Belfast. We've never had the need to be locking doors in Castlelough." Until now.

He couldn't recall Deidre McDougall ever leaving her home except for daily mass or the funeral of one of her sons, all of whom had died, supposedly in the cause of a united Ireland, although personally Michael had considered them little more than neighborhood thugs.

Wondering what had brought her here from the

north today, he reluctantly fell back on the manners first his mother, then the nuns, had drilled into him. "Would you care for tea?"

"I won't be staying."

That was a bit of good news. Perhaps he'd be spared the pestilence after all. "Suit yourself." He filled the copper kettle from the tap to make a cup for himself. "It's blowing like old Gabe's horn out there."

"I didn't come here to be drinking tea or discussing the weather with you, Michael Joyce."

"So why are you here?"

"Rena's dead."

His fingers tightened on the handle of the kettle. He felt the muscles in his back and shoulders clench.

"I'm sorry to hear that." He lit the burner with a thick kitchen match. "Had she been ill?"

He couldn't imagine such a thing. Rena McDougall had been so filled with life she'd reminded him of a dazzling flame. Or a comet blazing her way through a midnight sky. On some distant level he wasn't surprised that she'd flared out too soon.

"She was murdered. On her wedding day."

This time Michael flinched and briefly closed his eyes, fighting the images that flashed into his mind. Rena gazing up at him from sex-tousled sheets, her emerald eyes offering a gilded feminine invitation; Rena posing for him wearing nothing but lush, perfumed flesh and a smile.

Then finally, Rena cursing him to the devil on the dark day of her brothers' funerals, when he'd refused to join the gangsters whose terrorist actions had cost Tom and James McDougall their lives.

"I'm sorry," he repeated, knowing his words were sorely inadequate. When he turned back to her, his expression was stoic, meant to conceal the turmoil in his mind.

He couldn't help wondering briefly if things would have been different if he'd stayed in Belfast. Would they have wed and settled down to a mundane middle-class married existence in one of the dreary ubiquitous red-brick row houses in the Catholic section of the city?

The answer, of course, was no. Rena had been no more eager to settle down than he. Indeed, he'd often thought her as impossible to hold as the wind, as ethereal as morning mist.

"She was my last child," Deidre said.

"I know."

Michael shook his head, hissed a curse between his teeth, and considered the waste. Of all the atrocities he'd witnessed, this was the only one that had struck so close to home. He did some quick calculations and realized that more than eight years had passed since those fiery six months they'd spent alternately fighting and loving. Sometimes it seemed like another lifetime; other times, such as now, it seemed like yesterday.

A silence as thick and dreary as the weather fell over the kitchen that only minutes before had seemed so warm and welcoming. Assuring himself that he wasn't surrendering to her silent disapproval, Michael nevertheless yanked the damp sweater back over his head.

"She married a Unionist," Deidre grimly reported. "Against my wishes, of course, but when did the girl ever listen to anyone?"

When indeed? Michael echoed to himself. "That must not have been a very popular decision in the neighborhood."

"Her brother's mates took it as a betrayal. As did the boy's Protestant chums."

This time Michael's curse, in Irish, was harsh.

"There's more." From her tone, Michael didn't expect any good news to come from this visit. "She had a child."

A premonition flickered. Before he could respond, the kettle began to whistle. Turning away, he yanked it off the burner and turned off the blue flame.

"It's yours," she revealed before he could ask.

She dug into the black vinyl handbag she had been clutching in her red-knuckled hands and pulled out a piece of heavy, parchment-type paper. There was an official-looking gold seal in the lower right-hand corner.

"The girl's eight years old, and if you'd be thinking of denying paternity, Rena named you on both the birth and baptismal certificates."

Rena had been many things: quixotic, unreasonably—at least to his mind—partisan when it came to the Troubles plaguing her homeland, and the most tempestuous woman he'd ever known. She was also incredibly outspoken and had never, that he knew of, lied. If she claimed the child was his, Michael had no reason to doubt her word.

He skimmed the legal document, unaware that the woman who might have been his mother-in-law actually recoiled slightly at the absolute lack of emotion she viewed in his gaze.

"She's yours," Deidre said again, less firmly this time.

"So you said," he responded as he continued to read. Then he looked up at the older woman. "The girl's name is Shea?"

"Aye. Shea McDougall." Unwilling to allow herself to be cowed, Deidre set her chin. "Since her father was not around to be claiming her, she was given her mother's family name."

"I didn't know." Michael didn't realize his hands had clenched into fists until he heard the sound of paper crumpling.

"You'd have no reason to know. Weren't you already gone by the time she found out she was pregnant?" Having recovered her usual bluster, she spat the words.

"The news bureau could always find me."

That was more or less the truth. Michael conveniently didn't mention that he could disappear behind hostile borders for weeks at a time.

He decided that wasn't relevant since he certainly hadn't been out of touch for eight years. His work had been published in enough newspapers and magazines, had garnered sufficient awards to earn him a measure of public regard. In addition, there'd been that Sunday morning when the damn CNN cameras had caught him peppered by shrapnel in the marketplace.

Others had been wounded that day; people had died. But he'd been the one to show up again and again on nightly newscasts when various news organizations around the world picked up the story. Photos of him lying unconscious amid the carnage of what had only minutes earlier been a lively market had even made the covers of the *International Herald Tribune*, *Time*, and *Newsweek*.

Having always preferred the anonymity of being behind the camera, he'd hated being depicted as some sort of folk hero. There was absolutely nothing heroic about getting yourself caught in the line of fire. Still, he'd had not only his fifteen minutes, but nearly a week of fame, and if Rena had wanted to track him down it would have taken only a single telephone call.

Eight goddamn bloody years. He shook his head as the thought ricocheted inside it like rounds from an AK-47. He had an eight-year-old daughter named Shea. A daughter he knew not a single thing about. The idea was staggering.

"Rena should have told me." He felt like punching his fist though the wall, but, unwilling to give Rena's mother the satisfaction of knowing she'd gotten under his skin, he shoved his hands into the pockets of his jeans instead.

"You were always talking peace," Deidre reminded him scornfully, as if he'd been guilty of heresy. "She didn't want you influencing her child against our family's beliefs."

"Dangerously partisan beliefs that caused the death of her father, her brothers, and, it appears, herself," he said with open and bitter condemnation. "What of her husband?" The idea of Rena marrying a man she'd been brought up to consider a blood enemy was almost as much of a shock as her death.

"He's in hospital with gunshot wounds, but the doctors expect him to recover."

"Has he adopted the girl? Shea?" The name felt impossibly foreign on his tongue.

"No. Nor will he. The vows had not been exchanged before the killing. Besides, he and Shea never took to one another. Which is why I've brought her to you."

"To me?"

"Aren't you her father? She's your responsibility."

Father. The word was one he'd never thought he'd hear applied to him. Jesus Christ. What he knew about children could be stuck on the head of a pin and there'd still be enough room for a thousand—hell, a million—dancing angels.

"Where is she?" As unexpected and unwanted as Deidre's bombshell was, and despite his vow to retreat from the world, Michael's upbringing did not allow him to ignore responsibility.

"Waiting outside."

His gaze swung to the window, where sleet was pelting the glass. "You left her outside in this storm?"

Deidre McDougall was not easily cowed. She squared her broad shoulders before his furious glare. "She's in the car."

"She must be freezing."

Abandoning the last of his manners, he left the kitchen, went down the hall and retrieved a blanket from his bed. Without so much as a glance toward Rena's harridan of a mother, he yanked his jacket off the hook by the door.

"You'll be needing the keys."

Fury flared even hotter at the idea of an eight-year-old child locked in a car in the midst of a winter storm. Michael cursed again as he snatched the keys from her hand and marched out into the miserable weather.

The mud-splattered Toyota was parked in front of the house, which explained why he hadn't seen it when he'd first returned home on the tractor by the back fields. A small pale face dotted with freckles looked up at him through the passenger window.

"She favors you," Deidre, who'd followed him out to the car, said.

He couldn't see the resemblance, but there was no mistaking Rena in the child's thickly lashed eyes that were as green as the Emerald Isle itself, the fire of her unruly hair, and the scattering of freckles across the bridge of her nose.

She was, at the moment, too pale, even for a fair-complected Irish lass, yet he supposed some fresh country air would change that. Even so, she was a pretty little thing. Indeed, had it not been for her unhealthy pallor, she would have brought to mind one of the cherubs who smiled down so benignly from the gilded ceiling of the parish church. The only difference was, this cherub wasn't smiling.

"She'll grow to be as beautiful as her mother," he murmured as much to himself as to Deidre.

"So some say," she agreed grudgingly. "Which is why I've taught her that beauty is a tool Satan uses to trick girls onto the path of sin."

"She's too young to be fretting her head about sin."

"The girl was born into sin, outside the marriage bed." Her accusatory glare assured him that she held him solely responsible for that. "She's also a year past the age of reason," she added, reciting the Catholic dogma. "Which makes her responsible for any sins she may have committed. Even if she hasn't received her

first Holy Communion yet. Rena and Peter hadn't settled the question of which religion she'd be brought up
in when they were gunned down at the altar."

Michael didn't want to think about Rena's blood stain-
ing a lacy white wedding dress and wanted even less to
talk about it. "Have the Garda arrested the murderers?"

"Not yet. They were wearing the usual black ski
masks. But you can't be keeping a secret such as this in
the neighborhood. The rogues will not be getting
away." Both her tone and her eyes were like flint.
"Rena may no longer have brothers to defend her
name, but she wasn't the only McDougall in Belfast.
Her cousins will see that she's properly avenged."

Despite any peace agreements. Of course, Rena's
murderers would have cousins of their own, and so on
and so on, hate breeding like maggots on a dead,
swollen cow.

"I'll not be allowing anyone to teach my daughter
hatred." He was firm about this, even though the word
daughter still felt as alien as Martian on his tongue. He
unlocked the passenger door, yanked it open, and held
out his hand.

"Hello, Shea."

Serious eyes, far more grave than any child's had a
right to be, looked up at him. "Are you my father?"

"Aye." It occurred to him that she didn't exactly
look thrilled at the idea. *Well, join the club, lass,* he
thought grimly.

She blinked up at him. "Bad men killed my mum."

"I know."

"She left a letter saying that if she ever died,
Grandmother should take me to live with you. So"—

she held out her arms, the gesture unnervingly sacrificial—"here I am."

"So it seems." Damn Rena for keeping her secret for so long! And damn her witch of a mother for springing this sprite of a child on him when all he wanted from life was to be left alone.

He reached into the car and wrapped the blanket around thin shoulders clad in a cheap clear-plastic slicker that could be doing nothing to protect her from the cold.

Michael had trekked through the mountains of Afghanistan mostly on his own, with only a crazed mercenary from *Soldier of Fortune* magazine—who'd spent a great deal of time stoned on local hashish—as a guide.

But he had not a single idea how the hell he was going to find his way through this new uncharted territory of parenthood.

Arms nearly as thin as sally reeds twined around his neck as he lifted her from the seat. The soft scent of soap emanating from her skin carried a faint, underlying odor of fear. Michael could recognize it, having experienced it personally on more than one occasion. Her breath was like little puffs of gray ghosts on the cold moist air.

"I've never been on a farm before," she said as she looked with childish interest over the rolling fields dotted with sheep.

"It's a great deal different from the city."

"I think it looks lovely." Her gaze moved to the larger of the barns, curiosity appearing to overcome any nervousness she may have been feeling. "Do you have horses?"

"It wouldn't be a proper Irish farm without them."

"I've always wanted to learn to ride a horse. But there aren't hardly any in the city." Her smooth brow furrowed. "Only the police and soldiers have them."

His jaw clenched with remembered anger at losing a camera to a police horse's hooves while photographing a riot during the Orangemen's marching season through the Catholic section of Derry.

"A friend of mine just happens to have a sweet-tempered mare for sale that should suit you well enough," Michael heard himself say. Jesus, if anyone had told him only an hour ago that he'd be in the market for a horse for his daughter, he'd have accused them of being madder than he was reputed to be. "Her name is Niamh."

"Nee-av?" she repeated the ancient Gaelic. "That's a funny name." She almost, just barely, smiled.

"She's called after the daughter of the Son of the Sea. Surely you've heard the stories?"

The child shook her bright head.

"If she was to grow up in the north, it was important for the girl to be a realist," Deidre said brusquely. "I wasn't going to let her head be filled with foolish legends and fanciful stories."

Knowing that Deidre had her own stories, all of them hate-filled, Michael was once again forced to tamp down his temper.

"Well, aren't you here in the west, now?" he told his daughter placidly. "And we like our stories."

"I like stories, too." She leaned back a little so she could look up at him. Her face was small and worried. Michael suspected that her quivering lips were due to emotion rather than cold and felt another prick of conscience.

She was only an innocent child; she certainly hadn't asked to be born of the lust he and Rena had shared. The day he started thinking like Deidre McDougall was the day he may as well admit that he'd lost the last lingering bit of his humanity and throw himself off the edge of the cliff.

"But I might not be staying." Shea's tremulous voice broke into his grim thoughts and tugged at emotions too complex to analyze while they were standing outside in a winter storm.

His arms tightened around her. "Of course you'll be staying. Aren't I your da?"

A mere hour ago, the idea would have seemed impossible. Now, though Michael still wasn't certain what he was going to do with her, sending this child back to the north was equally untenable.

"You might not like me," she insisted with a faint flare of tenacity that reminded him of her mother.

He wondered what she'd been told about him, about why her father had never been a presence in her young life. "Why would you be thinking such a thing?"

"Grandmother doesn't like me," she informed him. "She says I'm a changeling."

"Does she now?" Michael managed, just barely, for Shea's sake, to keep his voice mild as he looked over his daughter's head at Deidre. "If she said that, I'm sure she must have been jesting with you."

"Grandmother never jests."

Michael decided that was undoubtedly one of the most accurate statements he'd ever heard.

"The girl's being truthful, for once." Deidre reached past him into the backseat and pulled out a green canvas duffel bag. "Either she was switched by faeries in her cradle or she's possessed."

She thrust the bag toward him as if anxious to turn over all control of her granddaughter—and the situation—to someone else. Anyone else, Michael suspected.

"That's a very harmful thing to say about your own granddaughter." Once again he was tempted to throttle her. "Especially coming from a woman who alleges she doesn't believe in the old stories."

"I didn't say I disbelieved. I said I didn't want to fill the child's head with fancy. But the faeries have already marked her, as you'll be finding out yourself soon enough, Michael Joyce."

She climbed into the driver's seat of the rusting Toyota and turned the key in the ignition. After an initial grinding protest, the engine came to shuddering life that kicked exhaust from the tailpipe, engulfing Michael and Shea in a cloud of acrid blue smoke.

"If I were you, Michael Joyce, I'd get a priest to perform an exorcism."

Leaving those less-than-encouraging words ringing in his ears, she slammed the driver's door and drove back down his driveway, turning on the road in the direction of the north.

❧ 3 ❧

Something to Believe In

Seattle, Washington

"$\mathcal{A}$re you certain you have everything you need?" Grace O'Halloran asked her daughter for the umpteenth time as they waited for the flight from SeaTac airport to New York to be called.

"Absolutely," Erin assured her yet again.

"I still wish you'd let me get you a decent set of luggage." Grace frowned at the battered canvas duffel bag that Erin had been dragging all over the world for the past six years since graduating from Johns Hopkins medical school. "Something like that." Erin's mother pointed out a lovely floral bag carried by a woman clad in a black knit suit, alligator pumps, and very good pearl earrings.

Dressed in her usual uniform of jeans, an oversized sweatshirt, high-topped sneakers, and Orioles baseball cap atop her short brown curls, Erin figured she'd be more likely to wake up one morning and discover that she'd turned into Gwyneth Paltrow during her sleep than to ever be able to pull off such a sleek look.

Erin knew that her mother was proud of her, but she also suspected that there had been times, like now, when Grace O'Halloran—a former Miss Washington runner-up who Erin suspected had been born knowing that she was a winner—found her only daughter a bit of a disappointment.

Erin had truly tried to learn what her jock brother had always referred to as "that girly stuff." Like an anthropologist studying a newly discovered tribe, she'd pored over *Glamour* and *Cosmopolitan* as if the glossy magazines filled with advertising for shampoo and makeup that promised to change her life might actually live up to their hyperbole.

Unfortunately, the makeup tips and charts depicting the best swimsuit for her body—which regrettably lacked both hips and breasts—could have been written in Sanscrit.

Erin knew she'd never be a Miss America candidate. But she *was* intelligent. Intelligent enough to skip the second, fourth, and eighth grades. While her freshmen classmates were stalking the aisles of the drugstore, searching for that perfect shade of lip gloss that would turn boys to putty in their perfectly manicured hands, she'd been in the biology lab, marveling at the flash of protozoa through the lenses of her microscope and tracing frogs' nervous systems.

When her brother's harem of wannabe girlfriends began conducting experiments to discover whether lemon juice or chamomile worked best to bring out blond highlights, Erin was rubbing poison oak leaves on her arm and testing various topical treatments on the itchy red rash.

By the time she'd headed off to college at fifteen, both she and her mother had accepted the fact that Erin's personal style could best be described as pre-makeover.

"I wouldn't want you to waste your money," she told her mother now. "Besides, this fits my lifestyle."

She'd never been a collector—of possessions or of people—and since her work with an international medical relief group required the ability to jump on a plane at any minute, it was important to travel light.

"A lifestyle that could get you killed." Worry lines etched their way across Grace's smooth forehead. "I never should have let your great aunt Ida give you that Doctor Barbie when you were ten." The frown deepened. "If only you'd liked Rock Star Barbie instead."

"Then you'd be worrying about me doing drugs and sleeping with Mick Jagger."

"You'd never do drugs. And Mick Jagger is old enough to be your father."

"Not *my* father." The idea made Erin smile.

"You'd be surprised," Grace said. "Your father wasn't always an accountant. When he was in school, he was quite an accomplished musician."

"Really?" Erin wondered why she had never heard that story. She found it hard to picture her father in a high school rock-and-roll garage band. "Are you sure we're talking about the same John O'Halloran? A tall, lean guy with a nice head of hair and a tattoo on his forearm?" Okay, she allowed, perhaps the tattoo suggested possibilities.

"I'll always hate the U.S. Navy for that." Grace's lips drew into a thin line. "It almost cost him his first job. Needless to say, accounting firms don't get all that many applicants sporting tattoos of mermaids."

"Especially applicants who can make the mermaid's tail move," Erin agreed with a grin as she remembered earning money for the Good Humor truck by getting her father to flex his forearm for third-grade classmates at her Coldwater Cove, Washington, elementary school. If she'd known about his having been a musician, she might have doubled the price of admission. "What did he play?" She was certain she would have remembered if she'd ever stumbled across an electric guitar stashed away in the attic.

"I can't believe we never mentioned it. He made the Washington all-star marching band his final year of high school, beating out trombone players from all over the state."

"He was a trombone player?" The mental image of a long-haired John O'Halloran clad in skin-tight black leather, playing hot licks on a Fender Stratocaster dissolved. Erin couldn't hold back a sputter of laughter.

"Don't laugh." Grace's own lips, lined in Raspberry Rose, twitched. "It did, after all, put him at the front of the parade."

They shared a mother-daughter laugh. Then, as Erin's flight was called, hugged.

"Promise me you'll be careful," Grace repeated what she always said as she dabbed a tissue beneath eyes that had been expertly enhanced with smoke-gray shadow.

"I promise." It was what Erin always said. "Besides, you don't have to worry this time. What could happen to me in Ireland?"

"How about terrorist bombs?"

"There aren't any terrorists in Castlelough." She'd never been there, but Tom Flannery had assured her that the most danger she'd face would be possibly dying of boredom.

"I still wish you didn't have to go," Grace fretted in an obvious attempt to stall Erin's departure. "You just got home."

"I was home for nearly two weeks." It had been the longest Erin had been in Coldwater Cove since graduation from medical school.

"You promised three. We never did go shopping to buy you some new clothes."

If she weren't so concerned about Tom, Erin would have been thanking God for small favors.

Still, she knew the complaint was about more than merely clothes. Her mother was sorely disappointed that neither of her two children had seen fit to get married and give her the grandbabies she so longed to spoil.

"Tom Flannery's my best friend, Mom. And he needs me."

"Now where have I heard that before?" Grace O'Halloran murmured. "One of these days, darling, you're going to learn that despite all your good intentions, you can't save the entire world."

"I don't want to save the world," Erin answered, not quite truthfully. "I just want to save Tom."

"Promise me you'll call when you get to Manhattan."

"I promise."

Erin had scheduled a day's visit with a doctor who'd been a tough, no-nonsense resident when Erin had been an intern. While their lives and practices had turned out quite differently—Julia Southerland was a world-renowned neurosurgeon who lived in a luxurious apartment on Park Avenue while Erin was a relief doctor who considered herself fortunate to sleep in a dry tent—they'd become friends. In fact, they were nearly as close as she and Tom were.

"Perhaps you'll have time to pick something up while you're in New York."

"Perhaps." Erin knew that Grace would love nothing more than to burn her jeans and sweats, then drag her out to some trendy boutique. Fortunately, the woman who epitomized style had given up trying to pass on the feminine wardrobe secrets that seemed second nature to her.

As the jet flew over America's heartland, Erin's mind returned to Tom. She still couldn't believe that the man she'd worked beside in so many refugee camps could be dying. As it had been since he'd first tracked her down in Coldwater Cove, her mind was tormented with shifting images of helicopters spraying the poisonous chemicals that supposedly were, two years later, eating away at his immune system.

After years of caring for all the world's people who couldn't care for themselves, her best friend had finally returned to the village in which he'd grown up to establish the family practice about which he'd always talked.

Dammit, it wasn't fair that he'd lose his dream just when he'd achieved it!

He couldn't die, Erin vowed as the wheels of the jet touched down on the runway at La Guardia airport.

She wouldn't let him.

"Sister Mary Patrick says it's a sin to use the Lord's name in vain," Shea volunteered when Michael cursed as Deidre drove away.

"Sister's right." Michael was getting weary of all this talk of sin. The sleet was forming wet droplets on the wool blanket and pelting down on their heads. "We'd best be getting inside before you catch pneumonia."

He picked up the small bag that presumably held all his daughter's worldly possessions and began walking back to the house.

"I had the pneumonia when I was six," Shea informed him. "But Mum prayed to Saint Jude, who made a miracle, so I didn't die."

"Then I'm indebted to Saint Jude."

Michael didn't believe in saints or miracles any more than he believed in God, but he wasn't about to get into a theological argument with an eight-year-old daughter he'd just met.

"I'm also not possessed," she assured him as they entered the house.

"It's pleased I am to be hearing that. Since I'm not certain Father O'Malley even knows how to perform an exorcism."

She looked up at him, green eyes wide and earnest in her pale-as-milk complexion. "Don't you want to know how I know I'm not possessed?"

"Only if you'd like to be telling."

"Mary Margaret Murphy told me."

"And I suppose she's your best friend at school?"

"Oh, no. She's my guardian angel."

"Is she now?" He plunked her down on a chair and touched his hand to the kettle to see if the water would still be warm enough for tea.

"Oh, aye. She's been watching over me since the very moment I was born. She and Casey."

"Casey?" He helped her out of the plastic slicker and thought about throwing it away, but, deciding he'd best keep it until he could get a replacement in the village, hung it next to his jacket on the coatrack.

"Mary Margaret's wolfhound."

"Ah. Would he be an angel, too?"

"Aye," she answered without hesitation, as if having a dog for a guardian angel was the most natural thing in the world.

"Mary Margaret died in a fire in a sewing machine factory a long, long time ago. In the old days, before television was invented. Or even automobiles. People used to ride around in coaches pulled by horses in that time." The expression on her face suggested Shea would find this to be no hardship.

"So I've heard."

"She always wanted a pet, but the sisters didn't allow any in the foundling home, so when she got to heaven, God matched her up with Casey."

"That was thoughtful of him." At least no one could accuse his daughter of lacking an imagination. In that respect, she reminded him of his father, who'd died last year of a sudden heart attack on his way to the Irish Rose pub in the village.

"Oh, God's very thoughtful and generous. One nice thing about dying is that you can have anything you want in heaven. Like ice cream in every flavor that you don't even have to pay for and horses with lovely pink satin ribbons in their manes that you can ride whenever you want.

"When she was alive, Mary Margaret only had pitiful rags to wear and no shoes at all," she continued her fanciful tale. "But now she has emerald slippers and lots of beautiful dresses in different colors to match her rainbow wings."

"I always thought angels had white feathered wings."

"Some do. Some have gold or silver. Casey's wings are sort of silvery white and sparkly, like a spiderweb that's all damp with the morning dew.

"Mary Margaret grew up in Belfast when the skies were always smoky, so when she first saw all the rainbows in heaven, she thought they were so beautiful, God took a piece from one and made her wings out of it."

Ah yes, Michael thought. *She definitely sounded like her grandfather.* He could only hope that she'd be easier to handle than Brady Joyce had been.

"Would she be having a halo, as well?" he asked while he made them both tea. At least while they were carrying on the fanciful conversation he didn't have to think about future plans.

"She used to," Shea answered matter-of-factly, "when she first got up to heaven. But it was always getting slanted when she flew through the clouds, so God decided to let her wear flowers in her hair instead. They smell really nice and they're very pretty. And they never, ever wilt."

"Mary Margaret sounds like a very special guardian angel, indeed."

"She is." His daughter beamed. "And she loves me best of all the little girls in the world. Even when I do something wrong, she never yells at me or hits me with a strap."

As he rummaged in the cupboards for the biscuits left over from his nephew Rory's last visit, Michael realized he'd just been given an unwelcome insight into his daughter's life.

He considered it ironic that he'd come back home to Castlelough to embrace the mundane and ordinary, yet here he was, talking with a newly discovered sprite of a red-haired daughter about guardian angels and wolfhounds who sported spiderweb wings. If he hadn't stopped drinking, he might have thought the entire experience was a hallucination born of too much Jameson's.

He heard the familiar sound of laughter first. Then a man who had the look of a leprechaun gradually appeared. He was sitting cross-legged atop the refrigerator, like some Indian swami.

"Doesn't the Almighty laugh while foolish man plans?" Brady Joyce reminded his son in the lilting voice that had made him one of the best storytellers in all of Ireland when he'd been alive.

It was not his father's first visit. There were times when Michael was able to convince himself that the apparition was merely a figment of his imagination, providing the conversations that he'd discovered had been the thing he'd most missed during his years away from home. Those other times, he didn't question it, choosing instead to just accept the fact that Brady was proving to be every bit as unconventional in death as he'd been in life. While he'd been searching for the biscuits, Shea had slid down from the chair and, dragging the blanket behind her, had gone over to the window, where she was gazing with a city child's obvious fascination at the rolling fields dotted with sheep and cows. The fact that she didn't appear to see her grandfather atop the icebox backed up Michael's imagination theory.

"So this is God's doing?" he muttered beneath his breath as he reached into the refrigerator for the milk.

Personally, Michael considered God as dead as a doorknocker, but that wasn't an argument he wanted to enter into with a hallucination who appeared to believe he was capable of bopping back and forth between heaven and earth.

"Aye. And, as I told the Almighty—"

"Now you want me to believe you speak with God himself?"

"It's not the same as you and I are speaking at the moment," Brady allowed. "But it's communication, just the same. And to be getting back to what I told God, when I first learned of it, it's a high grand plan. And isn't it a perfect solution to your problem?"

"Until thirty minutes ago, other than some stupid livestock and a sheep dog that could well lose her leg today, I wasn't aware I had a problem."

"Of course you do. Hasn't your mother been worrying that this scheme of yours to bury yourself in farming would prove so boring you'd take off again and get yourself killed in some godforsaken foreign hellhole?"

"That isn't about to happen."

"She's also concerned about you hiding away here on your farm like some mad Irish hermit monk."

Michael wasn't prepared to discuss his self-imposed celibacy with a hallucination. "I'm finding it depressing to discover that a person still has worries in the afterlife."

One more reason to doubt heaven. Hadn't the doctors at that military hospital in Germany told him that he'd died twice, once in the helicopter and again on the operating table? But Michael had no memory of any bright light leading him to still pastures.

"Death doesn't stop parents from loving their children," Brady informed him. "Why, only this morning the most interesting things in your life were a handful of pesky ghosts, your dog's broken leg and the possibility of losing two of your sheep to the sea. Now, out of the clear blue sky—"

"It's gray." Michael shot a look out the rain-streaked window at the view that seemed to be holding Shea spellbound. "And wet."

"I'll never know how a son of mine could be such a stickler for details," Brady grumbled. "I also don't recall you having such a negative view of the world."

"Not all the world is like Castlelough. There are all too many places where a human life has no more value than the horse shit I shovel out of the barn each morning."

"Now, you'd not be telling me anything I don't already know meself." There was a very un-Brady-like edge of frustration in his father's tone. "And don't you be forgetting that me own view of the world is a wee more clear than yours might be these days. Since it comes from a bit higher up," he tacked on pointedly.

Michael mumbled something that might be concession at that remark. He still wasn't at all sure how his father managed to just drift in from whatever afterlife realm he'd ended up in, nor did he really care. He'd abandoned his former curiosity about things that didn't directly concern him the same way he'd locked away a fortune in camera equipment in that trunk hidden in the loft of his barn.

"Me point is, Michael James Joyce," Brady said, "you've just been given the grandest gift of all. A child. And, if I do say so meself, from the tale of Mary Margaret and her furry angel friend Casey, it appears your wee darling daughter has inherited her grandfather's superlative knack for storytelling."

A very nonghostly grin brightened the apple-cheeked face, and strikingly young blue eyes twinkled merrily. "I believe you're in for some interesting days ahead of you, boyo. As well as a challenge that could make your former career as a war photojournalist seem like child's play."

Since for once he and his eccentric father were in perfect agreement, Michael didn't bother to respond.

∽ 4 ∽

The Lass with the Delicate Air

*H*aving no idea how to talk with a daughter he'd just met, Michael was relieved when Shea seemed willing and able to fill any potentially awkward conversational gaps. Indeed, over a dinner stew and slabs of bread lathered in butter, she talked practically nonstop, mostly about Mary Margaret and her equally fanciful, angelic Casey.

"Where will I be sleeping?" she asked as she helped him clear the table without needing to be asked.

"I was thinking I'd be putting you in the same room where my nephew Rory stays when he comes for an overnight visit. It's not a large bed, but it's comfortable. As a matter of fact, it was my bed when I was a lad."

"Oh, I like that idea." She tilted her head, her wide green eyes turning intent, as if listening to some voice Michael could not hear. "Mary Margaret says that you must have known I'd someday be coming."

"And why would she think that?" he asked, his arms up to the elbows in soapsuds.

"Because you kept your bed for me."

"Life in the country isn't easy," he warned her. "You quickly learn to make over, make do, or do without.

We farmers are not ones for throwing useful things away."

"Still, it's fortunate that you kept it," she decided.

"Aye." He rinsed her bowl and put it in the drying rack.

"Sometimes my mum let me sleep with her," Shea offered as she brought her empty milk glass to the sink. "When she was lonely."

"Fortunately, with Mary Margaret and Casey by your side, you shouldn't be lonely."

"Oh, they're grand company, sure enough. But they don't exactly sleep *with* me. Mary Margaret hovers over the bed, like this"—she held out her arms in front of her in a protective gesture—"and Casey curls up at the foot in case any bad men or monsters might sneak into my room while I'm sleeping . . . Do you have any bad men or monsters here?"

Michael decided internal monsters didn't count. Especially since he'd become so adept at ignoring them. Unfortunately, he hadn't quite exorcized all of the numerous ghosts that had followed him home.

"Not a single one."

"Good." She breathed a little sigh and gathered up the cutlery. "That's a very big relief."

The Irish might not be models of prompt efficiency, but actually getting his daughter to sleep tested even Michael's patience. There was a bath to take—next time perhaps he could have some bath salts like Mum always put in the water, she suggested—hair to wash, with shampoo, rather than the bar of plain, unperfumed soap he'd always found satisfactory.

"I'll buy both the salts and shampoo tomorrow," he

promised as he had her tilt her head back so he could pour the rinse water over the wet red curls.

"Mum always got the kind of shampoo that smells like strawberries."

"Then that's what I'll be getting."

"Good." She nodded. "It's my favorite."

He caught hold of her as she climbed out of the tub, slippery as a seal. "Here's a towel. Can you be drying yourself off?"

"Of course. I *am* eight years old," she reminded him. She frowned a bit at the roughness of the brown towel he handed her, but didn't comment on it. Michael dutifully made a mental note to add those pink fabric softener sheets his sister Nora used on her wash to his shopping list.

"It's a nice bed," she said as she bounced a little on the mattress.

"I'm glad you approve."

His dry tone flew right over her head, which currently was sporting a corona of wet corkscrew curls. "And the covering's lovely, as well." She ran her hand over the spread woven in the blue and green colors of Ireland.

"A friend made it for me when I moved into this home."

"A girlfriend?"

"No. A friend friend. My sister was married to her brother for a time. Then he died." Michael could have torn out his tongue for bringing up the subject of death at bedtime.

Her rosebud lips pulled down into a frown. "That's sad. Did he have any children?

"A son. Rory, who I told you sleeps here on occasion."

"Oh." She thought about that for a moment. "Did Rory's mum die, as well?"

"No. She married an American last year. They're visiting there now."

"That's nice." Her moods seemingly like quicksilver, the frown turned to a smile. "I've always wanted to see America."

"Perhaps someday you will."

"When Rory gets back, perhaps he can tell me stories about his adventures," she suggested.

"I'm sure he will." Michael was more worn out by the bathing and teeth brushing ritual—in which apparently each small pearly tooth had to be scrubbed ten times up and down—than he'd been after a midnight hike through the mountains of Kurdistan, where his boyhood friend Tom Flannery had been gassed, turning the Irish relief doctor into one more casualty—albeit delayed—of war. He reached out and turned off the bedside lamp, sending the room into deep shadows.

"Mum sometimes let me read a story before I went to sleep," the small high voice offered into the darkness.

Michael scrubbed a weary hand down his face. "Did she now?"

"Aye. Even though Gram said all a girl needed to read was her catechism, her missal at Sunday mass, and tales of our brave fighting men."

"Your grandmother was wrong." He sighed, turned the light back on, and took a book from atop a sturdy, scarred wooden table that had been crafted by his great-grandfather Joyce.

"Try this one on for size," he suggested. "It's a story set here by the sea in Castlelough."

She opened the old leather-bound text, stared at the ivory-hued page, blinked three times, rubbed her eyes with her knuckles, then frowned.

"I'm only in third form," she said in something perilously close to a whine that had him hoping she wasn't entering some difficult girlhood phase. What he knew about children was close to nil. He knew even less about young females. "These words are too hard."

Michael kept his surprise to himself even as he wondered how it was that the same little girl who'd been reading him the sports scores from the *Irish Times* while he'd been cooking her dinner could be having problems with a simple folk tale that he himself had probably read for the first time before his seventh birthday. He made a mental note to have Tom give his daughter an eye test at first opportunity.

"I suppose I'll just have to tell it to you myself. As my own father did to me. And his before him."

When he went to pull up a chair, Shea patted the muslin sheet beside her. "There's room for you to sit with me. Just like Mum sometimes did."

Michael would have had to be deaf not to hear the need in the all too obvious invitation. Having little choice, he joined his daughter on the narrow mattress. She cuddled up against him, a wee sprite wearing a pink flannel nightgown that even he could tell clashed with her wild mare's nest of wet red hair, smelling of soap and minty toothpaste.

Something unbidden in his heart, a touch of warmth he'd thought had died with him on that faraway operating table, stirred.

"This would be the story of Kevin James Joyce, a distant cousin of ours, who lived before you were born and was one of the best singers and dancers in the county. It was said that even the angels in heaven would weep when Kevin would perform his *sean-nos* singing at funerals."

"That's singing without music," Shea said as she nestled her head against his shoulder.

Michael put his arm around her. "Right you are, and I suspect you'll be hearing your grandda Joyce's friend Fergus performing it now that you'll be living in Castlelough."

"I'll like that," Shea said without hesitation. Since arriving at the farm earlier today there'd been nothing the girl hadn't liked, which made Michael wonder again what it was that caused Deidre to have such a negative opinion of her granddaughter.

"Well, as my da told the story to me, one rainy spring day Kevin was down by the sea, looking for one of his sheep who'd wandered away, when he viewed the most beautiful woman he'd ever seen sleeping on a rock. She was wrapped in a gray cloak and hood that kept her warm enough, but unfortunately the tide was coming in and Kevin feared for the woman's life."

"Because she could get washed out to sea."

"Exactly." Michael nodded. "He ran down to the rock and shook her awake and warned her that she must leave with him right away or she'd be drowning."

"Did she leave with him?"

"What she did was laugh at him. A laugh he'd later tell friends sounded like silver Yuletide bells. Then she dove into the surf and swam out to sea. Kevin watched as she disappeared beneath the waves, and for the next week he cursed himself for not saving her when he had a chance."

"She drowned?" Shea's eyes widened.

"So Kevin believed. But then one day, when he was cutting peat, he heard singing, in a soprano voice even sweeter than his own famed tenor."

"Was it the lady?"

"None other," Michael agreed. "Kevin left his spade and followed the song floating on the air down to the beach. There he saw her, on the very same rock. She'd taken off her gray cloak and was combing her long hair.

"Ah, she was a most winsome sight, with her skin gleaming like pearls. And Kevin knew, at that moment, that since God had brought her back to him, he was meant to take her for his wife. So, he sneaked up behind her and snatched the cloak away."

"Was she wearing anything at all underneath it?"

Michael winced a bit at the question he should have seen coming. "Actually, I believe she was clad in the very same flesh she was born in," he allowed. "Which was all the more reason Kevin felt he should marry her right away."

"But didn't you see my mother naked when you made me? And you didn't marry her."

Michael had heard complaints from married acquaintances that children were growing up too swiftly in these modern times, as if their internal timers had been set on fast forward. Having witnessed the horror of children dying in war zones, he hadn't honestly taken what he'd considered petty concerns that seriously. Until now.

"We're getting off the point of the story," he said

gruffly. "But if I'd known your mother was carrying you, Shea, I would have married her in a heartbeat."

It was a lie, but a well-meaning one, Michael reassured himself. He was not about to add that Rena had obviously neglected to notify him about his daughter because she herself had wisely not wanted to marry the wild Irish rover he'd been in those younger, more idealistic days.

Never knowing when a bullet could strike or a bomb could blow him to smithereens, Michael had lived each day as if it might be his last. Then, just when he'd forgotten to expect it, fate had caught up with him.

Shea smiled at his assertion, then wiggled impatiently. "Go on with the story."

"And so I will . . . Well, the woman made Kevin a fine wife. She cooked his meals, cleaned his house, spun his wool, gave him four beautiful children, and warmed his bed every night.

"Kevin's heart was so filled with love for her that he managed to overlook those times when he'd find her standing at the edge of that very cliff"—Michael waved toward the mist-draped landscape outside the window—"looking out to sea, silent tears streaming down her face."

"That's so sad." Her small, freshly scrubbed face puckered up; her eyes glistened.

"Aye. And didn't it become even sadder when a huge bull seal began appearing out in the surf, roaring all the day and night long, keeping the people from their sleep nearly as far away as Galway, and even Limerick, he was so loud, and made Kevin's poor wife cry all the more.

"Now, Kevin was not an unintelligent man. He knew that the wife he loved beyond distraction was no ordinary woman, but a selkie, a creature of the sea. When she took to her bed and could neither eat nor drink, and began to melt away, like sea mist warmed by the sun, Kevin knew what it was he must do."

"What was that?" She was practically holding her breath.

"He went upstairs to the loft, retrieved the sleek gray waterproof cloak he'd hidden away so many years before, and took it into the bedroom they'd shared for those seven years. Her beautiful pearly skin looked like wax, her eyes were closed, as if in death, and her hair was a limp dark tangle around her too thin shoulders, but she was still the most beautiful woman Kevin had ever seen."

"That was because he loved her," she said with a perception Michael would not have expected from an eight-year-old.

"Aye. With his entire heart and soul. Which is why he knew he must set her free to save her. The moment he wrapped the cloak around her, her eyes flew open, and color, like pink roses, flooded into her cheeks. She flung her arms around his neck and kissed him with so much feeling that his aching heart seemed to swell in his chest like a sea sponge dropped into water.

"Then he brought in their children, including the wee lass not more than six months old, and she kissed them, too, and stroked their hair and told them how much she loved them all. How much she'd always love them. Then, together, hand in hand the family walked down to the sea, with Kevin holding the wee babe, and he and his children watched as she walked into the surf, toward the bull seal, who turned out to be her father, come to fetch his darling daughter home."

"Like you would have fetched me, if you'd known I was in Belfast?"

"Absolutely," he agreed, his firm tone meant to address the insecurity he heard in her small voice.

He dropped a kiss atop her head and felt his heart lurch yet again when she wrapped her arms tightly around him and clung.

"Well," he said, roughly clearing his throat. "To be getting on with my tale, the woman's family stood on the rock where Kevin had first witnessed her sleeping and watched as the sea swirled around her ankles. Then her knees. When she'd waded into the surf up to her shoulders, she turned, gave them one last wave, then dove beneath the water."

When he heard Shea catch her breath, Michael instinctively ran a comforting hand down her hair and over her slender shoulder. "It was raining, hard, like it is today, but as she disappeared, back to her watery home, the sun broke from behind the dark clouds and a huge rainbow arced over the cliffs, all the way from the sea to the cottage where she and Kevin and their children had all lived together."

She was sniffling now. Damn. The problem with so many Irish tales, Michael had realized belatedly once he'd begun the story, was that even the ones that didn't involve war were very often bittersweet and ended with a death. And this had surely not been a proper tale to share with a child who'd just lost her own mother.

Cursing himself for a bloody fool, he scrambled to

tack on a new ending to the folk story he'd grown up with. "But it would not be their last time together."

"It wasn't?" Hope shimmered in the frail voice.

"Oh no," he assured her robustly. "For every evening, without fail, fair weather or foul, after the children brought the cows in from the fields, they'd go down to the sea and their mother would be swimming at the water's edge, and although they could not speak the seal language and she could no longer converse in either Irish or English, they managed to communicate just fine.

"Oh, and another thing I almost forgot to be telling you was that all four children had webbing, just like a seal, between their fingers and toes and even now, generations later, some Joyce babes are born with such webbing."

"Really?" Interest replaced sorrow on the small, intent face. She spread her own fingers, the pink tips of which were still slightly puckered from her warm bath. "I don't have any webbing."

"Are you certain?" He tugged the cover aside. "Maybe we should check, just to be certain."

Michael had never really believed the selkie story, but it crossed his mind, as he checked all ten childish pink toes for any sign of seal ancestry, that Kevin's wife's laughter could not possibly have been any more musical or pleasing to the ear than the sound of his daughter's breathless giggles.

~ 5 ~

The Moving Cloud

 $\mathcal{T}$ he walls of the bedroom were drawing in on him, as they so often did in the long, dark, lonely nights. Michael kicked off the top sheet, rolled over onto his good side, placed his arm under his head, and tried to find a comfortable position. On any other night, he'd simply give up the attempt at sleep and go walking along the cliff, sometimes until the sun rose.

But tonight was different. Different because of the little girl sleeping in his own child's bed just across the hall from his own room. What if he were to leave her alone and a fire broke out? That was admittedly unlikely, but if there was one thing Michael had learned, it was not to trust the status quo.

He yanked the bottom sheet from the mattress when he flopped over onto his back again. Death had been a grim companion, following patiently on his heels like a silent specter for years. It had lingered outside the American air base in Turkey, while Michael had undergone his first, lifesaving surgery. Then it had followed him to the ICU, practically daring him to surrender. But having so far won the battle against his nemesis, he damn well wasn't going to risk losing a daughter just for the need to get out of the house and walk off this damn unnamed anxiety. Even one who still seemed more stranger than child of his own blood.

"Didn't ye just meet the gel?" Brady Joyce asked from his perch atop the dresser. "Give it time, lad. Before you know it, you'll be teaching the wee sprite how to take award-winning photographs, just like her da's."

"Shea doesn't need any camera," Michael said curtly. "She needs to be concentrating on her school-work, not wasting time with foolishness."

"I don't seem to recall you calling it foolishness when you were a mere year older than she is now, and whenever your ma sent you to cut the peat, you'd sneak away to take photographs of the rich American tourists on holiday."

"We needed the money."

"That we did." Brady nodded. "Life in the west has never been easy. But believe me, boyo, it's the closest thing to heaven on earth."

With that pronouncement, he was gone, fading back into the mists of time and, Michael assured himself yet again, the murky depths of his own imagination.

As the plane descended on its approach to Shannon airport, Erin looked out the window and was hit with a rush of emotion so strong that tears welled up in her eyes, momentarily blurring her vision of the impossibly green island set like an emerald in a sapphire sea. She'd never considered herself a fanciful person, yet she couldn't ignore a strong feeling of déjà vu, and a distant sense of coming home.

Which was, of course, ridiculous, she reminded herself sternly as both a dazzling bliss and an aching sadness dueled in her heart and her mind. Ireland wasn't *her* home, it was Tom's.

She put the strange feeling aside as she dealt with getting through customs, enjoying a brief chat with the uniformed man who stamped her passport and welcomed her with great warmth to his country.

Erin's heart sank at her first sight of Tom. He'd changed, and not for the better. Her physician's eye skimmed over the slightly jaundiced cast to flesh that was stretched too tightly over his cheekbones, his obvious loss of weight, the thinning of his formerly thick hair.

She could hardly recognize the indefatigable man she'd witnessed working seventy-two-hour shifts in inhospitable regions and worse weather. He looked, she thought with a sinking heart, nearly as bad as some of the refugees he'd devoted so many years to treating. Not helping matters was the fact that he was standing beside a tall, broad-shouldered man who made him appear even frailer by comparison.

Then his lips curved in a bold, familiar grin that touched his brown eyes and made his face light up like a welcoming beacon, and he was once again the Thomas Flannery she knew and loved.

She was swept up into a pair of arms that lacked the strength that had once allowed him to carry her three miles over mountainous terrain when she'd broken an ankle. But as she closed her eyes and hugged him back, Erin could feel the incredible buoyancy of spirit that had always had her believing that things weren't nearly as bad as they might seem, that problems, no matter how immense, were merely obstacles to be overcome.

He put her a little away from him in order to study her.

"Sure and you're still the most gorgeous woman the good Lord ever created," he drawled in an exaggerated brogue that could always lighten her mood.

"And you're still full of blarney." She managed to smile up at him even as her eyes began to swim.

He put a hand on his chest in a gesture of feigned innocence. "Would you be accusing your dearest friend of telling tales?"

"Either that or you've gone blind since I've last seen you," she countered, falling back into their old pattern of teasing.

"Not yet." His gentle tone caused the reason for her being here to come crashing down on Erin again.

She lifted a hand to his cheek. "Thomas—"

"We'll talk later," he said with the same quiet authority that had always managed to create order from chaos. "Meanwhile, I'm forgetting my manners."

He swept his hand toward the man who was still standing silently beside him. "I'd like you to be meeting my old boyhood mate, Michael James Joyce."

The name rang an instantaneous and immediate bell. Erin's first day in Sarajevo had been a baptism by fire. Snipers hidden like the cowards they were up in the hills had attacked a popular Sunday market with gunfire, grenades, and rockets. The field medical office had been flooded with casualties. The stories that swept through the camp became more horrific, more unfathomable, as the seemingly endless day went on.

As she held a dying eight-year-old girl in her arms, at first Erin hadn't believed the tale circulating about the wounded Irish photographer who'd been swiftly airlifted to a trauma center out of the country while women, children, and old men were still lying wounded in the streets. The following morning she'd learned from a CNN reporter that the story was, indeed, true, and as she tried to comfort the child's grief-stricken parents, she couldn't help thinking that their daughter might well be alive if only she'd gotten the kind of VIP treatment Michael Joyce had received.

It was at Sarajevo that Erin had met Tom, who now seemed to be presenting Michael Joyce like some special gift. Her assessing gaze swept over the photographer. He was large, very large, towering over the other travelers in the crowded terminal.

Unlike the man who'd sat next to her on the plane and had seemingly drenched himself in an overpowering male cologne, Michael smelled like soap. His black hair needed a trim, falling carelessly over the collar of his thick Aran sweater. It was nearly as curly as her own, yet not the least bit feminine. Indeed, she thought, it only made his harshly hewn bones and strong square chin appear more rugged by comparison His jeans were faded and torn at the knee; his work boots scuffed.

Erin had met her share of hotshot photojournalists who only seemed to care about one thing—being the first to send home the most ghoulish pictures. The man standing in front of her was certainly the most famous of the lot. Having always considered herself a good judge of people—there had been times when her life had depended on that ability—she momentarily studied his face, trying to determine the truth behind the legends.

Was he, as some suggested, an idiot who earned his living by standing in the line of fire? Or a vulture who fed off the misery of others, who'd snap their pictures, then move on to other headline-grabbing stories?

There was also a third possibility: that he might actually give a damn about the people whose lives he earned his living by publicly invading.

Standing here in the terminal, looking a long, long way up at him, Erin vaguely recalled a tale, difficult to reconcile with Michael Joyce's macho cowboy image, about him rescuing a pair of infant twins along the road to a medical center, only to have them die after he'd reached camp. One AP photographer Erin had met in Kosovo had sworn she'd actually witnessed him burying the babies himself.

Unfortunately, there was no corroborating photograph, since Michael had reportedly snatched the camera out of the photographer's hand after she'd taken the photo and exposed the film to the light, effectively ruining it.

Considering that his reputation for recklessness was equaled by his reputation for the lusty enjoyment of women the world over, Erin would have expected him to be handsome, which he definitely was. What did come as a surprise was his remoteness. He seemed almost disconnected, as if he'd pulled some internal plug deep within him.

She searched the eyes of this man whose presence at any war validated its importance to the world, seeking to make sense of the contrasting stories of devil-daring and honest caring. His eyes were as deep blue as the sea, but hard, offering not a single clue to the inner man.

No, Erin corrected, not hard. But unnervingly flat and impossibly enigmatic. His expression was every bit as stony as the cliffs she'd just flown over.

"Hello, Mr. Joyce. It's a pleasure to meet you." It was a polite lie, but her mother had taught her manners. She held out her hand. "I've heard a great deal about you."

"People talk too much." He didn't return her wary smile. "And whatever you may have heard from Tom, I assure you, Doctor, it's all lies."

His voice was deep, like the rumbling of a war drum and almost as hard and flat as his disturbing eyes. His years away from home seemed to have worn away a great bit of the region's rough west country brogue along with any lilt of Irish charm.

Her hand had no sooner disappeared into his much larger, much darker one than she felt a sudden, inexplicable urge to reclaim it with a sharp tug.

"It's a sad day indeed, when the two people dearest to a man accuse him of telling falsehoods," Tom complained.

Erin reminded herself that she'd come here for Tom's sake and there was no way she was going to let Michael Joyce's unexpected appearance, or his strange assault on her nerves, make her lose track of her priorities.

"Poor abused dear." She went up on her toes and kissed the cheek that felt unnaturally dry, like ancient parchment that might crack and blow away at any minute. "Sure and it's a pitiful thing to be unappreciated." Her own feigned brogue was even thicker than his.

He laughed, tousled her hair in a gesture that was heartbreakingly familiar and grinned up at Michael. "Didn't I tell you she was wonderful?"

Michael's unfathomable gaze swept with excruciating slowness over her face. He was still not smiling.

"Wonderful," he agreed after a lengthy pause.

Michael had, indeed, heard all about the American doctor. Hadn't he spent many a long rainy night over pints in the Irish Rose, listening to his best friend wax enthusiastic about her intelligence, her bravery, her compassion?

But Tom had neglected to mention a complexion which needed no artificial enhancements from pots or creams. Beneath the baseball cap, her chestnut curls were as glossy as a selkie's coat; her eyes were the rich, tawny hue of Irish whiskey, and if they hadn't turned cautious at his rudeness, he suspected they could have been every bit as intoxicating. Her mouth was wide and unpainted, and she smiled easily.

She'd hidden her body beneath an ugly, oversized sweatshirt, but from what he could tell, she was as slender as a reed. While she wasn't a conventional beauty, there was something there . . .

Michael mentally struggled to name it, frustrated when he couldn't immediately come up with the proper word. His father would know. Language, along with a belief in leprechauns, lough creatures, faeries, and all things magical, had come as easily for Brady Joyce as breathing.

Michael may have stopped believing in God, but he was Irish enough to still believe in faeries. He'd just never expected to meet one in person. Vibrancy pulsed around her, shimmering out of her elfin body like star shine, brightening the gray and gloomy day.

He'd watched her making her way through customs, the usually bored immigration officer's already ruddy cheeks turning bright red at something she said. The man was old enough to be Erin O'Halloran's father, perhaps even her grandfather, yet Michael would not have been the least bit surprised if he'd melted on the spot.

"It's a bit of a drive to Castlelough," he said. "We'd best be going."

"Grand idea," Tom seconded with a show of enthusiastic spirit Michael hadn't heard for weeks. "That way you can have yourself a bit of a lie-down before I show you off at the pub tonight, Erin love. Everyone's been waiting to meet you."

If he hadn't been watching her carefully, Michael would have missed the brief flicker of dread in her eyes. In contrast, the smile she bestowed upon Tom as she assured him she was looking forward to meeting his friends, seemed to light her up from the inside out.

There was a brief tug-of-war over her well-worn duffel bag and laptop computer. Naturally, Michael prevailed.

"What the hell do you have in this," he asked as he slung the duffel bag over his shoulders, "rocks?"

"My medical bag. And some books."

"This may come as a surprise to you, Dr. O'Halloran, but we've had books in Ireland for quite some time."

"They're medical texts, no doubt," Tom explained as they walked toward the parking lot. "Erin refuses to accept the diagnoses of experts. Against all odds, she's determined to keep me alive."

"I'm a doctor," Erin argued, with an interesting flash of temper. Michael wondered if perhaps the woman wasn't quite the saint Michael had made her out to be.

While they drove north along the Shannon estuary from the airport, through the rich and rolling pasture lands that had once been inhabited by cattle barons, and before that, in times long past, by ancient kings, Erin questioned Tom seemingly nonstop about the surgery while still managing to rave about the countryside.

She talked with her hands, Michael noticed. They were never still, moving through the air like graceful birds, dipping and soaring to accentuate a point.

"It's so green!" she exclaimed again and again, the same thing Michael figured tourists had been saying since before the days of the Norse invasions.

As they approached Clarecastle, which Tom explained was the highest point inland on the River Fergus where ships could go, he suggested that Michael stop for a moment, so she could admire the sight of the Killone Abbey.

Ignoring the cold rain that was falling on the hood of her parka, she got out of the car.

"It's so quiet," she murmured, brushing at her curly wet bangs as she stood at the edge of the road and gazed out at the gray abbey on the shores of Lough Killone.

"A mermaid once lived in that lake," Michael volunteered.

"Really?" Since he hadn't uttered a word once

they'd begun their drive north to Castlelough, she seemed more surprised that he'd actually initiated conversation than she was by the idea of a mermaid.

"So the tale goes. It also alleges that she was brutally murdered, which is why the lake takes on the color of her blood on special occasions."

She went still. Shoulders, back, even her graceful hands in the pockets of her parka. "That's a tragic story."

"Too tragic for a grand day like today," Tom complained. "And shame on you for tellin' it, Michael."

Michael shrugged. "It's merely a legend. Unlike the tale of Colleen Bawn."

"Now, Michael," Tom protested. "This is no way to welcome Erin to our fair country."

"Don't worry, Tom." Erin patted his arm. "From what I've seen, Ireland is close to heaven on earth, and I strongly doubt there's anything Mr. Joyce could say that could convince me otherwise."

She was smiling up at him, in a friendly enough way, but Michael saw a sparkle of challenge in her brown eyes. He never had been one to turn down a dare.

"The tale of Colleen Bawn is a classic story of love and intrigue across the classes in the nineteenth century. Ellen Hanley was a farmer's daughter reputed to be of outstanding beauty and friendly disposition who made the tragic mistake of falling in love with a young man of the ascendancy, John Scanlin.

"Soon after their elopement, Scanlin tired of her. He plied his servant, Stephan Sullivan, with whiskey and convinced him to take fair Ellen on a boat trip down the Shannon. It was in mid-stream that Sullivan murdered her with a musket, removed her garments and wedding ring, tied a rope to her body, and threw her overboard. Her body later washed ashore in Killimer, where you can take the ferry to Kerry.

"The murderers were subsequently arrested and brought to trial. Needless to say, due to his family being gentry, the trial caused a great sensation not only in County Clare, but all over Ireland."

"Did Scanlin's social position allow him to get away with the murder?" Erin asked.

"There were many who thought he would. Especially since the general opinion at the time was that an aristocrat should not suffer for a crime against a mere commoner. But despite his family hiring the famous lawyer Daniel O'Connell, who was known across the country as the Liberator, Scanlin was found guilty and subsequently hanged on Gallows Green. Sullivan, of course, was hung as well, but not before confessing the entire plot on the gallows.

"A Celtic cross with the inscription 'Here lies the Colleen Bawn, murdered on the Shannon, July 14, 1819. R.I.P.' was erected on Ellen's grave in her memory, but souvenir hunters chipped the cross away bit by bit, and you'll be finding no trace of it today."

Erin tilted her head and looked up at him. "I've always heard of the Irish knack for storytelling, and surely Tom has always been a prime example . . . But tell me, Mr. Joyce, are all your tales so grim?"

Since she appeared honestly curious, he took the time to think about her question for a moment, remembering all too well how he'd been forced to change the ending of the selkie story he'd told to Shea. "Aye, I suppose they are."

She gave him another, longer, more searching look. "Then as sorry as I am for that poor Colleen Bawn, I'm even sorrier for you." That said, she got back in the car and shut the door.

Michael and Tom exchanged a look. Tom grinned. Michael did not.

∞ 6 ∞

The Shadow

*E*rin continued chatting with Tom as they made their way toward Castlelough. They were on the outskirts of the village when Tom pointed out another of the many grottos dedicated to the Virgin Mary dotting the landscape.

"It's lovely," she said, as she'd been saying about most everything along the road.

"It's a plaster statue standing in a tire," Michael pointed out derisively. The tire may have been painted white, but that didn't stop "Goodyear" from showing through. A few brave flowers were poking their heads from the damp ground in an attempt to rush spring.

"It's the Blessed Virgin standing in a garden," Tom contradicted him. "Created by one of our own."

He was clearly teasing one of them. And since it wasn't her, Erin glanced over at Michael.

"Did you make that grotto?"

"At the strict creative direction of my grandmother," he heard himself revealing. "Fionna Joyce is a fine, devout woman. But not always an easy one."

She gave him another of those long, steady looks. But this time Michael thought he saw just the hint of a smile on her unpainted lips.

"A trait, it appears, that runs in the Joyce family," she murmured, just loud enough for him to hear as they drove through the narrow streets of a tidy fifteenth-century town with its bright storefronts, artistically hand-painted signs, and stone church that she appeared to find even more charming than everything else she'd seen so far.

Having flown all this way to take care of Tom, Erin was frustrated at his refusal to let her stay with him in his rooms above the surgery he'd taken over from a retired physician.

" 'Tis bad enough that you're having to cut short your time with your family to help with my patient load," he told her the same thing he'd been telling her for days during their long transatlantic telephone calls. "I'll not be having you hovering over me, checking my vital signs and lecturing me about my bad habits."

"In case you've forgotten, it's you who asked me to come to Ireland to help you out. That's all I'm trying to do."

"I know that, lass," Tom said from the backseat. "But I also know that inside that fey exterior beats the heart of a Valkyrie and I'd just as soon forgo any more battles at this point in my life."

She knew he was referring to her refusal to accept the notion of his impending death and decided that she was too exhausted from the trip to march out onto that conversational battlefield right now.

"It's not that I don't love you dearly, Erin," Tom assured her in his lilting brogue. "But the bald truth of the matter is that having you staying under my roof would undoubtedly cut down on my success with the ladies, if you'd be getting my drift."

Frustrated as she was, she couldn't help laughing as he'd meant her to.

When her plane had landed, the sun had been gilding the island, making sea and land appear like sapphire and emerald stones set in gold. By the time she'd cleared customs and exited the terminal with the two men, a light rain had begun to fall.

Now, as the car made its way along the treacherous, narrow road that twisted along the edge of the cliff leading out of town, a veil of mist shrouded the horizon, merging sea and sky. Fog began to drift in front of the car like little ghosts riding the moist air currents in from the sea.

A particularly dense cloud floated by, draping over the windshield like an Irish lace curtain, blocking the roadway from view.

"We don't have far to go," Michael volunteered into the shrouded silence. "With any luck, we'll be reaching the cottage before the weather gets too socked in."

"Fog's never bothered me." Actually, she'd always found it somewhat romantic. When she wasn't having to drive through it, that is.

Wide, formidable shoulders lifted in a half shrug. "Then you're bound to enjoy our Irish west." He returned his attention to the corkscrewing road.

The fog thickened, a swirling white that wrapped around the car windows, concealing the sea on one side and engulfing the rolling fields bordered by stony mountains on the other.

Erin was admittedly relieved when Michael didn't drive like the daredevil cowboy he was reputed to be. The car was creeping through the seemingly impenetrable mist now, the headlights bouncing back from the dense white wall.

She shot a quick, surreptitious look to her right. Although he remained properly alert, she couldn't detect any sign of nerves and wondered whether such outward confidence displayed that same reckless disregard for danger that had gotten him shot in Sarajevo, or whether he'd merely driven this road so many times, he'd memorized its twists and turns. Despite her assertion that the thick fog didn't disturb her, Erin dearly hoped it was the latter case.

When what felt like another hour, but by her watch was a mere ten minutes, had passed without a word from either man, Erin glanced over her shoulder at the backseat, where Tom appeared to have fallen asleep.

She'd witnessed Dr. Thomas Flannery performing surgery for thirty-six hours straight in a mud-floored operating room under the most savage, inhospitable conditions that a long-ago American Civil War surgeon might have recognized, oblivious to extremes of sweltering heat or freezing cold, fueled only by caffeine and nicotine.

There had been more than one occasion—when her own head had rung with the shriek of incoming artillery fire and her T-shirt and jeans had been drenched in the blood of the seemingly endless stream of suffering victims—when the intoxication of shared purpose had worn thin, leaving her feeling on the verge of meltdown.

But then she'd glance across the plastic-draped green tent and view Tom tirelessly performing the amputations that unfortunately they'd all become expert at, and a surge of much-needed resolve would keep the doctor in her focused on the job at hand even when the woman longed to fling herself on the nearest cot and weep herself to sleep.

During their years working together, she'd come to accept his strength as a force of nature, like the ebb and flow of the tides, or the rising of the sun in the east every morning, wherever in the world she might be posted.

Since learning of his illness, she'd felt as if the planet had reversed direction and the world she'd known had suddenly started wobbling dangerously on its axis.

"We've still a bit left to go," Michael said after a time. His voice sounded even deeper and richer in the intimacy created by the fog. "If you'd be wanting to take a short nap."

"I'm fine."

She felt rather than saw his shrug this time. "Suit yourself."

She didn't go to sleep, but she did lean her head back, closed her eyes, and let her mind drift. Yet instead of focusing on the rolling green hills and craggy, mist-draped cliffs, Erin instead found herself thinking of Tom's dilemma.

So many deaths, she thought on a sad little sigh. Every relief worker she knew had warned her that in order to avoid burnout, she'd have to learn to distance herself from her work, to not take the brutal results of war so personally.

And she'd tried. Truly she had. She'd even developed a few mental tricks to keep from losing her grip.

But this dilemma with the man who'd been both mentor and best friend was different from watching a stranger die in some chaotic medical camp. It was extremely personal.

She wouldn't let him die, Erin vowed yet again. Admittedly, he looked even worse than she'd feared. But she was a brilliant doctor. Everyone had always said so. Hadn't she graduated at the top of her class at Johns Hopkins, despite being years younger than her classmates? She'd think of something, she assured herself. She may be brilliant, but Tom was the best diagnostician she'd ever met. They'd put their heads together and come up with something that would save his life. And then she'd get on with hers.

Shea stood at the window, shifting from foot to foot as she watched the rain streaking down the glass, impatient for the sign of her father's car coming down the narrow road.

"What do you think could be keeping him?" she asked for the umpteenth time in the past hour.

Fionna Joyce didn't bother to look up from her knitting. "It could be any number of things," she said calmly. "Perhaps the airplane was delayed arriving from the States. Perhaps the American doctor got stuck in customs. Or Michael could have had a flat tire on his motorcar. Fussing isn't going to make him arrive home any sooner."

Her tone was matter-of-fact, but not unkind. When her father had informed her that her great-grandmother Joyce would be coming over this morning to stay with her while he went to the airport, Shea had begged to be taken along. Her only knowledge of grandparents had come from her mum's mother, who'd never failed to remind her that she was Satan's child, born of sin and out of wedlock. Deidre McDougall had never liked Shea. By the time Shea had passed her third birthday, the feeling was mutual.

But this Castlelough grandmother—really her great-grandmother, her father had explained—was nothing like the Belfast one. It was more than the difference in their looks. Her grandmother McDougall was a large woman, while her grandmother Joyce was small and wiry, with a ruddy, kind face and hair that glowed as red as a fire, as brightly as Shea's own, which made her feel even more like a Joyce than a McDougall.

The two women were opposite sides of the coin in temperament, as well. While one would strap her for seemingly no other reason than her own foul temper, this one welcomed her into the Joyce family without so much as a blink of surprise.

She'd also, not once all morning, mentioned the circumstances of Shea's birth. And best of all, she appeared to honestly believe in Mary Margaret and Casey, something Shea suspected even her father—whom she already adored—did not.

"God gives us all guardian angels, of course," Fionna had said when Shea had told her about her constant companions. "But you're fortunate, Shea, darling, that you can actually see yours. Not many people can."

"Can you?" Shea had asked.

"No. Though last year I was in a store that was attacked by terrorists in Derry, and as the bomb went off, I knew I would survive because I felt protected."

She had nodded. "That's how I always feel."

Her grandmother had gone on to tell her all about her efforts to get a Sister of Mercy who'd grown up in Castlelough declared a saint. Sister Bernadette had worked for peace during the old days of the Anglo-Irish war and had been murdered for her efforts. *Just like my mum*, Shea had thought sadly.

"I'm getting closer to success," Fionna had revealed. "The Congregation for the Cause has been investigating Bernadette's case. All I need is one more miracle to set the wheels in motion for her beatification."

"I hope you find one," Shea had said earnestly, deciding on the spot to ask Mary Margaret to help her newfound great-grandmother in her quest.

"I intend to," Fionna had said in a way that had Shea doubting her not at all.

"I wish he'd hurry," Shea repeated now as she pressed her nose against the cold glass.

The view outside the window began to waver, and suddenly the car parked outside the house, painted all over with religious scenes depicting Sister Bernadette's life and times—Fionna called it her Miraclemobile— had a twin. Shea blinked furiously to bring the two visions back into one.

"Are you all right, dear?"

Her great-grandmother's voice, which had gone higher with concern, sounded as if it were coming from a long distance.

"Oh, aye."

"You've gone pale."

"There's nothing wrong with me," Shea insisted with a flare of desperation as she struggled to focus on the kind and saintly face of the martyred nun painted on the outside of the driver's door.

If her da knew about the headaches, he might think she was going to be too much trouble to take care of and send her away to an orphanage. Or even worse, back to her grandmother McDougall.

Just when she was certain she was going to embarrass herself by fainting, Shea felt Mary Margaret's rainbow wings folding comfortingly about her. Her blurry vision cleared; the headache faded back into the distance.

She was going to be all right, she reassured herself with a firm mental shake. After all, didn't she have her guardian angel to protect her?

The cottage Tom had booked for Erin boasted a rounded, yellow thatched roof and exterior that had been whitewashed to the hue of new snow. It was small, with only a kitchen-living room combination, bedroom, and, thankfully, modern bath, but wonderfully cozy. The deep windowsills had been painted, inside and out, in a rich apple red, and the door was the bright blue of a robin's egg.

A peat fire already lit by some unseen hand glowed welcomingly; a kitchen cupboard held substantial-looking pottery the colors of which could have washed off the landscape. In a single dinner plate Erin could view the green fields, blue sea, slate skies, and bits of yellow gorse that had gleamed like gold beneath the glowing rays of whatever sunbeams had managed to break through the clouds and rain on the long drive from the airport.

Handwoven tapestries depicting Celtic symbols brightened the white walls, and everywhere there were books. Ancient leather-bound volumes with gilt lettering on the spines jockeyed for space with glossy modern-day bestsellers and tattered paperbacks on nearly every flat surface, spreading over the kitchen table, the seats of the four chairs, the dresser, shelves, and even the floor.

A tower of what appeared to be mostly textbooks was being used as a doorstop between the two rooms; another nearby, made up of Irish-interest topics, served as a side table of sorts and was topped with a trio of fat beeswax candles.

It was like walking into a literary version of Aladdin's magic cave. Some people, more accustomed to order than chaos in their lives, might find it all a bit distracting. Despite having always believed in traveling light, Erin, who couldn't recall the last time she'd taken time to read solely for pleasure, found it wonderful. Unfortunately, remembering the medical books packed away in the duffel bag Michael Joyce was carrying into the cottage, she doubted that she'd have time to read them.

After she'd assured Tom that she'd be fine, and sent both men on their way, Erin resisted—just barely—a tempting book of Irish folktales, choosing instead a text on general principles of inhalation toxicology and clinical immunology. Drawn by the lure of the high bed she needed steps to climb into, she slipped beneath the quilts, opened to the first page, and promptly fell asleep, chased by the nightmares that had followed her to Ireland.

*   *   *

Not wanting word of his daughter's arrival to spread throughout the village until he could put the proper spin on the story, Michael had worried about what to do with Shea while he drove Tom to the airport to pick up the American doctor.

His sister would have been the obvious choice, but she was off visiting America with her husband, new baby daughter, and the rest of the family, and wouldn't be back until tomorrow, which left Fionna. While his grandmother wouldn't admit it, she'd entered her eighties, but despite her advancing years, had the energy of a woman decades younger. She should be able to tend to one eight-year-old girl for a few hours, he'd decided. Especially since, despite Deidre's warning, Shea was turning out to be an exceptionally polite child.

He'd been relieved at how well Fionna had taken the news of her great-granddaughter. Then again, his grandmother had experienced a great deal in her lifetime, including the loss of her husband and a son—Michael's father—as well as a bombing last year while shopping in the north.

"Is Dr. O'Halloran rich?" Shea asked when Michael entered the house. The enticing scent of his grandmother's nettle soup simmering on the stove reminded him that it had been a long time since breakfast.

"I have no idea." He made himself a cup of tea from the pot simmering on the stove. "Why would you be asking that?"

"Grandmother McDougall was always joining the letter writing campaigns to get money for the Cause from Americans because she said they were all rich."

The spoon of creamy custard Fionna had apparently prepared for Shea paused on the way to her mouth. "Do you think she'll be finding the cottage too small?" He'd taken Shea to the small home he'd lived in during the remodeling of this one after milking this morning, when he'd stocked the fridge for Tom's visitor.

"There's only herself living in the cottage, which is cozy enough for one," Michael pointed out. "She didn't arrive with much luggage. I don't think she'll have any reason to feel cramped."

"But Grandmother said Americans all live in fine mansions," Shea continued with a persistence that reminded him of her mother.

"It sounds as if your grandmother is an eejit who doesn't know the first thing about Americans," Fionna grumbled disapprovingly.

When Michael had first told her the news of the daughter he'd not known he had, she'd been typically outspoken against the McDougalls for having kept such a secret from him.

"But didn't you tell me that my aunt Nora's new husband is an American?" Shea argued. "And you said that he's rich."

"Aye, he's wealthy enough," Fionna allowed. "But that's because he writes movies and books."

"I don't think you need worry about Dr. O'Halloran's comfort," Michael assured his daughter. "While I've no idea whether or not she grew up in an American mansion, I do know that these past years she's been living in tents like Dr. Flannery used to before he took over for Dr. Walsh at the surgery. At least Fair Haven cottage will give her a proper roof over her head for a change."

"That's the same thing Mary Margaret told me," Shea said.

Michael had discussed his daughter's fanciful angel friend with his sister during a long-distance call to the States last night and had been admittedly relieved when Nora had assured him that imaginary playmates were normal enough at his daughter's age. Even more so for only children, as Shea was.

"So you and Mary Margaret have been talking about our visitor?"

"We talk about everything," Shea reminded her father. "She told me that Dr. O'Halloran has nightmares, just like I do sometimes."

"And how would your angel be knowing that?" Fionna asked, revealing that Shea had also told her great-grandmother the tall tale about her supposed guardian angel with the rainbow wings.

"Dr. O'Halloran's guardian angel told Mary Margaret," Shea said.

"I'm a bit surprised to learn that angels gossip," Fionna murmured as she returned to her knitting. She'd begun making the emerald green sweater for her new great-granddaughter as soon as Michael had rung her up with the surprising news.

"Oh, it's not gossip when angels do it," Shea assured her blithely. "They just like sharing stories in heaven the same way we do down here on earth.

"Mary Margaret says that Dr. O'Halloran's angel has been working almost around the clock to keep her safe these past years, and she's secretly looking forward to a wee bit of a rest now that the American has come to Castlelough for Dr. Flannery's dying."

Her words had Michael thinking of Brady's remark regarding a father's ongoing concern for his children. If any of these recent revelations were even partly true, it appeared that heaven was far more complex than the serene place of gilded clouds, lush green wildflower-dotted meadows, and placidly winding rivers depicted in the romanticized gilt-framed paintings that had adorned the walls of Holy Child School when he'd been growing up.

While heaven may remain a mystery, Michael had a very clear idea of hell, having visited it personally on more occasions than he cared to count. As, he knew, had Erin O'Halloran.

A vision flashed through his head—one of the female doctor performing battlefield surgery, up to her elbows in blood. Uncomfortable with the mental image of the fragile-appearing woman surrounded by such blood and gore and hopelessness, Michael was grateful when he realized his grandmother had asked him a question.

"Excuse me. My mind was drifting for a moment."

"So it seemed," Fionna said. "I asked what the American looks like."

"I didn't really notice." A sudden narrowing of his grandmother's still bright eyes suggested his tone wasn't as casual as he'd hoped.

"Did you happen to take note of what she was wearing?"

"Jeans and a baggy sweatshirt that looked as if it had seen better days. Sneakers." Also well-worn, seemingly chosen for comfort rather than style. The bright kelly green laces had been a whimsical, unexpected touch.

"And one of those billed sports caps Americans seem so fond of, but I wouldn't be recalling which team."

"Do you at least recall the color of her hair?" Fionna was clearly impatient at this scant bit of information.

"Brown."

"Long or short?"

"Shorter than your own. Longer than Sinéad O'Connor's when she shaved her head."

"That's hardly an insightful description to share with your sister who's going to be ringing me up from America tonight wanting all the details," Fionna complained. "But I suppose I'll just have to go to the Rose and check the woman doctor out for myself. Since my night eyesight isn't what it once was and I'd hate to run my lovely Miraclemobile into a hedge, you can pick me up at seven."

"I can't go running off to the pub every night now that I'm a father."

"You didn't spend that much time at the Rose before Shea's arrival," Fionna countered. "Indeed, there are those in the village who have accused you of being the only antisocial Irishman ever born."

"I wouldn't be caring what a clutch of small-minded gossiping hens might be saying."

"Of course you don't. You've always had a mind of your own, after all. But I'll not be having you use your darling girl for an excuse, since you'll be bringing her along to the welcoming *ceili* for Dr. O'Halloran."

"Really?" Shea's expressive eyes lit up as if backlit by two glowing lanterns. "Will there be music? And dancing?"

Known for having a mind of her own, his grandmother

blithely ignored Michael's warning look. "Of course. What's a *ceili* without music and dancing, after all?"

"Could we go, Da? Please?"

It was the *Da* that did it. She'd been in his life only a single day, yet already Michael was finding it difficult to deny his newfound daughter anything. It had been the same way with her mother, he recalled.

Rena McDougall had possessed the seductive powers of a siren of old. More than a little spoiled because of her beauty and spirit, men fought to give her anything she desired, to do her every bidding. Michael had proven no exception, until the end, when he'd refused to join the killing for her, and the siren had turned into a wild, raging banshee before his very eyes.

"Surely you wouldn't be begrudging your daughter her first taste of country fun," Fionna coaxed, as wily as the fox that kept trying to steal his plump laying hens. "Besides, the boys will be needing you to bring your pipes."

"All right." One female was difficult enough to resist. Two were proving impossible. Especially one who'd taken a sally rod to his bare behind on more than one occasion while he was growing up.

"But only for an hour or so," he warned Shea in what he hoped was a firm, fatherly tone. "You'll need to be getting to bed at a decent time if you're to be going to mass with your great-grandmother in the morning. This isn't the city. Farm people can't be lying about in bed all day."

"I never lie about." She tossed her bright head in a way that once again reminded Michael vividly of her mother. He wondered if she'd also inherited Rena's temper and found himself hoping they'd both be spared that particular McDougall personality trait. "I was up this morning before the cock crowed."

"So you were."

Michael had been surprised when he'd rather enjoyed Shea's seemingly endless chatter during the early morning milking. Even if most of her discussions, other than her fascination with all things country, seemed to revolve around Mary Margaret and Casey.

Knowing that violence had been part and parcel of her first eight years, Michael understood how she might want to create a friendlier, more caring world in her mind. However, he'd also been concerned that she might have lost touch with reality. Last night's discussion with his sister Nora and another talk with Tom on the way to the airport had reassured him that her ability to create fantasy worlds was perfectly normal for her age.

"The sad thing," Tom had concluded on a deep sigh, "is that we adults eventually lose most of that connection with childhood."

Despite the seriousness of his work, especially during his years of relief work, Tom had certainly managed to remain close to his inner child. With the exception of his deceased brother-in-law—who'd certainly had his share of faults, one of which was an aversion to monogamy—Michael had never met anyone who played with more vigor than Tom Flannery.

Even more reason it was so tragic to be forced to watch his lifelong best friend disintegrating into a shell of his former robust self.

On the drive to Castlelough from Shannon, he'd

watched Erin O'Halloran watching Tom, not so much like a woman concerned about a friend, but as a doctor, diagnosing an ailing patient she intended to cure. Which was, Tom had assured Michael on more than one occasion, a lost cause.

Michael suspected that like him, Dr. Erin O'Halloran was all too familiar with lost causes. The difference was that she appeared to still possess the ability to hope, while any natural optimism he might have once possessed had been destroyed during too many years spent living in a universe where murder and mutilation were the norm, rather than the exception. A world that seemed a violent dark parallel planet to the tidy, peaceful west Irish village he'd grown up in.

"Will you bring along one of your cameras?" Fionna asked with a sly subtlety that was distinctly different from her usual outspokenness.

"I don't believe so."

They both knew he hadn't picked up a camera since he'd returned home. First his father, now his grandmother. Michael was getting a bit weary of his family's well-meaning pressure to resume that part of his former life. How could he begin to explain that he no longer wished to look at the world through lenses that had seen too many horrors?

"Your daughter's first appearance at the Rose as a member of the Joyce family is, after all, an occasion of note. It should be commemorated."

Michael opened his mouth to decline again when his grandmother tilted her head. He followed her gaze to Shea, who appeared to be literally holding her breath.

Bloody hell. It was more than a little obvious that such a small thing was of vast importance to his daughter.

"Perhaps you could take a snapshot or two with your Kodak," he suggested to Fionna. "That way Shea and I can be in the photographs together."

"As father and daughter." Shea breathed the words in the soft, reverent tone a religious pilgrim might use when referring to her god.

"Aye." Michael decided that it would take a man much harder-hearted than himself not to smile at this half-pint redhead who had turned his life upside down. "The photos will be the first of many that I suspect we'll have taken together."

It was, apparently, exactly the right thing to say. While his daughter beamed like a thousand newborn suns and Fionna nodded approvingly, Michael rashly decided that this parenting business just might not prove as difficult as he'd first feared.

Later, when his entire life seemed to be falling to pieces, when he was on the verge of losing everything he held dear, he would look back on this moment and wonder if just perhaps his premature pride was partly to blame for the inevitable fall.

❧ 7 ❧

The Dreaming Sea

$\mathcal{A}$ cold, desultory rain was falling from a smoke-filled sky. All around Erin, buildings were smoldering, the early morning eerily lit by orange flames on the horizon. The mortar attack had temporarily ceased, allowing the civilian population to come out of hiding.

Men, women, and children walked like vacant-eyed specters through the rubble that had once been their homes, stepping over once-precious possessions. They could have been answering a casting call for extras for a remake of Night of the Living Dead.

The sun was slowly rising in the east, a stuttering pale ball valiantly attempting to shine through the acrid clouds of smoke. Somewhere in the distance, a dog was howling. The crack of a pistol rang out. The dog was silenced. Erin could only hope the animal had been shot to be put out of its misery.

She closed her eyes and took a deep breath. When she opened them again, she saw a little girl, somewhere between four and five years old, emerge from beneath a pile of what appeared to have once been her family's kitchen. The child's hair was a snakelike tangle of blond curls; her face was smudged with dirt and soot. She was crying—wailing—for

*her mama and papa when she was distracted by something
beneath the chair.*

A sickening too-late feeling swept over Erin. She tried to
shout out a warning, but the words stuck in her throat.
Tried to run, but her feet felt mired in quicksand.

A moment later, the world around her exploded in a horrific bang and a blinding flash.

Her own screams woke her, jolting Erin out of a fit-
ful sleep. She sat upright in bed, drenched in sweat, her
out-of-control heart hammering like a rabbit's.

"It was only a nightmare," she assured herself as she
sank back against the pillow.

Still struggling to breathe, she glanced at the oak-
framed clock on the wall and realized she'd slept the
entire day away. She was thinking that it was nearly
time to get ready for her command appearance at the
pub with Tom when the phone rang. Leaping from the
bed, she raced across the room, tripping over a stack of
books before finally managing to scoop the old-
fashioned black receiver from its cradle.

"Erin?" the familiar voice asked. "It's Tom . . . Are
you all right?"

"Of course." She was panting as if she'd just run a
marathon and her knee, which had hit the corner of an
end table on her way down, was throbbing.

"You sound a bit strange. Are you certain I didn't
interrupt you at a bad time?"

"I tripped over some books," she muttered, scowl-
ing down at the blood trickling from the cut on her
leg.

"Ah, I suppose that's easily enough done in that cottage," he agreed. "I was calling about tonight."

"I was just getting ready when you called," she said, fudging the truth.

"Well, that's what I wanted to talk to you about. Do you think we could make it tomorrow night instead?"

Every instinct Erin had went on full alert. "Are you all right?" she asked, her pain instantly forgotten.

"I'm right as rain. It's just that I've got a bit behind on my paperwork, and—"

"Dammit, Tom." Concern made her impatient. "We've been friends long enough that there's no need for you to lie to me. How are you really feeling?"

"I'm a wee bit fatigued," he admitted with obvious reluctance. "But that's to be expected, given my condition. I also wasn't lying about needing to catch up on my paperwork. Keeping billing records and such is not exactly something I had to do when we were working in the field together. I'll be fine by morning."

She weighed the logistics of getting into the village without a car to check on him, then reminded herself that he was, after all, a grown man.

"If you're sure that's all it is . . ." She hated her uncharacteristic vacillation.

"Absolutely."

"All right. Since we're being perfectly honest with each other"—she stressed the honesty issue—"I'll admit that I'm not quite up to an evening on the town, either."

"Then I'll see you in the morning. And, Erin love," he said, his voice thickening ever so slightly, "thank you. Not just for coming across a sea to help with the surgery, but for being the warm, loving person you are."

She felt the moisture sting behind her eyes as she

managed to assure him that an opportunity to visit Ireland was no hardship. Then, secretly relieved that she'd been given a reprieve on tonight's public appearance, she picked up the book that was still lying atop the quilt and took it into the kitchen area with her.

While the water rumbled to a boil in the kettle, Erin cut slices of cheese from a wedge she took from the refrigerator and spread them on a loaf of fragrant brown bread she found in a wooden box on the counter. The absolute stillness surrounding her was not something she was accustomed to, and it crossed her mind that she could happily luxuriate in this cozy little cottage for weeks.

"That's not what this trip is about," she reminded herself as she cut a crisp red apple into quarters and added it to the cheese-and-bread plate. "It's about Tom."

She felt herself sinking back into despair when the kettle whistled merrily. By the time she'd steeped the herbal tea bag to a rich black color that resembled coffee more than tea, she'd recovered her resolve.

After the light supper, she carried the medical book and one of the candles into the bathroom. While the water flowed from the surprisingly whimsical faucet shaped like a swan's head into the high claw-footed tub, she lay back in the warm water, sipped another cup of tea, and watched the sun sinking into the sea from the bathroom window, unworried about being observed since the cottage was perched on a cliff overlooking the Atlantic.

Then, even as she resumed plodding her way through the thick medical language research physicians seemed to believe gave weight to their message, Erin felt every bone and muscle in her body gradually begin to relax.

Michael wanted a drink. Worse yet, he *needed* a drink. As the night grew dark, he sat on a rough wooden bench outside the house and imagined the whiskey burning a fiery line down his throat and into his gut. He could feel the seductive siren's call of a binge that would comfortably fog his thoughts.

He lit a rare cigarette and drew in a stream of smoke that was a poor substitution for the Jameson's he'd once drunk for breakfast, dinner, and supper. Then there'd been the after-supper drinks—just to help him sleep, he'd told himself at the time.

It was the same thing he'd told Nora, who'd chided him on more than one occasion about his excessive drinking. She hadn't believed a single word and no wonder, since they'd all been lies. Hell, he hadn't really believed them either, he admitted, exhaling a stream of smoke. The ghosts who'd haunted his sleep were just excuses. Having never accepted excuses from anyone else, Michael was not prepared to accept them from himself.

The sorry truth was that by the time he'd poured the whiskey down the drain, he was drinking during most of his waking hours. The rest were spent in a somnolent state close to unconsciousness.

He may have used the ghosts as an excuse for his drinking, but they had, indeed, been real. They did not come as often as they once did, but a few still visited from time to time. Once Michael had stopped fighting the specters and learned to accept their presence, they, in turn, seemed to become more accepting of his inability to right the wrongs that had been done to them. More and more drifted away, out of thought and mind.

"Or perhaps," he considered out loud as the tobacco burned down to his fingers, "they've moved on to other lives." He thought back to an all too familiar pair of such ghosts—twin babies he'd come across in the killing zone of the Rwanda-Burundi border.

Their mother had died giving birth to them along a road packed with a tidal wave of displaced, emaciated, and wounded civilians. Others, shell-shocked and taxed to their emotional limits, streamed silently, relentlessly by the infants whose faint mewling had miraculously captured his attention.

Even sensing that his efforts were futile, unable to leave them behind, he'd scooped them from the bare ground that bore the craters of numerous land mine explosions and carried them—one in each arm—more than ten miles to the refugee center where the doctor had taken one look at them—premature and each weighing less than a kitten—and instructed him to leave them outside.

The facilities were already taxed to the limit, and there was nothing to be done for them. The doctor, whose T-shirt and jeans were filthy and blood-stained, had pointed out that all energies must be directed at those whose lives they could save.

Michael had argued. He'd cursed. But deep down in his heart, he'd known from the bedlamlike sight inside the army-green medical tent that the doctor had no other choice

Cots filled with the maimed and dying jammed a
floor of dusty volcanic rock awash in puddles of blood
and the chlorine disinfectant that was continuously
sprayed in a fruitless battle to prevent disease. Lobster-
clawed beetles buzzed around gaping wounds, while in
a nearby corner two rats fought over a piece of protein
biscuit dropped by one of the emaciated patients. The
ripe scent of death was everywhere, mingling with the
acrid odor of despair.

A harried nurse, who looked nearly as burned-out as
he felt, took time he suspected she couldn't spare to
inform him that things were even more chaotic than
usual today since one of the militias had crept back
into the hospital late last night and begun hacking
away at patients whose lives had been saved in frantic
struggles only hours earlier.

Having no other choice, Michael took the babies
back out beneath a rare tree. Shadows lengthened as
day turned to night. In the distance active volcanoes
glowed like hellfire in a midnight-black sky. He'd been
humming the "Connemara Cradle Song" that he
remembered his mother singing to his sisters, when he
felt first one tiny heartbeat, then the other, flutter like
hummingbird wings. Then go still. And still he sat,
holding the infants in his arms.

The same nurse he'd spoken with earlier came out
of the tent for a cigarette break. When she saw him still
holding the two small bodies, she tried to take them
away, but Michael refused to relinquish his young
charges. He stood guard, protecting them from the vul-
tures and jackals who were, like death, waiting
patiently for their next victims.

As soon as the predawn light began glimmering rose on the horizon, he borrowed a shovel from one of the aid workers and dug a small, deep grave. Then he wrapped both skeletal bodies in the single spare denim shirt he carried with him.

He did not say a prayer after the burial because sometime during his long night's vigil, any lingering belief in God had perished along with the infant twins.

The babies had been absent from his nightmares for a while, which had him considering the possibility that they'd already begun new existences in some safer, more hospitable place. Perhaps even here in Ireland. Michael decided that he rather liked that idea.

He lifted the cigarette to his lips for one final soothing drag, frowned when his hand shook ever so slightly, and reminded himself that alcohol would only make things worse. Besides, it wasn't ghosts who were haunting him tonight, but the more recent memory of shaking hands with Erin O'Halloran. He'd forgotten that anyone's skin could be so soft.

"Too damn soft," he warned himself. He stubbed out the cigarette, looked up at the sky, and just for a fleeting moment allowed himself to think of the warmth of the American doctor's whiskey brown eyes.

This time it was the call of the lark that woke Erin from a blessedly dreamless sleep. She lay in the high bed, listening to the sound of the rain drumming on the thatched roof, the distant sound of the surf cutting into the seaside cliff, the bleating of sheep.

Sometime during the night the fire had burned down, leaving the air smelling of smoldering damp peat and the room so chilly that frost had created lacy sparkles in the corners of the wood-framed windows. She tossed more of the coal-black peat on the fire, then dressed quickly, throwing on the first things she pulled from the chest of drawers in which she'd packed her clothes away after last night's long, luxurious bath.

She fixed a quick breakfast of scrambled eggs, toast, and coffee, blessing her absent host who'd thoughtfully supplied the electric machine and grounds for her morning caffeine fix. She continued to read from the medical textbook as she ate at an old farm table. Erin wasn't an antiques buff like her mother, nor could she date the table within a decade of its origin, but she suspected it was at least a century old. The top appeared to have been hewn from a single log, the legs were square and unadorned. It was a utilitarian piece of furniture, constructed to hold heavy platters of food for a large family. But the joints were square and tight, and there was an obvious pride in the workmanship she admired the same way she could appreciate a clean, trouble-free appendectomy.

She traced a set of initials—MJ—carved into the wood with a fingertip, remembering when her brother had done exactly the same thing to the Chippendale table her mother had unearthed at the estate sale of a former lumber baron in Gray's Harbor. Needless to say, Grace O'Halloran had not been pleased.

The rain faded to mist while she washed the few dishes and dried them with a soft linen towel. Struck with a sudden urge to go exploring on her own, she glanced at the clock on the wall, which assured her that she still had more than thirty minutes before Tom arrived to pick her up to take her to the surgery. She'd argued that she was perfectly capable of renting a car at the airport, but he'd been resolute about wanting to meet her, which had precluded that idea.

Unaccustomed to being dependent on anyone but herself and not wanting to make him drive back and forth every day when his strength was so obviously waning, Erin determined to locate an agency in the village where she could lease a serviceable, inexpensive sedan.

Patience had never been Erin's strong suit. Indeed, she'd often had to struggle to keep from causing diplomatic problems whenever petty bureaucrats or army officers tried to interfere with her medical care. Unable to sit still now, she retrieved her parka from the peg on the wall, pulled on the tall green wellies she found by the door—Tom's contribution, she suspected—and headed off for a walk along the cliffs.

As she carefully made her way along the rocks that were the last bit of land until America, Erin felt as if she could have been the only person in Ireland. Or the world, for that matter. Despite the always possible threat of trouble across the northern border, despite off and on peace accords, war and armed strife seemed a lifetime away.

She stood at the edge of the world, gazing out toward the horizon, where a gray veil of mist merged leaden sky with steely sea. She watched what appeared to be hundreds of seagulls ride on the air currents, saw a lone beachcomber gathering seaweed into a woven basket, and felt again that peculiar inner pull that was something more than peace.

Lifting her face to the mist blowing up from the sea, Erin inexplicably felt a deep, almost visceral sense of belonging. As impossible as it was, after spending her entire adult life as a medical gypsy, Erin felt as if she'd come home.

"That's not so unusual," she insisted as she turned away from the cliff.

Hadn't a nurse of Germanic heritage she'd worked with in the Sudan, whose grandmother had moved the family to France during the 1940s, professed to feel the same thing when she'd first viewed the Black Forest? The pull of ancestral roots was undoubtedly universal.

The sheep she'd heard upon first awakening were grazing nearby, their winter-shaggy bodies brightened with splashes of fluorescent red paint. One glance at the suicidal angles at which those woolly creatures were walking along the cliff made her wonder how any survived.

She was returning to the house when she saw a man coming toward her out of the gray gloom. Michael Joyce's stride was long and sure, his arms swung loosely at his sides. Despite the icy chill in the air and the light rain that was falling, he wasn't wearing any sort of cap.

His dark hair was ruffled by the sea wind, and his unrelentingly male face, chiseled by elements and life, had her thinking of marble halls and ancient pagan gods. He looked even larger, more formidable out here in his natural environment than he'd appeared in the airport terminal.

"Good morning," she greeted him.

His only answer was a brief, almost curt nod.

"The rain reminds me of my home back in

Washington State," she said, refusing to be intimidated by his lack of response. Perhaps he wasn't a morning person. After all, she was occasionally known not to say a word until after her second cup of morning coffee. "Is this what you Irish call a soft day?"

He glanced up at the dove-gray sky, almost as if surprised to see that it was raining. "Aye. I suppose you could call it that."

"It's lovely. And a nice change after the driving monsoons in Bangladesh. That was my last posting. Before I came here."

"To save Tom."

"Technically, I've just come to help out until he's back on his feet, but yes, that's my intention."

He arched a knowing, sardonic brow. "I may not have a medical degree, Dr. O'Halloran. But even I know that's not going to happen."

Her chin shot up. A touch of temper flared. "All those reports of your alleged feats of derring-do failed to mention that you were psychic."

"It doesn't take a psychic to see that he's dying. Everyone in the village has been watching his condition worsen these past six months."

That assertion caused a stab of guilt. If only she'd known earlier, she might have prevented the illness from digging its tentacles so deeply into her best friend. If she weren't so concerned for him, Erin would have been angry at Tom for having kept his secret from her for so long.

"Nothing's fatal until the patient takes his last breath," she quoted the words Tom had spoken on so many seemingly hopeless occasions.

"Then you'd best be believing in the Almighty. Because the only hope you—or Tom—has is a miracle."

"From your less than encouraging tone, I take it you don't believe in miracles."

The quirk of his lips was more smirk than smile. "Tom said you were clever, as well as beautiful."

Erin was momentarily distracted by the idea that this man—who'd been photographed with some of the most beautiful women all across Europe, including one voluptuous blond Scandinavian supermodel who couldn't seem to keep her clothes on—thought her beautiful.

Then, remembering that he was merely quoting Thomas, who tended to look at the inner person rather than outward appearances, she put the idea aside and thought instead of the story about Michael Joyce burying those babies in Rwanda.

He did not appear to be a man who cared about anything or anyone. Apparently, either he'd changed a great deal since then, or that anecdote was merely a fanciful tale that had been exaggerated each time it was told, helping build his larger-than-life reputation. Which in turn, she considered, undoubtedly sold more photographs.

"Have you always been so cynical?"

He folded his arms across the broad expanse of his chest. "I wouldn't be calling myself cynical."

"Then what would you be calling yourself?"

She thought she saw a glimmer of amusement in his eyes as she threw his Irish syntax back at him, then, when he turned away from her and stared silently out over the white-capped sea, decided she must have imagined it.

Michael Joyce certainly didn't contribute to the reputation the Irish had for loquaciousness. The February cold had begun to seep into Erin's bones. Part of her wanted to just give up on this conversation—and the plan she'd thought up while eating her breakfast to enlist this man's help in convincing Tom to seek further medical treatment. Another, stronger part was honestly curious about his answer.

She wasn't quite certain how long she waited him out, but she had begun to suspect that it was becoming a contest of wills when he glanced back toward her.

"Not a cynic," he decided. "But a realist. If you think you're going to be able to come up with a miracle cure to save Thomas, Doctor, you may have just as well stayed at home."

His deep voice was laced with a sarcasm that raised Erin's last hackle. Deciding that it was time to leave for town, and not wanting to keep Tom waiting out in the cold, she forced a blatantly false smile.

"I've always heard about Irish hospitality. But it's illuminating to see it in action." With that she turned and began marching back toward the cottage.

～ 8 ～

Bring the Peace

*G*ood going, Joyce, Michael told himself with a sigh. Personally, he didn't care if the woman cursed him to the devil. But Tom obviously loved her, and for that reason he owed her a measure of outward respect.

Since she actually hoped to save their mutual friend from the death that appeared inevitable, Michael wasn't overly surprised that despite all she'd obviously witnessed, Erin O'Halloran continued to believe in tilting at windmills. In that respect, she reminded him a bit of his grandmother, or Nora, who'd been a postulate in a Dublin convent before returning home to take care of the family after their mother had died giving birth to Celia, the youngest Joyce child. They, too, believed in miracles. As he'd told Erin, he did not.

He began walking alongside her, adjusting his long stride to hers. "I apologize if I offended you."

It was her turn not to answer. Although she barely came up to his shoulder, her slender legs were eating up the damp ground at a surprisingly rapid pace.

"Did you sleep well?" he tried again.

"Like a log." She didn't look up at him.

"It's the feather bed blending with the sound of the

sea. One embraces you while the other lulls you into a blissful sleep. I've a thoroughly modern box spring and mattress in my own house, but there have been times when I've considered switching them.

"The only problem with that idea," he continued in an uncharacteristically conversational manner, "is that the bed in my house is too large for the cottage. The mattress would undoubtedly stretch from wall to wall."

"I'd suspect the owner of the cottage might object to you switching furniture with him."

"Aye, he might, were it not for the fact I happen to be the owner of Fair Haven cottage."

That stopped her in her tracks.

It fit, Erin admitted reluctantly and wondered if he'd been the one to name it. She'd experienced the welcoming warmth and refuge the moment she'd walked in the door of the small, cozy cottage. "Are those your initials carved into the table?"

"Guilty." This time she knew she wasn't imagining the brief amusement that flashed in his eyes. "Gram tanned my ass with a sally stick for that one."

She thought back to her first sight of him, wearing those snug, faded jeans, and decided it was best not to spend too much time thinking about Michael Joyce's ass.

"Then those must be your books as well."

"Aye. Actually, they've been collected by my family through the generations. Nora has quite a few herself, but I'm the one who ended up with the majority of them."

"Have you actually read them all?"

"Not yet. But they provide a goal."

"I imagine so." She began walking again. "Tom failed to mention that you were my landlord."

"He's had a bit on his mind of late." He was right beside her, catching her arm when she almost slipped on a mossy rock, then releasing it just as quickly. "And I'm not exactly your landlord, because I told Tom that I wouldn't be taking any money."

Since he hadn't been very pleasant since they'd met, Erin didn't want to be beholden to this man for anything. "I assured Tom that I'd insist on paying rent." Several times. But when he'd gone into a coughing fit during one of their telephone arguments, Erin had decided to wait until she got to Castlelough to put her foot down.

"There's no need. The cottage hasn't been occupied since I moved into the larger house, and it's pleased I am to be able to do a favor for a friend."

"We're far from friends."

Erin usually had no trouble getting along with people, no matter what their differences. But if Michael Joyce's behavior thus far was any indication, she suspected Ireland would experience another Ice Age before the two of them worked their way up to friendly acquaintances.

"That's true enough. But it's Thomas I was referring to. Not yourself."

"Oh. Well . . ." Uncomfortable at having been caught jumping to erroneous conclusions, she began walking more swiftly. "You're right, of course. I suppose, for Tom's sake, I can pretend to like you, so long as you can pretend to be halfway civil."

He rubbed his broad square jaw as he seemed to be

considering that proposition. "It may be a stretch. But I'll try. For Tom's sake."

Erin never had been able to hold a grudge. Which, she'd always thought, allowed her to work in a world where centuries-old grudges proved deadly.

"That's quite generous of you," she said dryly. She might not hold grudges, but neither was she a pushover. "And now that we've gotten that little matter settled, I'd best be getting back." She glanced down at the wide-banded stainless steel watch with its large sweep hand her parents had given her for her graduation from medical school. "It's nearly time for Tom to be arriving to drive me into town."

"You'll soon find that time's relative here in Ireland. In fact, we have a saying, 'When God made time, he made plenty of it.' We aren't as wed to the clock as you Yanks, and Tom in particular isn't known for his punctuality."

"Still, I don't want to risk him waiting outside with his weakened lungs."

"There's no need to worry. As you pointed out, his lungs aren't at their strongest these days. Since he refuses to stop working, to help save a bit of his dwindling energy I volunteered to drive you to the surgery."

"That's very nice of you." And surprising. His show of concern made Erin consider that perhaps she'd misjudged Michael Joyce. That idea was to be short-lived.

"It was the sensible thing to do. And for the record," he said in a voice close to a growl as they approached the cottage, "I'm seldom nice."

The rain picked up again, hammering on the roof of Michael's car like stones, streaming down the windshield as he drove away from the cottage with much more speed than he'd demonstrated on the drive through the fog from the airport.

"I don't think I believe that," she decided after they'd gone about three kilometers.

He slanted her a sideways glance. "Believe what?"

"That you're seldom nice. Tom's a very good judge of people, and it's obvious that he admires and likes you."

"We were lads when we became friends. Perhaps his judgment wasn't as carefully honed then."

"Perhaps. Or perhaps you're just trying to scare me off."

"And what reason would I have to be doing that?"

"I haven't the foggiest idea." She frowned and combed her hand through her moist curls. "I'll have to think about it."

"Why don't you do that?" he suggested mildly.

"I will. Meanwhile, you can think about ways to help me talk Tom into fighting."

"He's always fought for the underdog. What would you be having him fight for this time?"

"For his life, of course."

He shot her a quick warning look. "What Tom chooses to do with his life is his business. Not mine."

Perhaps he hadn't been lying after all about not being nice, Erin considered glumly. "You said you've been friends since you were boys."

"Best friends," he elaborated.

"Then how can you not care that he's dying?"

"Of course I care." He turned his attention back to driving along the slick narrow roadway lined with stone walls. "But we all die. Some, like Thomas, too soon." He frowned as he thought about those doomed twins once again. "Then the worms eat us."

"Isn't that a lovely thought."

He shrugged. "You're a doctor. Supposedly you worked on cadavers in medical school, so the concept of death and decay can't be alien to you."

"Of course not. But the experience only intensified my respect for human life."

Unlike some who'd gotten through gross anatomy class by joking about the cadavers they dissected, Erin had always been humbled by the sacrifice some unknown person had made so she could learn to become a doctor. Her much older anatomy partners had laughed at her and accused her of being too sentimental to make it to her second year. But she had, with flying colors.

"You certainly picked an odd specialty for someone who values life," Michael said. "Surely you've noticed that most of your patients die. If not on your operating table, then later, when they get blown to pieces by land mines making their way back home."

She shook her head. "You really are the most cynical man I've ever met." If he'd worked for her relief organization, he would have been declared suffering from burnout and shipped back home.

"A realist," he reminded her.

"A true realist would notice that a significant number of my patients survive."

"Ah." He nodded. "Now we've sunk to the level of conversation where we argue about whether the glass is half full or half empty."

Erin had no doubt that Michael Joyce was in the latter group. While she may have gotten tougher out of necessity, she hoped that she'd never lose the ability to care.

"We're not discussing platitudes concerning glasses," she insisted on a frustrated huff of breath. "We're talking about Tom. And there's no way I can stand by if there's something—anything—I can do to keep someone I love from dying until he's lived a full life."

"The man's already lived a fuller life than three normal people combined. It's a natural law that the flame that burns brightest burns shortest. Besides," he continued, cutting off her intention to argue, "the decision not to take extreme measures just to gain a few days or weeks, or even months, is Tom's. If you really want to help him, Dr. O'Halloran, I'd suggest you honor his wishes."

He braked for a border collie herding a group of cows across the road. When the elderly man following in their wake waved, Erin automatically waved back. Michael, who seemed to have relapsed into full glower again, did not.

"I didn't come all this way not to save him," Erin muttered as they resumed driving.

"Then you'd better be as good at praying as Tom says you are at doctoring."

His curt tone declared the subject closed. Frustrated and saddened by his intransigent attitude, Erin reached behind her and retrieved the book she'd brought along with her medical bag and buried her nose in the pages.

While they drove through the rolling green landscape veiled in a soft silvery mist, she continued to search for an elusive cure for a fatal ailment that was so individualistic it didn't even have a name. Even knowing that Michael's earlier suggestion had been intended as sarcasm, Erin decided that any miracle would definitely be welcome.

Upon arriving at the surgery—a two-story building painted a summer-sky-blue with yellow trim and sporting a traditional hand-painted sign, an office on the ground floor, and living quarters above—Erin quickly discovered that a doctor's life in rural Ireland wasn't anything like she'd always imagined whenever she'd picture herself practicing family medicine in the States.

"How can you not keep office hours?" she asked, incredulous when Tom informed her that they were off to visit patients in the countryside.

"Ah, but I do," he assured her. "Once the house calls are completed."

That was another thing. She couldn't imagine a doctor in this day and age in America paying house calls. "And when will that be?"

"Oh, they'll be done when they're done. It varies from day to day, of course."

"Of course," she murmured. "How do you make appointments?"

"I don't. Once I get back from my rounds, I see patients on a first come, first served basis. The nurse I inherited from Dr. Walsh, Mrs. Murphy—you'll be meeting her when we return—keeps things running smoothly enough in my absence and has everyone all triaged when I arrive back here." He plucked a muffler from the back of a chair and wrapped it around his neck.

"I suppose that sounds like a fair enough way to manage things." She reached up to tuck the wool muffler into the front of his tweed jacket. "Did it ever occur to you that you're in no condition to be running around the country in the pouring rain?"

"Ah, isn't that what Michael keeps telling me?" Tom asked with his puckish grin. "You're two of a kind, you are."

"Hardly." Erin didn't want to sidetrack the conversation by getting into an argument about Michael Joyce. "But it appears we're in agreement about this, at least."

"It's not going to do any good, you know."

"What?"

"Hovering over me like some fussy mother hen. I'm going to die, darling. Getting wet isn't going to make any difference in the ultimate outcome."

"We're all going to die, eventually. But you can't be sure—"

"But I can, you see. I'm no fool, Erin. Nor am I all that anxious to depart this world. I've been to some of the greatest diagnosticians in the world and played the starring role in countless grand rounds show-and-tell sessions. Indeed, the magnetic resonance spectroscopy in both Chicago and London revealed that I have much lower normal levels of N-acetyl-aspartate in my brain stem and basal ganglia, much as they're discovering certain Gulf War vets do, which I suspect explains my trembling hands and my occasional frustrating lack of balance. As much as I'd wish otherwise, the conclusion has always been the same. I have, at best, two months to live."

"I don't believe any doctor, even the greatest diagnostician in the world, has any right to tell a patient how long he or she has to live," Erin said with heat. Coincidentally, she'd just read about the use of radio waves to measure body chemistry that morning. "Or did those eminent physicians possess crystal balls?"

"Not that I noticed." Despite the somber topic, the corners of his lips quirked as if he were holding back a smile.

"There, you see." Erin nodded decisively. "Medicine's coming up with new procedures and drugs every day. We just have to find the right one for you."

"Or we could pray for a miracle," he suggested as they left the office, unknowingly echoing his friend's earlier words.

While she'd certainly witnessed instances of a patient surviving against odds that could be considered medically impossible, Erin still preferred to make her own miracle where Tom was concerned.

Despite his insistence on independence, she noticed that he allowed himself to brace a hand on her arm as they made their way across the rain-slick cobblestones to where his car was parked. Having read the frustratingly incomplete medical records he'd faxed to her in Coldwater Cove when he'd first asked her to come to fill in until another doctor could be found to take over his country practice, Erin knew that Tom was suffering from early stages of phosphate diabetes.

For some reason, undoubtedly due to the chemical attack he'd suffered from those helicopters that had attacked the innocent civilians he'd been attempting to treat, his kidneys were not maintaining a sufficient level of phosphorus in his body, which was demineralizing his bones so that a mere slip and fall could easily cause a fracture. In the more severe cases, bones became so brittle that even shaking hands could break them.

"We'll find something," she repeated as she climbed into the car.

She considered it a major victory that she'd won the short argument over who was going literally to be in the driver's seat today. Of course the realization that he'd only let her win because he was obviously still tired from yesterday's trip to the airport and sightseeing tour made her victory less sweet.

"So, where are we off to?" she asked as she drove down the tidy street out of town.

"The Burkes' farm first, I believe. Maggie's water broke just before you arrived. We should be in time to catch the wee one."

"She's having the baby at home?" Castlelough might not be a large enough village to boast a hospital, but surely making the trip to Galway would be safer.

"As she has birthed her three sons. As she herself was born, and her husband, as well. These are country folk, Erin," he said gently. "Farm people. They're more comfortable among their own kind, more likely to have their children in old beds that have been handed down through the generations than in some impersonal city maternity ward."

"What if something goes wrong?"

He threw back his head and laughed at that.

"Strange words from a physician who specializes in performing field surgery where everything can go wrong. And usually does."

"You're right." She smiled back at him. "It'll be a pleasant change to deliver a baby I don't have to worry about getting blown apart by land mines on its way back home."

Erin frowned as she realized the words were the same that Michael had thrown at her. It wasn't the same, she assured herself. Having always been an optimist, she refused to surrender hope, as it appeared he had done.

The countryside they were driving through was so peaceful, so different from the rural war-torn areas she'd grown used to, that once again Erin thought she could have landed on another planet.

Whitewashed cottages gleamed in the stuttering sun that managed to break through the rain-soaked clouds, stone ruins dotted green fields, and every so often they'd pass a crumbling, brooding manor house that spoke of richer times and English occupation.

"Is that what I think it is?" she asked as they passed a network of soft green, grass-covered walls and ivy-mantled mounds. Looking more closely, Erin thought she could make out traces of footpaths.

"If you'd be thinking it's a former settlement, you'd be right. It's a lost village, a place depopulated a very long time ago. Perhaps during the Famine."

"That's sad." Despite the yellow gorse growing atop the ruins of the village, there was an aura of melancholy about the place.

"Aye. There are some who say the ghosts of those

who died rather than emigrate live on. Others believe that faeries have moved in."

"I think I prefer the faerie version."

"Just don't mention that to the Burkes," Tom advised. "It wouldn't do to have them worrying that you're in league with the wee folk."

"In league to do what?"

"Why, steal their child, of course," he said, his expression revealing surprise that she hadn't known this bit of Irish folklore. "Faeries are infamous for switching babes in the cradle, taking the innocent little mortal child and putting a weakened, wizened changeling in the cradle beside the poor unsuspecting mother."

"Surely you don't believe that?"

"Now, I can't say I do." He rubbed his chin. "And I can't say I don't," he answered obliquely. "But the Burkes do. So you'd best be blessing the baby straightaway when it slides from its mother's womb. That'll protect it from the evil eye, don't you see."

Erin shook her head. Tom was the most intelligent man she'd ever met. He was the last person she'd expect to believe in old folk myths, faeries, or the evil eye.

"There's a magic to this wild green land you're named after, Erin O'Halloran. There's no escaping it. The trick will be to tear yourself away from this place after I die and your duty to me is done."

"There will be no more talk of dying," she insisted.

Seemingly unwilling to argue further, Tom merely directed her to turn to the right at the next roundabout, then another kilometer and they'd be at the Burkes' farmhouse.

∾ 9 ∾

Miracles of Nature

The rain stopped as Erin pulled up in front of the farmhouse. A collie—ancient from the looks of her white muzzle—lay on an old car seat that had been pushed up against the outside wall of the house, basking in a thin beam of sun. She thumped her tail against the torn brown upholstery, yet didn't seem inclined to rise and greet her guests.

A clutch of scrawny white hens pecked at the gravel, and nearby a bearded goat was effectively mowing his way across a patch of spotty lawn.

Erin guessed Mr. Burke to be in his mid-twenties. The ruddy complexion above his red beard bore witness to a life spent outdoors, struggling against wind and weather and slim odds to eke a living from the bogs. He was a large man, nearly as tall as Michael Joyce, with huge arms, meaty hands, and muscled legs that filled his tweed trousers.

"Herself will be glad to see you," he told Tom. "And since Maggie's mother has arrived from Kiltamagh to help with the birthing, there's no need for me to be paying additional fees for your nurse."

"Ah, but she's not my nurse, she's a doctor, same as

meself," Tom responded, his brogue suddenly nearly as thick and incomprehensible as the farmer's. "And isn't it your lucky day, Brian, lad, that you'll be getting two such fine doctors for the price of one?

"Erin, may I introduce Brian Burke, descendant of the famed Richard de Burgo, who settled this land back in the twelve hundreds. Brian, this is Dr. Erin O'Halloran, a most brilliant physician from America, who'll be helping out at the surgery for the next few weeks."

The man's eyes narrowed suspiciously. "You look young to be a doctor."

Erin suspected it was more her gender than her age that so obviously disturbed him. "As do you, to be the father of three children with another on the way," she lied with a blithe smile.

He folded his enormous arms and looked down at her. "I began early."

The rain may have stopped, but the air was still pregnant with moisture that had begun to sink into her bones, and the cold wind blowing in from the Atlantic felt like needles against her face. Clenching her jaw to keep her teeth from chattering, she tilted her head a long, long way back and met his look with a level one of her own. "As did I."

The standoff between them was palpable. Just when Erin, who'd always prided herself on quickly adapting to any hostile situation, was beginning to wonder if she was fated to find herself in constant conflict with Castlelough males, Tom broke the heavy silence.

"Well," he suggested robustly, rubbing his hands together, "I suppose we should be getting in to see your wife, Brian. Before she has your babe on her own."

Brian Burke mumbled something Erin couldn't quite comprehend, but moved away, allowing them into the house that was, thankfully, a great deal warmer than the outdoors.

A peat fire glowed in the fireplace, offering both heat and cheer to the gloomy February day. The wall was papered in a forest-green-and-brown print decorated with photographs cut from magazines. Pope John Paul II and President Kennedy shared wall space with the ubiquitous Virgin Mary and a romanticized gilded portrait of her son, a glowing Sacred Heart taking up an anatomically impossible percentage of his chest.

Two small boys, with hair as fiery as their father's, played with trucks on the floor in front of the hearth, seemingly unconcerned that their mother was about to add to the Burke brood. They didn't look up as Tom and Erin entered, but a baby with curls the color of corn grinned and banged his wooden spoon on the tray of his high chair.

"This fine lad is Devlin Sean Burke," Tom advised Erin as he ruffled the child's unruly hair and earned a broad, nearly toothless grin in response. "He's a year old now, and the sturdiest lad I've ever brought into the world. I tell you, Brian, teach your son football, and you'll be able to retire in luxury."

"There's no retiring from farming," the child's father grumbled. "And football is a luxury the boy will be having no time for. He's needed in the fields. As me own father needed me." With that less-than-encouraging statement, the dour man led them into the bedroom.

The room was small, crowded by a double bed, oak

dresser, and rocking chair, but it was obvious that Maggie Burke had worked to make it a cozy haven from what Erin suspected was a hardscrabble life. A bright quilt adorned the wall, and hand-tatted ivory lace brightened the single window.

There was a fireplace, as well, and above the hand-carved mantel, in the place of honor, was a black-and-white wedding photograph of Maggie and Brian Burke. The bride, whose white dress was of a style that suggested it had belonged to her mother, looked shy and more than a little nervous, but undeniably happy.

The groom, on the other hand, displayed none of the ambivalence of his new bride. Indeed, the way he was beaming down at her, with his mouth and his eyes, suggested he'd just won the Irish sweepstakes. Erin could hardly believe that love-struck groom was the same sullen man who'd opened the farmhouse door.

A woman who could only be the bride's mother was sitting beside the bed in the wooden rocking chair. She looked up from her knitting when they entered. "It's about time you showed up, Thomas. I thought I'd be catching this babe on me own."

She may resemble her daughter, but her tone and unpleasant expression were twins of her son-in-law's.

"Surely you didn't think I'd be letting you have all the fun?" He crossed the room and sat down on the edge of the bed. "Good day to you, Maggie, darling," he greeted the young woman lying amid tangled muslin sheets. Her damp hair clung to her forehead and cheeks. "It's a glorious day to bring a child into the world."

"I was praying it'd be born on St. Brigid's day," the

older woman grumbled. "Then he'd be carrying the saint's blessing with him."

"I told you, I was trying, Ma," Maggie said. "But the babe wasn't ready."

"If you'd only drunk that herbal tea I brewed—"

"Babies seem to have minds of their own," Erin said, easily breaking into the woman's complaint.

"And aren't they often smarter than we adults," Tom said with a cheerfulness that, only because she knew him so well, Erin recognized as feigned. He was, she guessed, as irritated by the lack of emotional support Maggie Burke was receiving as Erin herself was.

Introductions were made quickly. Then Brian left— escaped, Erin suspected—leaving the birthing matters to the doctor and the women.

"I've never met a woman doctor before," Maggie told Erin between contractions. "I know there are ones in the city, but before Tom came back from the wars, we only had old Doc Walsh."

"Who was a fine enough doctor to deliver eleven of my fourteen children," the older woman said sharply. "The other three," she informed Erin, "I brought into the world myself."

"Dropped them in the field, no doubt," Thomas murmured for Erin and Maggie's ears alone as he monitored Maggie's blood pressure. "Then strapped them to her back and picked up her plowing right where she left off."

Maggie's giggle drew her mother's attention. "Giving birth is no laughing matter, girl."

"I know, Ma," Maggie said, exchanging a laughing glance with Erin. "It was just a pain that made me cry out."

"You were an O'Flattery before you were a Burke," the woman reminded her. "O'Flatterys don't cry."

"Aye, Ma." Maggie sighed. Then her face tightened up as she rode out another contraction.

"You're doing fine," Erin assured her, relieved that the delivery thus far was proving uneventful. Tom had turned control of the situation over to her, but so far, other than check vital signs, she had little to do but cool Maggie's perspiring face, chest, and arms with a damp washcloth. "Better than fine." She watched the swollen belly clench again, harder, longer. "I'd probably be screaming bloody murder by now."

"Oh, it's worth a little work and pain to experience a miracle firsthand," Maggie managed to gasp as she squeezed Erin's hand, her ragged, work-worn nails biting into Erin's flesh. "But I will admit that at this moment, I could easily take a cleaver and castrate Brian."

They all laughed at that, even Mrs. O'Flattery. Then, as the contractions came closer together, the birth obviously imminent, the mood changed to one of efficient seriousness.

"It's a girl," Erin said as the infant slid from the womb into her hands.

"A girl." O'Flatterys may not cry, but those were definitely tears of joy streaming down Maggie's pretty, flushed face. "Finally."

After suctioning the mucus from the baby's mouth and nose, Erin laid her on Maggie's stomach to cut the cord.

The new mother stroked the wet fuzz of black hair with her fingertips. "Welcome to the world, Kathleen

Rose Burke." She bestowed a watery smile upon Erin. "I dearly love my sons, but I've always so wanted a daughter. Perhaps I should have had a woman doctor before this."

Erin laughed at that as she cleaned the newborn up a bit and set to work finishing up the last details of the birth process.

It certainly wasn't the first child she'd delivered, yet as Maggie lifted her baby to her breast, Erin experienced a twinge of envy, which was odd since she'd never thought she'd want children of her own. The world was too fragile a place, and she'd seen too many mothers' hearts broken to willingly risk such emotional pain herself.

Even stranger, as the infant rooted in and began to suckle, she could have sworn that she felt a deep inner pull in her own breast.

Which was, of course, impossible.

Putting the puzzling sensation aside, Erin decided that Maggie Burke was right. The birth of baby Kathleen Rose was nothing less than a miracle. And it was wonderful.

Their next house call turned out to be three children with chicken pox, all living together with their parents and elderly grandfather in a cottage nearly as small as the one for which she still intended to pay Michael Joyce rent.

After dispensing some calamine lotion and antihistamine for the children, she prescribed a holiday for the mother, who only laughed as if Erin had suggested she climb aboard a rocket ship to the moon.

"Farming's always been hard," Tom murmured as they continued down the winding road through the rolling hills. "But harder yet here in the west. Which is precisely what Cromwell had in mind when he gave all the Irish landowning families the choice between hell or Connacht." His tone was flat, and although he'd only observed at the delivery, he looked distressingly tired.

"I could use a little energy burst," Erin said, concerned for him. "Do we have time to stop somewhere for a cup of tea?"

"Of course we do, darling, if that's what you wish. After all, as we say here in Ireland—"

"When God made time he made plenty of it."

"Aye, that he did. So you've heard the saying?"

"From Mr. Joyce, just this morning, when he dropped by the cottage to pick me up. The cottage you failed to mention belongs to him."

"I didn't see a need." He gave her a curious look. "Does it make a difference that the cottage is Michael's?"

"I just wish I'd known."

Tom gave her a long, thoughtful look. He'd always had the uncanny ability to read her mind. "Surely you wouldn't be blaming the man for what happened in Sarajevo?"

"He was airlifted out while a young girl died in my arms," she reminded him needlessly.

"That wasn't his choice," Thomas reminded her back. "He was, after all, unconscious. As for being given special treatment, I can't be denying that he was. As you or I would have been under the same circumstances," he said pointedly.

He was right, of course. Erin sighed and wished the

entire subject hadn't come up. She didn't want to argue with Thomas, especially about Michael Joyce. She didn't want to talk about the man, or even think about him. Which she realized was going to be a bit difficult to do now that she knew it was *his* books overflowing every flat surface of the cottage, that it was *his* bed she was sleeping in and *his* whimsical swan bathtub she'd found so soothing.

Erin was trying to think of something, anything to say to change the subject and had decided to ask more about their next patient—an old sheepherder with arthritis who was too crippled to drive his donkey cart into town any longer, Thomas had explained—when a teenager suddenly bolted in front of the car, arms outstretched.

Erin slammed on the brakes, sending the car into a skid on the wet, slick pavement. The tires squealed as she managed to stop mere inches from the boy's legs.

After assuring herself that Tom was all right, she jumped out of the car, heedless of the renewed drizzle. "Are you crazy?" she shouted. "You could have been killed."

"I'd have moved if you'd gotten any closer," he said, seemingly unnerved by the incident that had her pulse pounding like a jackhammer. "But I didn't have any choice, you see, since if I'd waited, you'd have already passed."

He glanced at Tom, who'd climbed out of the passenger seat. "It's Molly," he told the doctor. "She's sick as a dog, Doc. And now she's just lying down and can't get up. I think it's something she ate."

Thomas sighed and dragged his hand through hair

that had thinned considerably since Erin had last seen him. "No doubt. Well, let's be checking the poor girl out, shall we, Erin?"

They got back in the car and followed the boy, who'd retrieved his bicycle from where he'd dropped it by the hedgerow, down a muddy driveway.

"How old is Molly?" Erin asked as she stopped again outside a farmhouse that could have been a twin of the Burkes', though it was bright with whitewash, and the seemingly new green-and-yellow tractor in the field behind the house and the late model car outside suggested these people were far more prosperous. "Do you think it could be appendicitis?"

She hated that idea. Although she'd certainly performed emergency operations in far less hospitable conditions than a spartan Irish cottage, she'd mistakenly had the impression that family practice would be routine and uneventful.

"My guess would be that she's about four years of age. But we needn't worry about appendicitis. I suspect she's merely gotten into the poitin mash again."

"Poitin?"

"It's a homemade whiskey of the sort I believe you call white lightning in America."

"Moonshine?"

"Aye." Tom nodded. "The whiskey comes out of the still at four hundred proof, and even though they cut it considerably with water, the Gallaghers, at whose home we are, make some of the strongest in all the counties around. It feels like a bolt of lightning—or hellfire—going down your throat and is much in demand."

Erin did not share his apparent amusement. Indeed.

she was livid. "Are you saying these bootleggers"—she heaped an extra helping of scorn on the term—"actually allow their child to drink moonshine whiskey?"

"Oh, Molly isn't their child." He paused. For effect, Erin thought as she watched the familiar twinkle come into his eyes. "She's a nanny goat."

"A goat? Our patient is a goat?"

He chuckled. "Don't be forgetting that we took a Hippocratic oath to heal, lass. And fortunate we are that the Gallaghers pay with actual coin rather than poultry or fish."

"A goat." Erin shook her head as she took the bag from the backseat of the car and followed Tom, who was headed toward the barn.

The snowy lace curtains at the window of the Irish Rose pub should have been Erin's first clue that this was no ordinary workingman's bar. She paused a moment to read the message burned into the wooden sign nailed to the pub door: "Here when we're open. Gone when we're closed."

Yet more proof of the Irish concept of time, she decided. After the strange day she'd spent with Tom, first on his round of house calls, then later at the surgery— where he seemed to spend as much time chatting as he did examining patients or writing out prescriptions for them to take next door to the chemist—she'd come to realize that when it came to medical care, the west of Ireland could be the other side of the moon compared to what she'd become accustomed to.

Fortunately, she'd won the skirmish over the rental car and had driven herself here tonight. That would allow her to meet people, perhaps drink a glass of wine, then escape. Erin understood that remaining anonymous in a village as small as Castlelough would be impossible. However, she hated the idea of spending the entire evening being the center of attention.

Unfortunately, the moment she entered the pub, which could have come directly from the set of *The Quiet Man*, Erin realized that her hope of remaining somewhat in the background was a futile one. The buzz of animated conversation immediately ceased as every head in the place swiveled toward the door.

Glasses lowered to tables marred with rings that undoubtedly went back decades, perhaps even centuries. There was an aura of expectancy hovering over the room along with a cloud of blue cigarette smoke.

"Erin darling," a blessedly familiar voice called out from the back of the room. "Isn't it about time you got here? Everyone's been getting impatient to meet you."

She crossed the room to where Tom was standing, holding a yellow-and-blue feather-tipped dart. "Would you be saying that God only made plenty of time for the Irish, and not for the rest of us?"

The entire pub seemed to find amusement in her answer. Tom laughed as well, the bold sound reminding her more of the man she knew and loved. Unfortunately, his arms, as they wrapped around her, were heartbreakingly frail.

"Doesn't your blood flow as green as any native Irish man or woman I've ever met? So, love, consider me properly chastised." He paused, tossed the dart, hit the bull's-eye dead center, and grinned.

"That's two of the three games for me, Liam, lad,"

he called out to a man in his late fifties. "So, now that we've settled who's the best man tonight, a round for the house while I get me dear friend Erin O'Halloran a pint, then introduce her around to one and all."

That offer was met with unanimous approval and Erin was relieved when the conversations around her appeared to pick up where they'd left off.

"It's glad I am that you found your way," Thomas said as he put his arm around her shoulder and led her across the hand-pegged floor toward the scarred wooden bar. Behind the bar, the bottles atop the shelves on the dark-paneled walls gleamed like a pirate's booty in the muted light from brass hooded lamps. "I was getting worried about you, lass."

Erin was trying to decide if his brogue was thicker here in his own country, or, having been surrounded by myriad languages when they'd worked together, she'd never really noticed it as she did now. Like the pub, which she suspected was much the same as it was when the town had been built five hundred years earlier, Tom seemed an intricate part of this place.

"Since there's only one road from the cottage into town, it'd be a bit difficult to get lost."

"Oh, I wasn't worried about you getting lost. But there's always the chance of running into a cow. Or taking yourself a little detour to the lake and being spirited away by the Lady."

"The Lady?"

"Castlelough's own loch beastie. She's a bit like Scotland's Nessie, but with a story all her own, which I believe I'll have Michael Joyce be telling you, since the lough's on his family's land, after all . . .

"Two pints, Brendan," he said to the bartender. "You can't come to Ireland without tasting our most famous brew," he told Erin, who, for his sake, reluctantly decided to forgo the wine.

"A quick one," she said. "I can't stay long." She hadn't found anything encouraging in the medical books thus far, but she was determined to keep looking.

"There's no such thing as a quick pint. Besides, didn't you just arrive? You can't be leaving before the *seisiún.*"

As she watched the bartender fill a row of disturbingly large glasses three-quarters of the way full, then set them aside, Erin remembered from the tourist guide she'd managed to skim through on the plane after takeoff that a *seisiún* was an informal gathering of musicians.

"I suppose it would be futile to ask exactly when this *seisiún* would be occurring?"

"Oh, soon enough," he said airily with that total disregard for time she was becoming accustomed to. "We'd only be awaiting our piper."

Terrific. A headache had been hovering behind her eyes ever since her unexpected encounter with Michael on the cliff. A bagpipe was the last thing she needed. Not wanting to hurt his feelings, Erin merely smiled and watched as the bartender, now apparently satisfied that the dark brew had settled sufficiently, began topping the glasses off. When he finally set the tall glass in front of her with a flourish, she found herself hoping that there wasn't some sort of social custom that demanded she drink it all.

Other glasses were handed out, and every man,

woman, and child in the pub turned expectantly toward Thomas, who lifted his glass to Erin.

"Ah, Erin lass, love of me own true heart, I wish you health, I wish you well, and happiness galore.

"I wish you luck for you and friends; what could I wish you more?

"May your joys be as deep as the oceans, your troubles as light as its foam.

"And may you find sweet peace of mind, wherever you may roam.

"*Céad míle fáilte!* One hundred thousand welcomes."

The others in the room echoed the Irish toast. As glasses lifted, Erin took a tentative sip. The purple-black, foam-topped Irish beer was faintly bitter, but creamy and smooth.

"It gets better by the second or third sip," Thomas volunteered.

"Better yet by the second or third glass," piped up an apple-cheeked elderly man, who appeared to be at least a hundred, seated a few stools down from Erin. "If you're going to be taking a holiday here, lass," he said, "the first thing you have to learn is that Guinness is not merely a drink. It's a way of life as well as a fine and proper tonic."

"Erin isn't taking a holiday, Fergus," Tom corrected. "She's helping out with my practice until we can find a doctor who'll take it over when I die."

"There'll be no talk of dying tonight," the bartender said in a quiet but firm voice. "It's bad luck when welcoming a newcomer to town."

"Brendan's right," Fergus agreed. "Besides, Thomas Flannery, now that you've finally come back home to

God's country, where you belong, we're not going to let you get away so easily."

He lifted his glass to Tom. "Here's to your coffin. May it be made of one-hundred-year-old oak and may we plant the tree together tomorrow."

This toast was also affirmed by the others, who drank deeply. Then a man in the back of the pub got up to toast Fergus for having made that lovely toast to Tom, setting off what seemed to be a familiar pattern.

Toasts were made, more pints pulled. Erin managed to stay with her initial glass. As the level gradually lowered, foam was left clinging to the inside of the glass, the lacy pattern much like the frost that had been on her window that morning.

"Is your tongue finding it smoother?" Fergus leaned across Tom to ask Erin.

"I believe it is." The Guinness might be smoother on her tongue, but that same tongue was beginning to tangle ever so slightly.

"That's the way of it," he said as the door to the pub opened.

She wasn't drunk. Not by a long shot. But Erin had just begun to unwind when Michael Joyce entered, carrying a set of pipes and accompanied by an elderly woman and a child whose face could have washed off a Botticelli painting.

Without the slightest hesitation, his gaze bypassed the patrons seated at the round wooden tables around the room, homing straight in on Erin in a way that caused a little stutter of nervousness in her stomach and wiped away any Guinness-induced relaxation.

～ 10 ～

At the End of the Day

"*I* see you've found yourself a new friend, Michael," Brendan called out as he uncapped a brown bottle and set it on the bar. "Would you be introducing her to one and all?"

"I will."

Michael knew he'd not be able to keep Shea's presence a secret for long, especially since Fionna was taking her to mass tomorrow and he was enrolling her in school the next day. As he'd driven in from the farm, Michael had assured himself that announcing her existence at the Rose—where so many would already have gathered to take a look at the American doctor—was the best way to handle things.

He took a drink of the nonalcoholic beer made by the same brewers who provided the nation with Guinness, then lifted Shea up on the vacant stool next to Tom so that all in the pub could see her.

"This is Shea Joyce. My daughter."

Enough people gasped at this announcement that he realized his secret hadn't spread as he might have expected. Then again, he couldn't imagine Deidre McDougall stopping in at the Rose for a friendly pint on her way back to Belfast.

"Well, isn't that a reason for celebration," Brendan robustly broke the stunned silence. "And since you're new to our little village, lass, your first drink is on the house." He opened the door to the cooler. "Would ye be liking a lemonade or an orange?"

"A lemonade, please, sir," Shea said, speaking up in a way that tugged at chords of parental pride inside Michael that he hadn't even known existed.

"A lemonade it'll be," Brendan said, pulling out a can and pouring it into a tall narrow glass.

"And a round for the house," Fergus called out. "In honor of the lovely young lady." Since Fergus was known for his tightfistedness, this was a suggestion met with a great deal of enthusiasm by one and all. As the drinks were distributed, the people began calling out for the music to begin.

"It seems I'm going to have to work for our drinks," Michael told his daughter. "Will you be all right here with your great-grandmother and my friend Tom?"

"Aye." She nodded, her eyes bright with curiosity as she looked around the pub, taking it all in. There was something else there, too. Some deeper sense of concern that had Michael guessing that Rena's affection for drink may just have increased since the wild days and even wilder nights they'd spent together.

"There's no alcohol in Kaliber," he assured his daughter quietly. "You'll not be having to worry about your da getting drunk."

Her expressive eyes, so like her mother's, met his over the top of her glass of lemonade. "Oh, I wasn't worried."

But she had been. The way her childish brow had

instantly cleared assured him that his suspicions had been correct. He apparently had a great deal to make up for where his daughter was concerned.

Michael was walking across the floor to join the other musicians he'd played with since his teenage days, when he heard Shea's high clear voice pipe up above the low buzz of pub conversation.

"Would you be the American doctor?"

He missed Erin's answer but did hear Shea's response. "You're pretty," she said. "Like the faeries in the coloring book my great-grandmother gave me. Not at all like the doctor in Belfast who was bald and fat and smelled like the onion sandwiches he ate for lunch."

Erin's answering laughter was as enticing as a siren's song. Michael pulled up a chair next to Seamus Browne and watched as Tom put his arm around her and murmur something into her ear that had her smiling up at him. Even a blind man would be able to sense the unconditional love flowing between them.

While Seamus led the group into "The Call of the Sea," Michael felt a fleeting, painful stab of emotion and wondered what kind of unconscionable individual he'd become that he could feel envious of a dying man.

Since Castlelough was situated in the Gaeltacht—the part of the country where the Irish language had never been allowed to die out—Erin couldn't understand the exact lyrics of many of the songs, but the transcendent beauty of the music eliminated any real language barrier. It was obviously a tribute to this wild Irish west.

The instruments consisted of an accordion, a concertina, two fiddles, a bodhran—which Tom leaned over and explained to her was a goatskin frame drum—a pair of flutes, a tin whistle, and Michael Joyce's pipes. Certainly she'd heard larger orchestras, but never before had she heard any that could so perfectly capture the isolation and quiet beauty of their homeland.

Tom narrated the quintessentially Irish songs of wars, life, death, God, whiskey, the devil, and of course love, which was usually unrequited, Erin noticed.

Tom explained that the pipes Michael was playing—which were a great deal different from the larger war bagpipe Erin had been expecting—were uilleann pipes. Made to be played by a bellows attached to one elbow, rather than mouthed, they produced a soulful, achingly sweet sound that made her feel a little weepy and had her imagining solitary walks on the cliffs in a soft gray mist.

Michael's expression was brooding while he played, but she decided that seemed appropriate to the sad songs that spoke to so many of life's difficulties. From time to time he'd switch off, exchanging the pipes for a flute, producing a pure clear sound like liquid silver. She'd seen enough of his work to know that Michael Joyce was a brilliant photographer. Obviously capturing war images on film wasn't his only talent.

Then Fergus, whom she'd uncharitably thought to be merely a colorful pubfly, climbed down from his stool and joined the musicians, who immediately quit playing.

The old man's high voice was an instrument in itself as he sang of a sailor's love for the sea competing with the weariness of being away from family and loved ones.

A hush fell over the pub as Fergus's plaintive tale continued to chronicle the bonds of love enduring through good times and bad.

And then, without a note of warning, he stopped, the last reedy note hanging on the stilled, smoky air like the remnants of a dream upon awaking.

Everyone in the pub seemed to be holding their breath. Then Tom began to clap. Fionna Joyce, who'd been introduced to Erin as Michael's grandmother, followed suit; Brendan O'Neill and the rest of the listeners quickly joined in.

"That was remarkable," Erin said when Fergus joined them back at the bar and accepted another pint as a reward for his entertainment.

"It's pleased I am you enjoyed my little ditty," the elderly man responded with a false modesty she didn't believe for a moment.

"You were in rare form," Tom assured him, lifting his glass. His hand, which had been steady as a rock when he'd thrown that dart earlier, trembled in a way that caught Erin's immediate attention. "I don't think I've heard you sing so well and pure since Brady Joyce's funeral."

"I was moved by Brady's spirit that day. Tonight it was feminine beauty providing the inspiration." He swept a deep and dramatic bow toward Shea, who giggled.

"It is an inspiring sight," Michael agreed as he joined them. "Thank you, Brendan," Michael said as the bartender handed another bottle of Kaliber across the bar. "Playing is thirsty work."

"You were wonderful, Da," Shea said with a daughterly pride that Erin recognized well. Hadn't she always felt it for her own father?

"Thank you, darling. Like Fergus, I was inspired by your loveliness." Erin was surprised when he bent his head and touched his lips to the top of her fire-bright hair with a fondness that couldn't possibly be feigned.

She was thinking that it was certainly more emotion than she'd witnessed from the man thus far when he turned toward her. "So, did you enjoy your first *seisiún*, Dr. O'Halloran?"

"How could I not? I'm certainly no judge, but you all sounded like professionals."

"Some of the boys have played a professional gig from time to time," Michael told her. "In fact, Seamus there on the bodhran"—he pointed the bottle in the direction of the drummer, a fifty-something man with a smiling face and a corolla of carrot-hued hair—"has played on the Dublin stage with The Chieftains, in London with Clannad, and in studio sessions with various other famous musicians. But the rest of us are just amateurs who like to get together from time to time and fiddle around."

His easy pun drew a smile and had Erin thinking that the congenial atmosphere of the Rose, along with the presence of his daughter, seemed to mellow him.

"This is a country that's seen much hardship and deprivation," Tom told Erin. "Families split by emigration, the Famine, the sad sense that the only hope for a better life may lie across the Irish Sea or the Atlantic in America. Those who stayed behind found comfort through the long nights and wet winters in the pubs, sharing the old stories and songs. I doubt if you'll find a house, especially out here in the west, where there wasn't always music playing."

"It was that way at our house," Michael agreed. "Even after we got the television, coming here to the Rose was our favorite amusement. And of course it was always special when Da would tell his stories."

"My son was a marvelous storyteller," Fionna Joyce leaned past Shea to tell Erin. "The best in the country, most say."

"And couldn't he fill a pub better than any man in Ireland?" Brendan added with robust appreciation.

Erin, who long ago had gotten a handle on how things worked, was not surprised when this comment drew yet another round of enthusiastic toasts.

"You seem to have survived your day well enough," Michael said to Erin as the conversation buzzed around them.

"It was a long day, and a bit of a strange one," she allowed, thinking back on her experience pumping the drunken nanny goat's stomach. "But all in all, I enjoyed it."

"Perhaps you won't be having any nightmares tonight," Shea suggested.

Erin glanced at the little girl with surprise. "How did you—" She slammed her mouth shut as she realized that Tom and Michael, as well as Fionna Joyce, were looking at her intently.

Shea seemed unaware of the tension her innocent comment had caused. "Mary Margaret told me."

"Mary Margaret?"

"My guardian angel. She tells me everything."

"I see." Erin exchanged a look with Michael, who merely shrugged.

Then she remembered something she hadn't thought of in years. She'd had her own imaginary friend when she was about Shea's age: a little girl named Jolene who wore ruffled dresses and shiny black patent Mary Janes, whose long golden hair never got mussed and who would much rather have pretend tea parties than collect bugs in empty peanut butter jars with nail holes punched into the lid. The kind of girl, she'd believed at the time, and sometimes still suspected, that her mother would have preferred.

But still, an imaginary friend was one thing. An imaginary guardian angel who knew about her nightmares was something else altogether. Erin was attempting to think of some way to casually question the little girl further when Fergus asked her a question about how she was enjoying her time in Castlelough thus far, and the moment was lost.

It was well after midnight when Erin finally made her way back to Fair Haven cottage. She crawled into bed with yet another medical book, blinking as the words blurred on the page while the moon moved across a surprisingly clear sky outside the window and turned the distant sea to silver.

She wasn't certain when, exactly, she'd fallen asleep. One minute she was trying to decode a complex article about renal failure, of which she feared Tom's hand tremor could be symptomatic. The next thing she knew the sound of bells calling Castlelough residents to Sunday mass were tolling from the church in town.

Dragging herself out of the warm bed, she brushed her teeth, splashed cold water on her face, then plugged in her laptop computer and logged on to the Internet, seeking more information on Tom's condition and sending e-mails to colleagues around the world requesting assistance with his case while she drank her coffee.

It had obviously snowed sometime after she'd fallen asleep. A soft winter quilt of powdery white covered the ground outside the cottage. When her computer search proved futile, Erin decided to walk off some of her frustration.

It was when she was standing on the cliff, watching a tiny fishing boat pitch in a white-capped sea, that she belatedly recalled the dream she'd had just before awaking.

The dream was so vivid, Erin could recall every single detail as she brushed a dusting of snow from an outcropping of stone, sat down, drew her knees to her chest, wrapped her arms around them, and stared out to sea. However, it was not the waves she was seeing, but the vision that began to coalesce in her mind.

The huge hand-carved canopy bed was draped in a rich moss-green velvet. Vivid tapestries of Italian gardens and Flemish still-life paintings adorned the stone walls, silk threads shimmering like moonlight in the glow of candles in wall sconces.

She hadn't been sleeping; indeed, she'd been weeping in the arms of a man whose face was draped in shadows.

"This is nay a time for weeping, wife," he said as he brushed a tear away with the tip of his finger with a gentle touch. "But loving."

"I do love you, husband." She flung her arms around

his strong neck and clung, burying her face against his throat where his pulse beat strong and steady. "I heard Annie when she was working in the kitchen with Maeve only yesterday, repeating that foolish peasant prophesy: a wet winter, a dry spring, a bloody summer—"

"And no king," he finished the familiar words that had been whispered over the rolling hills, from sea to sea, from cottage to manor house, even to this very castle.

"I care naught of kings or rebellions," she insisted heatedly. "My concerns are for my family, and I'll not be having you leave me to go off with those who'd follow Fitzgerald and all the others who plan to risk their fool lives chasing dreams in Wexford."

Her hand fisted against his chest. She hit him, hard, feeling the jolt all the way back up her arm to her shoulder. As strong as the oaks that had once covered this wild land, he didn't even flinch. Rather, he caught hold of her wrist, lifted her trembling hand to his lips, unfolded the tight fingers and kissed them, one at a time in a way that, although the memory was of a mere dream, not reality, still sent a sensual shiver through Erin.

"A republic is a dream a man has no choice but to chase, love."

He threaded the fingers of his free hand through the tousled long brown hair he'd unbound earlier that night, framed her face, which was sorrowful and angry at the same time, in his wide palm, and kissed her. A slow, deep, drugging kiss that had her sinking into the feathers.

"Let us stop this arguing," he suggested as he touched the tip of his tongue to the hollow of her throat and made her heart leap. "And let me take you to magic places."

Oh, he could do that, she thought as the mere touch of his mouth at her breast set her bones to melting.

"And what of your child?" she managed to demand with a last flare of coherent thought. "Have you given any thought to your son?"

"It's for him that I'm doing this." He pressed his hand against her swollen stomach. "I'll be back in time to witness our son's arrival as a free citizen of the Republic of Ireland."

With that promise, he kissed her, longer, deeper, again and again, until a new day dawned with the sound of the lark in the meadows and the more ominous sound of hoofbeats headed toward the Norman castle his family had built upon first landing on Irish shores.

She stayed in bed, too upset and angry to get dressed and see him off. But after she'd heard his footfalls on the stone stairs, she wrapped herself up in the wool blanket and stood at the window, watching as he rode off with the contingent of United Irishmen into the mist toward the east.

Then, with tears trailing silently down her face, she dropped to her knees on the stone floor and began to pray.

∾ 11 ∾

On a Cold Winter's Day

Shea had never enjoyed going to mass in Belfast. She'd always been too aware of her grandmother McDougall beside her, alert for the faintest sign of inattention as she knelt on the unforgivingly hard wood. A wandering look could cause Shea's hair to be pulled so hard her eyes would water, a slight shifting from knee to knee could earn a pinch to the back of the leg. And the priest always seemed to be preaching about hell and sin and those damned Orangemen who'd never see God.

But this church was different. Shea could tell the moment she entered and viewed the lovely stained-glass windows that, unlike the Belfast windows depicting the seven deadly sins in gory, frightening detail, focused on wonderful miracles: curing the lepers, feeding the multitudes, changing water to wine. Better yet, the benches in front of the pews were padded in a lovely green vinyl ever so much more comfortable than the ones that had given her the occasional splinter.

Father O'Malley, a tall, lean man who reminded Shea a bit of a stork, but with kind and gentle eyes, had apparently been informed about her appearance here today.

After following the cassock-clad boys up to the altar, he'd publicly welcomed her to both Castlelough and the congregation. Pride had been one of the deadly sins portrayed on the Belfast church windows. Yet Shea nevertheless felt a warm burst of it when he introduced her as Shea Joyce, firmly establishing her place—and family ties—in the community.

Shea knew that she was proving to be an object of curiosity; more than once during the mass she felt eyes shifting toward her and did her best to remain as still as Lot's wife, so as not to cast aspersions on her newly discovered family.

But her great-grandmother once again proved to be nothing like her mother's mother. On the occasion when Shea's attention did wander, like to the boy behind her who waggled his fingers in a friendly wave when she glanced back over her shoulder, Fionna Joyce merely smiled and patted her knee.

Another thing that was different was that in Belfast, the lectern had been placed high above the people, as if to raise the priest above the common folk he preached to, while Father O'Malley actually came down in front of the altar to read the gospel story about how Jesus loved children. The sun began streaming through the Last Supper window behind the altar in a way that bathed Shea in a warm ruby and golden glow and made her feel as if she must look like one of the saints on a gilt-edged holy card.

She was hoping that the people of Castlelough, upon seeing this phenomenon, would realize that Michael Joyce's daughter was, indeed, special, when she heard a voice whisper in her ear.

"Better you concern yourself with the good father's words," Mary Margaret advised, "than allowing yourself to be puffed up with pride."

"I'm truly trying my best," Shea answered aloud, drawing another absent pat on the knee from her great-grandmother. Her murmured response also seemed to draw the priest's attention and when his eyes smiled directly at her, Shea smiled back, even as she felt the all too familiar twinges of a distant headache.

The headache built. As she'd been doing for weeks, Shea ignored it as best she could. It was during the preparation of the gifts that things began to go wrong. The smell of burning candle wax, which had seemed so pleasant when Shea had first entered the church, began to sear her nostrils like the acrid odor of burning tires the provos would use for their barricades.

"Jesus broke the bread." the priest said.

Shea blinked furiously, struggling to bring them into focus as his words began to sound like the drone of a swarm of angry wasps. "And gave it to his . . . buzz, buzz, buzz. . . . Take this, all of you buzz, buzz, buzz. . . . This is my body . . . buzz buzz buzz."

Mary Margaret's reassuring wings were folding around her. Shea could feel Casey's protective presence hovering close, his huge body pressing against her leg as the priest raised the host high over his head.

The bell rung by the altar boy chimed through the church; more ominous bells tolled inside Shea's head.

"At the end of the meal, Jesus took the cup," Father O'Malley was saying as he poured the ruby red wine and water into a pewter chalice engraved with a Celtic cross.

"He gave . . . buzz, buzz, buzz . . . this is the cup of my

blood . . . buzz, buzz, buzz . . . so that sins may be forgiven . . . buzz, buzz, buzz."

He lifted the chalice high for all to see. The bells chimed again.

There was another prayer. Then Fionna began making her way with the other faithful to receive communion. Shea, who'd not yet received her first Holy Communion, was required to remain behind, which she truly didn't mind since she wasn't certain she could stand. She was vaguely aware of the boy who'd been sitting behind her taking the host on his tongue, making the sign of the cross and returning toward his pew. This time he didn't smile at her, but tugged on Fionna's dress to gain her attention and said something to her that had Shea's great-grandmother looking down at Shea with a worried frown.

"You'll be all right," Mary Margaret was assuring Shea even as the pounding in her head escalated to that of a hammer on stone. Now Fionna was saying something to her, but she could have been speaking from the depths of the Irish sea for all Shea could understand.

She cried out as she felt the tremors take hold of her body and throw her toward the stone floor. She felt herself fighting against the hands that were reaching out from all directions toward her. Collapsing in a heap, Shea surrendered to the enveloping darkness.

Erin was reliving her memorable, disconcerting dream when she gradually became aware of someone standing behind her. Her eyes flew open and she turned around and looked up at Michael Joyce. She frowned as her stomach jittered in some strange new way.

"What are you doing here?"

"We're neighbors," he reminded her. "Like it or not."

Erin refrained, just barely, from voting for not. "Did you want something?"

You. The thought flashed surprisingly through his head before he had time to censor it. Michael immediately squashed the idea.

"I had breakfast with my grandmother and Shea this morning before seeing them off to church and Fionna suggested, in a way I've learned to heed, that I should be making a neighborly gesture by bringing you some fresh milk for your tea." He held up the bottle as proof of his honest intentions.

"I have trouble believing you always do what your grandmother tells you to do."

"After you've been here awhile, you'll discover that it's wise not to waste your time arguing with Fionna Joyce. She's already worn down the local bishop in her quest to get a hometown nun beatified, and now that she's turned her laser beam of intention toward the pope, it'll take all Gabriel's heavenly angels to protect the poor man from her holy crusade."

"Speaking of angels, I wanted to ask you something last night."

"And what would that be?" Ignoring the dusting of powdery snow, Michael sat down on the cliff beside her.

"How did your daughter know I've been having nightmares?"

He jerked a broad shoulder in a shrug. "Now that's a good question you're asking. It could be the simple

process of elimination. You've a bit of fatigue here"—
he rubbed the pad of his thumb between her brows—
"and here." He skimmed a touch beneath both of her
eyes and made her stomach flutter again. Stronger this
time.

"I think this is where I tell you that I really don't
like being touched."

"Well now, isn't that a shame, since you've got the
kind of skin that lures a man's fingertips," he said, even
as he slipped the hand that wasn't holding the milk
bottle in his pocket. "Your perfume drifted into my
sleep last night, Erin O'Halloran."

She looked up at him warily. Despite his seductive
words, he did not look like a man with lust on his
mind. In fact, he looked as if he wouldn't mind if she
got back on that Aer Lingus jet and returned to
America.

"I don't wear perfume."

"I suspected as much." He frowned. "Which means
we have ourselves a complication, since it was obviously your own unique scent tangling my dreams."

"There's no complication that I can see," Erin said,
not quite truthfully. She couldn't remember the last
time she'd felt this quickening in her blood. Wasn't
certain she'd *ever* felt it. "I'm not even sure I like you."

The kind of man Erin could have feelings for, the
kind she'd want to have feelings for her, wouldn't let
down a dying friend. As this man seemed prepared to
do. Tom would listen to him, she'd decided, observing
their close and easy relationship. Michael could convince him to fight against death.

"That's fair enough," he said. "And it's precisely why

it's a complication. Since I'm not at all certain I like you, either."

"Well." She didn't know exactly what to say to that. At least he was honest, she reluctantly decided. "Getting back to your daughter, I may admittedly look more tired than usual, but a few shadows beneath my eyes don't exactly reveal nightmares."

"It's always possible that Shea has the Sight," he said casually, as if possessing such mystical power was a natural thing. "Or, given the fact that she knows a bit about war and death herself, living her first eight years in Belfast as she has, she could merely be putting her own feelings upon you."

"I suppose that makes sense." A lot more than the magic. "I only took a rotation through psych when I was an intern, but I remember something about transference."

"That's undoubtedly what it is. However, were you to ask Shea directly, she'd undoubtedly tell you that Mary Margaret revealed you've been having difficulty with bad dreams."

Mary Margaret was the child's make-believe guardian angel, Erin remembered. "Do you believe in Mary Margaret?"

"No." His answer was quick and succinct. "But Shea does, and since she's had a hard go of it, I'm not about to dissuade her of whatever fantasies give her pleasure. Especially a guardian angel, which every little girl is entitled to."

"I suppose that's the wisest way to handle it."

Erin knew a great deal about taking care of the physical needs of a child, but hardly anything at all about emotional needs. There was a lesson she'd learned in Bosnia: get too close and you suffer so much psychic pain that you're no good to anyone.

"Thank you, but I'd not be claiming such wisdom for myself, since my sister Nora and Tom gave me the advice in the first place. Being a father is a new experience for me."

"So I gathered from the reaction of everyone in the pub." She supposed a child would have been a decided inconvenience for him as he'd roved the globe, taking his pictures and gaining international fame.

"I didn't abandon Shea and her mother, if that's what you'd be thinking. I didn't even know about my daughter's existence until a few days ago."

"That must have come as a surprise."

"Now isn't that an understatement?" he asked dryly. "Shea's grandmother brought her here to me because her mother's recently dead."

"I'm sorry."

"So was I, when I heard of it. Rena was a girl I was once quite fond of," he told her before she could ask.

Not that Erin would have, of course. Her mother had brought her up to have more manners than to delve into such personal matters. But she would have wondered.

"She was murdered by partisans in the north. Gunned down at her wedding, she was, in front of friends and family. And before Shea, who was her flower girl."

Even though she'd seen equally horrible things, Erin drew in a harsh breath at the image his words evoked. "That's a hateful thing to experience at any age. But for a little girl . . ." Her voice drifted off.

"Aye, it's an evil thing, and were it not for the fact that it would do my daughter no earthly good for me to land in some northern gaol, I'd have already gone to Belfast to find the men and deal with them myself."

"You wouldn't kill them." Erin decided that as much as the cold fury in his eyes caused ice to skim up her spine, she preferred it to his usual detached gaze.

"No." He dragged a hand down his face, the flare of emotion gone. "I've seen too much death to be adding to it myself. Yet I have no doubt I'll go to my grave feeling guilty for not being there to protect her."

Before she could give it any thought, she'd touched his arm. "You said you didn't know of her existence."

"True enough." He looked down at her gloved hand with mild interest. "So, does this seeming change in attitude mean that you've dropped whatever grudge you were holding against me?"

"I don't know what you're talking about," she lied.

"Don't you?" He lifted his gaze from her hand to her face. "You have a very open face, Erin O'Halloran. And it was obvious that you weren't particularly pleased to be meeting me."

"You were the one who was rude and uncommunicative."

"Aye, I was," he surprised her by allowing.

"Let me guess . . . You're one of those old-fashioned chauvinists who don't believe that women belong on the front lines." Hadn't she heard that enough times over the years?

"I've been called old-fashioned from time to time," he admitted mildly. "Even occasionally chauvinistic, which I'm not. I've spent too much time myself hunkering down in foxholes with female journalists to not consider them equals.

"Indeed, I've known some who've asked the kind of hard questions and sent back stories that resulted in terrorist leaders putting contracts out on their lives. I've no doubt that you're very good at what you do and people all over the world have been fortunate to have you caring for them so deeply, even at the risk of your own safety. As a matter of fact, Tom once described you as a cross between a wildcat and a mule."

"Well, that's certainly complimentary."

"He meant it as praise. I took it in the same vein. Yet, you see, his words had me expecting a different sort of woman than you turned out to be."

"And what sort would that be?"

She brushed an errant, windblown curl off her cheek, bringing Michael's attention to her hands, which, though they were currently covered by a pair of cranberry-red wool gloves, he remembered being as lovely as the rest of her. They were smooth and narrow, with long, slender fingers. Surgeon's hands, he supposed, though he preferred thinking of them as lady's hands. Or better yet, musician's hands.

Aye, it was a great deal more comforting to picture this woman strumming a harp, dressed in a silk blouse and velvet skirt that skimmed the floor, than cutting off gangrenous limbs in a battlefield hospital.

He realized she was waiting for an answer. "Well, for one thing, I didn't think you'd be so . . ." He struggled for the proper word, remembering why he'd taken up photojournalism for a career rather than using words to get his thoughts across, as his father had. "Delicate, I suppose."

"Delicate." She nodded at that in a way that, despite the rapidly dropping temperature, had Michael feeling vaguely as if he were sitting on the edge of a smoldering volcano about to blow its top. "You were expecting an Amazon with hips as broad as a battleship and arms the size of hams, I suppose?"

"I'm not certain I had any expectations. Still, Tom's tales of your heroic deeds—acts of bravery that would make Queen Medb's adventures appear to be child's play—I suppose had me envisioning you as being a bit more physically formidable."

"Maeve?" Her tongue had twisted a bit on her pronunciation of the Irish name, but she'd done well enough for a beginner.

"The Celtic warrior queen of ancient Connaught. A woman with blood rumored to be so hot her bath water would set to boiling whenever she sank into it. Surely, being of Irish ancestry yourself, you've heard the stories?"

"I'm an American. We have our own tales."

"And grand ones they are, I'm sure. But Tom's a natural born storyteller. I'm surprised he hasn't shared any of our Irish folklore with you. Especially since he was the one to compare you to Medb in the first place."

"We were a little too busy performing emergency amputations on innocent women and children to waste time spinning stories." Her tone was decidedly drier than the weather. "And I've certainly never thought of myself as heroic."

"True heroes never do. But I've met my share of relief doctors, Dr. O'Halloran, and it's my impression that many of you are, if not heroes, card-carrying idealists. Why else would you risk your life for the price of an airline ticket to misery-ridden places, primitive room and board, and a few miserable pounds per month salary?"

Erin had long ago quit trying to explain her motivation. "I may have been a bit of an idealist in the beginning." She was surprised to hear herself admitting anything so personal to a virtual stranger. It was the damn intimacy of sitting out here on the edge of the world together beneath a sky that seemed to have lowered to engulf them, she decided. "My first massacre changed that."

He was silent for a time, appearing to consider her words. "So, if you're not a hero or an idealist, how would you describe yourself?"

"I'm not particularly comfortable talking about myself." She wrapped her arms around herself, the gesture as much one of self-protection as an attempt to keep from freezing. Since the stone she was sitting on now felt like an iceberg, she stood. "In fact, now that you bring it up, it's always annoyed me that reporters seem to always zero in on me whenever they finally show up at the camps."

"That's because you're lovely," he told her, rising from the ground with a lithe, easy grace that was a bit surprising for such a large man. "Good looks are a plus on television, and any man would be a fool if he'd rather spend time with some male doctor than you."

"For an Irishman who claims to believe in women's equality, that's an incredibly chauvinistic remark."

"Perhaps," he allowed. "It's also true. You shouldn't let it disturb you so," he said when she snorted her dislike of this subject. "If it helps get your message out, why would you be caring that your gender and beauty cause you to be the doctor chosen from the crowd for an interview?"

Erin, who'd never considered herself the slightest bit beautiful, was unsettled by the way he had her almost wishing she was wearing something more feminine than flannel-lined jeans, a bulky down parka, and hiking boots with thick, heavy, practical soles.

"I care because whenever I take precious time away from my work to tell the world about the atrocities taking place around the world, reporters invariably waste time asking personal questions about my life and motivations."

"Personalizing a story tends to strengthen it."

"I can understand that, I suppose. But mostly I think all those pampered, well-fed, wealthy reporters find the idea of any doctor—but especially a young female one—turning her back on a nice, safe, lucrative suburban medical practice beyond their comprehension. So, in the end, the story becomes more about me than the message I'm trying to get out. Besides, as I said, I really don't like talking about myself," she repeated.

"Humility was yet another virtue Tom mentioned. But why don't you humor me and try?"

"Why should I humor you?"

"Because, despite your denial, I believe that deep down inside, you're an idealist, Dr. O'Halloran. And idealists—like saints and madmen—have always fascinated me."

"I'm neither idealist, saint, nor madwoman."

"Then how would you describe yourself?"

Erin shrugged. "Since you refuse to drop the subject, I suppose I'd have to consider myself a witness."

He nodded again. Slowly. Gravely. "Don't be looking now, Dr. O'Halloran, but it appears that we have something besides Thomas in common."

"No offense intended, Mr. Joyce." She kept her tone neutral. "But I truly doubt that."

"No offense taken, Dr. O'Halloran. But you'd be wrong."

There was a quiet force in his voice that made Erin go silent for a long moment.

"Don't they ever haunt you?" she asked softly.

"Who?" he asked, even though she knew that he knew exactly who she was talking about.

"The ones whose deaths you witnessed."

It was a question she'd only ever asked one other person. Tom.

His eyes narrowed. As she watched the quick click of comprehension, Erin belatedly realized that in the asking of it she'd revealed a secret she'd until now managed to keep from everyone but her dearest friend. The secret about the ghosts who dwelled in the private hell of her own personal nightmares.

❧ 12 ❧

Ancient Memories

Michael let the question hang as he thought back to the old woman who'd turned on him like a banshee after he'd photographed her keening over her dead husband and grandchild. She'd seen him standing nearby, seemingly so detached behind the lens of the camera, and, baring her teeth like some vicious, wounded animal, had turned on him, biting, scratching, screeching in a language he couldn't understand. The moment had been captured on film by not a few of his fellow photographers and had shown up in a few scattered newspapers and news broadcasts.

Despite the brief public embarrassment, he'd thought he'd escaped pretty much unscathed—a few fingernail scratches on his cheek that would heal, and no damage to his camera. Then he'd returned to the hotel to develop the film, which he preferred to do himself whenever possible, and viewed the shot of the woman just as she'd turned toward him.

Her eyes, wet with the sheen of furious, futile tears, were filled with such desperation and hatred, Michael had known that he could live another hundred years and not get those furious black eyes out of his mind.

The next day he was informed by a CNN reporter that his elderly attacker had later been killed herself during a midnight bombing run.

The photo, which first appeared in the *New York Times*, then was picked by papers worldwide, had earned him a Pulitzer Prize and a dark, lingering feeling of guilt.

Did they haunt him? The appropriate question for her to have asked, Michael considered, was how could they not?

"We're not that different, you and I," he said again, unsurprised when she opened her mouth to argue. He touched a leather-gloved finger to her lips to cut her off. The touch, which hadn't been meant as a caress, sent an unsettling sizzle streaking through him.

Complications, he mused on a frown, reluctantly accepting the irony once again that for a man who'd returned home to live a simple, unfettered life, he was running into one entanglement after another. What was that his father had said, about God laughing while man planned?

"We've both witnessed the same things." Again he was enticed by her fresh scent, so full of life. So different from the stench of death he'd feared had been forever seared into both his nostrils and his mind. To keep himself out of trouble, he reluctantly withdrew his impulsive touch.

"You may use a stethoscope, while my tool was a camera. But our goals were not that dissimilar. We were both diagnosing the conditions of the heart of people, the country, and even, in some small way, the planet."

Her lips drew into a tight line as she considered his

words. She looked out across the white landscape dotted with sheep placidly grazing in the mist.

"I was in Kuwait after the Gulf War," he told her when she didn't immediately respond. "It was like landing in the middle of an interactive science-fiction novel, one of those where you have to make up the plot as you go along, and any turn can send you off into a fatal direction.

"You criticized journalists for our high-flying expense accounts, but the hotel we were all staying in not only didn't have room service, it didn't have a restaurant, period. Nor did it have any water, electricity, or doors, because for some reason I'll never figure out, the Iraqi soldiers had taken them all when they retreated.

"There were days when I couldn't use my light meter because there wasn't any wind and the smoke from the fires that shot into the air and sounded like jets taking off all day and night blocked every bit of sunlight. It was like living in perpetual night.

"A mist of oil was everywhere, in the air, on the ground, on the clothes I had to throw away at the end of every day. Every so often, I'd come across the dead bodies of animals and people preserved in oil, like the pictures you've seen of the victims of old Pompeii, the ones caught for all eternity in volcanic ash?"

Erin knew the uplift at the end of his words was the Irish way of turning a declarative sentence into a question, but nodded anyway.

Seeming satisfied that he had her full attention, he stared out over the roiling sea and continued.

"Never had I so identified with Dante's *Inferno*. You

had to walk carefully because the place was littered with unexploded mines. A friend of mine—an AP reporter who often wrote the stories that accompanied my photos—was killed when he drove a truck over a lake of oil that caught on fire when he was halfway across it. I'd been best man at his wedding two months earlier, and a joyous occasion that had been.

"His bride, who was working on assignment for *National Geographic* and sitting beside him, wasn't so fortunate. It took her another brutal six weeks to die."

He ground the words out, his voice harsh and flat and strangely growing more and more detached in a way Erin was beginning to recognize as Michael's way of emotionally distancing himself from the scenes he was remembering.

Perhaps they did have something in common, she mused. Not just the fact that they'd seen uncivilized things most people, sitting safe at home in front of their television sets, watching the world through a twenty-one-inch screen, could not begin to imagine. Michael's way of retreating from the horrors, she realized, was to go deeper inside himself. While her own method was to work harder. Run faster. Then maybe the ghosts couldn't catch up with you.

"When I took a picture of a starving child, mass graves, or a stable of thoroughbreds that had been burned to a crisp in a cluster bombing run, was I portraying just that child, those corpses, and those horses, or just perhaps, was I showing through them the horrors of war?"

"I suppose that would depend on your motive."

She watched him pull himself out of the memories.

His eyes bore down into her, looking hard, looking deep. An equally strong willpower kept her from shifting her gaze from his.

"People aren't killed because photographers are taking pictures of them," he insisted quietly. "Wars and genocide have been going on long before cameras were invented. In fact, you could make an argument that photography forces the rest of the world into a discussion about the fact that all wars, whatever the justification, create death, mutilation, and destruction.

"And my job is—or more accurately *was*—to take the side of the people caught up in the middle of that chaos."

The grim set of his mouth and eyes told her that Michael was telling the truth, that he'd cared about more than just winning fame and leaving a war-torn land with the best picture. He appeared as emotionally involved in his work as she was in hers.

Perhaps even more, since he appeared to make no apology for political advocacy, while her job demanded the exact opposite approach. The mandate of her organization was, Thou shalt not take sides. To do so, it was felt, would squander the ethical credibility of everything they were attempting to do. Unfortunately, achieving such purity of purpose was often a great deal easier said than done.

"Perhaps you cared about more than just your career," she allowed. "But you can't deny that there are others—"

"I'm not them, dammit." He plowed his hand through his hair. "I may not have the calm and comforting bedside manner of Thomas Flannery. I might be more rough, more to the point. But there was a time when I cared."

"And now?"

"And now I don't think about it." They both knew that was a lie, but Erin decided that he'd already opened up so much more than she would have expected him to, there was no point in calling him on it and pushing him back into that self-imposed shell.

"What would you say to making another deal?" he asked suddenly.

"What kind of deal?"

"You quit tarring all journalists with the same black brush and I'll stop thinking of you as a crazy do-gooder with more nerve than sense."

Erin was about to flare at that description she'd heard too many times to count when she viewed a faint distant light in his eyes that almost seemed like a twinkle. Or, more likely, she considered pragmatically, it was merely a trick of the shimmering winter light.

"For Tom's sake," he pressed his case. "He may be dying, Erin. But that didn't make him suddenly turn naive, stupid, or insensitive. If we're carrying on some conflict between us, he'll sense it. And no man should have to spend his last days trying to play referee between his two best friends."

"For Tom's sake," she agreed. "So, does this mean you've changed your mind about helping me convince him to get proper treatment?"

He shook his head. The frown was back. In spades. "You definitely have Irish blood flowing in your veins, Erin O'Halloran. I know few individuals as stubborn."

"I believe Tom warned you about my mulish tendencies," she reminded him.

"Aye. And the wildcat ones as well." The quirk at the right side of his mouth suggested that she'd almost made him smile again. Once she was alone back in the warm comfort of the cozy cottage, Erin was going to think about why that gave her such a good feeling.

"Well?" She asked the question through her teeth, which were beginning to chatter.

"I'll be giving it some thought."

It wasn't the answer she wanted. But she was wearing him down. It'd just take a little bit longer, she thought with a renewed burst of optimism.

A little voice in the back of her mind whispered that she was running out of time. Erin didn't listen. After all, if one were to believe the Irish, and she chose to on this point, when God made time, hadn't he made plenty of it? Surely, after all the unselfish good he'd done for others, there would be enough time for Tom.

"My car's parked on the roadway," Michael said, breaking into her thoughts. "I'll drive you home."

Home. There it was again. That word she couldn't remember using about any place but Coldwater Cove. Which, to be honest, hadn't been much more than a recharging station since she'd gone off to medical school.

Since she felt on the verge of freezing, Erin didn't argue.

He turned on the heater, and she nearly wept with gratitude as she felt the blast of warm air blowing through the vents in the dashboard.

"Don't take this personally," she said as she held her

hands out in front of her, warming fingertips that had turned to ice. "But I think I may love you."

This time he did smile. Just a little. Like a glimpse of sun behind a dark cloud. "In that case, how would you feel about taking a little side trip back to the cottage?"

"How much of a side trip?"

"An hour at the most. There's something I want to show you."

"That sounds a great deal like when I was fifteen and Benny Robertson asked me out to the Dairy Queen for a banana split, then took me to the submarine races."

"Now, I've always thought I was a fairly worldly man, having traveled as I have. But I've never heard of submarine races in America."

"They don't exist. That's the point."

He thought about that a moment. Erin watched the comprehension dawn. Then he smiled. Really smiled in a way that had her thinking that perhaps it had been worth waiting for. "He was a right clever boy, Benny was."

"He was a right clever boy with a broken nose."

"You hit him? In the nose?"

"He took me there under false pretenses. Then tried to kiss me."

"You're a dangerous woman, Erin O'Halloran." His smile widened and there was a warmth in his eyes she was definitely not accustomed to seeing. "And I promise that I'll get permission before I kiss you."

"What makes you think I'll give it?"

"Because, like it or not, you're beginning to find me irresistible. As I find you." He reached over and took hold of her hand in the space between them. "Come with me, Erin, and I'll show you wonderful things and magic places."

Her hand froze in his. As she slowly retrieved it, Erin assured herself that it was only a coincidence his words came so close to echoing those in her dream.

"I don't suppose you're going to give me a hint as to where we're going?"

"Now wouldn't that take some of the magic out of it?" He smiled again in a way she found all too appealing.

Try as she might to deny it, she and Michael Joyce were beginning to have some sort of relationship. Erin just couldn't figure out what kind it might be.

Michael was so enjoying rerunning one of last night's dreams—the one where he'd been tumbling her in a meadow of spring wildflowers—through his mind that he nearly missed his turnoff. He braked, turning sharply in a way that had she not been wearing a seatbelt would have thrown her into his lap. Yet one more mark against progress, he considered. The idea of the lovely doctor sprawled across his thighs was not unappealing.

"I should have asked if you're up for another bit of a walk before we took off, I suppose," he said as he cut the engine on the car.

"How far?" Warm once more, Erin wasn't all that eager to trudge through the snow that had begun to fall again.

"Not very. And I promise that the scenery will be well worth the effort."

Reminding herself that she'd certainly survived far more hostile conditions under much worse circumstances, Erin agreed and followed Michael along a well-worn meandering path, through a local cemetery where high stone Celtic crosses were dotted with pale green moss.

As they crossed the meadows where a scattering of brave wildflowers were already beginning to thrust their heads through the snow from the moist earth, as hard as he tried, Michael could not ignore the fact that the faerie woman smelled of flowers herself.

She paused beside a mound of earth, decorated with stone. "Is this what you wanted to show me?"

"It's one of the things. But not the major attraction. This is a cairn. A pre-Christian tomb."

She was silent for a moment, studying the archaeological site harking back millennia to the Ancients. "You can feel them," she murmured in a hushed voice appropriate for a cathedral. "The pulse of them. And the heartbeat." She tilted her head. "The singing."

His eyes narrowed. If she could sense the presence of the Ancient Ones here, Michael wondered how she'd react if he took her to the circle of stones nearby that straddled Joyce and O'Sullivan lands.

"There are those who say they can hear the stones sing."

His sister Nora could. As could Kate O'Sullivan, who everyone in the village knew had the Sight. But Michael hadn't expected such clairvoyance from a woman who seemed to work overtime to appear briskly efficient and practical.

She ran her finger over a stone carved in ogham symbols, then looked up at him. "But you don't. Feel them, that is."

"I wouldn't exactly disbelieve. There are too many tales of magic in this land, and too many members of my own family who've experienced it, to ignore the possibility. But I've never experienced it myself."

They continued walking. Less than five minutes later, he came to a stop in front of a hedge that towered over them both and seemed to go on forever in either direction.

"Are you certain you know where you're going?" she asked, unwilling to go wading through brambles.

"There's a passageway. Not many know of it."

Erin followed him through the almost invisible break in the hedge. Then drew in a sharp breath at a picture postcard scene of unparalleled beauty.

"Lough Caislean." He used the Irish pronunciation for the glaciated lake that had given the town of Castlelough its name.

Located at the bottom of a small valley veiled in a silver mist, the lake was fringed with feathery-topped brown reeds and gleamed like sapphire on a bed of folded white velvet. Two white swans that looked as if they'd just flown in from Sleeping Beauty's castle glided as serenely as snowflakes on a liquid mirror.

The scene was familiar; indeed, from what Erin had seen thus far, it was duplicated, without such perfection, all over the west of Ireland. Indeed, it appeared to be the same one she could see from her office window at the surgery. But it was the stone castle, slowly crumbling in the ice-spangled light, that drew her like a lodestone.

"I dreamed of this." Her voice was faint, barely above a whisper, but easily heard in the stillness of the valley.

"Not a nightmare." Michael was not surprised. She'd already proved herself susceptible to the lure of his native land.

"No. Not exactly. I mean, it was sad. But not like the others I've been having about war . . .

"There was a man." She rubbed her temples with the tips of her fingers, struggling to call forth his name.

"Patrick Michael Joyce," Michael murmured.

Erin tore her gaze from the white-shawled castle up to his face. "Yes. Was he a real person?"

"Aye. Very much so."

"An ancestor?"

"I was given my name to commemorate him," he confirmed her guess. "There is, of course, a story about the man."

"Of course." Wasn't there a story about everything in this sad, stunningly beautiful country? Her gaze was drawn up to the open space that she knew, with every fiber of her being, had been the bedroom window Patrick's wife had stood in as she'd watched him ride away. "It's a tragic story, isn't it?"

Erin had known there would be no happy ending for Patrick Joyce and his pregnant wife when she'd dreamed the hoofbeats coming out of the thick morning fog to collect him.

"As you've already pointed out, many of our stories are. But aye, it's one of our family's sadder sagas."

"Will you tell me?"

"Why would you be so interested?"

"Because I know." She pressed her gloved fist against the front of her parka. "In my heart, I know that he died at Wexford."

A muscle flinched in Michael's cheek. "And would this knowledge come from some book you found in the cottage? Or your dream?"

"I realize that it sounds ridiculous and impossible, but I dreamed that two men came to get him." She closed her eyes, trying desperately to recall specifics. "Fitzpatrick. No, that's not right . . . It was Fitzgerald. And Walsh. They were all off to Wexford to fulfill some ancient prophecy."

She struggled to remember the words. "A wet winter, a dry spring, a bloody summer—"

"And no king," he finished just as Patrick Joyce had in her dream. But Michael's tone was flat where Patrick's had been optimistically determined.

Her eyes flew open and looked straight up into his, which had grown veiled again, as if he'd pulled down a heavy dark velvet curtain over his emotions. "How did you know that?"

"It was a popular prophecy in the late 1700s, and in more modern times schoolgirls have jumped rope to the rhyme. Unfortunately, it only got three of the four items correct. There was a wet winter, a dry spring, and a bloody summer. But when the summer ended, after one hundred thousand men had died, more than thirty thousand at Wexford, the English king was still on the throne."

"Tell me," she asked again.

"It's no myth," he warned.

"I realize that." Drawn to the site, she began walking toward the castle, unknowingly taking the old path that had led from the fields that had once fed so many of the castle's inhabitants. The skeletal web of bare beech tree branches stood out in stark relief against the stormy gray winter sky. When he didn't immediately follow, she paused long enough to look back over her shoulder.

"I want to know, Michael . . . I *need* to know."

He gave her another of those long, unfathomable looks. Then dragged his hand down his face.

"Aye, then I'll be telling you, and leave it up to you to decide the meaning of your dream."

❧ 13 ❧

Lament for a Hero

"*T*here was a time," he said, looking toward the castle as if picturing the long-ago scene, "one brief, shining moment in the latter part of the eighteenth century when both Protestant and Catholic in this country were of one mind. They both shared the dream of a free and independent republic and came together, as United Irishmen, to wrest back their dignity, their freedom, and their country from the iron fist of English colonial power.

"It was during May of 1798 that the rebellion in Wexford burst into flame. After skirmishes throughout the countryside, a rebel army made up essentially of peasants armed mostly with pikes, battled a detachment of the North Cork militia from the garrison at Wexford. Hundreds ran at the sight of the militia, but the main body, by standing their ground, destroyed the detachment of the king's troops."

His voice was flat, his delivery lacking any musical storytelling cadence, but Erin had no difficulty envisioning the scene. She shivered, not from the cold.

"After capturing the arms of the slaughtered militia, the rebels marched for some hours about the countryside, recruiting thousands of men, many of whom felt that since the fury of the military was being directed against guilty and innocent alike, they might as well become insurgents.

"The next major attack was at Enniscorthy. There was bloody hand-to-hand fighting in the streets. After three hours of fighting, the English garrison had, again, lost more than a hundred men. A retreat was sounded.

"The ragtag army then moved to set up camp on a prominence overlooking Wexford. For several days men—and some women as well—from all walks of life made their way to Vinegar Hill to swell the ranks of the rebel army."

"Among them Patrick Joyce," Erin murmured.

"Aye. With his friends John Walsh and Thomas Fitzgerald, who was a cousin of Lord Edward Fitzgerald. Edward Fitzgerald had fought for the British in the American Revolution, then later became acquainted with Thomas Paine and subsequently enamored with the idea of freedom."

"So it became much more than a mere peasant army."

"True enough. As I said, for that one summer, men of Ireland were united beneath the banner of potential freedom. Unfortunately, there was an absence of an overall plan.

"The English, who had no intention of losing another colony—especially one that could so easily fall into the hands of the French—counterattacked. Twenty thousand rebels packed together on a hill presented a sitting target for the cannons and howitzers, and eventually the green flag that had flown over

Wexford from the windmill atop Vinegar Hill came down, signaling the end of any hopes for a united republic. Along with the hopes of Patrick, who died there that day, and his wife for a long and happy life together.

"She screamed when she heard the news," Erin whispered.

"Aye." Michael had no way of knowing whether it was feminine intuition or something else that had Erin guessing this part of the story. "The shock of being widowed sent her into labor. Hours later, a son was born, a bit premature, but seemingly strong and healthy. A son, they say, who was the image of his father."

"He should have been some consolation for her loss."

"You'd be thinking so, wouldn't you? But the babe did nothing to ease the pain in Mary's heart. Two weeks after receiving the news that the man she'd loved since childhood had been killed, she slipped out of the castle one moonless night, took the path down to the sea, and drowned herself. Because both families were much loved hereabouts, the priest declared her death an accident rather than a suicide, allowing her to be buried in hallowed ground."

"What of her child? Their son?"

"Her sister took him and brought him up in their family. He later married himself, to a Maeve Burke, one of the region's strongest families, and continued that branch of the Joyce family tree. The same limb my grandfather, fathers, brothers, and sisters and I sprang from.

"Meanwhile, having learned their bloody lesson, the revolutionary army went to ground, outwardly appearing to go on with their lives and work. For a very long time, an unspoken conspiracy of silence wiped the concept of there ever having been a united Irish from folk history."

"You're right." Erin sighed. "That's a tragic story."

"I warned you," he reminded her. "There's also one interesting little side note I failed to tell you."

"And what's that?"

"I didn't reveal Mary's last name."

She knew, deep in the marrow of her bones. There was no need for him to say the name out loud. But he did.

"O'Halloran."

She dragged her gaze from his and looked up at the window again and imagined the feel of the hard cold stone of the floor against Mary O'Halloran Joyce's knees. "It's a coincidence."

"Aye. Undoubtedly so. It's not an uncommon name, after all."

"Not uncommon at all," she agreed. "Why, I couldn't begin to count all my cousins who live in Coldwater Cove alone. There must be hundreds of O'Hallorans in Ireland."

"Thousands," he guessed.

They were standing there, Michael looking down at her, Erin looking up at him. The crisp winter air turned unreasonably thick. Somewhere in the winter-barren trees a lone bird called out; a heron rose from the reeds at the edge of the lake; a black swan landed, causing barely a ripple in the glassy surface.

"A coincidence," she repeated, a bit more strongly, as if her words could make it true.

"If it's only that, then why do I know how you feel in my arms?" Michael moved closer, but did not touch her. "How can I know your taste?"

"You can't." Erin let out a shaky breath. Drew in another. "We can't."

"Perhaps not. Perhaps it's only coincidence. Or imagination." His mouth was a mere whisper from hers, his voice rough. "Perhaps I've been too long without a woman, you too long without a man. But tell me, Erin O'Halloran, how is it that I know you want this as much as I do?"

His mouth covered hers with a force that stole her breath. It was shocking that he'd think he had any right to kiss her. Even more shocking was the way her hands fisted in his hair, the way she pressed herself against him, kissing him back with an urgent need that bordered on desperation.

This was nothing like the slow, tender lovemaking of her dream. It was harsh, stunning, and wildly erotic. His hands thrust beneath her jacket and roamed down her back, locking her so tight against him that not a single whisper of wind could have gotten between them.

Tongues tangled, hearts drummed, and everywhere there was heat, surging through Erin's veins, scorching at her every nerve ending, curling into a fiery ball at her innermost core.

Never had any man taken so much with only a kiss. Never had she wanted any man to take so much more.

Her thoughts scattered, like wild swans soaring over the lake. Feeling as if she were teetering on the very edge of the castle's high tower, Erin struggled to call them back.

"I've come here for Tom," she managed to remind them both on a shuddering gasp as Michael's teeth nipped at her bottom lip and nearly caused her knees to buckle.

It was like turning off a light switch. He lifted his hands from her body so swiftly she swayed, forcing him to steady her with a hand to her arm. "Of course you have."

His breathing was labored, his eyes once again unfathomable, impossible to read. The wicked mouth that had so wonderfully plundered had been drawn into a tight line.

"And it's good that you would be reminding us both of that fact. Before we made a mistake we'd regret."

Seeming assured that she could stand on her own two feet, he backed away from her. This time her shiver was caused by the return of that eerie, absolute lack of outward emotion. What kind of man could go from molten to stone in a mere heartbeat?

"We'd best be getting you back to the house."

He didn't say anything all the way back to the car. Nor did he speak a single word as he began driving back to the cottage. At first, sitting beside him, Erin felt like a plague carrier. Then, the nearer they got to the cottage, the more her confusion turned to annoyance.

After all, she hadn't asked him to take her to the cairn, or the castle. And she certainly hadn't asked him to kiss her.

"And here I thought the Irish were famous for their loquaciousness," she muttered.

"I should have thought that during your relief work, you would have learned the dangers of stereotyping."

At least she'd gotten him to talk, Erin thought. "This from a man who thought I'd be built like an NFL linebacker."

He almost smiled at that. "I was mistaken about that. You're built just fine, Erin O'Halloran."

"I'm delighted I meet with your approval." Her tone was dry, but her mood was cheering, just a bit. It was difficult to stay angry when you were sitting so close to a man who, despite every bit of common sense you'd always prided yourself on possessing, you wanted to leap on.

"You do, indeed. But as you pointed out, you've come here for Tom."

Surely he didn't think that she had any sort of romantic relationship with Tom? Not that what she and Michael had shared at the lake had anything to do with romance, either. It had been a kiss born of lust, pure and simple.

No, not simple at all, she corrected. But wonderful and unsettling, all at the same time. The moment his mouth had crushed down on hers, his taste had flooded through her with such familiarity it was as if they'd kissed a hundred, a thousand times before.

"I still don't understand," she murmured, more to herself than to him, "how I knew."

He shrugged as he turned down the lane that would take them to the cottage. "It's an old tale. You've obviously heard it at one time. Perhaps from Tom."

"Perhaps." But she couldn't quite make herself believe that. "Or perhaps I could have picked up on some sort of psychic vibrations still hanging around the castle."

"That's also a possibility." He glanced over at her. "Have you ever experienced such a thing before?"

"From time to time, at ancient battle sites, but that's always a general sort of feeling of restless spirits, like at the cairn. This was different."

She turned toward him. "It was as if I'd experienced everything Mary was feeling the night before Patrick rode off to his death at Wexford."

"I'd imagine it wouldn't be so difficult for a woman to put herself in another's place."

Erin shook her head, bemused and more than a little frustrated. "I thought you said you believed in the magic."

"I said I didn't disbelieve," he reminded her. "There's a difference."

She thought again about Shea and Mary Margaret. "But you don't believe in angels."

"No."

"How about God?" She was genuinely curious now.

"I did at one time. But no longer."

Erin could understand that, she supposed, knowing what he'd witnessed. Even sympathize. But she couldn't empathize. "It must be hard, believing in nothing."

"I believe in myself," he replied. "It's simpler that way."

"Perhaps. But also lonelier. While I admittedly have no children of my own, I think that if I had a daughter, I'd want her to have the security of some sort of belief system."

The warning look he shot her suggested she'd gone too far. "Shea's got her imaginary angels," he reminded her gruffly. "They'll serve her well enough."

Since his tone didn't allow for argument, and she had to admit, at least to herself, that she honestly didn't have any right to be telling the man how to raise a child he'd only just recently discovered, Erin fell silent as they pulled up in front of Fair Haven cottage.

They'd just entered the cottage and Erin was putting away the milk when the phone rang.

"Erin, I'm glad I finally caught you," Tom said. "I've been ringing you for nearly an hour."

"Is something wrong?" She exchanged a look with Michael, who seemed to be taking up most of the small kitchen area. "Are you all right?"

"I'm well enough. But I'm afraid we've got a bit of a problem here. I've been looking for Michael. Would he happen to be there with you?"

"Yes." Although Tom's tone was matter-of-fact, Erin had known him long enough and well enough to sense that something was definitely not right. She handed the black receiver to Michael. "He wants to talk to you."

She watched Michael listen. Viewed his face turn dark and grim. "I'll be right there." He hung up without bothering to say good-bye. "Shea had some sort of seizure during mass," he told Erin. "She's been taken to the surgery."

Erin didn't ask to accompany Michael. Nor did he seem to be at all surprised when she got back into the passenger seat. In fact, she thought he looked slightly relieved.

"Has she been complaining about headaches?"

"She hasn't complained about a single solitary thing since she arrived. Except my shampoo," he recalled. At any other time the memory of that first hair-washing experience might have made him smile. Not now.

"How about double vision or lack of motor control?"

"Not that I've noticed," he said through set teeth as they raced down the road at a speed that was far from prudent.

"You realize," Erin said carefully, "that it isn't going to help your daughter if we get killed on our way into town."

His only response was a vicious-sounding curse muttered in Irish, which made Erin glad she didn't speak the language. But he did slow down. Slightly.

She used her cellular phone to call the surgery for an update.

"Tom says she appears fine now," she repeated what she'd been told. "He thinks it might be just too much excitement. Or perhaps an allergic reaction to the incense he says Father O'Malley is unfortunately so fond of."

Michael shot her a look, naked hope written in bold script across his handsome, tortured face. "Do you think that could be it?"

"At this point, according to Thomas, there's no reason not to believe that it's an isolated incident. She's certainly eager to get out of there. Apparently a little boy came with them from church. A Jamie something—"

"O'Sullivan. His mother's brother was once married to my sister Nora."

"Well, apparently he mentioned a stable of horses, and now she's trying to talk herself out of the surgery so she can go riding."

"Kate—Jamie's mother—runs a stud farm," Michael revealed. "And Shea wants a horse." Michael half smiled at that.

Erin half smiled back. "Which you'll be getting her."

"Every Irish child needs a pony."

The mood, which had been so tense it was palpable, eased ever so slightly.

"It was probably just the incense," Michael decided.

"Probably," Erin said encouragingly.

"I told her that porridge wasn't enough breakfast for a growing girl, but she insisted that was all she wanted. Next Sunday I'll be making her some bacon and eggs before she leaves the house."

Such obvious parental concern was additional proof that Michael Joyce was much more complex than the hotshot headline seeker Erin had originally thought him to be.

∼14∼

Distant Drummers

They found Shea propped up by fluffy goose-down pillows in Tom's bed above the surgery. A glass of juice and a plate of cookie crumbs were on the table beside her. Surrounded by well-wishers and family, she could have been a princess holding court.

"I'm all right, Da," she assured Michael.

"It's glad I am to be hearing that. But I'll feel even better when the doctors tell me, as well." Michael dropped a kiss atop his daughter's bright head.

Then, as Erin watched, he turned toward a gorgeous woman and swept her off her feet. "It's glad I am that you're home," he murmured. Erin had no trouble hearing the relief and unmasked love in his voice. She also recognized a prick of something that felt frighteningly like jealousy and wondered how he could embrace another woman in her presence after that kiss they'd shared.

"It's good to be home." She wrapped her arms around him, and buried her face against his neck for a brief, emotional moment. When he lowered her to the ground again, she turned toward Erin, her eyes bright with moisture.

"I'm Nora Gallagher, Michael's sister, home just this morning from America. And you must be the paragon."

"I'm Erin O'Halloran." She hated the relief she felt at learning that this beauty who looked as if she'd stepped off a painting by Titian was Michael's sister.

"Aye." Nora nodded, smiling through her unshed tears. Her face was as open as her brother's was usually closed. "The paragon. Hasn't Thomas told us all about you?" She held out her hand. "It's good to be finally meeting you, Erin. It's also probably just as well the others aren't here. The Joyce clan is admittedly a bit difficult for some to take in all at once. I well remember the first morning Quinn spent as a boarder in my home."

"The poor man looked shell-shocked," Fionna offered.

"Didn't he now?" Nora's rich, bubbly laugh was as warm as the peat fire glowing across the room.

"So you sent the others home?" Michael asked.

"Aye, I thought it best. Ellie—she's my new daughter," she explained to Erin with obvious maternal pride, "slept like an angel all during the long flight, but since she was getting cranky and hungry when Gram rang us up on the car phone, Quinn dropped me off here at the surgery so I could meet my darling niece and wait for you."

Nora went on to introduce Erin to a stunning dark-haired woman, Kate O'Sullivan, and her young son Jamie. As she exchanged polite greetings, Erin felt a bit like a sparrow in a room of swans and wondered if all the women in Ireland were as beautiful as these two.

Putting that oddly depressing thought aside, Erin

turned toward Shea. "I like your sweater. And the medal's lovely, as well."

Shea ran a small hand down the rolled lapel of the kelly-green sweater that proved a foil for her red hair and fingered the gold-tone religious medal. "Great-grandmother Fionna gave it to me. It's a holy medal of Sister Bernadette. She was a Sister of Mercy from Castlelough who got killed. And now Gram's going to get the pope to make her a saint."

"Well, isn't that nice." Erin sat down on the edge of the bed, touched the fingers of her left hand to the inside of the little girl's wrist and picked up the ophthalmoscope Tom had left on the table with her right.

Shea nodded. "Then Sister Bernadette can protect me, too. Just like Mary Margaret and Casey do."

"We can all use every bit of help we can get." Her pulse was strong and within the normal range for a child her age.

"And Kate gave me a stone." She uncurled the fingers of the hand Erin wasn't holding to show her. "She said the vibrations are good for health. She wasn't at mass, but Jamie rang her up when we got here."

Having seen the benefits of native treatments firsthand, Erin wasn't opposed to folk medicine. Pagan runes, crystals, and stones with supposed healing powers were another thing. But since the simple white rock Shea was holding could do no harm, Erin decided to overlook it.

"Isn't that nice," she said mildly. "Do you feel up to a little test?"

"All right."

"I want you to follow this light with your eyes."

"Dr. Tom already did that. He said I passed with flying colors. But I can do it again, if you'd be wanting to see," she said helpfully.

"I would." Again, normal. The pupils were both the same size, shrank properly at the bright light and tracked perfectly. Erin rechecked the backs of Shea's eyeballs, where the optic nerve attached to the retina. "You did it just right again, clever girl."

"That's because it's an easy test. Perhaps you could be making it harder next time by making loops with the light."

"Now there's a possibility." Erin took in her skin tone, which wasn't unnaturally pale for an Irish complexion. There were none of the spots that might suggest meningococcal meningitis, one of the possible causes of convulsions, and the child's temperature was normal. She was focused, her mind alert. And she was certainly having no difficulty speaking.

"Do you remember how you were feeling before you fainted?"

"I remember the singing, and the praying, which Great-grandmother's going to teach me to do in Irish. And I remember Jamie coming back from Communion"—she smiled at the boy standing by the window, who smiled back—"and then, the next thing I knew, I was here in Dr. Flannery's bed."

She shrugged, hands held out, palms up, in the universal gesture for *who knows?*

"But I'm fine, now," she insisted. "So there's no reason to be keeping me here when I could be home helping my da with the chores."

"There'll be time enough for chores." Michael

turned toward Tom. "Could we talk outside?" His gaze expanded to include Erin.

When they both agreed, he bent and brushed a kiss against his daughter's temple. "We'll be right back."

She smiled her assent, her heart in her eyes. That she loved her new father without reservation was obvious to everyone in the room. That the feeling was returned was also obvious.

"Well?" Michael demanded when the three of them were out in the hall. "What the hell happened?"

"Well, now it's a difficult thing to know, Michael." Tom rubbed his chin thoughtfully. "Are you certain the lass hasn't been complaining of headaches? Or behaving strangely?"

"Or, perhaps," Erin felt obliged to ask, "could there have been any possibility of her getting hold of any sort of drugs in the house?"

Temper flared, hot and savage in his eyes. Then was ruthlessly banked.

"There is not so much as an aspirin in my home. And certainly nothing illegal." His tone was cold steel, lethal as a stiletto. "Nor has she said a word of headaches. As for behaving strangely, how would I know how a young girl's supposed to behave?

"She's been well-mannered, talkative, and unrelentingly cheerful. In fact, she seems more than a little bit like my own little sister Celia, with the admitted exception of her fanciful tales of angels."

"Which, as I told you when she first arrived on your doorstep, is perfectly normal for her age," Tom allowed.

"Especially if you knew her grandmother," Michael muttered. "If I were forced to live with that harridan, I might be concocting tales of supernatural protectors myself."

Erin saw a sudden look of awareness come over Michael's face. "What?" she asked.

"It's nothing," he said, but his thoughtful frown suggested otherwise. "Just some ill-humored thing Deidre said before she drove off."

"What was that?"

"Nothing to take seriously."

"Perhaps you should let us make that decision," Tom suggested, earning a swift, dark look.

Michael swore. "It's nothing," he repeated. "Deidre merely accused Shea of being either a changeling, or possessed."

"Are we speaking possessed as in devil possession?" Erin asked.

"Aye. That was what she was suggesting."

"Do you believe that?" Erin asked carefully.

He snorted. "Of course I don't. I wouldn't have brought it up, except for you asking and Tom insisting."

"You know," Tom said slowly, thoughtfully, "if you'll both allow me to play devil's advocate here—no pun intended," he added quickly as Michael's dark brows dove downward, "perhaps the woman was referring to some behavior you haven't yet witnessed."

"Such as the seizure she had at mass?"

"That's possible. Would you happen to be knowing if there's any epilepsy in the family?"

"Not on my side. I don't know about Rena's family."

"Well, we can call the grandmother and ask," Tom said decisively.

"Good luck getting that witch to do anything to help."

"The girl's still her granddaughter, and if Shea's been having problems, it's possible that there have already been medical tests done that could save us precious time if something is seriously wrong with Shea."

"Is that what you'd be thinking? That something's seriously wrong with her?"

He'd gone the color of ashes. For a fleeting moment, Erin had the impression that he actually swayed just a bit.

"Tom didn't say that." Erin touched his arm and felt it stiffen like a boulder beneath her fingertips. "It's best to rule as many things out as we can, then we can zero in on what made Shea faint today."

"It was the incense," Michael insisted. "That and not enough nourishment. Jesus, the child's thin as a rail, it's obvious she hasn't been eating properly. She just needs a bit more time in the country air, eating nourishing farm meals, and she'll be fine."

Erin had witnessed the same desperate hope from parents all over the globe. The difference this time was that she could honestly be more optimistic than usual.

"I believe you're probably right. But surely you wouldn't want to risk overlooking any problems she might be developing?"

"No." He dragged his hand down his face, seeming to age years in that single moment.

Erin considered how new all this must be for Michael. When it came to taking care of a child, he was bound to be feeling as unprepared as a young father who'd been handed a helpless infant from the maternity ward.

"Of course I want to do what's best for her," he said. "What would you be suggesting?"

"There seems to be no reason to keep her here overnight," Tom said, exchanging a look with Erin, who nodded her agreement. "Why don't you take her home, keep her quiet for the rest of the day, then bring her back here in the morning so Erin and I can run a battery of tests. By then, I may have gotten more helpful information from Shea's grandmother and her Belfast doctor."

"For all the good that will do you." Erin could tell Michael was frustrated they couldn't give him a firm diagnosis.

She could sense his continuing irritation and concern as they left the village, Shea strapped into the backseat, chattering away like a magpie, seemingly unaware of the tension between the two adults. A new storm had rolled in from the Atlantic, bringing with it sleet that kept pelting against the windshield.

"You needn't get out," Erin said as they pulled up in front of the cottage.

"I'll walk you to the door."

"Really, that's not necessary."

"Aye. It is." The look he shot her was firm, allowing no room for argument. Deciding that he must want to ask her something about Shea in private, she merely nodded.

After assuring his daughter he'd be just a moment, he walked alongside Erin to the bright blue door. "Thank you."

She looked up at him, so surprised she didn't feel the sleet on her face. The same sleet that was melting in his hair, deepening its shade to a gleaming jet she had a sudden, unbidden urge to touch. "That's what you wanted to say?"

"As I said, this fatherhood business is new to me

You being there at Tom's, caring for my daughter, made a bothersome situation a great deal better."

"That's my job," she reminded him.

"Aye. And it appears you do it very well, Dr. O'Halloran." He lifted a hand, as if perhaps to touch her hair, as she'd wanted to do to his, then slowly lowered it to his side. "Thomas is a fortunate man, indeed, to have you in his life."

With that, he left.

The warmth created by those simple words continued to embrace her as she entered the cottage. Feeling a bit like the foolish, dreamy high school girl she'd never been, Erin stood at the window and watched Michael's car drive back down the lane until it disappeared behind a white curtain of sleet.

After having been examined top to toe by both Dr. Flannery and the pretty American doctor, Shea was sitting on a fragrant yellow bale of hay in the O'Sullivans' barn, watching Jamie currying his horse. Since the O'Sullivans were their nearest neighbors, her father had allowed her to visit her new friend after he'd returned home from school.

It would have been an easy enough walk, but her da had insisted on driving her and picking her up later, despite her assurance that she'd walked twice the distance to school all by herself every day in Belfast. She hadn't needed Mary Margaret to tell her that her father was worried about her. Or that the doctors were still puzzled at her reason for having fainted in church yesterday.

"My da said that he's going to be getting me a pony," she volunteered.

"If your da says he'll get you a pony, then you'll be having one soon enough."

As Jamie ran the currycomb through the black mane, Shea's fingers practically itched to touch it and see if it was as silky as it looked. The horse's coat was a reddish brown color, a bit like the nutmeg her mum used to sprinkle atop the eggnog each Christmas. A long white blaze ran down her face.

The mare kept nervously glancing in Shea's direction, and the way her huge brown eyes rolled back in her head made Shea think that she must be able to see Casey. While she was the only person she'd ever met who could actually see and hear Mary Margaret and her angelic wolfhound, she'd discovered that animals sometimes could.

"Everyone in Castlelough knows that Michael Joyce is a man of his word," Jamie continued to assure her. He frowned a bit. "Even if there are some who believe him to be mad."

The mare was a large horse, so tall that Jamie had to keep dragging a three-legged wooden stool around so he could reach her back, but she was so docile that Shea, more accustomed to watching policemen running down neighborhood boys on their steeds, wasn't the least bit afraid.

"Because he was always going off to take pictures of wars," she guessed. It was the same thing her gram had told her time and time again.

Jamie climbed down from the stool, picked up the horse's hind hoof, and began digging away with a tool that looked a bit like the lock pick she'd once seen atop one of her uncles' bedroom chest. Brendan McDougall had not just been a provo, he'd been a thief as well, arrested more than once for breaking into Protestant and Catholic houses alike.

Her new friend's movements were deft and practiced, which made him seem a great deal older than Shea herself, though she'd learned yesterday that the two of them were of an age.

"I like your da well enough," Jamie offered. "But running into the path of guns and bombs and nearly getting himself blown to bits doesn't seem like anything a sensible man would be doing."

From her grandmother's descriptions of her famous father's behavior, Shea had often thought the same thing herself. Since arriving at the farm, she'd begun to think that Deidre McDougall was as wrong about this as she was about Shea being possessed by the devil.

Her father certainly seemed sane enough. And far more sensible than anyone she'd ever known on the McDougall side of her family. Even if he did tend to brood.

Mary Margaret had assured her that was only normal behavior, considering all the death and destruction he'd witnessed. Which was something Shea had learned about firsthand. Strangely, the nightmares of her mother's death had stopped her first night at her father's house.

The bed her father had once slept in was narrow, with a white iron frame that carried a wee bit of rust, noticeable if one looked closely enough. But the fat feather mattress was so soft and puffy that first night, as she snuggled into it, Shea felt as if she were sleeping on one of Mary Margaret's clouds.

"But if Michael Joyce hadn't been taking pictures of the Troubles, he wouldn't have met me mum," she repeated what Mary Margaret had pointed out to her. "And I wouldn't have been born."

Jamie considered that a moment as he moved on to another hoof. "That's true enough," he allowed. He shot her a glance over his shoulder. "How do you like having a father?"

"Oh, I love it," Shea answered without a moment's hesitation. Just the glorious thought of it made her want to hug herself and dance around the barn with glee. "More than anything."

His dark frown reminded Shea, too late, that her da had warned her about talking about Jamie's father since his parents were getting a divorce.

"Would you be missing your own da?" she asked solicitously.

"I would not." His response was quick and as firm as his lips. But Shea, who'd learned early to watch out for the faintest signs of her mother's quicksilver mood changes, noticed that the hand industriously working on the left front hoof began to tremble. "I wish he were dead."

"Surely you wouldn't be wishing him shot?" Shea asked, truly shocked by his answer.

"No, I wouldn't be wishing for that," he said. A bit unconvincingly, Shea thought. "I'm sorry. I didn't mean to make you feel bad," he added. "I imagine you'd be missing your mum."

"I do."

The Troubles had cost her all her uncles as well as her mother. Not that she was alone in that. Indeed, most of Shea's friends had suffered some loss because of all the violence. She rubbed her temples as a twinge of another one of the headaches she'd been getting ever since the murders hovered on the horizon.

"Mary Margaret says my mum's in heaven." She'd been relieved to hear that news since her grandmother McDougall had always said that her mother had gone off on a sure slick downhill road to hell when she'd chosen to marry a Unionist.

Thinking of her mother finally happy with Jesus was a lot better than remembering all that bright red blood that had been spattered over the altar—and her own pretty pale green flower girl dress.

The inside of the barn began to waver ever so slightly and the mare suddenly had a twin. Shea blinked furiously to bring the two visions back into one.

"Are you all right?"

"I'm fine."

"You're pale as a banshee, the same way you were yesterday before you fainted at mass."

"And I suppose you've seen a banshee?" she challenged.

"No," he admitted. "But I've heard enough tales to know that they're as white as a winter moon. Just like you."

"There's nothing wrong with me," Shea insisted with a flare of desperation. "And you'll not be talking about this to anyone. Not if we're to be friends."

He reluctantly agreed, though she could tell he didn't like the idea. As her vision cleared—which it always did—Shea nearly wept with relief that she'd managed to keep her secret.

≈ 15 ≈

The Dispute at the Crossroads

"*W*ell," Erin asked Tom at the end of another long day, "what do you think about Shea Joyce?"

He locked the door and turned the hand-painted sign to Closed. "She seemed hale and hardy enough, though in the lower percentile on weight. But I have no doubt that a few weeks of hearty farm cooking will take care of that problem. And despite all she's been through, she appears to be a normal eight-year-old girl."

"It's not normal for a child to faint."

"True enough. It could be psychosomatic," he mused as he turned off the computer he'd bought in hopes of upgrading the billing system when he'd first taken over old Dr. Walsh's practice. Of course Mrs. Murphy refused to use it, claiming it was too impersonal, and continued to write out the invoices by hand, as she'd been doing since God was a pup. But Thomas remained hopeful.

"After all," he said, "the last time the girl was in a church, her mother and stepfather-to-be were gunned down."

"I was thinking the same thing," Erin agreed. She picked up the rubber hammer they'd used to test Shea's reflexes and began absently moving it back and forth from hand to hand. "There's also the outside chance she was merely trying to bring attention to herself. That fanciful story about her angels suggests that she has a vivid imagination. Perhaps she was acting."

"You sound as if you wouldn't be believing in Mary Margaret or Casey."

"Of course I don't." Erin looked at him more sharply, thinking back on his remark about faeries snatching infants. "Surely you don't?"

He waited a beat before answering. "I'd like to think that there's some helpful entity who's going to lead me to the next stage of my life. Like that Nicholas Cage fellow in the American video I rented last week from Mrs. Monohan."

"*City of Angels* was merely a movie," Erin said. She'd rented it herself while she'd been home in Coldwater Cove. "And those angels were fictional." Restless, she began to pace.

"Perhaps the ones in the movie. But that doesn't mean they don't exist. Both the Old and New Testaments are filled with such tales. Wasn't Jesus himself fed by angels, defended by angels, and strengthened by them? And didn't Luke write that 'God will order his angels to take good care of you'?"

She stopped in mid-pace and stared at him. "I certainly don't recall you being religious." Indeed, despite working in a field that might encourage a few self-protective prayers, he'd always been a self-professed lapsed Irish Catholic agnostic.

"True enough. But you know that old saying about there being no atheists in foxholes?"

"Of course."

"Well, there are probably very few on deathbeds, either."

"You're not on any deathbed." She hadn't meant to snap, but the thought of losing him was too painful to discuss calmly.

"Not yet," he agreed.

"Not for a long, long time," she countered. "And since you brought it up . . ." She stopped wearing a path in the rug long enough to dig into her medical bag. She came up with a small brown plastic bottle she held out to him. "I've brought you something."

He opened the lid and peered inside. "What are these?"

"Just a few pretty pills I picked up from the chemist next door while you were lancing Mr. Sheehan's boil. Just take them, okay?"

"Why?"

"Because I'm your doctor and I told you to."

"I realize that my memory's not what it used to be, but I don't recall appointing you my physician."

"Consider me self-appointed," she countered. "Besides, you did too, when you asked me to come to Castlelough in the first place."

"To help out with the surgery."

"Tough." She folded her arms. "Because I'm here now, you're not getting rid of me, and I'm changing the rules."

He arched a brow at the determined tone he'd heard her use so many times before, shrugged, then, curious at what she'd come up with, shook the colorful capsules and tablets into his palm.

"This is quite the cocktail you've mixed up."

"I called an old medical school friend who has a practice in New York. He specializes in autoimmune diseases."

Tom sighed. "Erin—"

"I'm not backing down on this one, Tom. There's nothing there that can hurt you, but according to my friend, from the information I faxed him this morning—"

"Are you telling me that you've been digging around in my private medical files?"

Erin flatly refused to let a little matter of personal privacy get in the way of her mission. She'd do the same thing again. As she knew he would do for her.

"I didn't have any choice. You weren't being very forthright."

"Perhaps because I considered dying a personal matter."

"Well, you're wrong. There are too many people who care about you, who love you, and who depend on you, dammit, for you to just give up without a fight."

"That's pretty much what Michael said."

"Michael called you?"

"Oh, it would have been too easy to ring me up because I could have simply hung up the phone. No, he asked Nora, who has to be exhausted from her long journey, to stay with his daughter so he could return here last night and harangue me nearly to death.

"Then, after he'd left me wounded, Nora and Fionna rang up, as if they'd plotted the attack." He shook his head in good-natured exasperation. "You all seem determined to beat back the Grim Reaper."

There was not an iota of humor in her eyes as she met his tender gaze. "You know as well as I do that death is always dogging us, Thomas. Especially in our line of work. Sometimes he wins. Sometimes we do." She set her jaw. "This time we're going to beat the bastard's bony butt."

He laughed at that, a rich, booming roar that send him into a coughing spasm and caused him to spill the pills all over the floor.

"So, your friend truly believes these drugs will cure me?" he asked, once he'd overcome the hacking and was sprawled in a chair, enjoying the view of her appealing jean-clad bottom as she crawled around the floor, retrieving the bright capsules.

"No," she admitted reluctantly. "But he does believe that they can buy you time. Meanwhile, he's sending your case on to every doctor he knows in the field. Someone is bound to come up with something." Once again Erin couldn't allow herself to believe otherwise.

"You realize, of course, that by sending out my medical records all over the world you're guilty of a terrible invasion of privacy?"

She lifted her chin in a pugnacious way that government and rebel soldiers around the globe had reluctantly learned to respect. "So why don't you stay alive long enough to sue me?"

He shook his head with mock frustration. Sighed. Then smiled. "I love you, Erin O'Halloran."

"I love you, too, Thomas Flannery." Refusing to let him see her cry, she turned her moisture-blurred gaze out the window. "So damn much."

Once she'd fought back the tears, she turned back to

him and held out a palm filled with the multicolored pills she'd picked up from the rug. "And now that we've got that settled, would you be wanting water or juice with your medication?"

Her first morning at Holy Child School wasn't nearly as bad as Shea had feared. In fact, just as her father had promised, it had gone very well. She'd been assigned a seat across the aisle from Celia Joyce, who was her own age, even if she was her aunt. Celia had smiled encouragingly at her when Mother Mary Joseph had introduced her to the class. When her turn came to do long division problems on the big green board at the front of the room, she got every single one right, which gave her a huge sense of relief and an even greater feeling of pride, since she was the only student in the class to do so.

Even recess started out well, as she jumped rope with Celia and the other girls. She was in line for her third turn when a group of boys came sauntering across the small courtyard playground. They were led by a large freckle-faced boy with hair the color of rust. Shea, who didn't recognize him from her own class, thought he appeared to be at least in the fifth form. Perhaps even sixth.

"You're the girl who had the fit at mass," he said, pointing a finger at her.

"It wasn't a fit," Celia shot back before Shea could open her mouth to respond. "So why don't you just go back to your own side of the yard, Gerry Doyle?"

" 'Twas too a fit," the boy insisted. "Me ma says that she shouldn't even be allowed in a proper Catholic school, being possessed as she is "

"I'm not possessed," Shea insisted, getting that familiar sick-to-her-stomach feeling she'd always got when her grandmother had claimed the same thing.

"Are too." The boy shot a pugnacious chin her way. "The devil's in you. He's probably made you mad as your crazy da who didn't even see fit to marry your mother."

That was it. Shea was used to having bad things said about her. She didn't like it, but until she'd arrived in Castlelough, it had been a fact of life, a part of her, like her red hair and white skin. But no one insulted her da and got away with it.

"He's not crazy." She pushed both hands against the bully's chest, but it was like trying to move one of the marble statues of Mary, Jesus, and Joseph that stood guard over the vestibule of the church. "And don't you be saying he is!"

"My brother isn't mad," Celia seconded, with a wide, roundhouse swing. "You're the crazy one, saying such things."

"Everyone in Castlelough knows that Michael Joyce is mad as a hatter." He easily dodged the blow, throwing Shea, who was still pushing against his chest, off balance. She tumbled to the ground.

"Hey!" A sound like a roar echoed across the courtyard.

As Shea rubbed her scraped knee, she saw Jamie and her cousin Rory Fitzpatrick Gallagher, whom she'd also just met on the steps before school, racing toward them, heads down like charging bulls. Both boys threw themselves at Gerry Doyle. But instead of bringing him down, they were shaken off as easily as water off a swan's back.

"Don't you be picking on my cousin!"

Rory was up like a shot, hurling himself against her antagonist, Jamie right behind him like a shadow.

"And you're just as bad," Gerry accused as he aimed a beefy fist at Jamie's jaw and sent him sprawling. "With your mother being a witch and damned to hellfire."

"You're a mean, horrid bully, Gerry Doyle!" Celia attacked like a banshee, wildly kicking at his knees. When she connected with bone with a satisfying crunch that had him yelling out in pain, his mates, who'd surrounded the group at the first sign of trouble, entered the fray. As did Shea, who quickly forgot about the stinging scrape on her leg when she saw Jamie being punched between the shoulders by a wiry blackhaired boy with squinty eyes.

Later, witnesses questioned by a furious Mother Mary Joseph would report that it had taken less than two minutes for events to go from playground argument to full-fledged brawl. All the participants had been marched to the office, where they were forced to wait in disgrace to learn their punishment.

"I'm sorry," Shea whispered to Rory. "I didn't mean to get you in trouble." Especially her first day at school.

"It wasn't your fault," he hissed back. "It's that Gerry Doyle. He's always been a big bully." He glared across the room, adorned with gilt-framed holy pictures, at the boy who'd started the fracas. Gerry, undaunted, glared back with eyes like sharpened knives.

"What do you think will happen to us?"

"Don't worry," Celia assured her. "Isn't it your first day? Nothing bad will happen to you."

"But I don't want you to be punished on my account." Shea felt miserable and guilty.

"It'll be all right," Rory and Jamie assured her in unison.

Shea wanted to believe them. Really she did. But the look on Mother Mary Joseph's face, when she called the four of them into her private office, was not encouraging. The stony expression reminded Shea of her grandmother McDougall. On a bad day.

Erin was preparing to suture up a ragged gash in Brendan O'Neill's top lip, which had gotten torn when a fishing hook attached to a fly had snapped back and attacked him, when Mrs. Murphy opened the treatment room door.

"Kate O'Sullivan's here to see the doctor," she said. "I told her he wasn't keeping office hours today."

Erin sighed inwardly and didn't bother to remind the woman—for the umpteenth time—that *she* was also a doctor. Thomas had warned her that the elderly woman didn't take to change easily. Erin had found that to be a vast understatement.

She squirted a small amount of lidocaine with epinephrine into the wound. She'd learned, during field work, that this technique provided for better hemostasis and made the insertion of the needle for the local anesthesia less painful. Unfortunately, she had rarely had the necessary supplies or time to use this knowledge, with the maimed and wounded stacked up like jets circling Kennedy airport waiting to land.

"Is it an emergency?"

"She says not." Mrs. Murphy folded her hefty arms

over a massive bosom that reminded Erin of a plump pigeon. "But there's something wrong with the woman, that's easy enough to see, even for someone who doesn't have a fancy medical degree hanging on the wall. Which isn't one bit surprising."

Brendan looked less than pleased by his situation when Erin brought out the long needle, but didn't so much as flinch when she injected the lidocaine.

Knowing that Mrs. Murphy had purposefully left her statement hanging, Erin refused to pick up on it. Having already been warned that Mrs. Murphy and her sister, Mrs. Sheehan, the butcher's wife, were the two busiest gossips in the village, she wasn't about to give the woman an opening.

"Being that the woman's damned," the elderly woman still managed to get in without an invitation.

"Conor Fitzpatrick's sister is no more damned than you are, Maeve Murphy," Brendan said, his words slurred from the effect the lidocaine was having on his lip.

"Do you have any feeling in your lip?" Erin asked in an attempt to forestall the fight she could feel brewing in the air.

"No. It's numb as a stone." Brendan's words were directed to Erin, but his glare was meant for Mrs. Murphy.

The nurse glared back. "Kate O'Sullivan's a witch, isn't she?"

"And not the only one in Castlelough," he mumbled just as Erin slid the first stitch through his desensitized skin.

Furious color rose in Mrs. Murphy's already ruddy

cheeks like a sky turning scarlet before a storm. "Like I was saying," she repeated stiffly, "the woman—the witch"—she elaborated sharply for Brendan's benefit—"is waiting to consult with you since the doctor isn't available."

Having managed to insult both Kate O'Sullivan and Erin in that single statement, Mrs. Murphy turned on her heel and marched out of the room, head high, back as straight as an iron rod.

"Sorry about getting her ire up," Brendan said to Erin. "It's just that Conor was a close friend when we were lads, and since he's not here to defend his little sister, I felt the need."

"That's very gallant of you." Erin slid the needle through the split flesh a second time. "But I suggest you wait to speak until I finish sewing up your lip."

Only one side of his mouth lifted as he flashed her a sheepish grin before turning as docile as a newborn kitten.

As she stitched, tied, snipped, then stitched again, Erin found it odd to be working in such stillness. A truck delivering milk to the creamery rumbled by on the cobblestones outside the office; in the distance she could hear the bleating of sheep on the hillsides. Having begun her relief work right out of medical school, she'd never practiced in peaceful surroundings. And certainly none as bucolic as Castlelough.

While she might have come here for Tom, the change in scenery had been good for her, as well. She'd only been in Ireland a few days, yet despite all the hours spent researching his disease, her body and mind had begun to relax out of her usual "fight or flight" mode. She was no longer running on adrenaline, and this morning a car had backfired outside the surgery and she hadn't even felt the need to dive behind a barricade.

And during the few hours of sleep she did manage, she was no longer haunted by all those patients she couldn't save. The ghosts had been with her for so long, she'd assumed they would always be part of her life.

Unfortunately, they'd been replaced by two others—Patrick and Mary Joyce. But now, whenever she'd dream of the couple's lovemaking, it would be Michael's kiss she was remembering, Michael's hands she imagined on her body.

"That's it." She tied the final knot and snipped the thread.

"You're very good," Brendan said. "I didn't feel a thing."

"That's the way it's supposed to be." She smiled. "But thank you for the compliment. Sometimes I get the feeling that not everyone in Castlelough is ready for a woman doctor."

"Don't be paying no mind to Maeve Murphy. We may be a bit behind the times, out here in the back of beyond," he admitted. "But she's always been a negative type, unwilling to say a pleasant word about anyone. Despite her outward show of piety every Sunday, she's a bloody hypocrite, which is another reason why I couldn't sit by and let her insult one of the kindest, most generous women in Castlelough."

"Kate O'Sullivan's fortunate to have such a friend." Erin peeled off her latex gloves and tossed them into the trash can beneath the sink.

"She's very special. And very dear to me," Brendan said in a way that had Erin wondering if perhaps there was a romantic relationship between the two. "Then there's the fact that patience has never been my strong suit."

"I never would have guessed that."

"Because of how I am at the Rose."

"You do have a quiet authority behind the bar that I'd suspect has kept things from getting out of hand more than once."

"That's necessary, since I won't be denying that sometimes the lads do tend to get a bit rambunctious. It's not all that natural, but I had to develop the ability when I took over the pub from my father last year."

"What did you do before that?" she asked conversationally as she put the stainless steel surgical equipment in the autoclave for sterilization.

"Oh, I was a barrister in Dublin."

"A barrister?"

"That's like an attorney in the States," he offered helpfully.

"I know what it is. It's just that I can't understand why—" She nearly bit her tongue in half as she realized she was about to insult him in the same way Mrs. Murphy had insulted her.

"Why a man would give up a fine law practice in the big city to tend bar in a wee village like Castlelough?"

"It *is* quite a career change."

"Aye, now wouldn't it seem to be," he agreed. "But it's really not so different. I'm still doing much the same thing—listening to people's problems, and offering a sympathetic ear and a bit of advice—just as I once did practicing the law.

"And if you'd be thinking that I regret moving back to help out my father, you'd be wrong, because I was never really cut out for the city and enjoy the freedom running the pub gives me."

Erin thought about the sign posted on the door of the Rose: Here when we're open. Gone when we're closed.

"Freedom to go fishing," she said with a smile. "I'll bet you never got attacked by feathered hooks in the city."

"No. But I was once hit over the head and robbed coming out of the Temple Bar." He shrugged as he slid off the metal table covered in the tidy white paper she hadn't seen since her internship at Johns Hopkins. "I'd much rather take my chances with our country perils."

He grabbed his cap from where he'd tossed it on the back of a chair. "Thank you, Dr. O'Halloran," he said. "Despite the circumstance of a wayward hook, it's a pleasure doing business with you. You're a very good doctor. And a fine addition to Castlelough. It's pleased we all are to have you join our community."

"Please, call me Erin." The professional title sounded unnecessarily formal under these circumstances.

"Erin it will be." His lips were still lopsided, but his friendly smile showed in his eyes. "As you'll be calling me Brendan."

"Agreed." Erin smiled back. Then she walked out of the small treatment room into the waiting area, where Kate O'Sullivan was waiting.

~ 16 ~

The Crow on the Cradle

$\mathcal{K}$ate really was an exceptionally beautiful woman, Erin thought. With her thick black hair, porcelain skin, and naturally dark red lips, she reminded Erin of Snow White.

She smiled up at Brendan when he greeted her, lifted her fingertips to his injured lips, and murmured some words of concern in Irish that Erin couldn't comprehend. He, in turn, touched her cheek in a gesture that appeared more fond than romantic.

Then, after tossing some bills toward Mrs. Murphy, who scowled and muttered something about the money smelling of fish and whiskey, he left the surgery.

"Good afternoon, Mrs. O'Sullivan. May I help you?"

"It's Kate." She held out a long, slender hand. Silver rings, formed into Celtic symbols, gleamed in the overhead light. "We're not much for formality in Castlelough."

"So I've discovered." Erin shook the beringed hand that was stronger than it looked. Which made sense, she realized, remembering Michael telling her that Kate bred horses for a living.

Across the room Mrs. Murphy appeared to be busy

with the green ledger book she insisted on using rather than the computer Tom had bought for the office, but Erin could sense that her internal radar was locked in on their conversation.

"Why don't you come back into my office," she suggested. "And you can tell me what brought you here today."

"Thank you." Kate smiled, just a bit, but what appeared to be deep concern shadowed her eyes.

Erin's office was small, with barely enough room for a desk, chair, bookcase, and two visitors' chairs. Diplomas her mother had, after saving them for years, sent to her in Ireland hung on the wall in plain wood frames. None of the furniture matched and the upholstery was a bit shabby, but Erin never walked into the room without experiencing a strange twinge of secret pleasure.

Mine, she thought as she sat down behind the old oak desk that faced the window. Since the surgery was located at the top of a hill, she had a grand view over the rooftops of the rolling fields and a glimmer of lake in the distance. She'd found her gaze drifting to that piece of blue on more than one occasion.

Refusing to indulge in woolgathering now, and curious as to what had brought Kate here, she folded her hands together atop the files Mrs. Murphy had left on her desk for her to sign.

"What can I do for you?"

"It's a bit difficult to explain."

Erin indulged in the previously unknown opportunity to wait for a patient to gather her thoughts.

"I know you haven't been here very long, but I'm guessing that you may have heard tales of me."

"I know you're Michael Joyce's former sister-in-law. That you have a stud farm. And that Michael's promised Shea a horse you've bred."

"Aye. Those statements are true enough." She tilted her head and gave Erin a longer, deeper look. "You've not heard that I'm a witch?"

Uncomfortable, Erin picked up a pen and began moving it from hand to hand. "I believe Mrs. Murphy might have mentioned something about that." She also recalled the small white stone this woman had given Michael's daughter with promises of healing powers.

Kate's laugh was rich and mellow and reminded Erin of woodwinds. "Ah, and wouldn't she be dying to tell the newcomer about the most infamous woman in Castlelough." Her smile faded. As did the brief light in her eyes. "It happens to be true."

"Tom said that you've been mixing up herbal drinks for him." Erin had experienced enough strange occurrences in too many countries not to have an open mind toward folk medicine.

"Which he hates. And you undoubtedly disapprove of."

"What he hates is being weak enough to allow people like you and me forcing medications on him," Erin said mildly. "And I wouldn't disapprove of anything that wouldn't interfere with a conventional medical approach."

"It's relieved I am to hear that. Since Thomas is very dear to me."

"As he is to me."

"So we have that in common." Kate took a deep breath. Another silence settled over the office as she seemed to be once again choosing her words with extreme care. "Do you believe in dreams?"

"My answer before arriving in Castlelough would have been an unqualified no." As she thought of her own dream, the one she hadn't wanted, the one she couldn't get out of her mind, the one that seemed so impossibly real, Erin began fiddling with the plastic pen again, unconsciously unscrewing the top.

"And now?" Kate coaxed.

The spring fell out, bouncing on the desk before hitting the oak plank floor. "Let's just say I'm an agnostic."

"It's the magic getting to you."

"Or the power of suggestion."

"You're a skeptic, then."

"I'm a doctor. I deal in medical facts. But I don't rule out miracles." Wasn't she praying for one for Tom, after all? "I'm not certain about magic."

"But you have an open mind."

"Yes."

"Good. Because what I'm going to be telling you will take an open mind."

Kate's slender fingers were twisting together in a way that Erin sensed was unusual for her. Beneath her obvious discomfort about whatever problem had brought her here to the surgery today, Erin had the impression that she was normally a very self-possessed woman. After all, it would take a very strong sense of self to openly declare yourself a witch in a country where the Virgin Mary stood watch over so many cross-roads.

"It's Michael's daughter, Shea," Kate said on a quick rush of breath, as if she wanted to get the unpalatable words out of her mouth as soon as possible. "There's something terribly wrong with her."

After enrolling Shea in school, Michael drove to Limerick, where he bought some tack he didn't need and suffered a stilted conversation with Mary O'Malley who'd inherited the store from her husband the previous year.

The widow O'Malley was not an unattractive woman, with her glossy chestnut hair and doe-brown eyes. Her figure was also womanly lush, the kind a man could sink into. As she had on previous occasions, she'd made it more than clear—with her eyes, her smiling lips, the seemingly random touch of a hand on his arm—that she was available.

The trouble was, she hadn't moved a single solitary thing inside Michael. Indeed, she'd only made him think all the more of Erin O'Halloran as he'd compared the two women, one who obviously wanted him, the other who didn't want to want him.

"It isn't going to work, you know." The voice drew Michael's attention to the passenger seat, where his father was sitting, puffing away on his pipe.

"What?" He cracked the window to let some of the smoke out and fresh air in.

"Trying to get the American doctor out of your mind with another woman. Even one as winsome as the widow O'Malley."

"That's not what I was doing," Michael lied. "I needed tack. O'Malley's carries the best selection."

"You can never have too much tack," Brady agreed with a grin that assured Michael he wasn't fooling either of them. In truth, Michael was now the owner of a new bridle he neither needed nor wanted, but like some foolish stumbling bumpkin of a *culchie*, had felt the need to at least pretend a reason for driving to the Limerick shop. "I noticed you sidestepped the widow's offer for supper."

"I have to get home to Shea."

"Your grandmother could always stay with her. Even overnight, if things came to that."

"Gram's getting on in years. I didn't want to take advantage."

"And haven't you always been a thoughtful grandson," Michael's father observed with a teasing lilt. He puffed some more on the pipe, sending smoke rings into the confined air. "At least you were more successful with your dog."

Michael glanced up into the rearview mirror and observed Fail sleeping on the tarp he'd spread over the backseat. It had been touch and go for a while, and as the vet had feared, the border collie had, indeed, lost her left hind leg to the German's speeding car. Yet from the way she was bouncing around the kennel, excited to see her master when Michael had arrived at the veterinary clinic, it appeared that she was already on her way to recovery.

"The vet believes she'll be back out herding sheep in no time," Michael revealed, not knowing whether or not his father had been hovering anywhere nearby when he'd had the encouraging conversation with the vet.

"Aye, I've no doubt she will," Brady agreed. "I saw many a three-legged dog outwork those with four legs during my lifetime."

It was, of course, a common enough problem. Take a narrow, twisting, two-lane road, line it with hedgerows and stone walls, send cars speeding down it, and you already had the potential for accidents. Add some dogs, cattle, or sheep into the mix and the situation turned even more dangerous.

"Fail's a grand dog," Michael said. Hearing her name, the dog woke up long enough to thump a stub of a tail on the backseat. The fog was rolling in from the sea. Michael turned on the windscreen wipers when it began to mist.

"Did you tell your daughter you'd be bringing Fail home today?"

"I haven't mentioned her to Shea at all. I didn't want to get her hopes up, in the event Fail took a turn for the worse."

"That was wise, especially considering all the grief and loss the lass has already suffered in her young life." Brady nodded his agreement. "But she's sure to find the dog a special surprise. And won't Fail also prove a big help in the days to come?"

There was something in his father's voice, something uncharacteristically serious. Michael shot him a suspicious, narrowed-eye glance. "You make it sound as if you know something I don't."

"Now, isn't it always that way with fathers and sons?" Brady's vague gesture with the hand that was holding his pipe sent some ashes falling onto his sweater, but unlike when he'd been alive, they didn't seem to burn any holes into the wool.

Michael didn't believe his father's sudden, offhand attitude. Hell, he still wasn't certain he even believed in his father's appearances, period. Even so, Shea's fainting spell came immediately to mind.

"I have the right to know if something's about to happen to my daughter. And if you know of it, you have a grandfather's duty to warn me."

"There are no crystal balls in heaven," Brady shot back in a way that led Michael to believe that his father was regretting having even brought the subject up. Once again it crossed his mind that Brady Joyce hadn't matured all that much in the afterlife; he still spoke without thinking, and acted more on emotion than reason. "The future is often as muddy for those of us who've passed on as it is for you."

"Yet you know something," Michael persisted, his blood going colder than it had turned in that instant between the mortar's hitting the center of the marketplace and its explosion.

"Now, I'm not saying I do, exactly."

Brady Joyce had never been the master of a direct statement. It had always been part of his charm. It could also be, on occasion, a major frustration.

"However," his father continued, "I *have* received the impression that Shea's going to be needing all the love she can get, and don't we all know that a dog is the one animal on God's green earth capable of unconditional love?"

"I love her unconditionally." As he said the words, firmly, unequivocally, Michael knew them to be true. Despite never having a desire for children, Shea had managed to slip past emotional barricades that had been years in the making like an arrow shot straight into his heart.

"Aye, I have no doubt at all about that. She's a for-

tunate girl to have such a loving father. Such knowledge will prove a comfort to her in times of trial."

There it was again. That goddamn not-so-subtle
hint of impending trouble. Michael shot another,
harder glance toward his father, but they'd suddenly
entered a huge fog bank that seemed to fill up the
inside of the car with wet cold mist, as well.

On the seat behind him, Fail, who'd herded sheep
in far worse weather than this, lifted her furry head and
whined a canine discomfort.

By the time the car had cleared the fog and run into
a thick slanting rain, Brady had disappeared, leaving
Michael frustrated and concerned.

"Tom and I gave Shea a thorough examination after
her fainting spell in church," Erin assured Kate. "She
checked out just fine."

"Then you had no further concerns?"

"I didn't say that." Something occurred to Erin.
Something she would have discounted out of hand
only two weeks ago. "Are you suggesting that you
dreamed something about Shea?"

"Aye." Kate took a deep breath. "I dreamed she was
sleeping in a cradle crafted from ancient oak. There
was a crow perched on the hood of the cradle."

"I see," Erin said, not really seeing anything at all. "I
take it that the crow has some negative symbolism."

"A crow, or raven, has been seen as an oracle for
thousands of years," Kate explained. "The early Druids
divined according to their flight and cries, and the Irish
war goddesses the Badbh and the Morrigan are said to
have often appeared on battlefields as ravens."

"As a sign of death?"

"Aye. It's believed, by the Ancients, and those of us who follow their ways today, that their presence was to remind the conflicting armies that in war, the only winner is death itself."

"I can certainly agree with that message," Erin murmured. "But how does a message about war supposedly have anything to do with Michael Joyce's daughter?"

"Along with its association with death, the bird was also identified with the Goddess. Raven women appear throughout Celtic literature, and the Druid seers considered raven knowledge to be a gift that allowed them to see into the past and the future. As well as beyond the veil of death."

"Well." Erin let out a breath and began fiddling with the broken pen again. "That's not a very encouraging dream." She reminded herself that despite her own recent experience, she didn't really believe in dreams. Or dream therapy.

"Like all signs, it's open to interpretation," Kate allowed. "Since the raven could travel to the darkest regions of the Underworld, it was also believed that it was capable of bringing back visions and wisdom to healers. Which explains the occurrence of raven images at a great many ancient Celtic healing sanctuaries."

Erin might have felt a sense of . . . something . . . at the cairn. But despite that, and the strange coincidence of having seemingly dreamed of Michael and Mary O'Halloran Joyce's last night together, Kate had gone beyond Erin's belief factor.

"As I said," she repeated, "Tom and I examined

Shea, and she seemed like a sweet, well-behaved eight-year-old girl."

"I have no doubt she is exactly that. Yet it isn't often that well-behaved eight-year-old girls get into brawls at school."

An icy shiver skimmed down Erin's spine. "A brawl?"

"She, and her cousin Rory, her aunt Celia, who's of an age with Shea, and Jamie all were sent to Mother Superior's office today for fisticuffs on the playground."

"She was physically fighting?" Erin tried to imagine the thought of the little girl engaged in violence and failed.

"She nearly broke a boy's nose. Now, he's a bully, to be sure, and I have no doubt that he deserved it, but Mother Superior was not amused. It didn't help that his parents run the largest hotel in Castlelough. Or," she said with a regretful frown, "that my son was involved, since a great many of the nuns—Mother Mary Joseph included—consider me a heretic."

It was Erin's turn to frown. "Were any of the other children hurt?"

"No. Though they're fortunate, because Mother is known for her belief in not sparing the rod. I received the call to pick up Jamie two hours ago, and Nora retrieved Rory and Celia, as well. But she had an appointment in the city and no one could reach Michael, so I rescued Shea and brought her along with me."

"She's with you now?"

"Aye. I left her in Tom's office, to keep her away from Mrs. Murphy's evil eye. I thought I'd take her home with us, but first I wanted to stop by and share my concerns with you and Thomas."

"I'm glad you did," Erin murmured. "I don't want to make a big deal of examining her again, especially without her father's permission. But observing her a bit more closely couldn't hurt." She tented her hands and brought her fingers to her lips as she thought the problem through. "I was just about to leave for home. Since we're neighbors, I could stop by Michael's, leave him a note telling him that Shea's with me, then take her over to the cottage until he gets home."

"That's a grand idea." Kate looked relieved and, Erin felt, not entirely surprised by this decision.

As she went with Kate to fetch Shea, Erin couldn't help thinking that, try as she might to avoid it, she kept getting more and more involved with Michael Joyce every day.

～ 17 ～

All the Ways You Wander

*S*hea appeared a bit more subdued than she had the other night in the pub. Then again, Erin considered, getting involved in a playground brawl and suffering the subsequent punishment from the principal would undoubtedly alter anyone's mood.

"I didn't mean to start the fight," she told Erin on their drive through the rain to the cottage. "I tried not to get mad, even when that big boy said I was possessed, which I'm not," she said firmly as if Erin might harbor any doubts.

"Of course you're not."

"But when he said my da was crazy, well I couldn't help myself." She sighed and tugged at an unruly red wave. "I got so angry, I shoved him."

"I can imagine how you'd feel that way. I know there have been times I've been so angry that I actually saw red."

"I never see red," Shea said.

"How about any other colors?" Erin asked with outward casualness.

"Sometimes I see a bright light. But that's just the halo surrounding Mary Margaret."

"And her rainbow."

"Aye." Shea nodded. Then sighed. "My da's going to be really angry at me for getting in trouble, isn't he?"

"You're not the first person to get called into the principal's office. I'd suspect your father got into a scrap or two when he was your age." And when he was older as well, Erin guessed, recalling a story about him supposedly ramming his Range Rover through a UN border barricade in Bosnia.

Shea didn't look very convinced. Her small brow was furrowed, her freckles standing out on her face, which was as pale as rice paper. "Do you think he'll be sending me back to Grandmother McDougall?"

"Of course not!" Erin might admittedly have her problems with Michael, but she had not a single doubt about this. "He loves you, Shea. Very much."

"But didn't he love my mum once? And he left her."

"It's not the same thing. Sometimes grown-ups fall out of love, but it's not the same between parents and children."

Shea seemed to think about that for a long time. As silence fell over the car, broken only by the swish, swish, swish of the wipers, Erin couldn't see a single sign that Michael's daughter was anything but a normal, spirited eight-year-old with a possible short-fused temper who'd felt the need to defend her beloved new father.

There were no outward symptoms, other than her little fainting spell in church the other day. No indication that further tests were needed. The simple truth was that Shea McDougall Joyce was a great deal healthier and well-adjusted than the refugee children Erin was used to seeing in her medical practice.

Still, though she considered herself too logical an individual to believe in witchcraft and dream omens, a little caution never hurt.

She stopped at Michael's house and found him still away, but the door was unlocked, which wasn't that surprising since from what Thomas had told her, Castlelough had thus far escaped any problems with crime. She pulled a page from her organizer, wrote a quick note letting him know that Shea was at her house, and inserted it into the refrigerator door in a way she hoped he'd notice when he arrived home.

She was about to leave to return to the car, which she'd left running with the heat on for Shea, when she caught sight of a sweatshirt that had apparently slid off the wooden wall hook onto the floor.

A tidy person by nature, made even more so by her medical training, Erin bent to pick it up. It was dark green, with the sleeves cut short in a haphazard way that left them ragged, and bore the insignia of Trinity College. It was worn nearly to the point when even she—who'd never been a clothes horse—would have turned it into a cleaning rag.

When she went to replace it on the hook on the wall, some errant impulse—much the same as the one that had made her kiss Michael back with such unrestrained passion—had her lifting the shirt to her nose. The fleece material carried the scent of leather and hay, which had her guessing that he'd worn it while working with his horses. She also breathed in a unique male essence that was his alone and would allow her to recognize its owner in the dark.

More than a little unsettled by the realization that

her mind had catalogued Michael Joyce's scent, Erin quickly hung the shirt back on the hook and turned to leave. It was then she noticed the man sitting in a wooden rocker by the peat fire, puffing away on a pipe.

"Good afternoon to you," he said cheerfully.

Erin knew that he hadn't been in the kitchen when she'd arrived. She shot a quick look toward the door, which was closed, and decided that he must have slipped into the room while she'd been mooning like a foolish schoolgirl over Michael.

"Good afternoon." She didn't recognize him. But there was a certain devilish twinkle in his blue eyes that was oddly familiar. Erin decided that perhaps he'd been one of the men at the Rose. "I didn't hear you drive up." Her gaze slid to the window, where the only vehicle she could see was her rental car.

"Oh, I'd be having no use for automobiles," he answered with a vague wave of the pipe. "You'd be the American doctor everyone's been talking about."

"I'm Erin O'Halloran," she allowed, deciding that if he'd been at the pub he would have already known that.

Though there was something about him she couldn't quite put her finger on, something not quite right, he was, nevertheless, sitting in the kitchen as if he had every right to, which she took as evidence that he hadn't come here to burglarize the house. It was also difficult to fault him for entering the house while Michael was away, since she'd done the same thing.

"I thought so." He nodded and resumed puffing away at the burning tobacco. Wreaths of fragrant white smoke encircled his head. Though older, he bore a

striking resemblance to Michael, which made her wonder if he might be a relative. "I know of some
O'Hallorans from County Meath, not far from
Drogheda, where, of course, the terrible siege took
place."

"Siege?" Erin asked before she could stop herself.
She really didn't have time for another tale.

"Of 1649," he said, seeming a bit surprised that she
hadn't heard of it. "And a terrible three days that was,
with innocent women and children slain in their
homes and gardens . . . It was another of Cromwell's
wicked deeds, but too depressing a tale to speak of
today, when we're just getting acquainted. But perhaps
your family might be one of those who survived the
carnage?"

"I don't know." During her brief time in
Castlelough, Erin had discovered that the Irish had a
way of making ancient history relevant to their own
lives. "My knowledge of family history is pretty spotty."
She wasn't about to admit that she'd never really asked
about her roots.

"Now isn't that a shame." He rocked back and forth
and observed her thoughtfully. "Perhaps you could
research your heritage while you're here. As so many of
your countrymen do when they arrive here in their
homeland."

Erin was about to point out that Ireland wasn't
exactly her homeland, then recalled those vague,
unbidden feelings of belonging she'd first experienced
upon seeing the island from the air. Then there was
that unsettling dream that she'd had again last night,
in even more detail, allowing her to see Patrick Joyce's

face for the first time. It had borne a striking resemblance to Michael's.

"I doubt I'll have time."

"Isn't that a shame?" he repeated. "Then again, you never know. As we say here in Ireland, when God made time he made plenty of it."

"So I hear. I suppose you're waiting for Michael?"

"Oh, I expect he'll be along by and by. It was you I was looking to find." He took the pipe from his mouth and gave her a bright, friendly smile. "And here you are."

"Not for long, I'm afraid." She glanced out the rain-lashed window toward the car. "I left a child waiting in the car, so I really need to get back to her."

"That would be Michael's wee daughter."

"Yes."

"Lovely lass."

"That she is." Since he didn't seem ready to wind up the conversation any time soon, Erin began edging toward the door. "Michael's a fortunate man."

"And isn't that what I'm always telling him? Despite all the troubles he's suffered, along with whatever misfortunes still await around the bend.

"But, isn't that the way with life, after all?" he asked rhetorically. "It's not so much the destination, but the journey itself that matters."

"I suppose that's true." Definitely not having the time to get into a philosophical question with a total stranger, Erin reached out for the old doorhandle that had been polished to a gleaming brass shine. "Well, it was very nice meeting you, Mr. . . ."

"Joyce," he supplied, confirming her guess about

him being related to Michael. "But ye must call me Brady."

The name was instantly familiar. She'd heard the men talking about Brady Joyce in the pub. But Michael's father was dead; hadn't there been mention of that seemingly ancient man, Fergus, singing at his funeral? An uncle, she decided. Or some sort of cousin.

"As much as I've enjoyed our little chat, I really must be going." She opened the door that was nearly torn from her hand by a wild gust of wind coming in off the sea.

"I'll tell Michael you came by to see him," he said, raising his voice a bit to be heard over wail of the wind that was threatening to blow her across the yard. "He'll be glad to know that his darling Shea is in such good hands. Especially with her having her little problem."

Something in his tone caused a warning bell to ring in her head like a klaxon. Erin paused for an instant and looked questioningly back over her shoulder. But his gaze was calm, pleasant, and unreadable.

When another strong gust sent bullets of icy rain stinging against her cheek like needles, she decided that he must be referring to Shea's fainting at mass. Pushing against the wind, she managed to shut the door, then dash back across the gravel driveway to the car, getting thoroughly drenched in the process.

It wasn't until she was back at the cottage, changing her clothes and running a bath for Shea, who was now also soaked to the skin from the dash from the car, that the problem that had been niggling at her mind since she'd first turned around and seen Brady Joyce sitting in that rocking chair coalesced.

He'd told her that he hadn't driven to the farm, and the absence of a car other than her own in the driveway had supported that statement. But it had been raining when she'd first left Castlelough, and by the time she'd written Michael the note telling him of Shea's whereabouts, the island—at least this western part of it—had become caught in the grips of a violent winter storm. Yet somehow, without wearing so much as a cap atop his hair or a jacket over his heather-gray sweater, the man in Michael's kitchen had remained absolutely dry.

Which was, Erin told herself as steam filled the small bathroom and rain lashed against the window-panes like bullets, impossible.

It was also, against all reason, true.

∼ 18 ∼

Playing with Fire

If Erin had been concerned about her unbidden attraction to Michael, she knew she was in deep, deep trouble when she opened the door of the cottage and felt her heart begin tumbling in a series of out-of-control somersaults at the sight of the man standing on her stoop.

"Is she all right?" he asked gruffly, dispensing with any polite hellos.

His concern, touched with parental fear, was so apparent, Erin had to tighten her hold on the edge of the door to keep from lifting her hand to his dark cheek. His rugged, weathered cheek. "She seems fine. As I stated in my note, there was just a little problem at school—"

"She didn't faint again?"

"No." This time she did touch him, on the arm, the gesture meant to reassure. "It's nothing, really. Just a silly playground incident. Apparently the school bully teased her and the Joyce and O'Sullivan children leaped in to defend her. Then the bully's pals entered into the fray and from what the principal told Kate, things turned into a bit of a brawl."

The rain had lessened, but was still falling on his head. "Why don't you come in," she suggested. "I'm not much of a cook, but I can fix you something to eat and we'll talk about your daughter."

She knew it was a mistake the moment she heard herself extend the invitation and for more reasons than the fact that her culinary skills didn't go much beyond scrambling an egg or pouring cold cereal into a bowl. There *was* the bottle of wine she'd picked up at the mercantile.

"That's a generous offer." Michael stepped into the book-filled cottage that seemed even smaller than usual when filled with his presence. The cozy comfort she usually felt here dissipated as the air in the room seemed to vibrate with electricity, as it might just before a thunderstorm. "But I should be getting Shea home."

Here's your out, Erin told herself. Just take it.

"She's taking a nap," she heard herself revealing. "It was an eventful first day of school for her. You may as well let her sleep for a while."

"She'll be needing to eat."

"I fed her a snack when we arrived." Peanut butter and jelly. Yet another thing she could whip up. "I also gave her a bath to warm her up after she got drenched running in from the rain." She gestured to the clothing she'd hung over two chairs in front of the glowing peat fire. "Really, Michael, other than fretting a bit about how you'll take her adventure, she seems fine. Why don't you let her alone for a little while. I'll fill you in on the day's adventure, try to scrounge us up something to eat, and by the time we're done she should be awake and ready for you to take her home."

For a man who'd seemed possessed with an abundance of self-confidence, he appeared strangely undecided about this.

"I'll just be staying for a short while," he decided.

He shrugged out of his jacket and hung it on the hook by the door with an ease that told her what she'd already figured out for herself—that he'd spent a great deal of time in this cottage.

"It seems I'm also indebted to you, once again."

"There's no debt involved," she insisted as she felt her throat clog. He was looking at her in a way that made her unruly heart skip a beat.

She took a careful breath before speaking, just to make certain she could.

"I was only doing what anyone would do under the circumstances. When the principal decided to suspend the children for the rest of the afternoon, but couldn't get in touch with you, Kate decided to take Shea home with her so she wouldn't have to spend the rest of the day in the principal's office. When she dropped by the office, I suggested I bring Shea home with me."

Not wanting to upset him unduly, Erin was a bit undecided about revealing Kate's supposedly prophetic dream. Especially since she still hadn't been able to detect any signs of a physical problem.

"It was a generous gesture."

The concern for his child that had been etching harsh lines on his face momentarily vanished as his eyes, as deep and dark as the sea, slid speculatively to her lips, then lingered. Erin resisted the urge to lick the lips that seemed to fascinate him even as her own unruly gaze took in his sexy, fallen angel's mouth.

Seemingly as complicated as the land he'd been born to, Michael Joyce possessed the face of a Celtic poet and the strong, hard body of his Norman invader ancestors. The two were, she was discovering, a very potent combination.

It was just a hormonal glitch, Erin assured herself. Like a major case of PMS.

"You were in my dreams again last night."

Erin could have gone all day without hearing him reveal that. Unwilling to share her own dreams with him, she felt another ragged thread in her self-restraint begin to unravel. "I don't think we should be talking about this."

"Why not?"

"Because the timing's all wrong for a relationship."

"Were we talking about having a relationship?"

Bull's-eye. If he'd wanted to make her feel foolish, he couldn't have scored a more direct hit. Erin was beginning to regret even inviting him to cross her threshold.

"No, of course we weren't. And it's a good thing, because I'm definitely not in the market for one and I'd assume you also have too much on your plate right now, what with a new daughter, to be getting involved with anyone."

"Aye. That's true enough."

The conversation drifted off as they stood there, Erin looking up at him, Michael looking down at her. The faint, teasing laughter in his gaze turned hot and dark and made her feel as if a storm were brewing deep down inside her.

Make that the mother of all PMS attacks, she

assured herself. That's all it was. That's all she could allow it to be.

"I met a relative of yours today," she said, seeking something, anything to say. "But, of course, you know that."

"How would I be knowing that?" he asked absently, seeming fascinated by her mouth again.

"Well, since Brady was in your house when I dropped by to leave you the note—"

"Brady?" Any trace of desire instantly vanished as he practically bit off the name.

"Brady Joyce."

Storm clouds gathered on his brow even as his eyes shuttered in that frustrating way and his lips, which, heaven help her, she'd been imagining on hers again, drew into a tight line.

"I assumed he was a relation of some sort?"

"Aye. He is indeed a relation of some sort."

Trust his father to go meddling in things he didn't belong in, Michael thought. Brady Joyce had always been a modern-day Puck, seeming to delight in stirring things up. Sometimes he wondered how his mother, a seemingly calm and logical woman, had been able to stay married to him for all those years.

Then again, he considered, she hadn't had a great deal of choice, what with divorce being illegal in Ireland in those days, and land rights belonging to her husband, not that Brady would have known a seed potato from a turnip. Farming had not been his father's forte.

Restless, he came farther into the room, picked up a book of myths from the kitchen table, flipped through the pages, put it down again, and exchanged it for another filled with colorful photographs of Irish country gardens. The book had belonged to his mother, who'd loved flowers, but had neither the time nor the money to plant anything that couldn't be used for food.

"An uncle, perhaps?"

"No." The garden book joined the myths in the stack as Michael admitted to himself that Eleanor Joyce had never seemed to consider herself deprived. Indeed, if a woman had ever looked at him the way his mother had looked at his father . . .

Not wanting to go down that road, he turned back to Erin, who was watching him with open curiosity. "Did you say something about supper?"

"Sure."

She let out a nervous breath and dragged her hand through her glossy brown curls. Imagining what those silken strands would feel like against his chest, his thighs, Michael felt a spike of hot desire shoot through him. He did not have to look down to know that his body had gone as hard as a pike. Feeling like some horny, oversexed teenager, he decided that he should have just taken the widow O'Malley up on her implied offer and been done with it.

The problem was, he hadn't wanted the widow. Against all sense, the woman he wanted was currently living in his old cottage. Sitting at his table. Sleeping in his bed. When that idea caused hunger to dig its claws even deeper, he leaned against the table, hands jammed deep into his pockets to keep them out of trouble, and watched as she searched through the ancient refrigerator.

"I have eggs. And some butter, so I suppose, if you're feeling brave, I could try to whip up an omelet. Or if you're not too hungry, there's a bit of cheese I could grill on toast."

When she bent down to check out the bottom shelf, her sweatshirt pulled up, just enough to reveal a slash of pale flesh between the shirt hem and the waistband of her jeans. The denim pulled snug over her tight little ass in a way that nearly had him swallowing his tongue. Slender as a sally reed she might be, but the woman had curves in all the right places.

"I don't want to be eating the last of your food."

Obviously she'd been telling the truth about not being much of a cook. It appeared she hadn't gone shopping since she'd arrived in Castlelough. Then again, Michael reminded himself, she had been a bit busy, what with trying to take over Thomas's medical practice, find a cure for whatever mysterious maladies were eating away at his immune system, plus rescuing his daughter from the Mother Superior's ire.

"That's all right," she said, her head still inside the ice box. "I need to go shopping tomorrow anyway. I meant to yesterday, but I got caught up in a book . . ."

Her voice drifted off. Apparently the bottom of the refrigerator held nothing edible. When she stood up, she slammed her head against the glass shelf holding the milk bottle he'd brought her.

"Damn." Her incredible whiskey-brown eyes watered as she began rubbing her temple with her fingertips.

"Forget supper." Drawn by a power too strong to resist, he crossed the small divide between them, stepping over a small pyramid of Yeats. "I had a large lunch of pub grub in Limerick today that will hold me just fine." His fingers curled around her wrist, lowering her hand to replace it with his own, which began caressing the flesh beneath the wild curls.

"What do you think you're doing?"

"Checking to make certain you didn't break the skin." When she would have ducked away, without an ounce of self-recrimination Michael, who'd never used his superior size to his advantage with a woman, nudged her a few steps backward, until she was up against the edge of the wooden counter. "You wouldn't want to be risking infection."

"I'm a doctor." She pushed against him, but since she was but a wee thing, faerie sized, he thought again, she couldn't budge him. "I'm perfectly capable of checking for myself."

"I wouldn't be having a single doubt of it." Even as he knew he should back away, Michael held his ground and tangled his fingers in the hair that was, amazingly, even silkier than it looked.

"Do you know," he murmured absently, as he brushed the curls aside in order to observe the lump that was already beginning to form, "I just realized what your scent reminds me of."

"Since I've been working in the surgery all day, I'd suspect antiseptic."

"Not even close." He felt her flinch when his finger-tips skimmed over the wound, then stiffen ever so slightly when his light touch continued down the side of her cheek. "It's like moonlight on the lake." He tucked an errant curl behind her ear, felt her shiver, and knew that he was not the only one feeling the pull.

"Moonlight doesn't have a scent."

"A woman with Irish blood in her veins should be able to catch of faint whiff of moonlight on a still Irish night."

"Michael—"

"I'm not finished." He caught her chin between the fingers that had been playing with her hair and held her gaze to his. "You smell of streaming moonlight silvering glassy waters and night-blooming flowers and faeries dancing in circles of stone. Try as I might, I've not been able to get the scent or sight of you out of my mind, Erin O'Halloran." He skimmed the pad of his thumb over her lips, which parted imperceptibly at the caress.

"I don't want this," she insisted in a soft, shuddering voice that suggested just the opposite. Her body was softening against his.

"Nor do I." It was only half truth.

"It's only physical."

And physical attraction was one thing. Acting on it an entirely different matter. Michael might not have lived up to all the commandments the nuns at Holy Child School had tried to drill into him, but he'd never stolen anything, never committed murder, and never coveted another man's wife or lover.

The part of him that had been friends with Tom since boyhood knew that he shouldn't be thinking of her, let alone touching her. But then there was that other part of him, the part that couldn't remember wanting anything more than he wanted Erin O'Halloran at this moment. If he believed in such things, Michael might have wondered if she'd be-witched him.

"You may be right." He skimmed a palm down her side, from her slender neck to her hips, just barely brushing her breast with his fingertips and making her shiver again. "But from your response to me, it's all too obvious that you need to be touched by a man, Erin O'Halloran." He retraced the scintillating touch back up to her neck, tugged lightly at the lobe of her ear, and watched the desire rise in her eyes. "Everywhere. And often."

"Even if that were true, and I'm not saying it is," she said in a renewed flare of heat that reminded him that the American doctor was not as soft and fragile as appearances would suggest, "and even if I wanted *you* to be that man, which I'm not saying I do, I've never permitted myself to be ruled by my emotions."

"Never?" That came as a surprise. From what he'd witnessed thus far, she was very much a woman driven by emotion.

"Never." She slipped free, putting distance between them. "Control is a necessity in my line of work."

He rubbed his chin as he studied her, letting the silence draw out. Living alone as he had these past years since returning home, with just Fail for companionship, Michael had grown comfortable with silence. Indeed, the Irish even had a phrase for the concept that was especially fitting out in this rural west countryside—*ciunas gan uagineas*. Quietness without loneliness.

"I don't believe that," he said finally. "Oh, not the part about your work," he said when she looked inclined to argue. "I can understand that all too well. But closing off your emotions goes against your nature.

I also believe that deep down, in the secret recesses of your heart and soul, you'd be admitting that."

She shook her head with frustration even as her chin—as delicately formed as a piece of Castlelough crystal—shot up. "You're a fine one to be talking about shutting off your feelings," she pointed out in a flash of white-hot heat. "Besides, if I were you, I'd not be so quick to be judging other people's souls."

Michael decided that nothing would be gained by pointing out that for a woman who alleged not to be ruled by emotion, her temper was easily and quickly fired. "So you've determined that I'm one of those bloodsucking journalists you dislike so well, after all?"

"No." She fisted her hands at her hips. "I'm talking about a child dying while practically the entire NATO command was busy saving your life."

He'd been momentarily distracted by the way her gesture had pulled the sweatshirt more snug against her breasts. When her words finally sunk in, they hit with all the force of a neutron bomb.

"What the hell would you be talking about?"

Erin had the grace to blush. Once she'd truly accepted that he'd been in no way to blame for the child who'd died in her arms, she'd decided that there was no earthly point in bringing the matter up with Michael. "It's not important."

She bit her lip as she turned back to the refrigerator, dearly wishing she'd only kept her damn mouth shut. "I bought some wine the other day at the mercantile." She took the tall green bottle from the refrigerator. "Mrs. Monohan assured me that it's a very nice dry French white. Would you like to try a glass?"

He took the bottle from her hand. "I don't drink."

"That's right," she belatedly recalled. "At the Rose, instead of the Guinness the others were drinking, you ordered nonalcoholic beer."

"When I first came back to Castlelough, I was drinking too much," he volunteered. "Most of the time, actually." He reached into the drawer, found she hadn't moved the corkscrew from where he'd once kept it, and drew the cork. "So now I don't."

"That's probably the shortest Irish story I've heard yet."

"Yet believe me, it's also the most grim of the ones I've told you." He took a glass from the open shelf and poured the straw-colored wine into it, then held it out to her. "What little girl would you be talking about?"

She moved her shoulders as she accepted the glass and took a sip. "It's not important." Her eyes were lowered, and although her voice was calm enough, she was holding the stem of the wineglass so tightly her knuckles had whitened.

"I wouldn't want to be calling you a liar, but you're dodging the question. I also suspect that it has something to do with the grudge you've been holding against me from the beginning."

"I don't hold grudges."

"Of course you do. You're Irish, after all. The ability to nurse a grudge until doomsday is undoubtedly imbedded in your genes."

"Like the ability to smell moonlight?"

He smiled briefly at that. "Aye."

"I'm an American."

"So you keep saying. But as a doctor, you should

know that there's no escaping genetics. You've O'Halloran blood, Erin. Which should also make you a fair teller of tales. So why don't you share this one with me?"

"It's a rather long story."

He pulled up one of the kitchen chairs, turned it around, straddled it, and folded his arms along the back. "I'll spare you the old proverb about God and time. But I'll not be going anywhere until you tell me. Especially since I can't leave without my daughter, whom you've put to sleep in your bed."

Erin heaved a huge sigh. Then threw herself into a chair across the table and slowly began to talk.

Minds Locked Shut

"Well." He'd kept his eyes directly on her face, not interrupting her once during her recital of that horrific day. When she was finished, he turned to stare out the window, over the fields to the sea beyond. "I didn't know."

"I realize that. Since, as Tom pointed out, you were unconscious when they airlifted you out of the country."

"True." When he returned his somber gaze to hers, his dark eyes were haunted, giving her the impression that, like her, memories of those killing days were never very far away. "But you said it was your first day, and to have such an introduction to the madness could not have been easy. Not that anything about that tragic country was easy."

"No. It certainly wasn't."

He fell silent again. Wishing, for both of them, that she hadn't brought the damn subject up, Erin waited.

"You must have resented me."

"I suppose I did, for a time."

When he arched a dark brow at that, Erin threw up her hands. "All right. Perhaps for a bit longer than that." She knew she was only reinforcing his words about grudge holding. "Which wasn't fair . . . There were reports at the time that you were near death."

"They told me I died twice." He said it in a casual, off-hand way. "Unlike that child you held in your arms, something kept dragging me back." He scrubbed a hand down his face, and when he took it away, she could see the pain and exhaustion she'd witnessed on so many faces during that horrible time. "For a long time afterward, while I was recovering in hospital, I kept wondering if I'd been saved for some special reason."

"I suppose that's a natural enough feeling," Erin said carefully. Hadn't she witnessed self-proclaimed atheists turning evangelical after surviving a near-death experience? Just as she'd seen believers turn to the bottle, as it appeared Michael had done.

"Perhaps. It's also a burden for a man who never sought to be a hero."

"Then perhaps you should count yourself fortunate that your grandmother is apparently too occupied with her Saint Bernadette campaign to expect you to start performing miracle cures," she said in a attempt to lighten the mood a bit.

"Now that would almost make it worthwhile. If I could cure Tom."

"By the way, speaking of Tom, I owe you a thank you. For going to talk to him," she elaborated at his arched, questioning brow.

"He's a strong-minded man. A few words from me aren't going to keep him alive."

"No. But they did encourage him to listen to reason. Now it's my job to cure him."

He looked skeptical, but didn't argue. "You take a great many burdens on those slender shoulders."

She shrugged, wondering why people seemed to think that size automatically denoted strength, and vice versa. "I'm tougher than I look."

"So it seems." Tough she might be, but Michael suspected she'd be as soft as he'd fantasized last night while lying alone in the dark.

He told himself that this was the trouble with feelings. Ever since Deidre had shown up in his kitchen with news of the daughter he'd never known he'd created, they'd begun slipping past the barricades, a trickle at a time. Truth was, he was finding his emotions concerning Shea an unexpected pleasure. Mixed with the occasional stark fear.

But Erin O'Halloran was another story altogether. She made him feel things he'd forgotten he could feel. Want things he'd never even suspected he wanted. If he wasn't careful, all the lust and hunger and need he'd dammed up would come spilling out like a flood, swamping them both.

"Da!" They both turned around to see Shea standing in the doorway, her hair tousled from her nap, pillow linen lines on her fair face. "You came to get me!"

The edgy, anticipatory mood was shattered. Michael exchanged a significant glance with Erin. Despite his efforts to make a home for his daughter, it was obvious to both of them that she hadn't quite shaken her insecurity. *And why should she?* he asked himself, knowing firsthand how unstable the world could be. Michael vowed that he'd do whatever it took to keep Shea's personal world in balance.

"Now why wouldn't I be coming to get my best girl?" He scooped her up into his arms and blew a noisy kiss against her neck in a way that made her giggle.

He could smell Erin's soap on his child's skin. But it smelled different on Shea. Fresh and innocent, while the subtle, sensual scent Erin exuded could tangle a man's mind and make his body ache.

"I was afraid you might be angry at me for getting in trouble my first day of school." Shea's face pulled into a frown; her red brows furrowed. "Mother Superior was angry."

"Ah, and hasn't she been a sourpuss all of her life? I have not a single doubt that she'll scowl at St. Peter when she gets to the pearly gates," Michael assured her, enjoying her obvious shock at his irreverence.

"As for your standing up to Gerry Doyle, well, I'm proud of you for not giving in to a bully. Besides, my brother Finn and I certainly got in our share of fisticuffs in our day, as he could tell you if he were here, and not in Australia."

Green eyes widened at that revelation. "But you told me that my uncle Finn is a priest."

"Aye, that he is. But he was a boy before he was a priest, and hotheaded to boot. Why, I couldn't begin to count the number of fracases Finn was involved in. Most of which he instigated himself, mind you."

"Mary Margaret says we're not supposed to fight. She says we're to turn the other cheek."

"Mary Margaret sounds like a wise angel. But humans oftentimes forget that advice."

"Aye." She sighed and her eyes brightened with a sheen of unshed tears. "Are you going to punish me?"

"Well, now I'd have to be giving that some thought." He pursed his lips. "Have you been fretting about being punished?"

"All afternoon. Even while the fight was going on, I worried that you'd be angry at me."

Obviously swamped with unpleasant thoughts again, Shea's narrow shoulders slumped. Sniffling at threatening tears, she turned away to look out the window.

"And maybe send me away," she said in a tiny, choked voice.

Michael's stomach burned at the insecurity he heard. His heart clenched, and although he could sense Erin watching him carefully, he didn't dare look at her.

"Shea." He caught her small, pointed chin in fingers that were less than steady and turned her gaze to his. "You're my own sweet girl, darling. Forever and ever. There is no way that I'm going to send you away. Nothing you could do to make me want to."

She thought about that. "What if I were to be throwing a rock and break a window?"

"If it's an accident, we'll let it slide. If it's out of temper, which you'd be coming by naturally enough, you'll be doing extra chores around the farm to pay for the window. As well as losing some television viewing privileges."

She seemed to accept that. "What if I run away?"

"Then I'd be very frightened. As, I imagine, you yourself might be once it got dark. But I'd come and find you, no matter how far you ran."

"Would you hit me when you found me?"

"Never."

"What if—"

"There's nothing you could do to make me turn you away," he cut her childish questioning off. "Aren't you my own flesh and blood, Shea Joyce? And family sticks together. Which has me thinking, what would you be saying if tomorrow, after school, we go in to the village clerk and see what must be done to make your new name official?"

"Oh!" Her indrawn breath was audible, her wide, teary smile was luminous. "I'd like that."

"As would I. Meanwhile, I think it's about time we thank Dr. O'Halloran for her hospitality. As it happens, I have something waiting for you at home."

"A horse?"

"Not quite. And not yet, since it was too late when I found Dr. O'Halloran's note to go to Kate's and fetch Niamh. But we'll pick her up tomorrow on the way home from the clerk's office, if you'd be wanting to."

"Oh, I would!" She clapped her hands. Michael doubted she could have looked any more beatific if God had suddenly appeared out of the storm and plunked Mary Margaret's discarded halo atop her bright head.

It was such a small thing, Michael thought. Out here in the country, a farm child could expect to have a pony. But Shea seemed as thrilled as if he'd just handed her the planet on a silver platter and declared her empress of the realm.

"Did you hear that, Dr. O'Halloran?" she asked Erin. "I'm to have a horse!"

"I heard, and I envy you. I always wanted a horse of my own when I was a girl."

"Then you can be sharing mine," Shea said decisively. "Can't she, Da?"

"I think that's a grand idea."

"And a generous one," Erin said. "Thank you."

"Thank *you* for watching out for me," Shea said, as politely as a princess at high tea. "And for giving me that lovely warm bath." Since Deidre had always been lacking in the simplest courtesy, Michael knew he had Rena to thank not only for his daughter, but for Shea's manners, as well.

"It was a pleasure," Erin assured her. Her words were the absolute truth. Except for all her second and third cousins back in Washington, most of the children she dealt with brought scant joy.

"And thank you for the peanut butter. It was very tasty. I liked the strawberry jam." Shea turned back toward Michael. "Could Dr. O'Halloran come for supper tomorrow and watch me ride my pony?"

"Oh, darling, I'd truly love to, but—"

"Surely you wouldn't be turning down a golden-crusted bread fresh from the oven," Michael deftly cut off her planned refusal.

"Don't tell me you bake bread."

Wasn't it enough that he had the looks of an ancient Irish king and was turning out to be, beneath the emotional barricades he'd constructed during his journalist days, a genuinely caring man? If her mother knew she'd met such a man who could cook, as well as kiss the thoughts right out of her head, Grace O'Halloran would be flying to Ireland on the very first plane to begin preparing for the wedding it was obvious she'd begun to fear Erin was never going to let her plan.

"The bread's from my sister Nora. Tomorrow's baking day. But I'll have churned the butter. And fixed a stew."

"A stew?" He could not have tempted her more with a velvet tray of Tiffany diamonds.

"In the interests of full disclosure, it's merely a mix of lamb and vegetables that will have bubbled away in the slow cooker all day and not nearly as fancy as those that the chefs in Kinsale are cooking up these days. But I can be promising you that it will be hot and filling."

"And a lot better than a grilled cheese sandwich," Erin murmured.

"Aye. Not that there's anything wrong with grilled cheese sandwiches," he said. "I've no doubt you grill a wonderful one."

She laughed at that, feeling a surprising release of the tensions that had been churning inside her since she'd first arrived in Castlelough and found Tom so much more ill than she could have imagined.

He'd spent the day upstairs in his rooms, pretending to transcribe his patient notes, which may have been partly the truth, Erin allowed. But she also suspected that he'd awaken lacking the energy to treat patients.

Erin thought about the books she still had to read, the medical data she'd downloaded from the Internet that she still had to wade through.

"The idea is admittedly tempting. And I appreciate the invitation. But I really do have a lot of work to do."

"Next Saturday, then," Michael suggested easily. "We'll make it an early evening," he said, as if reading her mind. "You can even bring your own car from the surgery, so you can leave whenever you'd like."

"Puh-leez come, Dr. O'Halloran?" It was definitely a whine. The first Erin had heard from Shea, and a bit of a departure from the Perfect Daughter persona, which suggested that she was already becoming more comfortable in her father's presence. "I could fix you custard with clotted cream for dessert. My mum taught me how to make it when I was just a wee girl."

"Did she now?"

Erin thought how tragic it was that Shea wouldn't have a mother to teach her all the other things a mother passed on to her daughter: explaining the wonders of the female body when she experienced her first period, bra shopping, listening about boys and heartbreaks, then the romantic flush of new boyfriends.

Not that Erin had ever had anyone that would even qualify as a boyfriend until medical school, when she'd purposefully given up her virginity to an ER surgical resident on a narrow bed in his hospital sleeping room. Afterward, the best thing she could say about the experience was that his swift in, swift out procedure undoubtedly suggested he'd make a great surgeon.

"You wouldn't be trying to bribe me with custard now, would you?" The smile in her voice and in her eyes kept the accusation light.

"Oh, no. It was just a suggestion," Shea said. "I used to fix supper for Mum and Grandmother a lot, and even Peter, who Mum was going to marry and didn't like me very much, said that I was a fair enough cook."

Cooking a few meals certainly wasn't child labor, but remembering her own carefree childhood, when she'd been putting Band-Aids all over her dolls and conducting experiments with the junior biology kit

Santa had brought her one memorable Christmas, Erin wondered if perhaps Shea hadn't had a tough go of it before the shooting that killed her mother and would-be stepfather.

She glanced over at the heavy medical books the Castlelough librarian had gotten for her from the inter-library lending system from Trinity College's medical school. Then, looking back at the hope blazing on Shea's thin face, wondered how Michael was ever going to be able to deny this beautiful child anything.

"Custard sounds wonderful," she agreed. "I haven't had it since I was a child." She did not add that she'd been sick as a dog with flu at the time and it was the only thing—along with 7-Up—she'd been able to keep down. "Saturday evening it is."

Shea's smile was dazzling. But it was the warm approval in Michael's gaze, as he looked over the top of his daughter's fiery red head at her, that caused Erin's unruly heart to do an unnerving little stutter dance.

Erin spent the week making the morning house calls by herself, since Tom, whose condition was worsening day by day, had finally admitted he didn't have the strength such long country drives involved. Erin took it as a positive sign that he hadn't taken to his bed, and even insisted on handling some of the clinic appointments on his good days, but she could tell from the way he tried to hide the grimace as he got up from a chair or walked across the room that his bones were getting increasingly fragile. And his hair, which had been distressingly wispy, now seemed to be falling out in clumps

"I still think I should be moving in with you," she insisted yet again as she prepared to drive out to the O'Neill place to check what she was guessing would merely turn out to be a bit of diaper rash on the newest O'Neill, rather than the dreadful condition—such as scarlet fever or measles—the frantic mother had been worried about when she'd rung up.

"It's one thing to be living above the store, so to speak," Tom said. "It's quite enough to turn my home into a bloody hospice."

"I hate thinking of you alone."

"I'm not alone. Friends drop in daily."

Erin knew one of those friends to be Michael's daughter. Shea dropped in at the surgery every afternoon after school. Someone in the family would pick her up to drive her back to the farm. Occasionally it was Fionna, or Nora, and once Kate, who'd come to town to buy Jamie a pair of new trousers. But usually it was Michael, who, before leaving for home would go upstairs and talk to Tom alone while Shea would move to Tom's office and draw pictures of angels and rainbows.

"You and Shea certainly seem to be getting along well," Erin said.

"The lass is a delight. And we have a lot in common."

"Oh?"

"We both believe in angels."

Growing more and more concerned about his lack of response to treatment, Erin glanced over at the picture tacked onto the wall of a heavenly angel with blond hair and stained-glass wings that Shea had drawn for him. It was, she assured him, his guardian angel whom Mary Margaret promised would take good care of him.

"At least promise me you'll think about my staying here," she asked as she gathered up her bag and pulled on her coat. "Just until you're back on your feet."

"For your sake, because I love and adore you dearly, I'll give the matter some thought. Though why you'd want to leave Michael's cozy cottage for a bedroom above where you work all day is beyond me."

He pushed himself up from the easy chair by the window, which gave a view of the lake in the distance, and using the hawthorn cane Fionna had brought him, laboriously made his way across the small sitting room. He opened a medical cabinet and took out a brown bottle from the chemist next door.

"If you could be dropping these by the Flynns' farmhouse on your way to the O'Neills', I'd be much appreciative. This is Eileen's sixth child in eight years, and since Liam died in a boating accident while fishing off Inishmaan four months ago, she had to take a part-time job as a clerk in the crystal factory gift shop. But even with a paycheck coming in, she can't afford prenatal vitamins, and she's too stubborn and proud to go on the dole, so it's up to us to see that her babe is born fat and healthy."

Erin knew that he'd paid for the vitamins, which weren't at all inexpensive, himself. Which was a kind and generous thing to do, considering that his relief work salary had skirted close to minimum wage and from what she'd seen thus far, his patients paid as best they could. Which tended to be not much and not often.

"I'll be glad to do it," she assured him.

"Tonight's your dinner at the Joyce farm, isn't it?"

"Yes." She tilted her head and gave him a sharp, vaguely suspicious glance. "How did you know that?"

"Shea told me when she visited after school yesterday. She can't wait to show off the pony Michael bought for her."

"That was a generous thing for him to do."

"He can certainly afford it," Tom revealed. "Even after building his house with that sexy-as-sin bathroom that provided pub conversation for a month."

"I heard all about that bathroom from Mrs. Murphy."

The nurse still hadn't come to accept her as a full medical professional, but since Erin was about the only person she could gossip to during the day, she'd become more accepting of the new doctor's invasion of what she'd always viewed as her own private female domain.

"Did she tell you that when he first bought it, bets were being taken on how many women he could fit in the Jacuzzi tub at one time?"

"She mentioned something about that." And had awakened a sleeping green monster Erin hadn't even realized had been lurking inside her with the words.

"His return to Castlelough caused a great deal of speculation in the beginning. Mostly because he's insisted on keeping such a low profile. In fact," he said slyly, "you're the very first woman he's had out at his farm since his return."

Erin couldn't decide whether that thought pleased her. Or scared her to death.

She'd cut out her tongue with her very own scalpel

before admitting that she'd changed clothes three times this morning, appalled to discover that she owned not a single skirt. No wonder her mother had found her a fashion failure, she'd thought as she pulled on her usual jeans and a heavy sweater.

What could a man who'd dated supermodels and movie stars possibly see in a woman who didn't even own a dress or a pair of high heels? She asked herself as she pulled up in front of Eileen O'Neill's tidy home on the outskirts of town. Nothing, she decided. Which was just the way she wanted it.

"Oh God," she moaned as she cut the engine and lowered her forehead to the top of the steering wheel. "You're such a liar."

❧ 20 ❧

Awakenings

The O'Neill baby's red spots did, indeed, turn out to be merely diaper rash, a mild case easily treated with some cream and encouraging words to the fretful young mother.

Erin only wished that Eileen Flynn's problem could be solved so easily. The poor woman had suffered a terrible loss, both emotionally and financially, losing both a life partner and a source of income to feed her large family when her husband had drowned. She looked absolutely worn out, her hair was dry and wispy, hanging limp to her slumped shoulders, and her cotton print dress covered with a heavy cardigan sweater hung on a frame much too thin for the state of her pregnancy.

Her hands, as she fed her one-year-old a bottle, trembled badly, and the bruise-like shadows beneath her eyes were even darker than Erin's own. After a bit of conversation, Erin became concerned that Eileen could well be suffering from clinical depression.

When she suggested to the harried working mother that she could find her treatment at a clinic in Galway, Eileen's response had been a flat, humorous laugh. Then she'd gone on to point out that even if Erin did arrange for free treatment, getting away from her new job and family was impossible. She did not, however, rule out accepting assistance from her neighbors when Erin suggested they would surely be prepared to help.

Not yet prepared to prescribe an antidepressant, Erin decided first to try easing whichever of Eileen's problems she could. The vitamins Tom had sent would be a start, since the one thing the poor woman didn't need was a sickly, perhaps premature baby to care for.

Then she stopped at the church on her way back to the surgery and had a little talk with Father O'Malley, who, it turned out, had been concerned about the family himself.

"The members of the Women's Club would be happy to drop by the Flynn home with meals," he assured her. "To save Eileen the trouble of cooking during this hard time. They'd done just such a thing directly after Liam's funeral, but Eileen's a proud woman, and assured everyone that she was fine."

He'd gone on to pick up the phone, and within twenty minutes a supper committee had been formed, along with a house cleaning committee, as well as a much needed baby-sitting committee.

"In addition, we'll be having a fund-raising supper with an auction and bingo at the parish hall," the priest told Erin after he'd hung up. "Liam was much liked in the county. I have no doubt that everyone will turn out, which should raise a tidy sum of funds to help poor Eileen."

He smiled at her, his eyes warm and kind. "You're a generous and thoughtful woman, Dr. O'Halloran. And as much of a force of nature as Tom described. Perhaps you'll be visiting us at mass some Sunday."

"Perhaps," Erin said vaguely, deciding not to mention that the only time she went to church these days was when she was back home and her parents automatically expected that she'd join the family in the pew the O'Hallorans had been claiming since the founding of the town. "I'll definitely be at the supper."

Some help with the dusting and cooking and some extra dollars wouldn't give Eileen Flynn her husband back, but as she returned to the surgery, Erin felt pleased that at least she'd been able to accomplish this small bit for the woman.

She still might need to go on antidepressants for a time, but since Eileen didn't seem a danger to herself or her children, Erin would just as soon watch things carefully before she wrote out the prescription. It was also possible that once her life got back to something resembling normality, many of the things that had her depressed in the first place might go away. Which was what Erin was hoping.

That idea had her, once again, contrasting her temporary medical practice in Castlelough with her relief work. Relief work was a great deal like her ER rotation. Patients would come in, you'd treat them and move them out as fast as possible, never knowing what happened to them after they left your treatment room. But family practice, most particularly that in a small town such as Castlelough, where everyone lived in one another's pockets, was far more intimate and involved a great deal more than writing prescriptions and handing out medical advice.

Erin saw the patients she was beginning to think of as both hers and Tom's at the pub, on the street, in the mercantile. She'd already been invited to one wedding and had attended the funeral of Maggie Burke's centenarian great-grandmother, where Fergus's singing had left not a dry eye at the graveside service. She hadn't planned it, but little by little, Erin's life was becoming entwined with those of the people of Castlelough, and she knew that when it came time to leave Ireland, she'd be leaving a little bit of herself—and her heart—behind.

When she entered the surgery, Kate O'Sullivan was in the waiting room. "I've come to take you to lunch," she announced.

Her thoughts immediately went to Shea, and she wondered if Kate wanted to share another dream. "Is something wrong?"

Kate laughed. "Isn't that just like a doctor, always thinking the worst. No, I was merely in town for some shopping, dropped in to visit with Tom, and he told me that your afternoon is fairly free."

"You never know," Erin said. "With his appointment system, people tend to drop in."

"Well, won't we be just down the street at O'Neill's Chicken and Chips if someone does? Mrs. Murphy can ring up the restaurant and you can be back here in a flash."

"I don't know." Erin glanced up at the stairs.

"Tom drifted off about ten minutes ago. Mrs. Murphy and I will never be friends, but I will give her credit for being an excellent nurse. He'll be in good hands, Erin."

"It sounds tempting." Especially since she'd come to

like Kate a great deal. Although their methods were different, they shared the determination to do whatever they could to alter Tom's apparent destiny.

"When was the last time you had a girls' lunch?"

"I can't remember."

"Well, isn't that a shame? Nora's coming to town to shop, as well. She said she'd meet us there."

"You two already had this planned?"

"Of course," Kate agreed cheerfully. "It's obvious to one and all that you need a break, Erin. You can't be helping Tom if you drop dead from overwork."

"That isn't going to happen."

"Probably not. But the poor man's worried about you, so the least you can do is come have lunch with Nora and me to ease his mind."

"Not only a plot. Now you've sunk to emotional blackmail."

Kate flashed a dazzling smile Erin suspected most supermodels would kill for. She also didn't deny Erin's accusation. "Is it working?"

"Aye," Erin said, throwing up her hands both literally and figuratively.

Which was how she came to be sitting at a lace-topped table sharing a thoroughly enjoyable lunch with the village witch and Michael's sister.

"Michael was thoroughly obnoxious with his camera when we were all living together beneath the roof where Fionna, Quinn, and I and the children live," Nora revealed. "There was hardly a single soul in the county he didn't photograph at one time or another. But always what he'd call candid shots, although in my opinion, they were a great deal more intrusive."

"Like before he went off to university and shot Clare Cairns and Francis Farelly supposedly making love in a casket from Cairns Coffin Carvers," Kate reminded her.

"And wasn't a fuss made about that?" Nora agreed. "It was a fine deep casket," she told Erin, "with a lovely silk lining. But all you could see was Claire's face."

"Which was twisted in the throes of passion," Kate broke in.

"She was acting," Nora said. "But it was quite convincing, nevertheless, which makes it not at all surprising that she went on to make a fine living for herself on the Dublin stage."

She turned back to Erin. "Michael needed an essay for civics that would reveal a day in the life of Castlelough."

"An essay usually implies writing."

"True enough, yet Michael always tended to leave the words to Da. But he truly was a wonder with his cameras, wasn't he, Kate?"

"No one could argue with that. Well," she said as an afterthought, "perhaps the bishop and Donal Cairn might have a bit of disagreement." Her eyes twinkled as she refilled their cups from the pot painted with rich swirling colors that reminded Erin of the sea.

"This pot and cups remind me of the dishes at the cottage," she murmured.

"That'd be Annie Kavanagh. She lives a bit outside of town, but is pretty much of a hermit, content to throw her pots in peace. She has a successful cottage industry going for her and sells to shops all over Ireland and the Continent as well. I've heard that she's been offered an opportunity to show at a gallery in America, but refuses to leave Ireland."

"You sound as if you're friends."

"We're friendly enough. But she's a difficult woman to get close to." Kate shrugged. "I suppose it's her artistic temperament."

"Getting back to artistic temperament," Erin asked, "whatever happened with Michael's casket picture?" From what she'd been able to tell of the citizens of Castlelough, such a photograph could still cause quite a sensation.

"Well, it got quite complicated," Nora picked up the story again. "Michael got suspended from school for two weeks for desecrating a cemetery by taking such a photograph there in the first place, and the Castlelough chapter of the Irish League of Decency tried to stop his entry into the countywide contest, but didn't succeed because the rules failed to state any prohibition against location."

"Or lack of clothing, so it seemed."

"Oh, but the photograph wasn't indecent," Kate assured her. "Michael shot Francis lying on top of Clare, and the closest thing to indecency was his bare bum sticking up."

"And a quite nice one it was," Nora said. "I was one of those who bought a calendar when they were printed."

"Weren't you about to go off to the convent about that time?"

"Aye. And didn't it make me one of the more popular postulants in the class?" Nora smiled a slow, reminiscent smile. "I kept it under my mattress with my contraband romance novels, and after lights out all the girls would gather in my room and moon over it by the light of my battery torch."

"Another reason why no one who knew you were surprised when you didn't become a nun," Kate said dryly.

"I thought I had a vocation," Nora said with a shrug.

"You were the only one."

Nora's only response to that was a slight smile that suggested Kate just might be right.

"So, if the photograph was made into a calendar, I suspect Michael won?" Erin asked. She tried telling herself her curiosity had nothing to do with her attraction toward the man and failed miserably. The truth was that she wanted to know everything about him, and since he was less than open about his past, she was willing to get her information secondhand.

"Oh no," Kate said. "There was no way the quincentennial committee was going to vote for what they all considered an obscene photograph to represent the town.

"They probably would have been less upset if he hadn't layered it in the developing with that other print of the witch's coven dancing in the circle of standing stones," Nora offered. "Or if Francis hadn't been wearing that priestly white collar."

"The juxtaposition of the Ancients' stones and the high crosses made a powerful statement," Kate argued.

"Nothing personal," Erin murmured. "But I think I have to agree with the committee. It doesn't exactly seem a proper photograph to promote the town."

"And why not?" Kate asked. "Don't we have both

high crosses and standing stones? And the idea of witches and priests being in bed together—"

"Not priests or witches that I know of," Nora broke in with a faint flare of heat that had Erin thinking that she might not be quite as docile as she'd seemed at their other meetings at the surgery.

Kate sighed dramatically. "I was speaking metaphorically. Don't all the high holy days in the Church spring from pagan celebrations? So all Michael was doing was showing how the Church came to Ireland and screwed the ancient religions."

"Donal Cairn wasn't being all that metaphorical when he threatened to throw Michael into the sea for photographing Francis seeming to be having sex with his daughter in a casket made by Donal's own hands," Nora told Erin.

"But it proved an extremely effective shot, all moody black and white and lit by hundreds of flickering candles and Kate herself just barely visible in the foggy background, clad in a druid's cowl.

"While he didn't win the prize, the fuss the town council made brought the photograph to the attention of a gallery owner in Galway, who passed it on to a colleague in Dublin, which was where an art professor at Trinity College saw it. The professor arranged for Michael to have a full scholarship."

"From art major to war photojournalist is a bit of a leap," Erin suggested.

"Not so major," Kate argued. She spooned some sugar into her tea, took a sip, and added another spoonful. "Before he made the sad decision to lock his cameras away, wasn't he continuing to film disturbing scenes that told more of the truth than many people would want to accept?"

And seen more of the truth than perhaps anyone should, Erin thought but did not say. She suspected the decision to keep personal ghosts private was another thing she and Michael had in common.

"But I suspect you know more about that than either of us ever will," Nora suggested gently.

"I suppose I do." While she liked Michael's sister a great deal, her tone did not invite further discussion of the matter.

"Do you remember when Michael was sixteen and snapped a candid shot of Mrs. Kelly from Dungarven having a little roll in the sand in one of the caves down on the coast?" Nora asked Kate, seeming to understand Erin's need to change the subject. Which made sense, since from what Erin could tell, Michael had refused to discuss his wartime days with anyone.

"Oh, that was a grand one," Kate told Erin with a bold, wicked grin. "Unfortunately, when the man rolled over, taking the naked Mrs. Kelly on top of him, it turns out that it wasn't Mr. Kelly at all, but a young artist who often showed his glasswork at the Kellys' gallery.

"The artist heard the whir of Michael's motor drive and leaped up and chased him across the field, only to have his way blocked by Donovan McLaughlin's prize bull, who decided, for one reason or another, that he was going to keep him in that field.

"The poor man was stuck there, stark naked, until McLaughlin returned home from the pub and rescued him," Nora continued the tale. "The story, needless to say, made for juicy talk at the Rose, although Mam made Michael throw away the roll of photos after she found them hanging on clips in the darkroom he'd built in the barn."

The three women shared a laugh.

"I remember thinking at the time what a great risk Mrs. Kelly was taking to behave in such a manner, where someone could stumble across them, as Michael did, and still wonder, on occasion, if artists are really as good lovers as novels and the cinema portray them to be."

"Yet another reason why you never would have lasted as a bride of Christ," Kate said with a rich, warm laugh. "You're definitely made for the secular world, Nora." She laughed again. "And don't tell me you'd be looking to compare them with writers, less than two years after your own marriage?" Kate teased.

"No." Erin watched the soft color rise in Nora's face. "I'd be needing no other man in my life, as my writer seems to be just fine in that regard. Actually," she confided, the color rising higher, hotter, "he's wonderful. It's like magic, making love with Quinn."

"I'd suspect love has a great deal to do with that magic," Kate said. "Since it's obvious that the man's even more head over wellies over you than when you first met. You're a fortunate woman."

"Aye." Nora nodded as she refilled their cups. "I'm well aware that men like Quinn Gallagher don't come along every day."

"That's the gods' own truth," Kate agreed robustly. "As for the artists, while I wouldn't be having any personal knowledge, my guess would be that they're not as good lovers as their reputations suggest, since most of the ones I've met are too self-indulgent to even begin to know how to please a woman."

"I'll bet Michael does." Erin could have slid beneath the table when the thought slipped out of her mouth.

"The man is a damn good kisser, I can vouch for that," Kate agreed.

"You can?" And just when Erin was starting to like Castlelough's witch.

"We've only kissed, nothing more," Kate assured her. "In the circle of stones when he was fifteen and I a bit younger. I'd never been kissed like that before or since. Why, I nearly had my first orgasm right on the spot, though I was too innocent to recognize the feeling until much later in life."

"I'm not certain I'd be wanting to know about you and my brother and orgasms," Nora said. She glanced down at her watch, which bore a dark green leather Celtic cross band and a face bearing the Claddagh symbol of two hands holding a crowned heart. "And not that I'd want to be rushing us, but if we're going to be solving Erin's problem before the children get home from school, we'd best be leaving soon."

"I wasn't aware I had a problem," Erin said.

"Oh, weren't you, now? Then why would you be mooning over that bright red sweater in Monohan's yesterday?"

How on earth did she know that? Erin wondered, then decided that Mrs. Monohan must have witnessed her stroking the cloud-soft wool. Obviously, just as the willingness to help others in time of need was one of the benefits of small-town living, a lack of privacy was definitely a downside. "I wasn't mooning."

"Well now, that's not exactly the way I heard it. But whatever, it's a lovely sweater and I think you should finish your tea so we can go and buy it before that Nadine Kelly gets her mitts on it."

"But this one is new." She plucked at the bulky sweater she'd bought yesterday in an attempt to upgrade from her usual sweatshirts. "Mrs. Monohan assured me that it'll wear like iron and last for years."

Kate gave the sweater in question a scathing look. "And so it will, more's the pity, since it's the color of mud."

"Mrs. Monohan called the color bark."

"Bark is brown, and isn't it also the color of mud?" Kate was on her feet in a flurry of velvet rainbow skirt that swished around the top of her lace-up boots. "You're part of the community, Erin. As a doctor, people look up to you. That being the case, you owe the citizens of Castlelough better than running around town looking like a frump."

"A frump?" Erin felt something dark and dangerous stir inside her.

"Not a frump," Nora, who was sitting between the two women, said quickly in an obvious attempt to soothe troubled waters. "Merely a woman who is unaware of her power."

"The only power I have—and that's highly questionable at the moment—is the ability to heal."

"Well, of course you do," Kate said. "Doesn't Tom speak highly of your medical talents? But surely it's possible to be both a physician and a woman?"

"I fail to see how wearing a bark brown sweater is denying my womanhood."

"Of course it's not," Nora assured her yet again. "But you're hiding your lamp under a barrel, Erin. What could it hurt to at least drop by the mercantile on the way back to the surgery and look at the sweater once again?"

"Before Nadine grabs it out from under you," Kate said again as she tossed some bills on the table to pay for her lunch. "The woman's a clothes horse, sure enough, and definitely knows how to catch a man's eye."

"I'm not in the market to catch any man's eye." Erin pulled some colorful bills out of her own wallet.

"You should know," she said as they entered the mercantile less than five minutes later, "that my mother's been trying to make me over for years and it's never worked. I'm hopeless when it comes to fashion."

"No female is hopeless when it comes to clothing," Kate assured her. "You just haven't had the proper motivation until now."

"And what would that motivation be?" Erin had a feeling she already knew what Kate would answer.

"Why, the same motivation we all have, if we're fortunate," Nora said.

"A man," she and Kate said together.

Erin thought about denying that she'd even been thinking about any man, then decided that not only would it be a lie, both women would see right through her denial.

"A sweater isn't exactly a magic glass slipper."

"Then isn't it fortunate that you're no Cinderella," Nora said as she plucked the sweater, which appeared to have escaped the clutches of Nadine Kelly, from the shelf.

Erin knew she was in trouble even before she looked in the mirror. The sweater draped over her bare skin like a warm, soft cloud. She could almost feel the atoms inside her body rearranging themselves to adjust to the remarkably sensual feeling.

"And isn't it just perfect," Nora said with obvious shared pleasure in Erin's new look. "And it brings out the red highlights in your hair."

Erin studied herself in the mirror and decided that Michael's sister was right. Her hair did seem to glow with a touch of dark fire she'd never noticed. Then again, she mused as she turned sideways and was surprised to discover she suddenly had breasts, she'd never had any reason to be looking for hair highlights. Having decided early on in life that she'd never be pretty, she'd concentrated on being smart.

Which wasn't bad, she reminded herself. But pretty was nice, as well.

"See," Kate pointed out, "your fashion sense was right on the spot. You knew this sweater would be perfect for you. You just needed some friends to push you into buying it."

Erin paid for the sweater, trying not to flinch too badly at the cost—more than she was accustomed to spending for an entire year's wardrobe—as she watched Mrs. Monohan swipe her American Express card through the machine.

"We're having a sale on the new spring cosmetics, if you'd be interested," the storekeeper informed them.

"Oh, I don't think so," Erin demurred.

"What a grand idea," Nora and Kate said at the same time.

Twenty more minutes passed while the three women played with Erin's face as if she were a Barbie doll. They seemed to be having a marvelous time. Erin was not.

Until Mrs. Monohan held up a mirror.

She was relieved that they hadn't made her look like a clown, as she'd feared. In fact, they'd left her looking like herself. But much, much better.

"You have spectacular eyes," Sheila Monohan said. "Poor Michael doesn't stand a chance."

"Michael?"

"Aren't you going out to his house for supper tonight?"

"Yes, but how did you know that?"

"Oh, that sweet little girl, Shea, told Celia, who told Mary Brannigan, who is my own daughter Margaret's cousin. You'll discover, dear, that we tend to live in one another's pockets a great deal in Castlelough. But you'll not find a village in Ireland where people are more supportive of each other."

Thinking about the rallying for the beleaguered Mrs. Flynn, Erin tapped down her momentary pique at having her private life become grist for the Castlelough gossip mill.

"I think you may have been wrong," she told Nora as they left the shop.

"About what?"

"About me not being Cinderella. Because I certainly feel like her right now." She was glad the sun had come out today, bringing with it the scent and warmth of spring so she didn't have to cover her lovely sweater with her bulky parka.

"And don't you look even lovelier," Nora said with a smile that warmed her eyes in a way that reminded Erin of her brother. Then again, too much lately reminded her of Michael Joyce.

"The poor man's a goner," Kate decided.

"And high time," Nora agreed.

~ 21 ~

Little White Lies

"**Y**ou're getting in too deep," Erin warned herself later that afternoon as she drove to Michael's farm past hedgerows that were beginning to burst into a riot of early color.

She knew that, although he'd backed away during that rainy day in her kitchen, he'd still wanted to repeat that mind-blinding kiss they'd shared at the lake. Neither of them had said a word about the incident, but the way the air in the room became charged with energy whenever he walked into the surgery nearly every afternoon to visit Tom suggested that she wasn't going to be able to keep hiding from the problem.

Unfortunately, she also sensed that in Michael's case, if she were to kiss him one more time, it would not be enough. Another kiss would lead to more. And more. And then . . . well, since he was a healthy male, and since her hormones started pinging around like a steel ball in a pinball machine whenever he was around, she feared that if she didn't stay on her guard, going to bed with him would be inevitable.

"If you didn't want him to notice you, you should have stayed with the mud-brown sweater," she reminded herself. Unbidden, a fleeting fantasy of Michael taking the new crimson one off her, crept into her mind.

"Making love with him would probably be incredible," she murmured as she drove into the setting sun. That idea was tempting and surprising at the same time. Erin had never found sex to be any big deal. She had the feeling that with Michael it would prove to be a very big deal indeed.

Which, of course, presented another problem. Having never been the kind of woman who'd ever gone in for one-night stands, she feared that going to bed with Michael, or even having a brief affair, would lead to her becoming hopelessly involved with the man. Something she had neither the time nor the energy for.

Not with Tom trying to die on her, and her still tilting at those damn windmills like a twenty-first century Don Quixote, trying to keep that from happening.

Shea was another obstacle. Erin could think of no way to have an affair with Michael without bringing his daughter into the equation. Hadn't the little girl already lost enough without risking her expecting Erin to fill her mother's shoes, then having her small heart broken when Erin moved on, which she would be doing once she got Tom back on his feet?

If only there were just the two of them, Erin mused. If only she and Michael had met at any other time, in any other place. If only there weren't so many other people to consider.

"If only," Erin muttered. Those were, she decided, two of the most impossibly hopeless words in the English language.

*   *   *

"You've come!" Shea came racing toward Erin as she climbed out of the leased car.

"I said I would."

"I know. And Mary Margaret kept telling me you were not the kind of lady who'd go back on her word, but I was still a wee bit worried." She might have grown to trust her father implicitly, but she'd not been at the farm long enough to rid her of deep-seated insecurities that had been eight years in the making.

"Well, you needn't be." A black-and-white border collie was jumping around Erin, surprisingly agile for an animal that possessed only three legs. She bent down, patted the dog's head, and was immediately rewarded with a wet lick on the back of her hand. "Who's this?"

"This is Fail," Shea announced. "Named after Failinis, the sun god Lugh's hound of mightiest deeds. She was irresistible in battle."

"Lugh or Failinis?" Erin reached into the pocket of her jeans and pulled out an extra biscuit she had left over from this morning's calls. Fail gave it a cautious sniff, then took it from her hand and swallowed it down whole.

Shea's small brow furrowed as she thought about Erin's question. "Both, I suppose. But Failinis had magical powers. Whenever she bathed in water, she turned it into wine."

"Well, that could certainly be a handy talent." Erin felt Michael coming up behind her. She'd gotten so she could sense his presence. She'd tried, without success, to convince herself that was merely the fresh green tang of his soap, but knew that it was much, much more than that.

She turned to him. "Hi."

Was that breathless voice really hers? She sounded exactly the same way Tiffany Britton, Yell Queen of Coldwater Cove High School, had sounded whenever she talked to Erin's older brother, who'd been the star quarterback. Tiffany had been the stereotypical high school siren, floating beneath a cloud of streaked blond hair.

Once, his senior year, when Erin had been fourteen, she'd made her brother laugh by making gagging motions with her finger down her throat behind Tiffany's head. Tiffany, who'd turned around just in time to catch her, was not amused.

The next day, after he'd come home at four in the morning following a homecoming date, he'd told her that someday she'd understand why he'd risked being grounded to stay out nearly all night with the girl Erin insisted on referring to as "that airhead bimbo."

At the time, Erin hadn't had a clue what he was talking about. She definitely did now.

"Good evening to you." He was smiling more often these days. Erin knew that it was Shea who'd brought those slow, smooth smiles out from whatever inner box he'd hidden them away in, but whenever she was fortunate enough to be the beneficiary, it was almost enough to make her go weak in the knees. "You're looking well."

"Thank you."

He rocked back on the heels of his boots and gave her a slow, masculine perusal, from the top of her head down to her high-top sneakers, which today were sporting scarlet laces. As his gaze slowly moved back up to her face, she imagined she could literally feel it caressing her body.

"You've done something to your face."

She felt the color flood into cheeks that had never, until today, known an artificial blush.

"Erin's got makeup on, Da," Shea explained. "It makes her look even prettier than ever, doesn't it?"

"Aye." His wicked dark blue eyes dipped down to her lips, which wore a very un-Erin lipstick the hue of crushed raspberries. The three women who'd seemed to delight so in playing with the pots and tubes had assured Erin that, with the admitted exception of the lipstick, it was a subtle, natural look. The kind a man wouldn't even notice.

Wrong.

"Not that you'd be having any need to gild the lily," he assured her. He skimmed another, slower masculine look over her. "I like that sweater as well."

"It's new." Heaven help her, the man had her sinking to Tiffany's less than scintillating conversational level.

"It suits you. You look lovely."

He looked pretty good himself. Too good, she thought as she struggled to tamp down that foolish pleasure his rare compliments could trigger.

As her mouth practically watered, she reminded herself that her reaction to him was sexual chemistry pure and simple. Erin had aced chemistry in both high school and college. Since coming to Ireland, she was discovering that she didn't know as much as she might have believed about biology.

She also should have paid more attention in physics

class, she thought as she felt herself literally being pulled toward him, like filings to a magnet. But she wasn't alone. Without realizing that either had taken a step, they were somehow closer. Too close. Yet not as close as she wanted to be.

"Da!" Shea tugged on his jacket. "I want to be showing Erin my pony."

"Dr. O'Halloran," he corrected, a bit distractedly, Erin thought. He was still looking at her in that hungry, almost desperate way she feared she was looking right back at him.

"Oh, let her call me Erin." Her body felt like it was burning up inside, making her wonder if she'd caught the flu from Terrence O'Flattery during Wednesday's house call to the elderly man who'd been too feverish to drive into the village. "The two of us have become friends, after all."

"You have to see her." Shea took hold of Erin's hand and pulled her toward the barn, effectively breaking the sensual spell. "She's beautiful. Her name is Niamh. That was the daughter of the Son of the Sea," she explained.

"She had lovely golden hair and eyes as blue as a dewdrop on grass. One day some Fenians—they were ancient Irish heroes—were hunting near Lough Killarney when Niamh came riding by on her white horse. She had gold rings in every one of her curls, and her horse had a golden bit, and four golden shoes, and a silver wreath on the back of his head."

"That must have been something to see."

"Aye, it was. The men had never seen anything so wondrous, and when she picked Ossian to be her husband, he got right up behind her and they rode off across the land toward the sea and when they got to the water, they rode right over the tops of the waves, because, you see, it was a faerie horse, so they could do that."

"I'd imagine a faerie horse could do just about anything."

"Oh, it could. Niamh showed him all the wonders of her world and he was so in love with her that he lived in her faerie palace for three hundred years."

She paused for a brief breath, then went charging on. "Then one day, Ossian suddenly remembered the friends he'd left behind and started desperately wanting to visit his own world and his own people again, so Niamh gave him a faerie steed for the trip, but she made him swear that he would not let his feet touch earthly soil, or he'd never be able to come back to her, you see.

"So he went back, riding the magic horse on the wings of the wind, but everything had changed, because three hundred years had gone by and all the men seemed like dwarfs, not at all like the giants from his time. When he saw hundreds of them trying to move a marble slab, he rode right up to them and lifted it with one hand, partly to help them, but partly because he was vain and wanted to show that he was the better man."

"Pride goeth before the fall," Erin murmured, expecting that this story, like the others she'd heard, would have a tragic ending.

Shea nodded enthusiastically. "That's what Da said. So, when Ossian lifted the marble, the golden girth on the saddle broke and his feet touched the ground and the faerie horse vanished. Poof! Just like that. And Ossian was changed from the young man who rode off with Niamh across the sea into an old blind man.

"Since he couldn't help himself, St. Patrick himself took Ossian into his own house and took care of him and told him wonderful stories about heaven and how, if he gave up the old ways, he could go there. But if he didn't, he'd end up in the fire with his old friends.

"But Ossian answered that he couldn't believe that St. Patrick's God wouldn't be proud to be claiming the Ancient Ones as his friends. So, unable to return to Niamh, he chose to join the Ancients, wherever they might be. And then he died. Because he was so old in real time.

"But that's all right, you see," Shea was quick to reassure, "because Da said that he ended up in heaven with his friends where they're spending the rest of eternity hunting and singing their songs and dancing with pretty ladies and drinking ale and listening to the bards tell the stories of when faerie kings were giants."

"That's a grand story, and you tell it wonderfully."

"I know," Shea said with a childish lack of guile. "It's because storytelling is in my blood, you see. My grandfather Joyce was the greatest storyteller in Ireland."

"So I've heard," Erin said. But the words were directed toward the little girl's back as she raced into the barn.

"That's still a bittersweet tale," Erin murmured to Michael as they followed the red-haired ball of eight-year-old energy. "But quite a step up from your usual ones."

He shrugged. "Shea's had enough tragedy in her life. I decided it wouldn't hurt to twist the original ending a bit."

"And to think someone once told me that you're not a nice man," Erin said dryly as Shea came to a stop in front of a stall.

"See," she announced in a tone Erin would have expected to have been accompanied by a flare of trumpets. "This is my Niamh."

The horse was white, but a bit stockier than Erin suspected a magical faerie horse might be. But her brown eyes were as gentle as a doe's.

"She's a fine horse."

"Isn't she just?" Shea's heart was in her emerald-green eyes. "When I first rode her, I was a little bit afraid," she admitted. "But Da taught me how to stroke her head and read her face."

"Read her face?"

"Kate's father taught me to read a horse's face when I was a lad," he answered her questioning glance. "See how Shea's pony has a long, narrow head, compared to the one in the stall beside it?"

Erin looked over, noting that the tall black horse in the adjoining stall was Roman-nosed, which in some way made him appear as bold as his owner.

"Da's own horse has a bigger head than Niamh, which made me first think he was meaner," Shea explained to Erin. "But Da told me that he's not ill-tempered at all. But he does tend to have a mind of his own on occasion, which can make him harder to handle.

"Horses with long narrow heads, like my Niamh"—

she reached up and stroked the white head, which ducked a bit to encourage her touch—"are more willing to do what you ask them to do. So long as you give them proper instruction," she tacked on in a way that suggested she was quoting her father.

Erin looked toward Michael. "Is that actually documented?"

"Well now, I wouldn't know about proper documentation. But I've been around horses all of my life, and seen the theory proven time and time again. Kate, who learned from her father and inherited his magic knack for handling horses, once talked Nora's first husband, Conor, out of buying a dish-faced horse she said would be too timid for steeplechase riding.

"She turned out to be right as rain. The stallion was fast and responsive to training, but he was nervous in crowds, and I witnessed him balking on more than one occasion at a hedge or fence. Unfortunately, Conor ended up buying one that was as fearless as he was himself."

Having heard the story from Mrs. Murphy of how Conor Fitzpatrick had died trying to clear a wall known to be dangerous, Erin privately thought perhaps if he'd chosen a horse a bit less fearless, he might still be alive today. Which would, of course, mean that Michael's sister's own life would have turned out entirely differently.

Erin thought yet again what a strange and fickle thing fate seemed to be. Which in turn brought her thoughts around to how, if Tom hadn't been in those mountains on that particular day the government helicopters had flown over, he wouldn't have been sprayed with the lethal gas that was slowly, inexorably killing him.

If only.

"Watch how she takes care not to bite me," Shea said as she held a sugar cube on her palm toward the horse, pulling Erin's thoughts back from the depressing idea that Tom might just be right, as he'd been so many times in the past. That his condition might not be reversible.

Shea's giggles, as the thick horse lips nuzzled her small palm, proved contagious, drawing Erin out of her deep concern enough to make her laugh lightly as well.

An instant later she was given something entirely different to worry about when she made the mistake of lifting her gaze from the contrast of huge teeth and childish hand and found Michael looking at her in a way that suggested if his daughter hadn't been in the barn with them, he might have pulled her down onto the nearest pile of straw.

Suspecting that she wouldn't do a thing to stop him—indeed, she might be doing more than a bit of the pulling herself—had Erin thinking that there wasn't enough air in all of Ireland to replace what his dark and dangerous eyes had just sucked from her lungs.

The suspended moment passed, as so many others they shared had done, as Michael helped Shea saddle and bridle the horse.

"Da says that saddling is an important part of owning a horse," Shea quoted her father yet again in a way that had Erin thinking of how much she'd adored her own father when she'd been Shea's age.

"I was a little afraid, the first time, when I got on

Niamh's back," Shea revealed as Michael helped her up into the saddle. "But Da said he'd not be letting any harm come to me."

Erin, who'd ridden through Washington's Olympic forest with her cousins as a child, could remember how nervous she'd been the first time she'd been set astride a horse, so far off the ground.

"My father told me the same thing," she remembered.

"And did he keep you safe?"

"Yes." Erin wasn't certain she'd ever really appreciated how fortunate she'd been until she'd compared her own growing up to that of the children she treated all over the world.

"That's what a da does," Shea said.

Michael walked the horse out to the pasture, then he and Erin stood side by side, watching as Shea rode her white pony around in circles.

"She sits well," Erin murmured.

"That she does," Michael agreed. "She's come a long way in just a few days. I'm thinking she might be a natural born horsewoman."

"As well as a natural born storyteller."

"Aye. Which isn't surprising, since it's in her blood."

He gave her one of the few natural, unguarded smiles she'd had directed her way from this man. As the low winter sun began to dip into the sea, Erin decided that Shea wasn't the only member of the Joyce family who'd come a long way in such a short time.

"Da?" Shea called out to him.

"What is it, darling?"

"You remember at the pub, the night of the *ceili*

when Great-grandmother Fionna made the photograph of us together?"

"Of course."

"Well . . . I was thinking that perhaps you could be making a picture of me riding Niamh."

Michael went as still as a stone. Erin could feel the easy mood turn suddenly tense. She watched his hands, which had been hanging loosely at his sides, curl into unconscious fists before disappearing into the pockets of his dark jeans. Erin wasn't certain what had caused the sudden change in him, but when a muscle jerked in his cheek, she found herself having to stifle the urge to reach up with her fingers and soothe it.

"The light's getting too low for a decent shot," he said. His voice was as smooth and rich as always, but since she was watching him closely and listening to him carefully, Erin could hear the faint tinge of stress in his tone. "Perhaps next time."

"All right."

"One more trip around the pasture," he said. "Then we'd better put Niamh back in her stall so we can feed Erin supper as we'd promised."

The tense moment had passed. But remembering what he'd told her about his experience filming in the pitch-black dark of Kuwait, Erin knew that he'd just lied to his daughter.

≈ 22 ≈

The Trespasser

Erin was relieved when the supper, which she refused to consider a date, went very well. As she enjoyed the stew Michael had prepared and the custard Shea was so proud of, she actually found herself almost forgetting about her problems concerning Tom.

She certainly had a more relaxing time than she'd expected, since she'd been a nervous wreck while driving the last kilometer to the Joyce farm. She would have felt like a teenager suffering from a foolish, girlish crush, except for the salient fact that Erin had never experienced a crush.

Not that this was a crush, Erin told herself as she insisted on washing the dishes, with Shea standing on a stool drying, while Michael sat at the kitchen table and braided a rope. It would have been positively homey were it not for the fact that every time her gaze drifted from the iridescent detergent bubbles to his strong dark hands, she'd find herself fantasizing how they'd feel on her body. Touching her all over. All night long.

Oh, Lord. This was becoming worse than a mere crush. She was drawn to the man in a way that was beginning to feel almost like obsession. Despite all her reservations, Erin thought that perhaps they might have been able to explore these feelings it was obvious to her that he was experiencing as well, were it not for Michael himself.

It seemed that every time he found himself loosening up with her, whenever he allowed himself to look at her in that hot, needy way, something inside him shut down and he'd back away emotionally.

Perhaps, she thought fancifully, now that she and Kate O'Sullivan were becoming friends, she could ask the village witch for a spell. A love spell. The idea, of course, was ridiculous. Which only proved that she was obviously losing her mind.

"What's funny?" Shea asked, making Erin realize that she'd laughed out loud. Undoubtedly the next step on this slippery slope to insanity would be to start babbling incoherently to herself.

"I was just thinking about something."

She could feel Michael looking at her.

"What?"

"What a good time I had tonight," she hedged.

"You'll have to come again," Shea said.

Erin smiled at the way she could sound like the child she was during dinner while discussing how many times she'd managed to jump rope at recess, then suddenly become her father's hostess. "I'd like that." It was the truth.

"So would we. Right, Da?"

"Of course Erin is always welcome. But I imagine she's a bit busy at the surgery these days."

Erin couldn't tell which one of them he was warning that their next dinner together might be a long time in coming. The congenial, even sexy man who'd sat across the dinner table from her had disappeared. In his place was that remote stranger Tom had introduced to her at Shannon.

"Your father's right." There was a clink of pottery as her hands trembled a bit beneath the water. "But I'll try to get back to watch you ride Niamh again. Perhaps you can come to my house some day and visit. With or without your father," she tacked on for Michael's benefit.

"I'd like that. The cottage is nice, isn't it?"

"It's lovely."

"But not too small?"

"Not at all. I think it's perfectly cozy."

Erin thought she looked a bit relieved at that. "Perhaps you'd like to be staying for a long time, then."

"I'll be staying awhile longer. But only until Dr. Tom recovers."

"Jamie says that Dr. Tom is going to die."

Erin was beginning to fear Jamie just might be right. "No one can know for sure about such things," she said mildly.

"That's what Mary Margaret said when I asked her if Dr. Tom was going to go to heaven soon, like my mum. She said that's in God's hands."

"Mary Margaret has a point. But I'm going to do my best to help God keep Dr. Tom alive."

"Good." Shea nodded as she dried the glass Erin handed her with a linen towel and put it on the open shelf above the wooden counter. "I like Dr. Tom a lot. I wouldn't be wanting him to die until he's an old, old man. At least forty."

"At least," Erin agreed.

When they'd finished putting the last dish away, Michael tossed down the rope and stood up. "It's past your bedtime, darling. Why don't you go brush your teeth and put your nightgown on while I walk Erin out to her car?"

"But I thought maybe she could stay for story time."

"It's getting late. And I'm sure Erin still has a great deal of work to do tonight."

"That's true." But it didn't make her feel any better about his eagerness to get rid of her.

Michael's no-trespassing signs were up again. As were the barricades, which almost had Erin thinking she must have imagined the way he'd looked at her when she'd first arrived this afternoon in her new red sweater and makeup.

"I wanted you to tell me the story of the Lady in the Lake again." Her full cupid's lips pouted.

"I'll be back in by the time you're in bed. Then I will."

"But I wanted Erin to hear it."

"Perhaps another time," Erin suggested gently.

"Promise?"

Erin was frustrated when Michael's expression didn't give her a clue as to how to handle this situation and decided that if he wasn't going to help, she wasn't going to concern herself with his feelings, whatever they might be.

"I promise."

"Oh, good. It's a wonderful story. And Da tells it almost as well as Grandpa Joyce."

Erin's first thought was that Shea would have no

personal way of knowing this, since Michael's father was dead. Then she decided that for a little girl who was so obviously desperate for a family to love her, inventing conversations with her deceased grandfather wasn't all that different from the imaginary Mary Margaret and Casey.

She turned to assure Michael she could walk herself to her car, when she realized that his shields had dropped long enough to let her see that he was not as sanguine as she about Shea's offhand remark.

She shared a good-night hug with Shea, and when he insisted, let Michael walk her out to the gravel driveway where she'd parked her car.

"I'm no child psychologist," she said, "but I wouldn't worry about Shea's imaginary conversations with her grandfather if I were you."

"While I might not have known about them, I doubt they're imaginary."

"Surely you're not saying . . ." No. Michael might be complex and difficult to understand, but as a self-proclaimed realist he couldn't believe his daughter carried on conversations with a ghost. Could he?

"Do you know that old saying about not being able to keep a good man down?"

"Yes."

"Well, that adage seems to apply to my father. Brady Joyce was irrepressible in life, and he is even more so in death. Apparently it takes more than a bad heart and six feet of earth to keep my father subdued." Michael shook his head. "I only wish he'd warned me that he'd planned to talk with Shea."

"That sounds as if you talk with him as well." Erin

was willing to admit that her work had driven her very close to the brink of burnout, and perhaps worse, on occasion. So why should she be surprised that Michael might be suffering the effects of mental trauma?

"I do." His jaw hardened as he read the obvious doubt on her face. "As did you."

"I have my own ghosts," she reminded him. "I certainly don't need to take on yours." Something clicked. Something so impossible to accept that Erin stared up at him. "That man in your kitchen . . ." The one who'd stayed dry in a driving rainstorm.

"Was Brady Joyce. My father."

"I don't believe it."

"I don't blame you. There are times I don't either."

"And the other times?"

"As I said, he was always an irrepressible man."

"Well." Erin couldn't think of anything else to say to that. Even stranger than the idea that she may have had a conversation with a ghost was that here, in this place that, for her, epitomized magic, she was actually considering the possibility.

"The idea takes some getting used to," Michael said encouragingly.

"Now that's definitely Irish understatement." She decided to take advantage of the small chink she sensed in his formidable personal armor. "I truly had a lovely time. Shea's a delightful child. You're very fortunate."

"I'm realizing that."

"Yet you don't sound exactly thrilled."

He shrugged. "I suppose I don't quite trust when things seem to be going well."

Erin could understand that. "You're not in a war

zone any longer. As Tom assured me, there are no terrorists in Castlelough."

"With the possible exception of Mrs. Sheehan and
her sister, Mrs. Murphy, I'd suspect that's true."

He still sounded less than convinced. "Yet?" she
encouraged.

"I can't help feeling as if someone's handed me a
grenade with the pin pulled. The question is not if the
damn thing will blow up, but when."

"I imagine that it's difficult, settling back into a normal life. I haven't been able to stay home more than
two weeks at a time because I don't want to crack in
front of my family and have them realize that I'm not
quite the hardened war-zone physician they believe me
to be. They worry enough as it is."

"As I imagine I'd worry about Shea, were she to
decide to take up such an occupation." He skimmed a
look over her. Another chink surfaced. "And not to
argue with you, but I wouldn't be believing there's a
hard spot anywhere on you."

"There's an easy enough way to find out." She'd
never flirted with a man in her life. And she wasn't certain how she was doing now. All Erin knew was that
there was no way she was going to go home to her
empty bed—Michael's bed—without taking with her
the memory of his kiss.

Awareness flared in his eyes. "Would you be trying
to seduce me, Dr. O'Halloran?"

"Not exactly." Feeling more reckless than she ever
had in her life, Erin lifted her arms and twined her fingers together at the back of his neck. "I'm just testing
the waters."

"Are you now?" His hands settled on her waist. Since the night had turned seasonally cold, she was wearing her parka, which made it even more amazing that she could have sworn she felt the sizzle of his hot fingertips against her flesh.

"I just have one little problem," she said.

"And what would that be?"

"I can't decide whether to wade in slowly, or just dive straight in off the cliff."

"It would probably be safer if you just stayed on the shore," he suggested, even as she felt his fingers tighten.

"I probably should." She moved closer, near enough that her thighs brushed against his. She felt him stiffen and knew, with a woman's instinct that she'd never even suspected she possessed, that it was now or never. "But I've never been a real fan of safe."

Deciding that she could well die of the wanting if she waited for him to kiss her again, Erin went up on her toes and pressed her lips to his.

A punch of sensation rocketed through his system at the first touch of her mouth—that soft, sweet, luscious mouth—on his. He'd been thinking about her too often, craving her since that day at the castle. He'd even tried to tell himself that he'd exaggerated the experience. After all, while he'd never felt it himself, Michael was Irish enough to believe that there was magic in the air at Lough Caislean. Perhaps it had clouded his mind, confused his senses, played with his memory.

Fearful of what might happen if he unleashed the

passion that was clawing away inside him, he focused all his energies on remembering that it wouldn't do to rip off the woman's clothes and drag her to the ground while his daughter was getting ready for bed just inside the house.

Even as he kissed her back, even as he allowed his tongue to slip between her parted lips—just a bit—and was instantly rewarded by her seductive response, Michael was being bombarded by thoughts blasting through his mind and sensations exploding through his body like the flare of fireworks, sizzling at his every nerve ending.

One of the random thoughts that shot in and out of his consciousness was the story he'd told Shea, her first night at her new home, about the selkie who'd so bewitched a poor farmer with her beauty and voice. For the first time in his life, Michael fully understood exactly what Kevin had been feeling the day he'd stolen her cloak and taken her home.

He was bewitched. Definitely bothered. But not so bewildered that he didn't know that what he was doing was wrong. He didn't believe that Tom had any future with this woman who fit so perfectly in his arms. Even as need curled hotter in his gut—and lower—Michael told himself that the fact that his best friend was on the verge of death was even more reason not to want this woman. This was the last time, he swore to himself. Knowing he was rationalizing his uncharacteristic behavior, he decided that since he'd already committed the sin, he might as well let it go on a little longer.

She tasted fresh, like a long cool drink of clear sparkling spring water after a long thirst. He sipped slowly, drew a soft moan from her throat, then drank deeper still.

She smelled like moonflowers. He buried his mouth against her throat and inhaled the scent that sent the blood swimming hotly in his head and blurred his vision.

She felt like heaven. He unzipped the bulky parka, slid his arms around her and drew her closer against him. So close, he could feel her heart pounding against his chest in a rhythm as fast and erratic as his own. Despite the chill in the air, her body was throwing out heat like burning peat. No, he amended as he returned his mouth to hers, deepening the kiss, degree by erotic degree. This was not the warm comforting glow of the peat fires he'd grown up with. This was like a blazing wildfire that tore through a forest, destroying everything in its path.

She was close, hot, and, if the way she was moving against him—as if trying to start new fires with the friction of their bodies—was any indication, as hungry as he. Michael's needs had always been simple; never would he have thought himself to be a greedy man. Until now.

Figuring he was already damned, he shifted angles so he could kiss her harder, deeper, devouring her fire-drenched mouth with lips and tongue. When he nipped at her bottom lip, she trembled. When he put his hand on her breast, which was covered in that red wool that was as soft as a cloud, but, he suspected, not as soft as her fragrant flesh, she shuddered. Her nipple pebbled beneath his touch.

"Oh, God, Michael." Her hands managed to slip

between them to fret across his chest. Her fingers clutched at his sweater. "I was afraid of this."

"You're the one who kissed me," he reminded her.

"I know. And it was a mistake. Dammit," she moaned as he lifted her off the ground, so he could put his mouth against that softly rounded breast that had fit so perfectly in his hand. "I knew you'd be good at this."

"This?"

"Kissing." She sucked in a harsh breath when his teeth tugged at that turgid nipple through the scarlet sweater. "All that sex stuff."

"I thought women wanted men to be good at that sex stuff."

"Some women. I've never cared about it all that much." She locked her legs around his and clung. "It's messy, and if you really stop and think about it, the positions, and all the heavy breathing, the act itself is rather ridiculous."

"I have a suggestion for you." Blood was racing from his head to his groin. How could he have forgotten how it was to ache with every fiber of his being? To be drunk with lust, driven to the very brink of control.

"What?"

"Why don't you just stop thinking about it? For another minute or two."

"Oh, God," she repeated as his mouth moved to the other breast. "We can't do this, Michael. We can't have sex. Not here. Not now."

"I know." If she didn't stop moving against him that way, he was going to explode.

He hadn't been so sexually frustrated since Father

Murphy, who'd preceded Father O'Malley, had told an entire class of seventh-form boys that masturbation was a mortal sin that could send you directly to hell. Still young enough to believe the clergy was speaking for God, Michael managed to hold out for three long, torturous nights. Then, driven by demands stronger than religion, he'd decided that some things were worth risking hell for.

"I didn't want to want you," she complained as he lowered her back down to the ground.

"Nor I you." His lips skimmed over her face. "I didn't want anyone."

"No kidding." She tilted her head, luring his mouth back to hers. "Geez, I never would have picked up on that."

"The minute I saw you, flirting with that customs guy, I knew you had complication written all over you."

"Like you didn't?" Belying her words, she framed his face between her palms and this time it was she who deepened the kiss. "And I wasn't flirting."

"You left the guy in a puddle of testosterone."

"Really?"

She tilted her head back to look up at him. Viewing the honest surprise in her eyes, Michael realized that even after today's makeover, she still didn't truly believe that she was beautiful. Not that she lacked self-esteem. It was just apparent that she defined herself by her work, rather than her gender. He decided that if she ever did realize how much feminine power she could wield without even trying, she'd be even more dangerous than she was now.

"Really." The heat was subsiding, the mood changing from lust to like. That was another thing that made her dangerous. As much as he wanted to rip her clothes off her and bury himself deep inside her, Michael enjoyed just being with her. Talking with her. Watching her concern for others. "It's no wonder Tom is in love with you."

"What?" She leaned back even farther, her body at such a slant that, if he wasn't still holding her, she'd probably fall flat on that curvy little ass. "Tom's not in love with me."

"Of course he is." Stifling his sigh of regret, he zipped the parka up again to protect her against the cold wind that had picked up strength. "It's more than obvious."

"I've always admired your ability to capture a mood, Michael. But you're flat wrong about this. Tom and I are friends. As you and he are." She slipped the hands that had practically been ripping off his shirt into the pockets of her jacket.

"Believe me, Tom has never looked at me the way he looks at you. It's love shining on his face, Erin. Like a beacon for all to see."

She thought about that for a moment, which made Michael realize that he even enjoyed watching her brain work. He could practically see the circuits buzzing like some high-speed computer.

"He may love me," she decided. "As I love him. But not in any romantic way."

Michael wasn't surprised by her take on the situation. After all, he'd already determined that she was a woman of honor. Not the kind who'd cheat on any man, let alone one who was so obviously dying. But he still thought she was wrong about Tom's feelings.

"You're not exactly an expert on noticing men's

reactions to you," he pointed out. "You missed the customs agent entirely."

"I didn't miss anything. He was a grandfather, for heaven's sake. His daughter lives in Seattle. He's hoping to visit this summer and I was giving him some tourist suggestions."

"Yeah. He looked like he was fantasizing going to the top of the Space Needle."

"You're being cynical again."

"And you're being naive." He put a finger beneath her chin and held her frustrated gaze to his. "It's one of your many charms."

"I never would have kissed you like that . . . Good Lord, Michael, I practically devoured you."

"And I you. And it was quite enjoyable."

Enjoyable didn't even begin to describe what could well have been one of the most thrilling events of her life. "My point was that if I thought for a moment that Tom was even remotely interested in me in any romantic or sexual way, I never would have acted the way I did just now. Or at the lake."

"I know." Because she looked so serious, he couldn't resist just one more quick kiss. It lasted only an instant, but still managed to pack quite a jolt. From the slightly dazed look in her eyes, he knew he wasn't the only one affected. "Perhaps I'll be talking with Tom tomorrow."

"Even when he tells you that you're dead wrong, there are still too many complications to make any relationship work," she warned.

It was nothing he hadn't been telling himself. Over and over again. "Why don't we burn that bridge when—and if—we get to it?" he suggested.

Having no better idea, Erin merely nodded as he opened the car door for her. Before she could climb into the driver's seat, he surprised her by lifting her hand to his lips and kissing the tips of her fingers. Having never had a man kiss her fingers before, she was surprised to discover that their nerve endings were directly connected to other regions of her body.

"I was remiss in not telling you that I had a highly enjoyable time tonight."

"Before or during the kiss?"

"Both. Whatever Tom says, perhaps we should do it again."

"I still think you're wrong. But if it turns out that he is in love with me, in any romantic way, I'd feel as if I were cheating on him if we took things beyond a friendly dinner."

"We'll keep Shea as a chaperone. She'll be wanting you to visit again anyway."

"Good idea." Even as she warned herself that she was getting in deeper and deeper, she couldn't resist a glance up into her rearview mirror as she left the farm. Michael was standing, hands in his pockets, watching her drive away.

∾ 23 ∾

Angels Among Us

The day after the dinner with the American doctor, Shea was in seventh heaven. Since the sisters and lay teachers were having some sort of morning staff meeting on Monday, school wasn't going to begin until ten o'clock, which allowed her to attend Celia Joyce's birthday sleep-over on Sunday night. Shea had never really had a friend before. Her family's involvement in the Troubles made her home too dangerous for other mothers to allow their children to visit.

Now she had Jamie, along with Celia and Rory, who were not only friends, but family as well.

"I've been thinking about Gerry Doyle," she announced to the others. They were in one of the many rooms that had been added onto the farmhouse after her aunt Nora's marriage to Quinn Gallagher. There was now a large master bedroom suite for Nora and Quinn, with an adorable nursery for their baby, and this room, which boasted a fancy talking electric dartboard, a green-felted pool table, shelves filled with books luring readers to far-off places and thrilling adventures, an oversized fireplace, and a multitude of electronic equipment. Quinn called it the media room,

Nora called it the family room, because, Rory said, it was where the family gathered most in the evenings, and Celia called it wonderful. Shea definitely agreed.

It was like no other room she had ever seen. The television took up nearly the entire wall and blasted sound from speakers in every corner of the room, making it seem as if Spyro the purple dragon, who lived in the magic land being displayed in dazzling 3D, really was breathing flames and rescuing his dragon friends that the Gnasty Gnork had turned to stone.

The video game was one Quinn and Nora had bought in America for Celia's birthday. Rory had grumbled a bit about wishing they'd bought Bomberman Hero instead, but his mum had pointed out that it wasn't his birthday, and besides, she wasn't about to be getting her son a video game that involved throwing bombs at anyone.

"I don't want to think about that mean old bully on my birthday," Celia announced.

"I don't want to think about him either," Jamie seconded as he pushed a button that had Spyro blasting a creature with a roar of fire that turned into a bright butterfly. "Ma almost didn't let me come to the party today because of getting into that fight."

"It was the fight I was thinking of," Shea said. "I was lying in bed last night, trying to come up with ways to get revenge for what Gerry did. But Mary Margaret said that we should turn the other cheek."

"The mean bugger would just punch it if you tried," Rory grumbled. Jamie and Celia cheered when Spyro burned down the monster soldier's tent in the Peace Keeper's world. Shea, who'd seen the devastation of such fires in real life, didn't. "I wish this game was real," Rory said. "Then we could have Spyro go blow flames on Gerry."

"It wouldn't hurt him. It would only turn him into a butterfly," Celia pointed out. A year older than her nephew, she considered herself far more mature.

"That'd be okay. Because then we could get a big white net and catch him." Spyro had just found a gleaming hoard of treasure stolen from the other dragons. "And pin him to a cork."

"Mary Margaret says we should make friends with him."

"Of course she'd say that. She's an angel, isn't she?" Jamie retorted. "So she has to be kind to everyone or God would take her rainbow wings away."

Celia huffed a frustrated breath. "Jamie O'Sullivan, would you hurry up and destroy Gnasty Gnork so I could have a chance to play my own birthday game?"

"I'm pretending I'm Harry Potter," he responded as he determinedly pressed more buttons. "Un-cursing takes time."

"God would never take Mary Margaret's wings away," Shea said in staunch defense of her angel. "But what if she'd be having a point? Maybe if we're really nice to Gerry, he'll change his ways and become a nice person back to us."

"I'm sure Mary Margaret must be a very good guardian angel," Jamie said without taking his eyes from the screen as he and Spyro moved up another level. "She did keep you from getting killed."

"She and Casey."

"Yeah." The dragonfly Sparx, who also served as

Spyro's health-o-meter, was beginning to turn dusky green, signaling that Spyro was getting tired. Jamie zapped another creature, giving birth to yet another butterfly, which Sparx transformed into much needed fuel, turning his body back into a bright and glowing gold. "I've never heard of a dog being an angel before."

"Casey's special."

"Still, I don't think Maeve likes him all that much. She hid under the bed when you came into the room."

"Maeve's afraid of a lot of things," Rory said, reaching out to pat the head of the huge wolfhound that had finally emerged from beneath the bed, but was still looking with obvious doggy trepidation in Shea's direction. "She used to be the most scared dog in all of Ireland, but she's been getting better since Quinn came to Castlelough."

"We've all been better since Quinn came," Celia pointed out.

Rory nodded. "Aye, that's true enough. Especially Mam. And now I have a new sister, which is neat."

"I'd like a baby sister," Shea said. "Though my pony is nice for now until my da finds someone to marry."

"Someone like the American doctor?" Rory asked. Shea had told them all about last night's dinner.

"She looks as if she'd be a grand mam," Celia said.

"Oh, I think she would. I'm hoping that she and my da will fall madly in love and get married and have lots of babies. But I'll always be the oldest." This was said with an obvious sense of pride.

There was a flare of fireworks exploding from the screen. When Maeve whined fretfully, Shea absently patted the dog's head and tried to ignore the headache that had been building all day and wasn't helped by the noise booming from the speakers. "It's okay for you to be afraid, Maeve," Shea assured the dog. "We all get scared sometimes . . .

"What if we just tried to do something nice for Gerry?" she brought the conversation back to her original point.

"Like what?" Celia asked with obvious reluctance.

"Sneak into his house and put syrup between his sheets," Jamie suggested.

"And hot pepper in his underwear drawer," Rory said, not to be outdone.

"Those aren't nice."

"Neither is Gerry," Jamie pointed out. "He's just a big bully who'll always be a bully and when he's a grown-up he'll beat his wife and children."

Shea tilted her head, her eyes wide as she listened to the voice only she could hear. "Mary Margaret says that's all the more reason we should try to make friends with him."

"It'll take more than that to change him," Rory muttered.

"Yeah. Can Mary Margaret do miracles? Because we'll be needing one to keep Gerry from killing us if we ever get near him again. I heard from his cousin Liam that his dad switched him good for getting in trouble again."

"Mary Margaret can do anything," Shea said, not quite knowing if that was true. But she didn't want to encourage any more arguments. "Perhaps we could take him a leftover piece of your birthday cake," she said, turning to Celia.

"I suppose it wouldn't hurt. Nora certainly made a large enough one that there's plenty to spare. If Mary Margaret says that's what God wants us to do, maybe we could try it. But I still think that whatever we do, he's going to stay stinky old Gerry Doyle."

"Next thing you know, Mary Margaret's going to want us to be nice to that horrid Mrs. Murphy at the surgery," Jamie muttered.

"Mary Margaret says that her husband left her for another woman when they were barely a year married, which soured Mrs. Murphy on life."

"She's sour, sure enough." This from Rory. "Worse than a lemon ball."

"Maybe we could take her a piece of cake, as well."

Celia shot Shea a frustrated look. "You are certainly generous with my birthday cake."

"I was just trying to do a good deed."

"You know," Rory said slowly, "Father O'Malley said in his homily this morning that we should all try to be like angels on earth, performing acts of kindness."

"That's what I was trying to say," Shea said.

"It might be fun," Celia suggested, slowly. Shea could see that she was finally considering the idea seriously. "We could be like an angel squad."

"That's a good name for it." Shea beamed that she'd finally gotten her idea across to at least one of them. "It could be like a club."

"Would we be having a secret password?" Jamie asked.

"We'd *have* to have a password," Rory echoed.

After more discussion, the password *Wings* was chosen, and once Spyro finally blasted the Gnasty Gnork and rescued his fellow dragons, the angel squad settled down to plan their campaign to perform acts of angelic kindness all over the village of Castlelough.

It was raining as Michael drove into the village, the cold and gloomy day matching his dark mood. He'd rather face the entire Yugoslavian army than have this talk with his best friend. But things had already gone too far. He had to know what Tom's feelings for Erin were. It was a logical enough question, and if only Tom wasn't dying, it wouldn't even be that much of a problem. Tom would either claim her or not, a claim Michael would respect, as hard as it would prove to be.

Michael was glad that the sour nurse Tom had kept on after Dr. Walsh's retirement was on her way out as he entered the surgery. While she hadn't said anything—at least to his face—he suspected that Mrs. Murphy was one of the harpies in town spreading the word that his daughter was possessed.

"Good day to you, Mrs. Murphy."

"It's far from a good day when the doctor calls me in on a Sunday to do the monthly billing, which I couldn't get done during the week because patients kept dropping by the surgery."

"I can see how patients showing up at a surgery might be a distraction."

She looked at him sharply, as if seeking the joke at her expense. "Aye, they can be. Especially with the doctor sick as a dog and unable to keep hours these days."

"Tom has nothing but good words to say about Dr. O'Halloran. I've no doubt she can handle things well enough."

"She seems hardworking enough. But she's a mere girl. Besides, it's obvious that she's using her feminine wiles to get Dr. Flannery to leave her the surgery."

"And how would that be obvious?"

"The way she's taken to dressing," Mrs. Murphy sniffed. "Why, yesterday she came back from lunch wearing a scarlet sweater!"

From her scandalized tone, Michael thought Erin could well have been wearing a scarlet A rather than that lovely sweater. "I suppose all women enjoy buying a bit of new clothing from time to time."

"Red isn't a seemly color for a physician. And she was wearing makeup."

"As do most women, I believe," he replied, resisting, just barely, the urge to grind his teeth. Or pointing out that the two red circles of rouge on Mrs. Murphy's face looked like clown paint.

"She never has before. I tell you, she's out to take advantage of poor Dr. Flannery's weakened condition."

Since Tom had shared Mrs. Murphy's refusal to take him as seriously as his predecessor, Dr. Walsh, Michael found this sudden concern more than a little hypocritical. He wondered if the woman could be any relation to Deidre McDougall. The two harridans were definitely sisters under the skin.

"Well, it was lovely chatting with you, Mrs. Murphy." He opened the door, hoping to hasten her departure.

She muttered something he took as a negative response, then swept out of the office like a huge ship leaving the harbor.

～ 24 ～

Confessions

"*W*hy do you keep that woman?" Michael asked as he entered the upstairs bedroom.

It took a Herculean effort not to flinch at Tom's condition, which appeared to be going downhill day by day. Even Michael, who was no doctor, knew that the yellow tint to his skin was a sign that his kidneys were giving out. According to Erin, he'd flatly refused to consider dialysis, insisting that he had no strong impetus to prolong this stage of his life. His hands trembled almost all the time now, he was beginning to have difficulty with speech on occasion, and his head had taken on a strange twitch that came and went.

"What woman is that?"

Michael exchanged a few words of greeting with the private duty nurse who was one of two Erin had insisted on hiring, over Tom's protestations, for those hours when she couldn't be at the surgery. As the nurse left them alone, he took note of her pale blond hair, which she'd twisted into a long braid that fell down her back, enjoyed the sway of her lushly feminine hips, and decided that as pretty as she was, she didn't affect him in the way that Erin did.

He pulled up a hard-back wooden chair beside the bed, which offered a view of Lough Caislean in the distance and had him thinking of that kiss he'd shared with Erin at the castle. Then again, he considered as he picked up a bottle of moisturizing lotion Kate had made from seaweed she'd gathered by hand and various secret herbs from her garden, it seemed everything these days made him think of the sweet-tasting American doctor.

"I was referring to that clone of the Wicked Witch of the West who claims to be a nurse." He poured a bit of the white lotion that smelled like almonds into his hands, rubbed them together to warm it, then began smoothing it onto Tom's hands.

"Ah. The formidable Mrs. Murphy. Well now, there's an easy answer to that question."

Tom closed his eyes, relaxing as he did each afternoon when Michael dropped in at the surgery and gave him the massage that seemed to increase his ability to communicate. He'd begun the daily ritual as a means to comfort Tom and had discovered that it had, in some odd way, proved beneficial to himself, as well. Always close, they'd begun to connect on a level Michael thought they might never have reached otherwise.

"The pitiful truth, I'm ashamed to say, is that I'm terrified of her." He drew in a ragged, pained breath that sounded as weak as a sparrow's. Michael reached out to the green oxygen tank beside the bed and gave Tom a hit that quickly soothed out his breathing. "Thank you," Tom said, his voice stronger. "My plan is to let Erin deal with her after I'm gone."

"Erin?" Michael frowned as he switched to the other hand and arm that had lost so much of its muscle tone.

"I thought she was only staying until—" He slammed his mouth shut so hard and so fast his jaw rattled.

"Until I die?" It took an effort, but Tom gingerly managed to roll over on his side. Michael knew that rolling over unaided was a matter of self-esteem for Tom, and wondered how long he'd be able to do it. "Surely you can say the word, Michael. Having witnessed a great deal of death firsthand yourself."

"That's exactly the point, dammit."

When Tom had resisted wearing hospital gowns—and no wonder, Michael had thought at the time—Nora had come up with a compromise, slitting oversized shirts down the back, then fastening them with a tie at the back of the neck. Michael unfastened the tie on today's white cotton shirt that reminded him a great deal of the one his grandfather Joyce had worn, and began rubbing the scented lotion into his friend's paper-thin flesh.

"I don't like thinking of it in regards to you." When Tom flinched, he realized he'd used too much pressure and told himself that he should just speak his piece and get it over with. "This wasn't the way it was supposed to turn out, dammit. We were supposed to be elderly, cranky old men, sitting at the bar at the Rose, watching the pretty girls walk by the window, and reminiscing about the good old days."

He began the chest physiotherapy Erin had taught him earlier in the week, tapping Tom's back to help clear the damaged lungs and hopefully prevent pneumonia. Personally, there had once been a time when he might have considered pneumonia a blessing, since it would speed Tom's passage, but Michael had changed his position on that issue since Erin's arrival.

Only a few weeks ago, he'd truly believed that fate—and Tom—would decide when Tom would die. Now that the time when he would lose his best friend was growing closer, he'd moved over into Erin's camp. He'd even dropped by the church yesterday afternoon and lit a candle in the wrought-iron rack below the altar, though he still had scant hope that the act would prove beneficial. Even if there actually was a God sitting on some golden throne somewhere, surely he was too busy trying to handle the major problems of the unruly world he'd created to take note of a tiny flame flickering in some rural west Irish church.

"They were grand days, weren't they?" Tom glanced back over his bare shoulder, his eyes lit with a spark of the spirit that still dwelt in the frail body that was betraying him more with each passing day. "Even the"—he sucked in another short, painful breath—"wars. Oh, I'm not saying that I wouldn't have preferred a peaceful world," he said, when Michael looked inclined to argue that point.

At other times, when Michael had visited, Tom had displayed a tendency to drift off in the middle of a sentence. But today his voice, while far more reedy than his usual smooth tenor, was easily understood.

"But if men continue to wage wars . . . and it appears they will . . . then there's probably no greater adrenaline rush than being in the thick of things. Other than tumbling the sheets with an equally eager woman."

"Speaking of women," Michael began carefully.

"Most certainly a much more pleasant topic than war." Tom rolled back onto his side, this time with Michael's assistance.

"I need to talk with you about Erin."

"About my hopes"—Tom drew in a shallow breath, then let it out in a rattling wheeze that had Michael reaching again for the oxygen—"that she'll stay on here after I'm gone?"

"No. I mean yes. I want to hear your thinking on that topic. But that's not . . . hell . . . I'm a shit of a friend, Tom."

"Nonsense. You're my oldest and best friend."

The guilt was gnawing at him, like a rat eating away at his insides. "I kissed Erin."

"Did you now?" Tom did not look all that surprised.

"I didn't want to. But I'd taken her to see the lake—"

"And to tell her the story of the Lady?"

"I was going to. But I never quite got around to it."

"Because you kissed her."

"Aye." Michael decided that trying to explain the coincidence of her having dreamed about his ancestors was too difficult to tackle while he was attempting to unburden his soul.

"Did she kiss you back?"

Damn. He should have expected that question. "Aye," he said reluctantly, now feeling as if he were betraying Erin. Christ, a man couldn't win in a situation like this. He'd known she was a complication. A sane, sensible man would have just stayed the hell away. Once again Michael wondered if the villagers who thought him mad might just have an argument.

"So, it was just once?"

"No. It happened again. Last night."

"Ah." Tom nodded. "I thought that red sweater might get your attention."

"She had my attention before that." Michael shook his head with frustration and regret. "I'm sorry. What I've done is unconscionable."

"Why would you be considering kissing a beautiful, willing woman unconscionable? I assume she *was* willing the second time as well?"

"She was."

Willing was a weak word for what Erin had been last night. Just thinking about it was almost enough to make him hard. Almost. Guilt was proving even stronger than the memory of that shared lust, which just went to show, Michael thought grimly, that you can take the altar boy out of the church, but you can't entirely take the church out of the altar boy.

"Then why would you be thinking this was a bad thing?" Tom appeared truly puzzled, making Michael wonder if perhaps Erin wasn't mistaken about her and Tom's relationship being only that of true and good friends.

"Because you love her."

"Of course I do. Enough that I want her to be happy and safely settled down. Which is one of the reasons I brought her to Castlelough."

"I don't understand—"

"Jesus, Michael, for an intelligent man, you're behaving as dense as a stump." The burst of passionate frustration began a bout of such furious coughing Michael feared Tom might crack a rib. "I brought Erin here for you, of course," he managed, once the spell had eased.

"For me?"

"I have concerns about her continuing to work in

such a dangerous profession." He gestured toward the oxygen tank. "Could you be helping me out by putting that tube on me? I need it more often these days."

"Should I call Erin?" Michael strapped the tube so the vents went into his nostrils and tried not to think what this latest stage of the dying process might mean.

"Not on my account." The shallow breathing that had so unnerved Michael deepened and became less labored as he began drawing the life-sustaining oxygen into his damaged lungs. "I'm doing as well as can be expected. It's you I'm worried about, since you've not been yourself since you returned to Castlelough. I always envisioned that someday Erin would visit me here and you'd both meet and find each other appealing.

"But when I accepted the fact that I was, indeed, going to die, I decided I'd have to move up the timetable a wee bit. So I asked her to come here to help out in the surgery, which she seems to enjoy well enough."

"I've heard good things about her bedside manner." Michael moved on to Tom's legs, which, like the rest of him, were losing muscle tone at an alarming rate.

"She's always had a special way about her. I've seen people who've suffered unspeakable horrors visibly calm when she lays her hands on them."

Those words brought up an image Michael had been trying to avoid.

"But what makes Erin a great physician, rather than just an adequate one, in addition to her depth of caring, is her ability to make a snap decision in a high-stress situation where time is of the essence. Her instincts are the best I've ever seen. She's grace under pressure personified in one small, fey, gorgeous faerie female."

Michael managed to smile a bit at that. "I've thought of the faerie analogy, as well."

"Of course you have." Tom looked pleased. "I love Erin, Michael. As I would my younger sister, were I to have one. Which is why I thought it was a grand idea to match her up with the man who's been like a brother to me."

"Did it ever occur to you that I could get my own woman?"

"I've no doubt you could in a heartbeat. If you were to want one. But from what I could tell, you were living the life of a Trappist monk out there on your farm with your sheep and cows and dog."

"It's a life that suits me."

"Perhaps in the beginning, when you first came home. You had, after all, been through a physically and mentally grueling time. But there's more to life than farming, as satisfying as that might be to some people. The old cliché about this not being a dress rehearsal is all too true, as I'm finding out for myself . . .

"You hadn't been living life, Michael. You'd put your life on hold. Well, I brought Erin here to jump-start it for you."

"That's very considerate of you," Michael said dryly. "What would you have done if I hadn't found her appealing?"

"As I said, you're an intelligent man. You're also not blind. Nor long dead, which is what a man would have to be not to find Erin O'Halloran appealing."

Michael couldn't argue with that. "She doesn't realize the effect she has on men." He put the cap back on the bottle and returned it to the bedside table.

"And isn't that part of her charm?"

"Aye. It is." Once again Michael felt his lips curving in a reluctant smile. "Did it occur to you that there's one flaw in your cleverly woven scheme?"

"And what would that be?"

"You said she was good at her work."

"The best I'd ever seen."

"Then she must enjoy it."

"One usually enjoys doing what one does well," Tom conceded.

"So what makes you think she'd be willing to stay here in this out-of-the-way small Irish village when she's undoubtedly an adrenaline junkie who needs to be in the thick of things?"

"As did you. At one time."

"I had that blown out of me."

"True enough, and as bad as that experience was, perhaps it all turned out for the best, since it brought you back home where you belong."

"Perhaps you're right about me. But what makes you think that Erin belongs here in Castlelough?"

"I know that she's been in full-time relief work longer than is emotionally healthy. Most people burn out much sooner. I've also this feeling, I can't quite explain, that she belongs here. A feeling that was confirmed when I watched her coming through customs, looking as if she'd come home. The lass is Irish to the core. The island's obvious in her blood."

"If every Irish American showed up in Ireland, it would sink beneath the sea under the weight."

"True enough. Yet haven't you noticed how she's bloomed here? Like a primrose that's been in the desert too long, and has finally been transplanted into the proper spot?"

She *had* bloomed. Despite her long hours, and the fatigue circles that still bruised her skin beneath her eyes, she was more at ease. More grounded.

That idea made him think of her dream about the castle. And how, though he never would have admitted it to her that day, he'd experienced the same dream himself on occasion, which had never struck him as significant, since he'd known the story all of his life.

"I've been meaning to ask you something."

"Ask away."

"Did you ever tell Erin the story about Patrick Joyce?"

"The Patrick Joyce who was killed at Wexford? The same one whose wife walked into the sea?"

"That's the one."

"No. There was enough death in our daily lives." He briefly closed his eyes, as if to shut out unsavory memories. "Whenever I told her stories about this place, I tried to make them amusing." Tom opened his eyes again and looked up at Michael. "Why?"

Michael shrugged. "I was just wondering."

"You shouldn't lie to a dying man. You may not have the time to apologize, then think how guilty you'd feel."

Once again there was a spark of the old Tom in his eyes. Michael found himself wishing he'd believed in miracles. "You'll think I'm mad."

"Well, of course you are. That's always been one of the things I liked best about you."

Michael muttered a curse. "So you'd be wanting to fix your dearest friend up with a madman?"

"Erin has always thrived on challenges. I'll bet you could give her one that would keep her interested into the next millennium. So, tell me why you asked about Patrick Joyce."

"She dreamed of him."

"That's not a surprise. She's undoubtedly read the story. Lord knows it's bound to be in at least a dozen of those books you keep in the cottage."

"She says she didn't. And I believe her."

"Perhaps one of the patients mentioned it."

"No." Michael shook his head. "I know it sounds crazy, but it's as though she was remembering. And not just the dying. She knows things about Mary and Patrick. Private things. Personal things between a man and a wife."

Tom closed his eyes and was silent for a long moment. So long, Michael had begun to think he might have fallen asleep when those calm, thoughtful eyes opened once again. "Reincarnation is an interesting concept. Especially to one facing the void. I, myself, would personally prefer another shot at life than to spend eternity sitting beside a peaceful creek in placid green pastures."

"It's only a concept. An unproven concept, at that."

"True enough. Yet to play devil's advocate, there's no proof of the Lady in the Lake. Yet there are those—including your own father and nephew—who claim to have seen her."

"Aye. That's true enough."

"What about you?"

"What about me?"

"Did you feel anything when you were with her at the castle?"

"I don't know." Michael shook his head and decided that the need to drag her to the ground and take her then and there wasn't relevant to this discussion. "As you pointed out, my life hasn't exactly been filled with a surfeit of women since my return. I suppose it would only be natural that my juices would be stirred by such a woman."

"True. But there's a difference in having your juices stirred and feeling an internal familiarity. Still, stranger things have happened. Especially around here," Tom said. "So have I eased your mind?"

"About some things."

"Such as my relationship with Erin? And where you'll be going when you leave here?"

They both knew Michael would be going to Fair Haven cottage. "Aye."

Erin was restless. Unable to concentrate on her reading when her mind was filled with thoughts that tumbled around, constantly shifting from Michael to Tom to Patrick Joyce, she pulled on her parka and boots and left the cottage.

She told herself that she was going to just aimlessly drive along the coast to clear her mental turmoil, but soon found herself taking the roundabout toward the road that led to where Michael had pulled off when he'd taken her to Lough Caislean.

"You really have gone around the bend," she muttered as she parked and climbed out of the car into the mist that was more fog than rain. "You'll undoubtedly get lost and freeze to death before anyone finds you."

Thanks to the benevolence of the Gulf Stream, the weather was a great deal warmer than she would have expected this far north. Still, the way the damp winter chill was seeping into her bones had Erin thinking that the travel agents certainly wouldn't be booking tropical winter cruises to Ireland, either.

She found the cemetery with ease. Once again she experienced that same sense of hallowed ground as she made her way past the high stone crosses and more modern graves adorned with plastic flowers encased in plastic domes. She paused a moment at the cairn.

"Restless spirits," she murmured to herself, remembering how she'd heard the same low hum at a mass grave site in Kosovo. When she'd realized that the blue helmeted UN officer accompanying her hadn't sensed the souls that hadn't yet departed, she'd kept her thoughts to herself.

She was both amazed and more than a little relieved when she walked straight to the hidden passageway through the hedgerow. And there, rising like an Irish Brigadoon from the mist, was the square Norman tower of the Joyce castle.

Images flooded her mind, tumbling pictures she tried to assure herself were memories of dreams, not reality, which would be impossible since, according to Michael, the last time anyone had lived here had been over two hundred years ago.

Still, drawn by forces stronger than she could explain, she walked across the damp field. "It's only your imagination working overtime," she assured herself as she approached the crumbling gray stone structure. "You're overworked, stressed out, and you've been overdosing on estrogen, thanks to Michael Joyce. It's no wonder you're not in your right mind."

She placed her hand against the stone and felt a sharp tingle, like a quick jolt of electricity, arc from her fingertips straight up her arm.

"Maybe I'm dreaming now," she thought as the stone seemed to warm beneath her touch. "Maybe none of this is real."

The stairs to the second floor had long ago been eroded by wind and weather. But she entered the ruin anyway and stood at the center, head tilted back, looking up to where she knew Patrick and Mary's bedchamber had been.

In the distance, the steely gray Atlantic Ocean spewed waves and foam against ancient cliffs. The wind, which had been stinging at her cheeks, suddenly ceased, and a fire began to blaze in a stone fireplace.

Erin saw Mary sitting alone in the high bed, reading from a piece of parchment. The young woman's eyes were moist; tears streamed down her face.

"My dearest love," Mary read aloud. Then she sank back onto the pillows as she continued to silently read the remainder of the letter, which Erin knew could only have been written by Patrick from Wexford.

She watched, feeling Mary's sense of dread turn to despair.

Mary closed her eyes, crumpled the letter against her breast, and began to sob.

She was not alone. Two hundred years later, in that same place, Erin O'Halloran leaned against the wall that had turned as cold as a tomb, and wept.

Much, much later—she'd lost track of the time—
Erin left the Castle Joyce, pausing before going back
through the hedgerow for one last look. The castle was
once again swaddled in a filmy silver mist, but a single
slanting ray of sunshine managed to show through the
low-hanging clouds and shimmer on the still waters of
the lake. For one fleeting second, Erin thought she
viewed a flash of sparkling emerald beneath the surface, then told herself that it was merely a large fish. A
trick of the light, perhaps.

She was back in her rental car, headed for home.
Despite the heat blasting from the vents in the dashboard, her body was numb from the cold, her mind
even more numb from what she'd just experienced.

"There must be an explanation," she assured herself.
She was a doctor, after all. She dealt in medical facts.
Surely such a phenomenon must be explainable in
some rational way.

She remembered a quote from Descartes she'd
learned from a senior resident during her neurology
rotation: I think, therefore I am. "If that's true," Erin
muttered, "I'm in one helluva mess."

～ 25 ～

I Will Find You

Erin was lying back in the tub, warming her chilled body, her arms stretched out on the high rim, her eyes closed, when the *boom boom boom* of what sounded like drums overcame the lilting music from the Celtic CD she'd put on the compact stereo she'd found atop the bedroom wardrobe.

"Just a minute," she called out, as she realized that the sound was not drumming, but someone pounding on the cottage door.

She pulled the towel from the rack above the tub, made a half-hearted effort to dry her body, then, as the pounding increased in volume, shrugged into the top of the pajamas she'd brought into the bathroom with her.

"I'm coming!" Jumping on first one leg, then the other, she pulled up the matching bottoms. Fortunately, they were as concealing as sweats, so she didn't need to bother taking time to grab her robe from the wardrobe.

Her mind spinning with who could be causing such a ruckus at her door—in her practice as a small-town doctor, it could be anyone with any emergency from a sprained ankle to someone suffering a heart attack—she raced across the living room, following the narrow, serpentine path she'd made through the stacks of books.

She threw open the door to find Michael standing on the stoop, filling the small, low space.

"What's wrong?" His eyes were blue fire, his jaw so tight, she believed that only an injury to his daughter could cause him to look this intense. "Is it Shea?" She glanced past him toward his car, which appeared empty. "Is she hurt?"

"She's fine, so far as I know she's happily playing with the other children at Celia's birthday sleep-over."

"Oh." When the blue flame of his gaze swept over her, heating both flesh and blood in a way the warm bath hadn't been able to, Erin desperately wished that she'd given in to Kate's urging and bought that lovely ivory silk nightgown that had been hanging in Monohan's small lingerie section. She grasped the lapels of the old green-and-red plaid flannel pajamas that had served her so well for so long a little more closely together, hoping Michael wouldn't notice that a strategic button was missing.

"Is something wrong with Fionna?" she asked. His grandmother was not young, and Erin had watched how long and hard she'd been working in her beatification campaign.

"Gram is also fine. I've come from Tom's. He's fine, as well. At least as well as can be expected, under the circumstances."

"Oh."

"You were right. About him not loving you as a man loves a woman he wants to go to bed with."

"Oh." The fire flamed hotter in his eyes as his gaze settled on the triangle of damp skin framed by the neckline of the pajama top. Her blood flowed warmer. Thicker.

It was a single step across the threshold into the cottage. For one long, suspended moment, as he looked down at her and she looked up at him, Erin feared he might not take it.

But then he did, and she was in his arms, and he was kicking the door shut behind him and plundering her mouth like his ancient Norman ancestors had once come to plunder this lush green island for which she was named.

"I want you." His mouth was everywhere—on her lips, streaking up her cheeks, nipping at her chin. "I didn't want to." Biting the sensitive lobe of her ear. "But I do."

"Then take me." Her lips were no less eager, avidly recapturing his and drinking deeply of a taste as dark and rich and intoxicating as mulled wine. "I've been waiting for you. All of my life. Longer." She clung to him, her throaty moan echoing the ache spiraling up from deep inside her. "Please, Michael," she whispered with a painful sense of urgency. "End the waiting."

"Aye. Heaven help us both, that's what I've come here this day to do."

And that wasn't all. He told her, between deep, drugging kisses, in exquisitely erotic detail all the things he planned to do to her, for her, with her. When he went to pick her up, to carry her into the bedroom, caught up in the fever created by his suggestive words and promises, she grasped hold of his wrists and lifted his hands to her breasts, which were literally, painfully, aching for his touch.

"Here." Her nipple was taut and tingled at his stroking touch. She could wait no longer. "Now."

"Here." He took advantage of the gap caused by the missing button, tore the pajama top open, and replaced his fingertips with his mouth. "Now." Tremors shook her body. Hot moisture began to flow between her legs.

He dragged her to the rag rug, somehow managing to push away books at the same time he stripped off her pajama bottoms and sent them flying.

Erin had never thought of herself as a particularly sexual woman, yet there was something wonderfully wanton about lying naked on the floor, totally exposed to a fully dressed man's hot and hungry eyes.

"I was right." His midnight blue eyes were lush with promise as he skimmed a fingertip along her collarbone. His skin was callused and felt a bit like fine-grade sandpaper, stimulating nerve endings that leapt beneath his touch.

"About what?" Her pulse was racing, her body burning.

"That you'd be soft." The treacherous touch continued down the axis of her body, then caressed each breast in slow, erotic circles, from her rib cage out to the taut tip, his rigid discipline a direct contrast to the hunger in his dark, fathomless gaze. "Sweet." When he closed his teeth around each nipple in turn, then tugged, a sexual frisson fluttered through her from her breast, through her vagina, stimulating a series of little explosions. "Luscious."

Her body beaded with a hot red flush, like a fever.

She arched her back off the rug, wanting—needing—more. It seemed that he owned her body, that she'd been created specifically with this man in mind. That she belonged to him, had always belonged to him, and would always, forever and ever.

"Please." No other man had ever made her beg. No other man had ever made her feel such a dizzying blend of need and greed that she'd even have considered begging.

"I need you." She lifted an arm that felt unnaturally heavy and pressed her hand against the placket of his jeans. He stirred against her, and the feel of him, hard and hot and ready, was almost more than she could bear. "All of you. Inside of me."

"Once I start, I won't be stopping for a long, long time," he warned. His own fingers trailed downward, pressing against the flesh of her torso, then her stomach, then lower still until first one, then a second, dipped into that damp warmth between her legs that was so aching to be filled.

"And wouldn't I be hoping you don't?" she breathed softly as she tightened against his stroking fingers, then gasped as his mouth found her ultrasensitive clitoris.

He laughed at her teasing, exaggerated brogue, the rumbling vibrating deep within her, causing another chain reaction she knew he could feel against his mouth.

"Jesus, you're hot." *And mine,* a little voice in the back of his mind whispered.

"Only with you," she whispered as she reached up and boldly ripped open his shirt as he had hers. When she stared at his chest, looking like a twisting red and white patchwork of roads on an Irish map in the dimming of the day, he knew that the involuntary cry wrenched from her lips was not one of passion.

"Hell." This was only one of the reasons he hadn't been with a woman since he'd returned to Ireland. Obviously, he was as physically disgusting to a woman as he'd feared. He took his hands from her body. Her warm and willing—that is, until she'd seen the truth of him—female body. "Look, we can just forget about this—"

"Not on a bet." No longer submissively pliant, she went up on her knees, pressed her palms against his shoulders, and this time it was she who pushed him back onto the rug.

"If you think a few wounds would make a difference in how I feel about you . . ." She touched her silky lips to one particularly nasty scar that roped its way from his nipple to his groin. "You'd be mistaken, Michael James Joyce."

She kissed her way over his chest, revealing a restrained passion blended with an honest acceptance that humbled him. "We all have scars."

Unzipping his jeans, she retrieved the penis that had gone limp as a burst balloon the moment he'd witnessed the shock on her face as she'd viewed his damaged body. "Some scars are on the outside." Her fingers curled around him. Began to move. Up and down. Up and down. For a woman he'd already determined had not had a great amount of sexual experience, her instincts were exceptional. They were also merciless.

"Others are on the inside." When she skimmed the tip of her tongue along his growing length, Michael felt the life force returning with a vengeance. "But I've come to the conclusion that it's impossible to get through life without collecting our share." Her tongue gathered in a drop of dewy moisture from the tip and drew a ragged sound that was half curse, half groan from his throat.

"Oh God, I've always loved your taste," she murmured as she took him into her mouth, deeper than any woman had ever swallowed him.

That it was Erin, his glorious faerie woman, treating him to such sweet torture made the experience even more erotic, and Michael understood all too well why Ossian had not hesitated to climb upon Niamh of the Golden Hair's white faerie horse and ride with her to the Land of the Young. At this moment in time, he would have followed Erin to the lowest rungs of hell and enjoyed every step of the journey.

"And I've always loved your body," she said. Together they dragged at the rest of his clothes, while all the time she reassured him with murmured words and tender kisses that she found him wonderful. Perfect. As he found her. "Just as I've always loved you."

He stiffened at her words. And not his cock, which was already as stiff as a tinker, but his entire body— arms, shoulders, thighs. Mind.

"Erin . . ." How in the name of all that was holy could he respond to something like that?

Sensing his discomfort, she framed his face between her palms and smiled at him. With her luscious lips and her warm, whiskey hued eyes. "I'm not asking you to say the words back to me, Michael. And I don't want you to worry about it. I'm not. Because it's right and natural and wonderful."

Still not knowing what to say, Michael kissed her greedily. His hands, which had never been anything but tender with any woman, grasped at silken skin and plundered, the need to possess overwhelming both body and mind.

Her own hands were not idle as they raced down his back, her short, neat nails digging into his flesh, her hunger feeding off his. He'd wanted her like this, dreamed of her this way: hot as hellfire, her slick body gripped with this grinding ache, tense one moment, then limp the next, as he relentlessly drove her up again and again.

Climax slammed into climax. As Michael watched her expressive eyes glaze over, that little voice repeated—louder this time, to be heard over the sob he'd wrenched from her—*Mine. Forever and always.*

She was still shuddering when he surged into her, driving hard and deep as she wrapped her satiny legs around his hips and met him thrust for thrust, their rhythm perfectly matched, as if they'd made love a hundred times before. The orgasms rocked through her, again and again, stronger, longer.

He touched his tongue to the silken hollow of her throat and felt her blood hammer hot and fast.

A red haze came over his eyes as Michael took them both into the void.

As her body gradually cooled, Erin slowly became aware of the world beyond the man who was sprawled on top of her, his mouth buried in her hair, the man whose heart, even as it slowed to a more natural beat, continued to echo the rhythm of her own.

"I never understood sexual passion," she murmured. Not quite ready to fully return to reality, she thought she could stay here like this forever, despite the fact that sometime during their lovemaking, they'd rolled off the rug, which left her lying on the hard, cold wooden floor. "I thought I'd never know it." She idly combed her fingers through his damp hair. "But I was wrong. I did know. I've always known, deep down inside."

The red cloud was still hovering over his brain, tangling his thoughts, making speech difficult. Michael felt as if he'd been on a two-week bender, then had been beaten up by a gang of waterfront thugs. He managed, with effort, to roll off her, opened his eyes and viewed the marks on her fair skin.

"I should have been gentler. This first time."

She smiled a bit at that, but kept her lids closed. "We both know it wasn't the first time. I still don't understand how that could be, that all this could be so wonderfully familiar, but not understanding doesn't make it not true. After all, I'm still not certain I understand electricity. Or computer chips." She snuggled up against him. "And despite having spent a glorious few days of R and R in Scotland, I'll never, if I live a thousand years, understand haggis."

"That's simple. The Scots are even more mad than we Irish." Michael put his arm around her and kissed her. Slowly. Sweetly. "We'd best be talking about this."

"Yes." She sensed that despite everything, he still didn't believe her. Which wasn't surprising, because if she hadn't gone to the castle earlier today, she wouldn't believe it herself. She tilted her head back and looked up into his face, which, while not as shuttered as she'd feared it might be, was still guarded. "But what would you say to moving the discussion to the bed?"

"I'd say that not only are you beautiful, you're every bit as brilliant as Tom has always said." He pushed himself to his feet, pulling her with him. "Though if you expect me to keep my mind on the conversation, I'd suggest you put some clothes on." Her rosy, love-flushed flesh was unbearably tempting.

"You tore my pajamas."

"I'll buy you new ones."

"Ah, but I suspect you'd be thinking of replacing those fine serviceable jammies with bits of silk and lace frippery."

"Absolutely. I'm a man, and call me a chauvinist if you will, but we men like our women in frippery."

It crossed her mind that his possessive comment might once have offended her. But the truth was she liked him thinking of her as "his woman." Especially since it was true, and had been for such a very long time. Forever.

He scooped her up in his arms as if she weighed no more than a feather and carried her into the adjoining bedroom. Erin, who had only ever had one other man carry her—and that had been Tom when she'd broken her ankle—nearly swooned from the romance of it.

"A wee bit of lace sounds lovely," she admitted. Such underwear had never been practical or possible in her line of work. "Yet it does make me wonder how you'd be expecting me to stay warm wearing such nightclothes."

He dropped her onto the bed, where she sank into

the thick feathers. "Why don't you let me worry about keeping you warm?" he suggested as he joined her beneath the quilt and pulled her against his body, which was, amazingly, hard again.

She laughed a little, drew in a sharp breath as he cupped her with his palm, then as she gave herself up to the wonder of Michael's caressing touch, decided that since they'd somehow waited more than two hundred years for this sublime lovemaking, there would be plenty of time for talking later.

Much, much later.

Michael left the bed only long enough to ring up Nora and tell her where he was, in the event of an emergency. She assured him that his daughter was fine and having the time of her life. She also volunteered to run by and take care of both his evening and morning milking, and did not sound even the slightest bit surprised that he was spending the night at the cottage with Erin.

"I wouldn't think so," Erin answered when he'd shared that with her. "Since Nora and Kate were the ones who dragged me into the mercantile to buy that sweater that caught your attention."

"Believe me, Dr. O'Halloran, you'd caught my attention long before you showed up at the farm in that sweater. And while it's quite appealing, I think I prefer you this way." Warm, soft, naked, and so very, very willing.

When he skimmed a hand from the nape of her neck, down her back, and over her bottom, she giggled in a very un-doctor-like way. "I think I do, too," she decided as she allowed him to carry her back into the mists.

Hours later, as the sky outside the cottage lightened from deep blue to silver, then rose, finally ending with a buttery yellow glow that suggested the country was edging closer toward spring, Erin tilted her face up to the warmth filtering through the lace curtains at the bedroom window and wondered if it was possible to be happier than she was at that moment.

"As much as I'd love to stay here, like this, with you, forever, one of these days we're going to have to leave this bed to get something to eat."

"I knew I should have put it closer to the fridge," Michael said, belatedly remembering that the last time he'd eaten anything had been at yesterday's noon dinner. Now that other hungers had been satiated—for the time being—he was becoming aware of his stomach. "We could try living on love."

"Now there's an idea," she murmured, then looked up at him, feelings glowing in her eyes. "I do, you know. Love you."

"You don't know me."

"I know that you're a brilliant photographer, that despite your decision to return home to Castlelough, you care far more about the world—and not just this charming little corner of it—than you'll readily admit. I know that you're a good brother, a grand and loyal friend, a wonderful and caring father, and a spectacular lover." She drew in a deep breath. "I also know that you—in our previous life—wrote me a letter from Wexford." The words tumbled out, like crystal-clear water falling over a mossy mountain cliff, as if she was eager to get them said.

Michael had been nuzzling at her neck, inhaling her

moonlight scent, enjoying the feel of the tips of her breasts against his chest, and her top leg draped over his, when the last of her claims caused a chill to skim up his spine.

"A letter?"

"Aye," she said in the language of his country. Of his heart. "And as delightful as the idea of living on love sounds in concept, I'm starving." She slipped from his arms and out of the high, feather-soft bed. I'll tell you all about the letter Patrick wrote to Mary over breakfast."

Michael knew they were entering dangerous territory. It was difficult enough for him to believe that there was any true future for the two of them. To be forced to face the possibility that they'd had no choice in the matter, that they were somehow predestined to end up together in this place and this time was more than he could handle. Especially on an empty stomach.

"I'm not certain I'd want to be knowing how you know about such a letter."

"Too bad."

She shot him a saucy look over her shoulder as she retrieved a heavy chenille robe from the wardrobe. The color of slate, it was impossibly ugly and did little to complement either her skin or her hair, but Michael still found her the most beautiful woman he'd ever seen. He also vowed to buy her a new robe at first opportunity. Something sleek and silk, that would cling to the slender feminine curves she'd become so good at concealing.

"Because I'm going to be telling you about the letter," she said. "Then I'll leave it up to you to decide the meaning. As you did when you told me about Patrick and Mary in the first place."

～ 26 ～

The Dangerous Reel

"I'm not certain that this is a very good idea," Rory said as they made what felt like a hundred-kilometer trek across the playground to where the older boys were playing mumbletypeg. They'd just gotten off the bus, and they had a little less than ten minutes to complete their mission before school began.

Invading the territory of their opponents was fool-hardy enough. When those very same opponents just happened to be armed with knives they were throwing into the ground near the brick south wall of the school was more than a little dangerous.

"Mary Margaret says we'll be fine."

"Mary Margaret's *your* guardian angel," Rory pointed out. "That doesn't mean she'll be protecting the rest of us."

"You all have your own guardian angels," Shea assured them. "Practicing acts of kindness was Mary Margaret's idea in the first place, and angels always stick together." A frown crossed her brow. "Except the dark ones, but so long as we don't listen to them, our angels will always keep us safe. Even if yours wouldn't be talking to you."

"Mine has," Jamie offered.

Rory spun toward him. "You never told me that."

"You never asked."

"But I'm your best friend, and best friends share everything."

Jamie's freckled face closed up. "It had to do with me da. I didn't like to talk about him."

"Oh." Rory appeared to consider that idea. "I suppose that would be all right then. But you should have been telling me."

"What does your angel look like?" Celia asked. "Is she a girl, like Mary Margaret? Does she have rainbow wings and flowers in her hair?"

"I wouldn't be knowing. Because I've never seen her. But she talks to me sometimes. Less now that things are so much better at home."

"She's probably resting up a bit, after having to watch over you so much when your da lived with your family," Shea suggested.

"Aye." Jamie nodded. "That's what I've been thinking as well. But she still watches out for me."

"That's why she's a guardian angel," Rory said. "That's her job."

They were closer now. Close enough to hear the *thud thud thud* of the blades as they hit, then sunk into the damp earth.

"I hope Gerry doesn't throw my cake on the ground," Celia said.

"I hope he doesn't slug us," Jamie said.

"I hope he doesn't stab us with his knife." This from Rory. "I once heard Mrs. Sheehan telling Mrs. Gallagher that his father slashed Brian O'Murphy's arm in the Rose one night when Mr. Doyle was drunk. He had to spend six months in the gaol for assault."

"Gerry won't be hurting any of us," Shea insisted even as her fingers tightened on the paper plate covered with the clear plastic wrap they'd found in her aunt Nora's kitchen.

Mary Margaret had never led her astray before. But sometimes keeping the faith was not so easy. Especially when she could feel the familiar aura leading up to one of her headaches, which were getting worse by the day, hovering in the background.

Fortunately the older boys were ignoring them, which allowed Shea to choose her moment. She waited until Gerry released the knife, which arced through the air, then landed a mere breath from the wall, closer than any of those thrown by his mates.

"Good day to you, Gerry Doyle," she said.

He spun around and glared at her, with his sneer of a mouth and his angry eyes. "What the feck do you want?"

The profanity didn't faze her. Hadn't she heard that and worse from her very own mother?

"We brought you something." She held out the plate.

"What's that?"

"It's a piece of my birthday cake," Celia said. "And if you wouldn't be wanting it, we'll just take it back." She reached out to do exactly that, but Gerry was quicker, snatching it from Shea's outstretched hands.

"What kind would it be?"

"Devil's food. With fudge icing."

"Devil's food," one of the other boys said on a scoffing laugh and punched Gerry's upper arm. "Sure, it sounds just right for the likes of you, Doyle."

"Shut up." Gerry didn't look at him. Instead his gaze bore down into Shea's face. "Why would you be bringing me a piece of cake?"

"Because it's very, very good. Because Celia had some left over after her party yesterday."

His expression was as unreadable as a blank slate wall. He was going a bit blurry around the edges, but as she blinked to clear her vision, Shea thought just perhaps a bit of the sneer had softened on his lips. Taking a quick, deep breath, she remembered what Mary Margaret had taught her about always telling the truth.

"But mostly because my guardian angel told me that I must practice acts of kindness, even to those who've harmed me."

"How do you know that it's not the devil talking to you, cursed as you are?"

She heard Jamie mutter behind her and felt Rory getting ready to leap. "I'm not cursed." Shea was growing weary of having to explain this point. "But if you'd be afraid to eat a piece of cake from me, Gerry Doyle, then you're not only a bully, but a coward as well."

Her piece stated, she took hold of Celia's hand and turned away on legs that had begun to tremble like sally reeds in the wind. The boys followed her, but a bit more reluctantly.

"You should have let us fight him for saying such a mean-spirited thing to you," Rory complained.

"That's not turning the other cheek."

"I still think it's a waste of my cake," Celia muttered.

"Hey!" the bully called out.

They paused and glanced back at him.

"It's not so bad," he said around a mouthful of dark chocolate cake.

"I told you he'd like it," Shea said once they were back on their side—the safe side—of the playground.

"What's not to like about any cake that Nora would be baking?" Celia asked.

"My mum's the best cook in the county," Rory said. "But just because he likes her devil's food cake still doesn't mean that he's not going to try to knock the stuffing out of us the next time he gets mad about something."

"That's true enough," Shea conceded. "But at least we've done our part to make Gerry Doyle a nicer person."

The others weren't so certain, but then the bell rang, calling them into the building to begin the school day, and the subject was dropped.

As if by mutual unspoken consent, neither Erin nor Michael discussed the subject she knew they were both thinking about over breakfast. Fortunately, she'd bought some scones at the market, there was jam in the cupboard, and even she could scramble an egg, so preparing breakfast proved a great deal easier than the supper she'd offered him the last time he'd shown up at her cottage door.

Fair Haven cottage wasn't really *hers*, she reminded herself. It was Michael's. But it had certainly begun to feel as if it belonged to her. Once Erin had thought it would be difficult to leave it. Now she wondered if leaving just might not be impossible.

"I went back to the lake yesterday."

"To the castle." He refilled her cup from the teapot she'd put in the center of the table.

"Yes."

"I'm surprised you didn't get lost."

"I thought I might. But I knew the way as if I'd walked those hills a hundred times before."

"Which you believe you have."

"I know it sounds far-fetched, especially for someone who's supposed to be a logical, science-oriented physician. But I don't just *believe* it. I *know* it."

"Because of some letter you say Patrick wrote to Mary from Wexford."

Erin nodded. "The night before he was killed."

Michael eyed her over the rim of the green-and-blue earthenware mug. Where she might have expected skepticism, she thought she viewed resignation in his gaze. "Would you happen to be knowing what this letter was about?"

"He told her he loved her."

"A logical assumption."

"It wasn't an assumption." She stirred sugar into her tea. "I know exactly what the letter said."

"What you'd be dreaming it said."

She tossed up her chin. "I wasn't dreaming. It was day, I was fully awake, and I went inside—"

"You went inside?" Resignation turned to frustration. "Do you realize how dangerous that place is? The castle's crumbling, Erin. You could have had stones falling on you."

"Well, I didn't. It also felt exactly right to be there, Michael." She reached across the wooden table, unclenched his hand, which unconsciously had formed into a fist, and linked their fingers together. "It was as if I belonged there. As if it was my home."

He shook his head, but didn't argue that point. "Tell me what you believe the letter said."

"It began, 'My *dearest love*.'"

"Not so unusual, in a missive from a husband to his wife."

"I suppose not. Yet I'm not certain that romantic love was a widely held concept between husbands and wives in the eighteenth century. 'I am writing this on what will undoubtedly be the last night of my life,'" she continued quoting the letter she could still see so clearly in her mind. " 'I realize now the folly of my mission, yet, were I to choose again, I would undoubtedly make the same risky choice in hopes that the son created from our loving bond would grow to manhood in a free and united Ireland.

" 'We are—approximately twenty thousand of us—encamped atop Vinegar Hill. Down below the English are amassing troops and heavy artillery and I fear we've become sitting ducks and will suffer the same consequences.

" 'I am sending our groom Liam—who insisted on coming with me on this quest for deliverance—back down the far side of the hill before dawn in hopes he will be able to slip through enemy lines and get this letter safely into your hands.'"

Erin felt the dull deep pain of regret and lost opportunities. "I don't understand. If Liam could escape, why didn't Patrick, as well?"

She could so easily picture Mary sitting alone, pregnant and forlorn in the tall empty bed.

"The bed!" Realization dawned on Erin. She glanced back toward the bedroom door.

"Is the same one," Michael answered her unspoken question. "The posts were cut shorter sometime over the centuries to fit beneath the lower ceiling of an Irish cottage. But it originally came from Castle Joyce."

Somehow, Erin wasn't surprised. She'd already come to accept so many things that only a few weeks ago she would have considered impossible, so that now the discovery that she was sleeping in Mary Joyce's marriage bed seemed almost logical.

"As for why Patrick didn't leave, when he had an opportunity, he was a man of his word," Michael answered her earlier question.

"He gave his word to Mary to love, honor, and protect her."

"Until death did them part."

"That's what the vows say," she agreed quietly. "Do you believe that in some cases, love can survive even that?"

"There have been many such tales. Including ones from this very island, such as the saga of the fair Una MacDermott and Thomas Costello. Their families were the Irish version of the Montagues and the Capulets, and so their love affair ended badly with them buried side by side on an island in the Shannon in County Roscommon. A pair of ash trees grew from the ground where each was laid to rest, and eventually the branches twined together, forming a bower over the lovers who were finally, in death, united."

"Well, that's certainly another tragic tale. But what if that wasn't the end of it? What if they met in some other time, as different people? Do you think they would recognize each other? Do you think they'd know?"

"I suppose it would depend on the strength of the bond. And each one's willingness to suspend disbelief . . .

" 'I understand that you may never truly believe me, Mary love,' " Michael continued quoting from the letter where Erin had left off. " 'Tis a complex problem I'm facing, but as much as I love you, and I do, with my entire heart and mind and soul, I cannot abandon those who joined us along the way to Wexford. The loyal men and women who put their trust in me. As you did when you agreed to become my wife.

" 'It is with a heavy heart I write these words, knowing the wound they will inflict on your own sweet and generous heart. But know this, wife—even death will not stop me from loving you. My heart will always belong to you, muirneach'—that roughly translates to 'beloved,' " Michael said.

" 'I will love you forever, beyond even eternity,' " he continued the letter that seemed as familiar as his own name. " 'And, if God and the Ancients allow, some day we'll be together again.' "

"You knew." Her voice was quiet, her eyes as somber as he'd ever seen them. "About the letter. About what Patrick had written."

"Aye. But not until you began to quote it. Then it came back to me."

"As it did to me at the castle." She shook her head, appearing more than a little bemused. "I never expected this."

"That would make two of us."

"I never would have believed it. Not before coming here. But thanks to Tom's bringing me here, we've found each other again. After all this time."

"It would appear so." He lifted their joined hands and brushed a kiss against her knuckles. Then laughed, feeling bold and free and truly happy for the first time in ages. He stood up, bringing her with him, scooped her up in his arms, and began striding through the stacks of books back toward Patrick and Mary's bed.

"Michael! I have to get going on my rounds."

"Then you'd best not waste time by arguing. Don't worry, love," he bent his mouth to hers and stole both her breath and her heart. "I promise, just this once, to be quick about it."

"Da!" Shea ran down the steps of the school bus into Michael's outstretched arms. "Did you miss me?"

"Aye, that I did."

He lifted her up and twirled her around, this wee sprite who'd claimed so much of his heart.

"I had the most special time at Celia's party," she chattered away as he carried her back toward the house. "She got lots of gifts. A new Sleeping Beauty Barbie that's the most gorgeous doll I've ever seen in all my life. And a sweater from Great-grandmother Fionna, who knitted it just for her, like she did mine, but in blue instead of green, and a pearl necklace from Nora and Quinn. Nora told Celia that they're going to be adding a pearl every year, isn't that a grand idea?"

"It is, indeed," Michael agreed, filing the gift idea away in his own mind for future use.

"And today we took a piece of her birthday cake to Gerry Doyle, you remember, that mean boy who got us suspended from school for a day?"

"I wouldn't be forgetting that." Indeed, he'd rung up the elder Doyle and suggested the man teach his son that prejudice and spreading lies was not a proper way to live. From the reaction he'd gotten—a threat to come over and knock his block off, then the slamming down of the receiver—Michael had better understood why Gerry was growing up to be such a terror. "That was a very generous thing to do."

"It was Mary Margaret's idea."

"Was it now?"

"She said we should practice acts of kindness. So we began with Gerry. Next we're going to be trying to soften up Mrs. Murphy."

"Well, wouldn't that be something to see," he said as they entered the house. "I'm not one to be discouraging kindness, but I'm not certain how much luck you'll be having with that particular project."

"Oh, I'm sure it will work," Shea said blithely. "Mary Margaret's never wrong."

Not wanting to suggest that his daughter's imaginary angel just may have taken on a challenge beyond even her heavenly capabilities, Michael took the tin of biscuits down from the cupboard and poured a glass of milk.

"I'll be out tending to the cows. Do you have homework?"

"I only have to be studying for a spelling test tomorrow." She took a frosted chocolate biscuit from the plate he set in front of her and bit into it.

"Well, why don't you do that after you eat your snack," he suggested. "Then when I finish up with the milking, I'll quiz you on the words."

"Okay," she said around a mouthful of biscuit. He was at the door when she called out to him. "Da?"

He turned. "What is it?"

"I love you."

"I love you, as well, *Inghean*." Daughter. It was a word he'd never thought he'd ever be using, yet just saying it had come to please him immensely.

As he fed the cows to keep them calm and contented during the milking process, and hooked up the machine to their swollen udders, Michael thought about how greatly his life had changed in just a few short weeks. His father had been right. Before Shea and Erin had arrived in Castlelough, the most interesting thing in his life had been the potential loss of some fool sheep to the sea. Now he had a daughter whom he adored unconditionally and a woman whose shared love had survived over the centuries.

Michael still didn't believe Mary Margaret was anything but a figment of Shea's active Joyce imagination, but the past few weeks were almost enough to make him believe in miracles. Miracle or not, he couldn't deny that he'd changed. No longer the man who'd returned home physically, mentally, and emotionally wounded, determined to shut himself off from the world, now he was not only capable of loving others, he could accept love himself.

Still feeling on top of the world, Michael was on his way back to the house to prepare supper and help Shea with her spelling test when he heard a keening wail, like what a banshee might make on a moonless night. With his heart in his throat, he threw open the kitchen door. The disastrous scene that greeted him resembled the aftermath of bombings he'd photographed in his past life as a journalist.

Shea was seated in the middle of the kitchen floor, surrounded by broken crockery and hunks of fiery hair that appeared to have been ripped out by her bare hands. Dark red lines of blood trailed down her face and her arms, revealing that she'd been ripping at her skin while he'd been foolishly waxing romantic about his future. As she stared up at him as if he were a stranger, the unearthly sound coming from her lips chilling his blood, all Michael's optimistic feelings disintegrated like a sand castle battered by storm tides.

❧ 27 ❧

Isle of Hope, Isle of Tears

*E*rin was still floating on a gilt-edged cloud when she arrived at the surgery after her morning rounds. Despite the fact that she and Michael hadn't discussed any plans for the future, she felt wonderfully optimistic. So much so, she even found herself once again hoping that something could be done to save Tom. After all, she thought as she reached for the door handle to open the building, he needed to recover so he could be best man at their wedding.

She almost fell into the room as the door suddenly opened.

"Good morning," she greeted the tall, lean man who was leaving.

"Good morning to you," he responded, a bit brusquely, she thought.

"If you're here for an appointment, I'm sorry I'm running a bit late today, but as the saying goes, when God made time—"

"I'm no patient." He drew himself up to his fullest height and looked down his beak of a nose at her as if she'd offended him greatly. "I'm a physician. Dr. Kavanagh, from Dublin."

"Are you a friend of Tom's?"

"We attended medical school together. When I heard he was dying, I decided that the timing was indeed opportune for both of us."

"Opportune?" Erin echoed, wondering how on earth Tom's dying could be considered anything but a disaster.

"I've recently lost my position as a research physician at Trinity, and thought I might offer Tom my services here."

"Oh." Even though she knew it to be an anatomical impossibility, Erin felt her heart lurch, then sink.

Apparently Tom had finally found someone to take over the surgery, which meant that she was once again technically free to return to her former life. Erin didn't care for the way Dr. Kavanagh made it sound as if he was stooping to the bottom of the barrel of medical possibilities, but she was certain that once he got to know the people of Castlelough, he'd realize what a marvelous opportunity Tom was offering.

"Well, it's certainly a wonderful practice." She studied him a bit more carefully, wondering if he'd be open to taking on a partner.

"It's a miserable joke of a practice in a backwater village populated by individuals who don't even pay their bills. Bills that are still written out by hand. My God, the office isn't even computerized."

Obviously he'd looked through Mrs. Murphy's records. "We're working on that." Meaning that she'd been asking Mrs. Murphy from day one if she could at least attempt to type her exam notes into the patients' files. Thus far, not a single diagnosis or comment had been entered electronically, but Erin remained hopeful.

"As for the bills, it's a bit difficult, since the practice isn't on the Irish plan." Indeed, the government selected which villages received medical care, and Castlelough had proved too small and remote for a doctor to be assigned to the community. "But most are eventually paid," she argued, feeling a need to defend patients who'd begun to feel like family. Tom had willingly accepted that lack of government financial support, as had old Dr. Walsh before him.

"There's no earthly way any physician could earn a living in this place." His scathing look encompassed not only the surgery itself, but the tidy town she'd come to love so well. "Tom never was good at the nuts and bolts of a situation. So far as I can see, the only intelligent thing he's done here is keep on the previous doctor's office nurse."

Erin was still laughing at that idea when she went upstairs to Tom's room. Laughter which immediately ceased when she viewed him, seeming even more frail than he had yesterday. He was literally wasting away before her eyes and there seemed to be not a single damn thing she could do about it.

"Don't be stopping your laughter on my account," he said, smiling up from his bed at her. He'd seemed in much cheerier spirits since she'd put him on a morphine pack. It eased the pain in his chest, which in turn allowed him to breathe more freely. "What has you in such a grand mood today, darling?"

Deciding that letting him see her heartache about his condition was not good for either of them, she sat down in the chair beside the bed. "I just met your old colleague. He was leaving the surgery as I was arriving."

"You're undoubtedly the only person George Kavanagh has ever put in a good mood. He was always quite the sourpuss when we were in medical school together, and it didn't appear he'd changed one whit."

"It was certainly obvious that he didn't approve of much around here." She took his hand in hers. His skin still felt too thin to the touch, but less dry than it might have been, suggesting that Michael was still rubbing that herbal lotion Kate had concocted into it each day. "However, he does believe that keeping Mrs. Murphy on was your single intelligent decision."

They shared a laugh over that. Then he looked at her more closely. Erin was about to tell him about Michael and Patrick and Mary when she heard the sound of someone clearing a throat behind her, turned, and found the formidable Mrs. Murphy standing in the doorway.

"Michael Joyce is here," the woman announced, her face stony, her lips grim. "With that possessed daughter of his."

"I'll be right down," Erin said. "And she's not possessed."

"That's a matter of opinion. You'd better be hurrying," the nurse advised. "Since the lass appears to be unconscious."

After sternly instructing Tom to stay in bed, Erin flew down the stairs and found Michael in the waiting room, his limp daughter in his arms. His complexion, nearly as pale as Shea's, was the unhealthy color of ashes.

"She passed out on the way here," he informed Erin. "She comes around every so often, but she's incoherent."

Erin pressed her fingers against Shea's throat. The child's pulse was thready and as rapid as a rabbit's. There were bare patches on the top of her head which allowed her pink skull to show through the tangled red curls, her hands were cut and bloody, her nails torn and ragged.

Her eyes were rolled back, and all the blood appeared to have drained from her face, making her freckles stand out and bringing to mind the old verse an ER nurse had taught her during the first days of her internship: If the face is red, raise the head, if the face is pale, raise the tail.

Tugging Shea from Michael's arms, which wasn't easy since he seemed to have a death grip on her, she lay her on the sofa and stacked pillows beneath her feet.

"Call St. Patrick's Hospital in Galway," she instructed Mrs. Murphy, practically barking the order as she slipped back into her old crisis control mode. "Tell them we'll be bringing a possibly comatose patient in."

Mumbling something about changelings and women doctors who didn't know their rightful place in the world, Mrs. Murphy nevertheless picked up the phone and placed the call.

"What happened?" Erin asked Michael, who looked on the verge of passing out himself. She knew that like her, he'd witnessed more medical trauma than any person should. She also knew that this case was different. Because Shea was his own flesh and blood.

"Christ, I don't know." He plowed an unsteady hand through his thick hair. "There wasn't anything wrong with her when she got home from school. I left her to do the milking, then, when I returned, she was sitting in the middle of the kitchen, surrounded by broken dishes and wailing like a lost soul."

"She was crying? As from pain?"

"Keening was more like it, though I suspect that part of it was from pain, given what she'd done to her hair and to her poor wee hands, breaking all that pottery as she did. She's scratched her face and arms, as well."

"So I see." Erin had witnessed such occasions of self-mutilation before with horrendously depressed patients in the camps. Also from psychotic ones who swore that insects were crawling beneath their skin. "You don't have any idea what triggered this?"

"No. She seemed fine to me. Better than fine. She was probably as happy as I've seen her since she's come to live with me. But when I tried to get her into the car, she began fighting me with the strength of a man. I tell you true, Erin, I was almost relieved when she passed out, so she wouldn't be causing me to wreck the car on my way here."

That explained the swollen flesh around his eye that was turning an ugly shade of black and blue. Obviously, he'd been struck with one of those small hands that were still curled into tight fists.

"Shea, darling." Erin knelt down beside the sofa and shone a light into the child's eyes, noting that this time the pupils were not reacting as they should. What the hell had she missed the first time? "You're going to be

all right, sweetheart. Don't worry. Just try to relax."
Fortunately, her flesh felt cool to the touch, eliminating any indication of fever.

"Now I know what Deidre was talking about," Michael murmured. "It was as if some dark soul had taken hold of her."

"Surely you don't believe that?" Erin asked, realizing it was the same question she'd asked the first time he'd brought the subject up after his daughter's fainting spell at mass. Reincarnation was difficult enough to accept; there was no way she was going to buy into a case of demonic possession.

"Of course not. I'm just trying to explain that the girl in my kitchen, the child you're examining, is the polar opposite of my Shea."

"Damn." Erin shook her head. This time it was she who dragged her fingers through her hair. "I should have done more tests."

"What is it?" Michael grabbed hold of her arm, his strong fingers digging painfully into her flesh. "What's wrong with my daughter?"

"I can't make a diagnosis without the proper tests," she said softly, her head turned away from Shea to keep the little girl from hearing her.

"Then why don't you try an educated guess?"

She knew better than to try to hedge with this man. He'd seen too much, knew too much. Then there was the fact that she loved him too much not to be completely honest.

"I don't have any proof. But if you're sure that she couldn't have ingested any foreign substances—"

"None."

"Then I think we might—possibly—be dealing with some sort of lesion in her brain."

He literally recoiled at that, reeling back as if she'd taken a hammer and hit him square between the eyes.

"Are you thinking she has a tumor? Cancer?"

"No, I'm not presuming to make that leap in judgment. Even if it turns out that she *does* have a tumor, the odds are that it's not malignant."

"And if it is?"

Still watching Shea carefully, Erin put her hand atop the one that was still gripping her arm and drew him a bit away. "You're leaping ahead."

Michael swore. "Just answer the goddamn question."

"We shouldn't even be approaching that bridge yet, but if your daughter does have cancer—and there's certainly no indication that she does—her condition wouldn't be nearly as critical as it would have been when I began practicing medicine. At least fifty percent of the children diagnosed with cancer today will live and suffer no recurrence."

"Which means that fifty percent don't make it."

"Michael . . . Listen to me. You're the only person in this room who's mentioned cancer. Shea's given all indications of being a strong, healthy child—"

"Strong healthy children don't wreak havoc in a house, then try to tear their hair out and their flesh off with their own bare hands. Strong healthy children don't have seizures and become unconscious."

"No. Of course they don't. My point is that whatever is wrong with Shea, we're probably getting it at an early enough stage that it'll be treatable."

"But you can't promise me that."

She shook her head, feeling like the world's worst doctor. Her best friend was lying at death's door upstairs and here she was without a clue as to what was wrong with the daughter of the man she loved.

"Don't do this," she pleaded, torn between the physician who needed to keep a cool and calm head and the woman who wanted to take him into her arms and soothe the misery etched into his handsome Celtic face. "You know I can't promise anything except that I'm going to see that Shea has the best treatment available." She turned back to Mrs. Murphy, who was hanging up the phone.

"Well?"

"They'll be expecting you."

"Good. We'd best be leaving." She reached into her bag, took out her address book and tossed it onto the appointment desk. "Ring up Jessica Southerland in New York City and ask her to stand by and be prepared to get on the first plane she can book to Shannon. Inform her as to what's happening, leaving out any mention of possession," Erin stressed, "and tell her that I'll keep in touch."

Michael already had his daughter back in his arms. "Who's Jessica Southerland?"

"The top pediatric neurosurgeon in the world."

His face was even more grim than it had been when she'd first come downstairs. But Erin thought she viewed a flicker of hope in his eyes that hadn't been there earlier.

She took a brief moment to run upstairs to tell an impatient Tom what was happening, then joined

Michael outside. He'd already gotten Shea strapped into the backseat. Erin climbed in beside her.

"You'll save her."

Erin couldn't decide whether he meant those words as command, prayer, or belief in her abilities. Whichever, she vowed that she would not fail as she had with Tom. Somehow, whatever was wrong with Shea, Erin would not let Michael's daughter die.

They reached Galway in record time, but even driving as fast as he had, the trip had seemed to take an eternity.

"Da?" the little voice whispered as he lifted her from the car.

"Don't worry, *Inghean*," he assured her. "You're going to be just fine."

"I'm not worried." Her green-as-Ireland eyes opened and cleared momentarily as they looked straight up into his. "Can you hear them?"

It had begun to rain. Michael held her tight against his broad chest, trying to shelter her as best he could. "Hear who, little one?"

"The angels." Her ghostly pale lips curved into a soft sweet smile. "They're singing."

≈ 28 ≈

Broken Wings

"*I*t's going to be all right," Shea assured her da as he hovered over her while all the people in the white coats poked and prodded and stuck needles into her. Only Mary Margaret and Casey's calming presences kept her from crying.

"Of course it is." He brushed some hair from her forehead with the gentlest touch she'd ever felt from him. "You just had a little spell, darling. But the doctors are going to find out why. Then they'll fix it."

"Did I faint?" Memories of the last few hours were a little foggy, which worried her, since it was not the first little bubble of time she'd lost. But, it appeared, this had been the longest.

"Something like that." His hands were trembling. It was hard to see him, with the light glaring in her eyes from the overhead lamps, but even so, Shea could tell he was very worried, which made her feel bad. "Which is why Erin and I brought you here to the hospital in Galway."

"I won't be dying."

"Of course you won't."

His voice sounded funny, too. It was rough and

scratchy, not at all like his deep, rumbling one, and his eyes looked wet, like he might be going to cry, but surely she was wrong about that, since she had the strongest, bravest da in the world.

"Mary Margaret says that it's not my turn to go to heaven," she assured him yet again. "There are no shortcuts, and everyone has to wait their turn," she explained earnestly.

She wished all the people crowded into the little curtained-off room wouldn't be shouting at each other so. It was making her headache worse.

Before her da could respond, the loud group of doctors and nurses began wheeling her down a hallway. If her head hadn't been pounding like an Orangeman's drum, Shea thought she might have enjoyed the fast ride.

"We're going to take some pictures of your head, Shea," Erin explained.

"I'd like that. Great-grandmother Fionna keeps telling Da that he should be making a photograph of me, but he still hasn't."

"Well, this is a different kind of photograph. It's an X-ray that will show us the inside of your head."

"I read about that in my science book at school. Will you be showing me the picture when it's done?"

She watched Erin and her da exchange a glance over the top of the wheeled cart she was lying on. "I don't see why not," Erin finally said.

They wheeled her into a big room. A plump woman with bright yellow hair, wearing a gray metal sort of apron that Shea thought must be very heavy, smiled down at her.

"All right, darling," she said. "I'm going to set this plate against your head, then take a picture, all right?"

"I suppose so," Shea answered, feeling a wee bit of fear as she stared at the big machine hulking over her. As he had done on so many other occasions in the past when she'd been afraid, Casey hovered close and Mary Margaret's wings folded around her. "I'll be fine," she repeated what she'd told her da.

"Why, of course you will. Now, I'm just going to leave the room for a wee second. But I'll be right back . . .

"Shooting," she called out from behind the door.

"Nooooo!" The flash of adrenaline hitting her brain made Shea forget how badly her head ached. She leaped up and tried to scramble off the metal table. "Please don't shoot me."

Michael, who'd been forced to wait outside, burst through the door and caught his daughter just before she fell on the floor. "It's all right, sweetheart." He held her against his chest. "It's not like in Belfast. The lady didn't mean she was going to shoot you with a gun." He glared at the woman who looked properly chastened. "She just meant that she was going to take your picture."

"Oh." Shea's arms were wrapped tight around his neck. He was so strong, she thought. Strong enough to help Mary Margaret keep her safe. She was still sad whenever she thought of her mum dying, but the good thing was that she never would have lived with her da if those bad men hadn't done the shooting at the church. "Then maybe she should be telling me to say cheese, like the man who took the pictures before mum's wedding did."

"Aye. That's a fine idea," Michael agreed.

"I'm so sorry, Shea," the woman said. "Why don't I just call out 'X-ray'?"

"That would be all right."

Shea sniffled and rubbed at her nose with the back of her hand. She hated that she'd cried in front of everyone like a baby and hoped her da wouldn't be too disappointed in her. Not that she worried about him sending her back to her grandmother McDougall anymore. He loved her. Just as she loved him. Which was another reason Shea knew that she wasn't going to die. From everything Mary Margaret had told her about God, he was much too kind a person to take her away from her father now that they'd finally met.

This time Erin, wearing an apron like the yellow-haired lady had on and a huge pair of heavy gloves, helped reset the machine. "I'll stay with you, sweetie," she said. Then turned to Shea's da. "Please, Michael, we'll be able to finish much more quickly if you'll only wait outside."

Shea didn't really want him to go, and she could tell that he didn't want to leave either. But he bent down and brushed his lips against her cheek. "You're in good hands, *Inghean*. I'll be just on the other side of that door if you need me."

Shea sniffled a bit more, but did not cry as he left the room.

"That's the good lass," the kindly yellow-haired lady said as she adjusted the controls on the machine, then left the room again.

"You're doing great, Shea," Erin said.

"X-ray," the woman called out.

There was a whir and a click. "That's one." She came back into the room. "Now that didn't hurt, did it?"

"No," Shea answered.

"Do you think we can do a few more?"

"Aye. I suppose so." Shea just wanted to leave this big noisy place and go back home. Lightning was flashing behind her eyes, it felt as if someone had blown up a balloon inside her brain, and she knew that if she could only crawl into her own bed instead of this cold metal table and pull the covers over her aching head, she'd feel ever so much better.

There was more adjusting, more calling out and clicking and whirring, then, just when she thought the ordeal was finally over and she'd be able to return to the farm, Shea was wheeled down the hall again to another room where she was put in a big tube that looked like something from a spaceship, which Erin told her was a CAT scan, which made her giggle, just a little, at the funny name that didn't seem to have anything to do with cats.

Erin also told her she had to lie very, very still, which Shea did her best to do since she was beginning to figure out that the only way to escape this place was to follow all the grown-ups' instructions.

Finally, they moved her upstairs to the children's floor into a room that had two beds and a lovely view of the River Corrib and beyond that, the looming hulk of the Catholic Cathedral. The setting sun was turning the rose windows all sorts of pretty colors, but Shea thought that Galway still wasn't nearly as nice as Castlelough and her da's farm. The other bed was empty, the sheets stripped off down to the bare black-

and-white mattress. Shea wondered if the child who'd been in it had died.

"Will we be going home soon?" she asked her da, who was still hovering over her, reminding her more and more of Casey with each hour she was in hospital.

"Not for a bit more yet," he said. "First we must let the doctors find out what's wrong with you."

"If we went home to Castlelough, we could go to the surgery and Erin could examine me like she and Dr. Tom did before."

"It's Erin who wants you to stay, darling. She needs a bit of help with her doctoring."

"All right." Shea closed her eyes. She was exhausted from all the poking and prodding and the needles being stuck into her and thought if she could just take a wee nap she'd be feeling all better by the time Erin and her da were ready to take her home. "I hope they hurry." A thought suddenly occurred to her. "Who'll be taking care of Niamh? And Fail?"

"Nora sent Rory over to fetch Fail. And Kate's taking Niamh and the other horses over to her stud."

"That's nice of her."

"Aye." He touched a roughened fingertip to each eyelid, encouraging them to close. "Get some rest, Shea, darling. I may have to meet with the doctors for a few minutes in a bit, but I promise not to leave the hospital."

"All right." She sighed and let blessed sleep and Mary Margaret carry her away.

Michael was sitting beside the bed, trying to remember how to pray, when Erin came into the room.

"How is she?" she whispered.

"Why don't you tell me?"

She sighed, which Michael did not take as a good sign. "Let's talk in the quiet room."

Michael hated the quiet room. They'd tried to stick him there earlier, but one look at the place, with its expected niche for the Virgin and the romanticized painting of St. Patrick hung on the wall beside the pope had given him gooseflesh. It was obviously a room designed for family members of gravely ill patients to sit idly by while waiting for Death to put in an appearance. Michael refused to accept the idea that Shea wasn't going to be back home by nightfall, in her own bed where she belonged.

"I'd rather be getting some tea in the dining room." What he wanted was a drink, but he realized that one would lead to another, and then still another, and getting rip-roaring, falling-down drunk would only make a horrendous situation worse.

"Fine." She nodded, appearing, in the white coat she'd donned, much more like a brisk, competent physician than the faerie woman he'd tumbled this morning. Had it only been this morning? he wondered with a bit of surprise as they stood silently side by side during the elevator ride to the ground floor.

Neither mentioned the subject that was hovering over them like Cromwell's ghost, until they'd taken trays through the line and picked up two cups of tea and a bowl of lamb stew, which Michael didn't want, but had only bought because Erin insisted he eat something and he didn't want to waste time and precious energy getting into an argument over such a foolish thing as supper when his daughter could be lying upstairs on the brink of death.

"Well?" he asked once they'd found an empty table and sat down.

"The tests were inconclusive."

Michael swore. "Then we may as well have just stayed in Castlelough, if all these fancy city doctors and goddamn modern machines can't tell me what's wrong with my daughter." He'd raised his voice, drawing the attention of several other white-coated strangers seated nearby.

"It's not that simple." She covered his hand with hers. It was the first time she'd touched him since they'd arrived at the hospital and Michael was surprised at how comforting it felt. "The X-rays show a shadow. A dark, abnormal, indeterminable mass in Shea's brain."

"A tumor?" Even though he'd known, deep in his gut, that this was coming, Michael felt his blood chill.

"Or a cyst. Whatever, it obviously doesn't belong there and is going to have to come out."

"You're going to be cutting into my daughter's brain?" The idea was unthinkable.

"Not me. I don't have the training for that kind of delicate surgery. But I've spoken with Jess and she's already on her way here."

"That would be your friend. The pediatric neurosurgeon."

"That's right." Her fingers tightened around his when he would have pulled his hand away. "She's very good, Michael. The best."

"So you said. Does this mean she'll guarantee that my daughter won't be left some sort of vegetable? Or end up spending years in a coma?"

"No doctor would possibly give you that sort of

guarantee, but I promise, Michael, that Shea's going to be in the best hands possible. I understand how you feel, but—"

"No." He cut her off with a wave of his free hand. "No offense intended, Erin, but you're not a parent. You cannot understand how I feel."

"Point taken," she said quietly.

"Tell me about this . . ." He couldn't say the word again. It made it too real, too terrifying. "This thing in Shea's brain."

"As I said, it's a mass, which the CAT scan revealed to be about the size of a walnut—"

"Jesus."

"There's more. She's got some edema. Not much, but enough that it's a concern. The bad news is that when a patient gets fluid on the brain, the resultant swelling has nowhere to go. The good news is that the pressure from the buildup of that fluid often calls attention to the primary problem by creating major symptoms that can no longer be ignored. Which I believe is, fortunately, what happened in Shea's case."

"Why, thank you, Dr. O'Halloran. I never would have suspected my daughter was so fortunate to have her brain swollen up like a goddamn vinyl balloon. Isn't that the best news I've had all day?"

Michael read the hurt in her eyes and knew that he should have refrained from sarcasm, but it was too late to pull the words back. "I'm sorry."

"You're upset," she said calmly, once again giving him a glimpse of the doctor Tom had told him could keep her head when everyone around her was losing theirs. "You're allowed."

"That's not true. But I appreciate your saying it." He sighed. "What's next?"

"If the cortical steroids don't reduce the swelling, we'll have to put in a shunt to drain the fluid. But that's a fairly benign procedure."

"I'm truly trying not to overreact to Shea's condition, Erin. But it's hard when you keep talking about cutting into my daughter's skull and mucking around in her brain with plumbing materials."

"I realize, to a layman, that it sounds unnerving—"

"You're definitely becoming more and more Irish by the day, Dr. O'Halloran, because that's one of the most major cases of Irish understatement I've ever heard. How about barbaric? Or horrifying?"

"It's not barbaric. But I do understand how it might sound that way. There's a mistaken, commonly held belief that someone diagnosed with a brain tumor is going to die. That's not the case. They're much more common than we think."

"I've never met anyone with one."

"Well, you have now. So you'll just have to deal with it."

"If you were trying to wound me, Dr. O'Halloran, that was a direct hit."

"I'm sorry. I don't want to hurt you any more than you're already hurting. But Shea's going to need the strong, loving, protective father I've watched you become since she entered your life, Michael. There's no time for you to begin wallowing in self-pity."

He shot her a look. "Is that what you think I'm doing?"

"Not yet. But it wouldn't be unusual in such a circumstance. Especially since you've just discovered that you had a daughter in the first place."

"Which is why I won't be losing her." It was his turn to squeeze her fingers. "I realize it's an unfair burden I'm putting on you. But I'm counting on you to save my child, Erin."

Her eyes suddenly swam in a very unphysician-like way, and her hand shook just a bit as she lifted her cup to her lips, which trembled. Not much. But enough for anyone who was watching her as closely as Michael was to note.

"I'm going to do my best."

It was, after all, all she could do. Michael realized that he was being incredibly selfish, putting such pressure on her. But right now, with Shea's life in the balance, he couldn't quite care.

"Would you be having anything important to do for the next few minutes?"

"No. I'd planned to go upstairs and check on Shea again, then talk some more with the staff neurosurgeon and prepare for Jess's arrival."

"I have to go out for a while. Would you mind staying with her? I wouldn't want her waking up and finding herself all alone."

"Of course I'll stay. May I ask where you're going?"

"First I have to call Nora and Gram and fill them in on the situation so far." Michael pushed away the stew he hadn't wanted in the first place and stood up so abruptly, he knocked the chair over. "Then I have to find a camera store."

~ 29 ~

Ready for the Storm

$\mathcal{W}$hen Erin returned to Shea's hospital room, she saw a familiar man seated beside the sleeping girl's bed.

"Good evening, Mr. Joyce."

"Ah, so Michael's told you about me."

"Some." He appeared so real. So solid. Erin was half tempted to reach out, to see if her hand might go through him, but afraid that it might, she slipped it into the pocket of her white jacket instead. "May I ask a personal question?"

"Ask away."

"Can everyone see you?"

"Ah, now that is a fine question you'd be asking." He smiled up at her. "And the answer would be, only those with pure hearts."

"So, if someone just happened to be walking by—"

"They'd undoubtedly think you were talking to yourself."

She shook her head. "You Joyce men do provide complications."

"There are those who might say that we can be a wee bit difficult to handle from time to time. But I've been told that we possess enough attributes that we're worth a wee bit of trouble. Which you seem to have discovered yourself." He looked back at Shea, who barely made a lump beneath the sheets. "The lass is going through a rough spot, but she'll be all right."

"Am I to take it that you have that on a higher authority than yourself?"

"No. But you're a fine doctor, Erin O'Halloran, and I have a world of faith in you. You've no idea what a relief it is to both Michael's mother and meself that our darling granddaughter is in such good hands. But it may be Michael who'll be needing your comfort soon enough."

There was something in his tone. Something that hinted at more than the problem with his daughter. "I don't suppose you'd give me a hint as to why?"

"Oh, I couldn't be doing that." His leprechaun's smile faded as he gave her a long hard look that reminded her of his son and made her realize that Brady Joyce wasn't quite the perpetually friendly ghost he appeared to be. "It's a fortunate man my son is to have found you again. And it's pleased I'll be to have you in our family."

"Thank you. But nothing's definite yet."

"And isn't that the way of the world? Nothing's ever definite, life with its twists and turns and surprises." He'd taken out a clay pipe and was turning it over and over in his hands. Hands that, unlike Michael's, didn't appear to have done much farm work. "I'll be lighting a candle for our darling Shea in heaven and will be looking forward to dancing at your wedding once the lass is cured of her little problem."

With that he was gone. One minute Erin had been

talking with him, the next he'd vanished into thin air. She shook her head bemusedly, thinking that if Shea did survive her surgery, and she and Michael did actually marry, her prospective father-in-law would definitely keep her family from being boring.

"You'd hate being bored," Brady's voice echoed in the room, even as he remained invisible. "Which is why you fell in love with me son."

"I'm beginning to admire your wife more and more, Mr. Joyce."

"Don't we all, lass. Don't we all."

Erin felt a difference in the room—a distinct lessening of energy—and realized that this time Brady truly had left the building.

"And isn't it high time you finally got around to taking a picture of your lovely lass?"

Michael glanced over at his father, who was walking beside him on the sidewalk back to the hospital. "I was wondering when you were going to show up."

"Oh, I've been here all along," Brady said blithely. "I just didn't want to be in the way. Besides, weren't you and that lovely woman doctor handling things well enough without my assistance?"

"This is what you were talking about, isn't it? That day in the car coming back from Limerick."

"The day you were foolishly trying to get the O'Halloran lass out of your mind by buying that tack you didn't need from the widow O'Malley."

"All right, so that might not have been one of my more stellar ideas," Michael admitted. "Tell me about my daughter. Will she live?"

"So far as I know, she will."

"So far as you know?" Michael stopped and turned toward him. "What the hell does that mean?"

"It means that I've received no personal notification that she'll be joining your mother and me in the afterlife. But then again, I'm not privy to all God's works. I'm still trying to receive an answer to my question regarding those mad Scots' affinity for haggis."

"You and Erin." If he still hadn't been so concerned about Shea, Michael might have found some amusement in the idea that his father and the woman he loved had something as inexplicable as sheep innards in common. "I tried to pray."

"I know." There was both sympathy and empathy in the rosy-cheeked face.

"It doesn't come easily. The old catechism prayers seem too rote for such a problem. But I can't think of any proper words to say."

"They needn't be proper. Speak from the heart, boyo. That's all that's needed." He reached up and patted Michael's shoulder. "Now, I'd best be getting back."

"Got a tight schedule up in heaven, do you?"

Brady shook his head. "You're still having a problem with faith, which is too bad, since I fear it'll soon be tested. There are three things I want to tell you, father to son."

"What are they?"

"It's lovely to be self-sufficient, but we all need someone. Wasn't Paul blinded on the road to Damascus?"

"Are you suggesting that faith can cure Shea of her tumor?"

"No. But it can bring you comfort . . . The second thing I would be telling you is that God's grace fills an empty cup. Not a full one. Open your heart, lad. You might be surprised by what happens."

"What's the third homily of the day?"

"Sarcasm doesn't suit you, Michael."

"That's it?"

"No. That would be merely a comment from your da. The third, and most important thing to be remembering, is that love is always the answer. Whatever the question."

With that he was gone, leaving Michael standing alone on the sidewalk, holding his new camera and several rolls of film.

"That's the inside of my head?" Shea, who'd recovered remarkably from this latest seizure during the night, was seated in a wheelchair, wrapped up in a blanket, studying the X-rays hanging on the light board.

"That's it," Erin said. "See that shadow?"

"Aye."

"That's what's been giving you the headaches and the double vision you told us about. But they'll be gone soon."

"Good, because I haven't been liking them." She heard the whirring of the film being rewound in her da's camera. He'd been taking pictures of her for hours. At first she'd kept turning toward the camera and smiling her very best smile. But now she'd gotten so used to him snapping away, she barely noticed.

"You should have told someone you were feeling

poorly earlier," he said as he reached into his pocket and took out a new roll.

"I know. But in the beginning I was afraid you'd send me away."

"I never would have done that."

"Well, I know that now. But having a da was a new thing to me. Didn't I have to be getting used to the idea?"

"She definitely takes after her grandfather," he said to Erin, who smiled a bit at that.

"Grandda came to visit me. He said that I'm in good hands."

"Aye. That you are."

This time the look he gave Erin suggested what Shea had been hoping for. That her da and the American doctor would fall in love and get married and then they could be like the real family she'd always wanted.

"Would you like to be taking a picture of my arm?" she invited. "It has a sticker on it."

It was a sticker of a shamrock with a smiley face. The man who'd come and taken her blood had given it to her. He'd also told her that after her surgery she could come down to his laboratory and look at it through a microscope, which she thought would impress all the children at Holy Child School. Even, perhaps, Gerry Doyle.

"It's a very nice sticker." The camera clicked and flashed as he focused on her outstretched arm.

"I know. He put one on my bear, as well."

"Your bear?" Erin asked.

"The one Grandda Joyce brought me from the gift shop."

"My father bought you a gift?" Her da frowned at this news.

"Aye. It's a very nice one. It's Winnie the Pooh, wearing his slicker and rain hat. You'll probably be wanting to take a picture of me with it."

Erin appeared puzzled. "But how could he—"

"It's probably best not to ask," Michael replied.

"Excuse me." There was a light knock on the door-jamb.

"Jess." Erin crossed the room and hugged a tall woman with very good bones and sleek pale blond hair that curved just beneath her chin. She was wearing black knit slacks with a matching sweater and what appeared to be very good pearls. For someone who'd just spent the night on a plane, Michael thought, she looked pretty damn good. Though she didn't affect him in the same way Erin had when she'd arrived from the States. "Thank you so much for coming."

"We're friends. You'd do the same for me," she said simply. She held out a slender hand to Michael. "Hello, I'm Dr. Jessica Southerland. And you, of course, are Michael Joyce. I recognize you from the cover flap on your last book." She studied him through cool gray eyes that had him thinking of ice princesses. "I've also been waiting for your next for some time."

"Grandda Joyce said that my da stopped taking pic-tures because they made him too sad," Shea offered. "But he's been taking ones of me all day."

"I've no doubt they'll be wonderful." She crouched down beside the chair, putting herself at eye-level with Shea. "You must be the little girl I've been hearing about."

"I'm Shea Joyce. I have a brain tumor. See?" She pointed up at the shadowed X-ray.

"So I've been told. But we'll be getting rid of that in no time."

"Good. Because I don't like getting headaches."

"Of course you don't." She stood up again and studied the films in silence. "Where are the CAT scans?" she asked Erin.

"Here." Erin offered the test results. They all waited while she studied them for a long, silent time. "Well, it looks as if I'll be able to take care of this and still have time for some quality retail therapy before I return to the States."

She smiled down at Shea in a way that warmed her eyes to a soft pewter color and made her appear more accessible. "You're a lucky girl, Shea Joyce. Not only do you appear to have a highly operable tumor, you've got the best hands in the business going after it."

"When will you want to perform the surgery?" Erin asked while Shea beamed.

"As soon as I shake off the jet lag, meet with the staff, and perform a few more tests. Let's tentatively schedule for Friday."

"That's three days away," Michael complained. Now that Erin had convinced him of the need for Shea to have surgery, he just wanted to get it done and over with.

"My goodness. The face and body of an ancient warrior king, artistic talent, and the man can count, too." Jessica flashed Erin a wicked grin that was at odds with her Grace Kelly looks.

Michael normally wouldn't have minded being the

focus of the ice princess's barbed humor. But as far as he was concerned, there was nothing humorous about this situation.

"Shouldn't you be operating as soon as possible?" he asked. After all, she hadn't been brought here to catch up on old times with her friend or go shopping for Irish curios.

"One of the reasons I'm so good at what I do is because I find it advisable to spend sufficient time preparing for surgery before I go spelunking around in a person's brain." Both her tone and her gaze were those an empress might use to keep a peasant in his place. "Nothing against your Irish doctors, but I prefer to run my own tests. I also like getting to know my patients, if time permits."

The smile she bestowed upon Shea was worlds warmer than the cool one she'd frosted him with. "Fortunately, in this case it does. Why don't we have dinner together in the cafeteria, Shea? And you can tell me all about yourself and your school and your favorite things."

"Oh, I like the food in the cafeteria," Shea said enthusiastically. "Brian—he's the man who took my blood and gave me this sticker"—she held out her slender arm—"brought me some scones and bacon from there this morning, and they're ever so much better than the food the nurse brought me."

"Then it's a date." Michael watched as she shook hands with Shea, treating her as, if not an equal, at least someone to be respected. Which had him feeling a bit better about the ultracool American doctor. Despite the fact that she was so different from Erin, from what he could tell, one thing the two women had in common was that neither was like so many of the physicians he'd met over the years—egotists with God complexes.

She gave Erin another brief hug, promised to visit Shea in her room in just a bit, then, with a nod toward him, left the room, pausing just inside the open doorway.

"Do you know the difference between God and a surgeon?" she asked Michael, giving him the strange, uncomfortable feeling she might have actually read his mind.

It was an old joke, and he wasn't in the mood to play games. "God knows he's not a surgeon?"

She clucked her tongue against white teeth that appeared as perfect as the rest of her. "Clever, too," she said past him to Erin. She nodded approvingly. "Looks as if you've caught yourself a keeper."

As she breezed away with a long-legged, purposeful stride, the low heels of her black suede pumps clicking like castanets on the tile floor, Michael couldn't decide whether or not he liked this supposedly renowned pediatric neurosurgeon. But he was definitely grateful to Erin for having brought her into Shea's life.

During the next two days, Dr. Jessica Southerland earned Michael's respect as she got every department in the hospital—including housekeeping—working at a higher level in preparation for Shea's surgery. He still didn't particularly care for her cool, brisk attitude, but he couldn't fault either her energy or her high standards.

Meanwhile, nearly half the population of Castlelough had arrived in Galway to give blood in the event Shea might need it. Michael himself had donated to the reserve and wished he could do more.

"If only she needed a kidney or a bone marrow transplant, I'd feel I was doing something more than just standing by like everyone else," he complained to Erin on the eve of Shea's surgery.

"You're here for her. You've also taken enough photographs to fill a hundred albums."

"I know. Once I got started, I couldn't stop." It had been like opening the floodgates on a dam. "I keep thinking I'll take one more, just in case . . . Hell."

He pressed his fingers against his lids, refusing to acknowledge the frightening image that was never entirely out of mind. As good as Dr. Southerland was, that didn't preclude something going wrong. What if he lost her? Michael knew he'd never forgive himself for not giving in to her repeated requests for a photograph of herself riding her beloved Niamh.

He looked around the waiting room at all the people who'd felt the need to be here and wait with him, and as much as he appreciated their concern, he couldn't help thinking that it wasn't the same for them. After all, they'd be returning to their normal lives, in their normal world, while his was in danger of lying in ruins by this time tomorrow.

"I'm her father, dammit. I'm supposed to make it better."

"Your job is to love her. Jess's job is to make her better."

"Look who's here, Da!" a voice called out from the

hallway. A moment later, Michael watched his daughter being wheeled into the so-called quiet room—which wasn't quiet at all, with so many people crowded into it—by, of all people, Gerry Doyle. She was wearing a joke arrow that appeared to pierce her skull.

"Gerry brought me this to wear when the doctors ask me how my head is feeling."

"Shit," Michael murmured to Erin as he took in the sight of the juvenile delinquent wannabe and his wee daughter together. "I'm afraid we may have just used up our share of miracles for the millennium."

✆ 30 ✆

Shadow of Turning

During her forced stay in Galway, Shea discovered that there were a few good things about being in hospital. One was having breakfast in bed and being able to watch television while you ate it. Another thing was the visitors and the gifts. She couldn't remember ever receiving so many presents, many from people she'd never met but had only seen in the store or in church with her grandmother on Sunday. Even Celia had tried to give her Sleeping Beauty Barbie, and although Shea had been very tempted to accept, at Mary Margaret's coaxing she suggested that perhaps they could just share the doll from time to time.

Gerry Doyle visited every day, each time bringing some little gift that made her laugh, like the arrow headband and the fake plastic vomit that at first had made the nurse think she'd thrown up on her sheets. Shea enjoyed his visits and was not as surprised as the grown-ups since Mary Margaret had assured her that miracles happened all the time. She also suspected, having a sense of the horrid home Gerry was growing up in, that all he'd needed was for someone to be nice to him to help him change.

"Are you afraid?" he asked the night before the operation.

It was nearly midnight and everyone else had been sent home so Shea could be rested for tomorrow's surgery. Gerry had sneaked in while she'd been lying in the dark, wondering what it felt like to have your skull cut into. Would she be able to hear the drill? she wondered. Like when her da had put the new hinges on the barn door?

Gerry was seated cross-legged on the end of her narrow bed, a pile of fish and chips from McDonough's between them. Gerry had told her that the restaurant on Quay Street had once been voted the best chipper at any port of call in the world by the old Soviet fleet.

"The chips at the Rose are good, though," Shea said loyally.

"True enough. But they'd have gotten soggy by the time I got here on the bus."

"You didn't steal these, did you?" She'd heard Mother Superior yelling at him behind the office door the day of the brawl, and several instances of former transgressions, including an instance of shoplifting from Monohan's, had been mentioned.

"Jaysus! Sure I didn't." He frowned darkly. "I got the money for the bus fare and the chips by cutting peat for old man Murphy."

"That's said to be hard work."

"Backbreaking is what it is."

"Then I'm honored that you'd be doing it for me."

"Ain't I eating them as well?" he said gruffly, apparently embarrassed by her compliment.

Shea was reminded of a starving feral cat who'd

lived in her neighborhood in Belfast, who'd refuse food from her hand, but would snatch it and run away as soon as her back was turned. By the time her mum had been killed, the cat had allowed her to pet it once in a while. She hoped she'd have the same success with Gerry, since he'd be ever so much better off spending time with her and Rory and the others than the bad mates he hung out with now.

She reached out a salty finger and touched a bruise beside his left eye. "You've been fighting again."

"It's nothing," he said around a mouth of cod. "A few of the lads thought I'd be having better things to do with my time than come here to see you."

"You probably do."

"No one will be telling Gerry Doyle what to do and when to be doing it." His jaw firmed, and his eyes were as hard as they'd been the day she'd given him the cake as a peace offering. "And that's all I'll be saying on the matter."

"Then what shall we talk about?"

"How about tomorrow? Are you scared?"

"A little. But Mary Margaret's going to be there. And Erin. And Dr. Southerland."

"Then you're in good enough hands, so all should turn out just fine." She could tell he didn't really believe about her angel, but that was all right. She understood that some things took more faith than others.

"Will they be shaving your head?"

"Aye." She hated that idea.

"Your hair will grow back," he said reassuringly.

"Aye. That's what they say." Her voice was as flat as her spirits whenever she thought about that.

"You'd best be finishing up your snack," he said, looking up at the round clock on the wall. "It's nearly midnight." Dr. Southerland had explained that she wouldn't be able to eat or drink anything after midnight. Despite the risk that he might be caught, Shea wasn't quite ready to let him go, because she would be left all alone.

"These really are good chips."

"It's glad I am you like them."

"I'm even more pleased that you're such a good friend." When she impulsively leaned over the food between them and kissed his cheek, a dark red color rose from the collar of his green football jersey.

"I'd best be going." He didn't wipe her kiss off his cheek, but Shea thought he might want to. *"Seamhas."* Shea's da and gram had taught her enough Irish to allow her to understand that he was wishing her luck.

"Thank you." she said. "You're a very nice boy, Gerry Doyle, despite what anyone else might say."

The flush deepened. Muttering something about making the last bus to Castlelough, he escaped only seconds before the nurse arrived.

"Where on earth did all this come from?" she asked, looking with obvious disapproval at the greasy newspaper the chips came wrapped in that Gerry had left on the bed.

"From a friend."

"Well, there will be no more eating for you, lass," she said briskly as she scooped up not only the rest of the chips, but the pitcher of water on the table beside the bed as well. "Tomorrow's a big day. You should already be asleep. Didn't the nurse on the earlier shift give you a sleeping pill?"

"Aye."

"Well then." She fluffed Shea's pillow and straightened the sheets that were spotted with grease. "I should be changing these, but it's more important for you to get your rest." She turned off the light and bustled out of the room, leaving Shea all alone, with nothing to do but stare up at the ceiling and hope that Mary Margaret was right about tomorrow, as she'd always been about everything else in Shea's life.

It hadn't been easy. When the floor nurse had first tried to kick Michael out of Shea's room, he'd refused to leave. Even the threat of security being called could not dissuade him from spending the night before the surgery at her side, as he had the others, until Erin quietly took him aside and suggested that watching her father getting led away in handcuffs was undoubtedly not the thing his daughter needed to see.

It took more coaxing, and some tough talk from Fionna regarding his need to be rested so he could be properly supportive of his daughter when she came out of the surgery, to convince him to return to the nearby hotel where Nora's wealthy American husband had booked an entire floor specifically for everyone from the village who'd come to offer support.

Erin's heart took a little dive when she came out of the bathroom of their suite after showering off the scent of antiseptic and rubbing alcohol she'd carried back from the hospital and found him sitting in the dark. The streetlight outside the window provided enough illumination so that she could see that he was pouring something from a small bottle into a glass. She didn't need to turn on the light to know that it was whiskey from the minibar.

"She's going to be all right."

He didn't look at her, but instead stared down into the whiskey as if searching for something—hope? faith?—in the brown depths. "You once told me that no doctor can ever guarantee such a thing."

"True." She crossed the plush carpeting and knelt down beside the brocade-covered chair. But she did not reach for the glass. That, she knew, was a decision he'd have to make on his own. "But her chances are excellent."

"Do you remember the story you told me? About your first day in Sarajevo?"

His voice was rough and thickened with a bitterness Erin feared was directed inward. She had a terrible feeling she knew where he was going with this line of thought and wished, not for the first time, that she hadn't shared the details of that nightmarish day with him.

"I remember."

"You said the girl who died in your arms was eight years old."

Dread was a ball in her throat; a cold iron fist squeezed her heart. "Lots of people died that day."

"But she's the one I can't get out of my mind." His fingers tightened around the glass. "Don't you find it a coincidence? That she was the same age as Shea is now?"

"That's all it is." She placed a hand on his thigh and

felt it tense beneath what she'd meant to be a soothing touch. "A coincidence."

"What if it isn't? A child died that day while my life was being saved. What if taking Shea away from me is God's way of evening the score?"

"You don't believe in God," Erin reminded him.

"Aye, so I said. It's coming as a surprise that I'm not quite the atheist I thought I was."

"Perhaps it's a surprise to you, but not to those who know you, who realize what a loving, wounded heart you've tried so hard to hide." She took a deep breath. Let it out in a soft shimmer. "Those of us who love you."

He was disappearing on her again, retreating back behind those damn barricades that she understood but hated. His only response to her declaration was to lift the glass. Erin watched him inhale the aroma of Irish malt.

He shook his head, seeming bemused by the emotions churning around inside him. "That little girl. The one who died from the marketplace shelling. Was she an only child?"

"I don't know." The day had been a horrifying blur. "But whether she was or not, you weren't responsible for her death, Michael. Those terrorists hidden up in the hills were."

"I was airlifted out." His voice was as flat as his eyes, which appeared black in the deep shadows of night.

"And thank God for it. Since it would have done your daughter no earthly good to end up an orphan."

He appeared to consider that. "Nora and Fionna said much the same thing. That perhaps God kept me alive for Shea."

"Fionna's faith is such a part of her, while it might not be a proper medical view, I wouldn't be at all surprised to discover that it actually flows in her veins along with her blood. Nora's is admirable, as well, but I suppose that's to be expected from someone who was once going to become a nun."

"You don't sound as if you believe that my being saved was part of a master heavenly plan."

Erin had never lied to him and knew this was no time to start. "I honestly don't know. I quit trying to figure out cosmic mysteries a very long time ago. When I first began relief work, I wasn't certain I was going to make it. Every time I lost a patient, I felt as if a little part of me died, as well.

"Tom was the one who taught me that if I spent too much time trying to understand why good people died horrible deaths and evil people got away scot-free, that if I let it eat me up, I'd never be of any use to anyone. So, I just tried to do what I could, where I could, and hoped—and prayed—for enough faith to believe that in some small way I might be making a difference."

"You have. And not just to all those refugees you've treated. To Shea." He sighed and put the glass down on the table and covered her hand with his. "And to me. I may have my doubts about God and angels and all those other supposed heavenly things, but I do believe in you."

Her eyes welled up with tears. "As I believe in you." She laced their fingers together and lifted their joined hands to her lips. "I love you so much, Michael."

He managed a weak, exhausted smile at that. "I know. And that alone should be enough to make me believe in miracles."

"We're the miracle," she told him as she wrapped her arms around him and held him tight. "Together."

"Aye." He buried his lips in her hair, which she'd only taken time to towel dry after her shower. "I need you, Erin O'Halloran. So much." He touched his forehead to hers and sighed. "Perhaps too damn much."

"No." She turned her head and kissed his temple. His cheek. His lips. "Never too much." She framed his handsome, tortured Celtic face with her palm. "Come to bed with me, Michael. Let me love you."

"I don't know how good I'll be tonight," he warned.

"You could never be anything but wonderful. But it doesn't matter. Because tonight, I'll be doing all the work. All you have to do is take."

She stood up, leading him by the hands to the wide king-sized bed some unseen maid had turned down while they'd been at the hospital.

She undressed him slowly, and told him, with gentle hands and tender kisses, how precious he was to her.

"I love you, Michael Joyce." She straddled him and pressed hot, open-mouth kisses over his chest, which she'd come to realize was not nearly as scarred as his heart. When she skimmed over his stomach, a moan rumbled deep within him.

Despite his doubts, his body was responding to her sensual ministrations, but unlike so many times in the past, Erin wanted to draw their lovemaking out. She wanted to soothe. To savor.

She took her time, even as her own needs spiraled higher and arousal began to cloud her mind.

"You have the most amazing body." Her palms skimmed down his rock-hard thighs. "All over

America—probably even the world—at this very minute, men are paying big bucks to go to gyms and get sweaty working out on ugly machines and they'll never come close to equaling you."

"It's the peat," he managed, his breath heaving as if he'd just cut a mountain of it. "It's hard, physical work." He was wild to take her, to bury himself deep inside her, but understood that she needed to give him this pleasure as much as he needed to take.

"God bless peat." A rich, sexy laugh bubbled out and sent heat surging into his groin.

"You're killing me, woman," he groaned as her teeth skimmed up the flesh her hands had warmed.

"I'm loving you," she corrected, switching to the other thigh, causing one of the muscles to tremor beneath her mouth.

He lifted his hands to the sash of the heavy white terry-cloth robe embroidered with the gold crown insignia of the hotel. "Take this off."

Slowly, wanting to draw out every sensation, she untied the sash and let the robe fall open. It might not be the sexiest piece of lingerie ever invented, but when his gaze slid down to her breasts, Erin felt her stomach tighten with the sexual desire that had replaced the despair in his midnight-blue eyes.

"I want to feel your body against me." He lifted a hand that felt unusually heavy and brushed a finger over her nipple, watching the heat rise in her eyes as it hardened beneath his touch. "Around me."

He wet his fingertip with his tongue, then circled the other nipple, feeling her blood burn and leap to the surface, on some level amazed that her hot flesh didn't sizzle.

He pushed the bulky robe off her shoulders, dragged it down her arms, then, when she was gloriously naked, her satiny skin glistening with a sheen of moisture, he pulled her down onto him, deciding it was time to quicken the pace.

"Oh, God." She clung to him as they rolled over the wide bed. She was small and warm and wonderful. And, amazingly, his. She tasted of peaches, from the cream she'd rubbed into her body after her shower, flavored with a tinge of salt, like a selkie woman who'd just walked out of the sea. "I think I could easily become addicted to this."

"Perhaps you should try going cold turkey." He pulled away, just a little, to tease them both.

"Don't even think about it." Her legs, which were surprisingly long, wrapped around his hips. As he slipped into her, the immediate shocks of pleasure surrounding him caused him to swell even larger. He braced himself and sank deeper into her wet, welcoming warmth, the friction of their bodies moving together in a way that stimulated his every nerve ending.

She was liquid beneath him, fueling his own driving desire by a rippling series of climaxes that had him feeling that at this, at least, he was no failure.

"Erin." His control was slipping away from him. But there was something he needed to say. Something he'd never said to any other woman. "Look at me."

She opened her eyes, which were glazed with passion and an emotion he recognized all too well since it was currently filling him as he was filling her.

"I love you."

He'd known she'd been waiting. But he hadn't expected the words to make her weep.

Before he could worry about that, despite the tears, she was coming again, her body clutching at his like a silken glove. The last of his tautly held restraint snapped, and Michael cried out her name as he gave in to his own long, shuddering release.

His mind was in a fog, his body lax. As badly as his body craved sleep, Michael couldn't leave things like this.

"Are you all right?" He touched a hand to her wet cheek.

"If I were any more all right, I wouldn't be able to move from this bed for a month." She caught hold of his wrist, brought his hand to her lips, and kissed his palm. "But I wanted to be the one making love to you."

"Is that why you were crying?" Hell, he shouldn't have taken the control away from her.

"Of course not." Her golden brown eyes widened with surprise and studied him in the slanting light from the sliver of moon hanging outside the window. "You're serious, aren't you?" She sighed. "God, men can be idiots. I was crying because you said you loved me."

"Now, admittedly I've never told any other woman I loved her, but—"

"You haven't?"

"No." Michael's gut twisted as the waterworks started in again. "Jesus, Erin, I'm sorry."

"Don't be an idiot." She managed a wobbly smile. "You'd think a man with three sisters would know that I'm crying because you made me so happy. I thought maybe I was going to have to wait another two hundred years to hear you say those words."

"I love you." It was easier this time. He kissed the new tears away. "I love you." Easier and easier. "Love you." Hell, it was becoming a snap. He kissed her temple, the tip of her nose, her sweet, luscious mouth.

Later, as she slept snuggled in his arms, Michael lay awake, thinking about Erin and Shea and how much his life had changed in a few short weeks. Surely God wouldn't be so cruel as to give him a taste of everything he'd ever wanted, without even knowing he'd wanted it, only to snatch it back again?

As the hours passed, the time for his daughter's surgery growing nearer and nearer, it crossed Michael's mind that he might still be undecided about heaven, but during that stolen time when he and Erin had been making love earlier, he'd definitely experienced paradise on earth.

The operating room was as cold as the North Pole. Shea lay beneath the thin blanket and tried to keep her teeth from chattering. People were bustling all around her again, sticking and poking and putting a needle attached to a tube into the back of her hand, but they were so busy chattering on about what they'd done last night, that she could have been invisible for all the personal attention they were paying to her.

Understanding that because she was just a little girl, they didn't take her very seriously, Shea vowed that if she were ever to become a doctor or a nurse, she'd treat patients—especially children—with more care.

Doctor Southerland still hadn't shown up, but a

nurse she'd asked had told her that surgeons never arrive until everything's ready for them. Shea had seen her da and Erin right before a grumpy nurse had harpooned her bottom with a needle, telling her that the shot would help her relax. So far it wasn't working.

She stared up at the high ceiling, blinded by the bright lights, and thought that it might be more restful if someone would have thought to paint a picture. A painting of heaven, with Jesus holding the children on his knees and the angels smiling down on the patients, might be nice, like the one on the nave of the church back home, but then Shea decided that a picture of heaven might make some people afraid they were going to die, which wouldn't exactly be relaxing.

Not that anything about this place was relaxing.

"Good morning, Shea."

She tried to focus on Dr. Southerland's face hovering just a few inches above her. "All ready for our adventure?"

Her mouth was dry as cotton. Shea licked her lips. "Aye," she whispered.

"Fine. That's a brave girl. You go to sleep now. And the operation will be over before you know it."

It would be easier to sleep if they'd be turning down the radio, which was tuned to a loud rock station that jangled her nerves. Celtic Twilight might be nice, Shea considered as yet another nurse stuck yet another needle in her and instructed her to begin counting backward from one hundred. Or Loreena McKennitt, who had a lovely voice that Shea suspected was how angels must sound when they performed concerts for God.

Her last thought, as she drifted off into a floaty, gilt-edged sleep, was that she knew what they should paint on the ceiling: Niamh, running along the shell-strewn beach, with the sun shining down on her beautiful faerie white mane and the wild sea foaming and spewing in the background. She'd have to suggest this to Dr. Southerland. After the operation.

～ 31 ～

I Can't Face That Lonely Road

Michael had spent the last hour on his knees, making deals with God. If only God would save Shea's life, Michael would return to the Church, attend mass every Sunday, and never miss another holy day of obligation again. If he'd only guide Dr. Southerland's hand skillfully and safely through the labyrinth of his daughter's mind, Michael would give a year's worth of royalty checks from his last book of photos from Kosovo to Father O'Malley's seemingly endless building and repair fund. Whatever it took, no sacrifice was too great, no burden too difficult, if he could only keep his daughter from dying.

Erin found him in the chapel, alone, as he'd chosen to spend so many of the past years of his life. She was trying to decide whether to interrupt his prayers so she could get back to the surgery, which was still in progress, or talk to him later. But the news from the lab was too personal, too potentially devastating to allow some stranger to break it to him.

She moved quietly down the carpeted aisle and had almost reached him when he turned, sensing her presence.

"I'm sorry. I didn't mean to interrupt your prayers."

"They weren't exactly prayers." He dragged a hand down his weary face. Erin doubted he'd gotten a bit of sleep since this ordeal began. "I was negotiating."

"Ah." She nodded and slipped into the polished pew beside him. "I've done that from time to time myself."

"Did it work?"

"I don't know. That's the mystery of it, I suppose."

A little silence drifted between them.

"I'm desperate for you to tell me what's happening up there," he admitted. "On the other hand, I'm terrified to hear if it isn't good news."

"The tumor is benign."

He exhaled a breath on a huge, relieved whoosh.

"It turned out to be a very rare form of tumor—a ganglioneuroma—which is slow growing and contains cells from the neurons from tissue between the nerve cells and blood vessels."

"Would you be saying the prognosis is good, then?"

"Absolutely. Jess hopes to get it all without any problems. There may be a need for a few radiation treatments, just as a precaution in the event any little bits of it get left behind. But unless some unforeseen complication occurs, I'd say she should be back home within a week to ten days. And riding Niamh soon after that."

"So you did it."

"I wasn't the one operating."

"No. But you were the one who called Dr. Southerland. You were the one who diagnosed Shea's problem—"

"A bit later than I should have." Erin would always feel a bit guilty about that. As it was, she'd lucked out that the tumor had not been a more virulent malignant type.

"It doesn't matter." He lifted his eyes to the cross at the front of the chapel. "I guess I'll be going to mass."

"It'll be nice for Shea to have her father with her."

"Aye. She asked once about that possibility, but I'd put her off. The same way I'd refused to take her photograph."

"Well, you've certainly made up for the latter. You will for the other, as well."

She paused, gathering up strength to tell him the rest. "I want to be getting back, but there's one more thing I need to tell you."

He didn't say anything. But she could feel him tense, as if preparing for a body blow.

"You know the blood drive?"

"Of course. Even Mrs. Sheehan showed up, which was yet another miracle. Would Shea be needing more?" He started to stand up. "I can go right now—"

"No." She urged him back onto the pew again, feeling that he should be sitting for this bombshell. "There's more than enough. In fact, most of it went into the blood bank, which was in need. But you realize, when people give blood, it's tested and categorized by type—"

"Of course." She watched the color drain from his face. "Are you saying that there's something wrong with Shea other than her tumor?" She heard the edgy fear in his voice and realized that she was handling this badly.

"No." She took a breath and tried again. "What I'm trying to say, and doing a damn miserable job of it, is that from the typing that was done on your blood and Shea's, there's no way that you can be her father."

He looked at her as if she'd just beamed down from some far distant planet and informed him his daughter was some sort of alien being. "Of course I'm her father. Didn't Deidre bring her to me? Aren't I listed on the birth certificate?"

"Hospitals take the word of the mother in such cases," she said carefully. "And Rena isn't alive for us to ask her why she chose to lie about such an important thing. But she did, Michael."

The silence was deafening, broken only by the trickling of water over the pebbles of the meditation fountain set into a niche in the chapel wall. It did not last long.

"There had to have been a mistake. That lab—"

"I had them run the test three times. The results came out the same each time."

It was as if she'd shot an arrow directly into his heart. Michael put a hand against his chest, where he actually felt a sharp pain. "Well." He let out another slow breath. His brain desperately struggled to plod its way through this latest dark and muddled development.

He was so damn weary. Now that the tumor crisis appeared to have mostly passed, Michael belatedly realized that he was physically, mentally, and emotionally drained. He knew he should be feeling something, but in truth, all he could feel was numb.

"It's hard to believe what you're telling me, Erin." His words echoed in the chapel, sounding every bit as slow and sluggish as his mind. "Rena was always truthful when I knew her, so I'd be having no idea why she would lie about such an important thing as Shea's paternity."

"Perhaps she knew who the better man was," Erin suggested quietly. She put her hand atop his; he absently linked their fingers together against the front of his sweater. A distant sense of comfort filtered through the numbness. "Who the better father would be, in the event anything ever happened to her."

If Michael hadn't been so exhausted, he might have thought it ironic that he'd returned home to shut out the world, only to have his little corner of it invaded by two females he'd inadvertently stumbled into love with. Erin and his Shea. Both had become as important to him, as vital, as the air he breathed. He could not imagine a life without them.

"It doesn't matter." The words rang infinitely true in both his head and his heart. "Shea's my daughter in all the ways that count. She may not be the daughter of my blood." The thick torpor began to lift like winter fog, replaced by a crystal-clear certainty. Surely no biological father could love a child more. "But she's the daughter of my heart."

Erin's warm and loving eyes filled up with tears. "Shea's a very fortunate girl."

He managed to return her wobbly smile with a faint one of his own. "I'm the fortunate one."

As he drank in the lovely face of the woman he adored, and thought of the enchanting child he'd been miraculously blessed with, Michael knew he'd never stated truer words.

*　　*　　*

"You don't look so bad," Jamie assured Shea the day after her surgery. He tilted his head and studied her. "Sorta like one of those cotton swabs."

She lifted a hand to the bandage that had been wrapped around her head, still dreading the moment when Dr. Southerland would unwrap it and she'd be forced to look at her bald head.

And, speaking of bald heads . . .

"I can't believe you shaved your heads," she said, staring up at her friends surrounding the bed.

"We didn't want you to have all the fun," her cousin Rory told her.

"And it's ever so much quicker to get ready for school in the morning," Celia said.

Shea still couldn't get over her aunt looking like a billiard ball. "I'll bet Aunt Nora and Gram were really angry at you."

Celia shrugged. "They were a wee bit surprised. But Nora was her usual understanding self. And Gram said that there was no harm done, since it'll grow back."

Shea's eyes swam at the sacrifice they'd made just for her.

"Jaysus," Gerry said. "If a little thing like us cutting off our hair is going to make you all weepy, I'm almost afraid to tell you that most everyone at Holy Child School did the same thing."

"Really?" Shea couldn't imagine an entire school of bald children.

"Some of them did it because they didn't want you to be the only bald student in the school," Rory explained.

"Others didn't want to be left out," Celia added.

"And the rest just did it to piss off Mother Mary Joseph," Gerry concluded.

Shea giggled at that idea.

"When would you be coming home?" Jamie asked.

"Dr. Southerland says that she wants me to have a few days of radiation treatment. Then I can leave."

"That'll be good. Because I think Niamh has been missing you."

"I've been missing her, as well. And Fail."

"Fail keeps waiting by the door, as if she's watching for you," Rory said.

Shea bit her lip to keep from crying at this news. She couldn't believe how fortunate she was. It almost made having a brain tumor worthwhile.

"The rule during visiting hours is only two people in a room at the same time," the afternoon shift nurse said as she marched into the room. She gave them all a warning look. "Let's see," she began counting, "one, two, three, four. Aye, it appears that there are only two visitors." She plumped up Shea's pillow. "Don't be tiring yourself out, lass. You'll want to be fresh for your radiation." With that little advice, and a suggestion to the others that they be thinking about wrapping up their visit, she bustled back out again.

"She seems nice enough," Celia said.

"Everyone's been very nice," Shea agreed. But she was still desperate to get back home.

"Do you think you'll glow after your radiation treatment?" Rory asked.

"Jaysus," Gerry muttered. "What a question. Can't you keep your bloody mouth shut, Gallagher?" The glare he shot Shea's cousin was reminiscent of the old Gerry, before the kindness cake.

"That's all right," Shea said quickly, thinking that people might not continue to be so nice if a brawl were to be breaking out in her hospital room. It was strange thinking of Gerry Doyle as her protector. Strange, but rather nice. "I asked Dr. Southerland the same question. She says I won't."

"That's good news," Jamie said.

"Aye."

There was a bit more discussion about school, and how Kathleen O'Neill had gotten the flu and thrown up all over her desk during a long division test, and how they picked some early wildflowers for Mrs. Murphy, who hadn't seemed very grateful and tartly told them that she didn't need to be getting yellow pollen all over the surgery. Also, how Father O'Malley had made a special intention for her at mass.

"And the ladies' guild will be having a party in the parish hall to welcome you back home," Rory told her.

"You're not supposed to be telling her that," Celia snapped. "It was to be a surprise."

"Geez," he complained. "A body can't even open his mouth around here without getting jumped on."

"Don't worry," Shea assured him. "I'll pretend to be surprised."

On that note, they all trailed out, but then Gerry ducked back in. "I almost forgot to give you this," he said, shoving an envelope toward her. He was gone before she could thank him.

She opened it and found a greeting card with an angel on the front. It wasn't Mary Margaret, but a cartoon angel, with a big halo of bright red hair.

"Friends are angels sent down to earth," she read.

"I'm glad you're mine." It was signed simply with a scrawled "G."

Shea hugged the card close to her heart. "You were right, Mary Margaret," she said on a soft, happy little sigh. "About turning the other cheek."

"I told you it would work," the silvery voice, like Yuletide bells, answered in her ear. "Most people just need a little love and kindness in their lives. Though I must admit," she said in a very unangel-like frustrated tone Shea had never heard from her before, "that Mrs. Murphy at the surgery is proving unusually impervious to heavenly intervention."

The radiation wasn't nearly as bad as Shea had feared. The nice man had explained how he was lining up the crossbars so that the gamma rays would beam at exactly the right spot. Then, like the X-ray lady, he'd scampered out of the room and the machine had buzzed. The strangest part of the experience was how, each time, just as he'd leave, music would begin coming from the speakers in the wall at the same time the buzzing began. It was, almost, Shea thought, as if both the music and the machine were connected to the door in some way so that they'd begin as soon as he closed it.

Eight days after her surgery, wearing one of Erin's billed caps, which had a picture of what she said was a Baltimore Oriole, Shea was on her way back to the farm.

"Jamie says that he saw the Lady again yesterday," she told her father as they drove away from the hospital.

"Did he now?"

"Aye. He says that he's going to take me to the lake and perhaps I'll be seeing her, as well."

"Now wouldn't that be lovely."

"I keep hearing about this lady," Erin said. "But I still haven't heard the story."

"We had other things on our mind when we were at the lake," Michael reminded her.

"Oh, it's a grand story, isn't it, Da?" Shea asked.

"It is, indeed. One of our better ones, I'm thinking."

"Shall you tell it?"

"Why don't you?" he suggested. "Since you're the new storyteller in the family."

"All right." She took a deep breath. "I'll try to remember to tell it like my Grandda Joyce told it to me . . . Once upon a time, in the very same spot the lake is now, there was a splendid kingdom ruled over by a queen with long flowing gold hair that fell down her back all the way past her waist and glistened in the sun like leprechaun's gold. Because she was as kind and generous as she was beautiful, the ancient gods had rewarded the queen and all her people with a most wondrous gift: a sweet-tasting spring whose waters brought youth to all who drank of it.

"The only problem was that every night the spring had to be capped with a large stone, you see, so that the water wouldn't overflow and flood the valley. Which wasn't that much of a problem, since the queen's husband always took care of that chore.

"But—and here's the bad part—a faerie lived in the glen. Unlike the beautiful and kind queen, she was ugly as a boar, sharp as a briar, and as evil as the devil. So of course no man would ever fall in love with her."

"Sounds as if she needed an angel squad to perform an act of kindness," Erin suggested.

"Aye. But I don't believe it would have worked, she was so very, very bad. Then the worst thing happened . . . She fell in love with the queen's husband!"

"Who didn't love her back because she was so ugly," Erin guessed.

"Aye, that's what the faerie thought, as well. So she did a spell and turned herself into a lovely lass, but still the prince stayed true and faithful to his wife, who he loved very much.

"Three times he turned down her advances, which made the faerie—who also had a very bad temper— very angry. So, on the night of the summer solstice celebration, she did another spell that made the prince get so drunk that he forgot to be putting the capstone on the spring. And all night long it flowed, flooding the kingdom."

"Oh, dear."

"But it was all right, because the water was magic, you see, so no one drowned and people continued their lives beneath the lake, just like nothing happened. Except the queen had to change her beautiful beaded gowns for emerald scales, which were much more practical, and every so often she comes to the surface to look over the land she loves so well and to visit with mortals, like Jamie."

"That is a lovely story."

"Aye. I know," Shea said in that self-confident, matter-of-fact way that reminded Erin so of Brady Joyce. Perhaps the elderly ghost and the young girl might not be related by blood, but the two definitely shared a love of storytelling.

"They also say that when the moon is full and the water is very, very still, you can sometimes see the castle and all the people going about their work."

"I'll have to remember to look for that. Perhaps we can look together," Erin suggested.

"I'd like that," Shea said with a huge smile. Beneath the brim of Erin's baseball cap, her eyes sparkled like the Lady's emeralds.

The last time Shea had ridden in a car to Castlelough had been when her grandmother McDougall had brought her to live with her father. Despite Mary Margaret's assurance that everything was going to be all right, Shea had been nervous and felt sick to her stomach. This time she was happy and excited to be going home.

∾ 32 ∾

Into the Light

*E*rin had talked with Tom every day by phone, keeping him updated on Shea's progress. She'd been able to tell, by the tremor in his once strong voice, that he was weakening, but even so, she wasn't prepared when Shannon Kennedy, the pretty blond private-care nurse Erin had hired, reached her at Michael's house as they were tucking a very sleepy Shea into bed.

"I think you'd best be coming straightaway," the nurse said. "In my hospice work, I've seen a great many unexpected turnarounds, but I have a feeling that it's Tom's time."

Erin felt the blood leave her face and managed to assure her that they'd be there within minutes.

"Erin?" Michael reached across the small mattress and took hold of her ice-cold hand.

"We need to go to the surgery."

"Is Dr. Tom dying?" Shea asked.

Michael and Erin exchanged a look. "Aye, darling," he answered for Erin, who was biting her lip to keep from weeping in front of the little girl. "I'm afraid he might be."

"Would you be asking him to do me a favor?" she

begged, seeming to take the issue of death in stride. Erin thought that undoubtedly had a great deal to do with Mary Margaret, in whom she herself had begun to believe. Just a little.

"Would you ask him to tell my mum that I still love her? And in case God's had her too busy with her angel training to be watching me all the time down here on earth, would you have him tell her that I love living with my da and that I have a pony named Niamh. And a dog named Fail?"

"I'm sure Tom will be pleased to pass those messages along," Erin managed.

"Good." She was nodding her approval when something outside the window captured her attention. "Look!" She pointed up at the star-spangled sky. A flare of light flashed toward earth, then twinkled out. "A falling star is an angel coming to earth to help someone." She smiled at that idea. Then quickly slid into sleep.

Michael arranged to have Nora come spend the night at the house, so he could go to the surgery with Erin.

Erin, who went upstairs first, had been watching Tom fade away for weeks. Even so, partly due to their recent days apart, she wasn't prepared for the skeletal man who greeted her when she entered the room above the surgery.

Refusing to flinch at the painful sight, she forced a smile. "So, I hear we've lost Mrs. Murphy." Shannon had passed the news on during the brief call.

"Aye. It seems she received a better offer."

"Oh?" Tom might be on the verge of death, but the familiar light still twinkled in his eyes

"She took a position working with George Kavanagh at his new practice in County Waterford."

Despite the grimness of his condition, Erin laughed at the idea of the two unpleasant individuals collaborating. "I pity the poor patients. But it's a blessing for us."

"Aye. One would almost say heaven-sent. There's a part of me that wonders if perhaps Mary Margaret didn't realize that the angel squad was overmatched in this assignment and decided to give them a wee bit of a miracle."

"Whatever the reason, I'm not about to question it." She touched her fingers to his wrist. His pulse was painfully weak and thready. "Shannon said she'd be willing to stay on."

"That she did. So, as the English bard said, all's well that ends well . . . It's good that you got home when you did," he admitted. "I've been trying to hold on so we could be sharing one final good-bye."

She bit her lip, felt the tears begin to swell, and wished that sometime during her relief work she'd learned to harden her heart a bit more.

"I can't imagine a world without you in it," she said as she brushed a wisp of hair from his forehead with trembling fingers.

"Oh, I'll be around. In one way or another. You won't be getting rid of me that easily, darling." When his smile this time turned into a grimace, Erin realized that he'd reached the point where even the morphine wasn't doing its job to block the pain, and knew that it would only be selfish on her part to fight the inevitable any longer.

"Did I tell you when I called last night that Michael's been taking pictures again?" she asked, seeking something, anything, to say that would forestall their parting.

"Aye. And pleased I was to hear it."

"It was as if Shea's illness unlocked something inside him. It was amazing watching him bond with the children in the hospital ward. He's thinking of putting the photos together into a book he's calling *Faces of Courage*."

"He's always had a knack for getting to the heart of his subject. I've no doubt that it will be a bestseller."

"That's what I was thinking." She'd already seen the proof sheets and believed that, as striking as his earlier war photographs had been, the photos of the children, who somehow managed to remain strong and optimistic in spite of sometimes debilitating illness, was his most stunning work. "There's something else."

"Oh?"

"I'm in love." The words sounded as wonderful as they had when she'd admitted them to Michael.

"Ah, well, isn't that the best news I've heard in a very long time."

"There's more."

"I rather thought there might be."

Erin drew in a breath. "We haven't discussed any long-term plans, but I'd like to stay here in Castlelough and continue your work here at the surgery, if that's all right with you."

"How could it not be?"

"Well, I know that the deal was I'd only watch over things until you found another doctor to take over the practice—"

"Darling, I'd already found a doctor when I tracked you down in the States."

"You had?" The answer sunk in, making her wonder why she hadn't realized it earlier. Because she'd been too distracted, Erin thought, what with trying to save Tom, learning a rural medical practice, and falling in love. "You knew I'd stay, didn't you?"

"I'd hoped you would. For all our sakes. Yours, mine, Michael's. The two of you were a perfect match, having so much in common—"

"You couldn't imagine."

"Aye, I believe I can. Michael told me about your dreaming about Patrick and Mary Joyce when he came to confess to me that the two of you had kissed."

She felt herself flush a bit at that, feeling strangely once again like a schoolgirl experiencing her first crush. Not that what she was feeling for Michael was any mere crush.

"Do you believe in reincarnation?"

"As I told Michael, the idea is quite comforting to a man facing his final days."

"I never believed in past lives. I suppose, like many doctors, I was a bit of an agnostic." She could no longer argue that Tom wasn't dying. It would be a lie and they'd both know it. As much as Erin hated to admit it, during the past days, her duty to her best friend had changed from trying to cure him to simply being here for him at the end. "Yet my feelings and memories are so strong, I can't disbelieve, either. There's just one problem I haven't been able to work out."

"And what would that be?"

"If I truly *was* Mary Joyce in a former life, I can't imagine committing suicide and leaving my child an orphan."

"It's difficult for me to conceive you doing such a thing, either." He shook his head with obvious effort. "Well, whatever, it's pleased I am that you and Michael have fallen in love. I only wish I could be dancing at your wedding."

Erin's eyes began to swim. She felt absolutely at home in Ireland, she was in love with a wonderful, caring man, and although he hadn't yet officially proposed, she was about to become mother to a darling little girl. Life would be perfect if only she weren't also on the verge of losing her closest and dearest friend.

"I wish that as well."

"Would you be doing something for me?"

"Anything."

"There's a blueprint in the top drawer of my desk over there. Would you get it?"

"A blueprint?" She stood up, crossed the small neat room and took the roll of drafting paper from the drawer.

"It's a medical clinic I've been planning for a long time," he revealed. "I had a chap in Cork draw up the plans."

"A clinic?"

"More like a hospital. A small one, granted, but fully equipped with state-of-the-art technology. It was my plan that the people around here wouldn't have to be going all the way to the city for tests and treatments of more serious maladies than I could handle here at the surgery."

"That's a wonderful idea." She thought about George Kavanagh's negative appraisal of the town and its medical potential.

"So I thought when I first came up with it. Now, since I won't be around to see it built, I'm taking advantage of our friendship to leave you in charge."

"You could never take advantage of our friendship. But I wouldn't begin to know how to fund such a project."

"Ah, you wouldn't have to be worrying your pretty head about such a thing," he assured her. "Because I've already got the money to build it."

"You do?" She glanced around the room, which certainly wasn't that of a wealthy man.

"During the time I was working in Somalia, I saved the life of a young man who was covering the tragic story there for the Associated Press. His father was quite grateful."

"I'd imagine he was."

"He also turned out to be a Greek shipping tycoon supposedly worth billions."

"He's the one funding your hospital?"

"None other. He told me at the time, if there was anything I ever needed, all I had to do was pick up the telephone because there was nothing I could ever request that could equal what he felt he owed me, for having given him back his only child."

"Wow. What a windfall. Why didn't you tell me about this earlier?"

"Because I didn't want to pressure you to stay here in Castlelough. I know your sense of responsibility, Erin, love. I've also watched how you've come to care for our patients. I didn't want you to feel you had to give up your relief work to fulfill my dream."

"I've come to realize that I was probably about to change careers anyway."

"You've lasted far longer than most, and it was more than a little obvious that it was beginning to take its toll. However, now that you're in love with Michael and will be staying here in Castlelough, then it seemed to me that this would prove a nice challenge for you."

"It definitely will be that," she agreed. "But it's not just your dream, Tom. It's mine as well." Even if she hadn't realized it until now.

"Then you'll be building my hospital?"

"Absolutely." She leaned over and touched her lips to his hot, dry ones. "It will be an honor."

"There's just one more thing."

"What's that?"

"You're not to be naming it anything fancy, like the Thomas Flannery Memorial Hospital, or such."

"But—"

"I'm serious about this, Erin."

She sighed. "All right. But it's going to take a lot of persuasion to keep your patients from overriding your wishes on that point."

"I have faith that you and Michael will handle things. Together."

Together. That was, Erin decided, after years of depending mostly on herself, the most wonderful word in the world. "We will."

She hugged him tenderly, taking care to be gentle so as not to injure his fragile bones.

"Would you be doing me yet another a favor?" he asked.

"Anything," she repeated.

"Would you be ringing up Father O'Malley? I think it's time for a last confession. He'll also undoubtedly be delighted to finally be able to bring out his holy oils."

Erin knew that the parish priest had visited daily, each time trying to convince Tom that the sacrament of Extreme Unction, which was now called the Anointing of the Sick, was no longer just for the dying. But Tom had been adamant that there would be no anointing before his time had come.

Unable to answer past the huge lump in her throat, Erin nodded and blindly picked up the receiver of the bedside phone to make the call she'd so been dreading.

"And while we're waiting, could you be sending in Michael? I'd like a word with him in private."

"Of course."

Michael stood up when Erin entered the downstairs waiting room.

"Is he—"

"Holding on," she said. "He wants to see you. Alone."

Michael closed his eyes briefly, took a deep breath, then touched his fingers to the side of Erin's face, the light caress meant to soothe them both. As he squared his wide shoulders, preparing to climb the steep stairs, he reminded her of a man going into battle.

"You missed all the adventures in the big city," he said as he entered the room and pulled up his usual chair beside the bed.

"Erin's been keeping me updated. You must be hugely relieved."

"Relieved doesn't begin to cover it. It's strange. Only weeks ago I didn't even know that I had a daughter. Now I love her so much that from the moment she became ill, I kept thinking that I wouldn't know what to do if I lost her."

"Hopefully you'll never find out."

"From your lips to God's—and Mary Margaret's—ears," Michael said. He passed on Shea's request to his friend, who promised to seek out Rena McDougall first thing upon arriving in heaven.

"Speaking of love," Tom said, "Erin shared some grand news with me. I assume you'll be making an honest woman of her?"

"Absolutely. And it's you I have to be thanking for bringing her to me in the first place."

Tom waved away the statement with a weak hand that barely lifted off the sheets. "You would have met somehow. I've come to the conclusion that you can't fight destiny." Obviously exhausted from his conversation with Erin, he closed his eyes and seemed to sink even deeper into the pillows.

For a fearful moment, when Michael couldn't hear his breathing, he worried that Tom had died on him. But then there was a rustle in the doorway and Tom roused to greet Father O'Malley, who'd arrived with his blessed oils.

Michael and Erin left the men alone as the priest performed the sacrament of Reconciliation. "Personally, I don't believe that Tom could have all that many sins to confess," Erin murmured as Michael made them both a pot of tea—the Irish remedy for all problems.

"He's a good man, that's the truth. We'll all be missing him greatly."

"He assured me he'd be around."

Michael managed a smile at that. "Aye, if anyone can pull off such a feat, it'll be our Tom."

Our Tom. Best friend to them both and the man who'd brought them together. Erin knew that she'd be grateful to him for that act of brilliant matchmaking for all the days of her life.

They sipped their tea in silence, each thinking thoughts of the man lying upstairs. Then Father O'Malley returned and invited them to join in the final sacrament.

Since Tom appeared to be weakening by the moment, the priest kept the prayer of faith brief, then performed the ritual laying on of hands before anointing Tom's forehead with the oil he'd brought with him.

"Through this holy anointing may the Lord in his love and mercy help you with the Grace of the Holy Spirit," he murmured. Then he moved on to Tom's hands, which were lying limply on the coverlet. "May the Lord who frees you from sin save you and raise you up."

Tom's eyes were shut again, but he smiled, comforted by the age-old sacrament, which made Erin remember his earlier words about there not being any atheists in foxholes.

They sat there, one on either side of the bed, silent, waiting, unwilling to leave this man who meant so much to both of them alone during this final stage of a time on earth he'd managed to fill with more vibrancy than many men could have managed in three lifetimes.

Downstairs, a clock announced midnight with a peal of chimes. After the twelfth note sounded, Tom's eyes suddenly opened, appearing more alive than Erin had ever seen them. "Ah, now isn't that splendiferous?" he asked, his gaze directed not at either Michael or Erin, but toward the window. "Tell Shea that she was right. About the color of the wings."

With that he sighed slightly, but not sadly, and both Erin and Michael could feel the once mighty life force slipping away from them as he took his final breath.

"Erin, look." Michael nodded toward the wall, where Erin had hung the picture Shea had drawn of what she'd assured Tom was his own guardian angel. The richly colored wings resembled stained glass.

"Tom was right." Erin managed a faint smile through the tears that had begun to flow down her cheeks. "They are splendiferous."

Since the Irish wake had mostly gone out of fashion, even in this corner of the world, Castlelough had recently acquired a funeral home, run by Dudley and Patrick McShane, a father and son who had operated a similar business in Dublin before choosing to give up the greater income in the city for the slower and friendlier pace of west Irish life.

Tom and Erin waited until the men had, with a gentleness that was a relief to them both, carried Tom's body from the bedroom out to their hearse.

The public mourning for Tom Flannery would begin in the morning. But for now, needing to be alone, by unspoken agreement, they went to the lake.

The water was silvered by the light of the moon, the air perfumed by the scent of the sea. They were passing by the shadowed ruins of the castle when a far distant memory suddenly stopped Erin in her tracks.

"Michael!" She spun toward the darkened sea. "There's a cave down there on the beach."

"There are a lot of caves. Along with tales of pirate stashes."

"A special cave," she insisted, momentarily side-tracked from tonight's painful loss by a mental image so strong it could only be real. "Where Patrick and Mary made love one summer's day soon after they'd married . . .

"The night she died, she took this same path down to the beach, to the cave, to remember. But she spent too much time there, and when the tide came in, she was trapped."

"So, she didn't commit suicide."

"No." Once she'd accepted the idea that she might have lived Mary's life, Erin had known that was an impossibility.

"I suppose that's a wee bit of good news."

"Yes." Erin no longer questioned how she knew such things. It was enough to know that a part of the tragic tale would be changed.

The ebony sky was clear, studded with stars. Erin gazed up at the glittering lights. "I wonder which one is Tom?" she murmured.

"The brightest," Michael said without hesitation. "I know I was unkind when you first arrived, but, like you, I'd begun to hope for a miracle recovery."

"I know." She sighed.

"But while we might not have received the response we wanted, that's not to say that all our prayers went unanswered." He turned her in his arms and drew her close. "You're my own personal miracle, Erin O'Halloran. I love you to distraction and if you'd be having me, I want us to spend the rest of our lives together as husband and wife."

It might have been her imagination, but Erin could

have sworn that she heard a familiar, rich male laugh of
pleasure riding on the night breeze. The painful chains
that had been gripping her heart since she'd first
arrived at the surgery and finally accepted that they
were about to lose Tom eased.

She lifted her face to this special man she'd loved
and lost, then, amazingly, had been blessed to love
again.

"Aye, I'll be your wife, Michael Joyce," she promised
as still more stars blazed and wheeled overhead. "For all
our lifetimes."

As they had for Tom's funeral, and Michael and
Erin's wedding, the entire village turned out for the
groundbreaking of the Sister Bernadette Mercy
Hospital. As Erin had predicted to Tom, it had taken a
great deal of argument on her part to keep the citizens
of Castlelough from naming it after the man who'd
meant so much to them. The late spring day had
dawned warm, the sun shining down on the building
site like a benediction.

The inevitable speeches were made, the ceremonial
shovels of dirt overturned. As Erin took her turn with
the spade, she heard the now familiar whir of Michael's
camera motor drive. His publisher had been so
impressed by his hospital photographs, they'd offered
him a generous contract to capture everyday life in
Castlelough. While she would have been perfectly
happy to be the wife of an Irish farmer, Erin was also
pleased that he'd found a way to return to the work
he'd once loved.

In the distance, sunlight glinted diamond-like off

the limestone cliffs that shone like white marble and the sea gleamed like endless sapphire. Nearer to Castlelough, Erin could see the lake. She and Michael had exchanged vows on the bank of Lough Caislean, in front of the ruins. The perfect day had also been blessed with sunshine and friends, and when her mother had told her that she'd never seen a bride look more beautiful, Erin had believed her because she'd discovered since coming to Ireland that love made any-thing—and everything—possible.

As she handed the spade over to the Greek shipping tycoon whose generosity had made all this possible, Erin caught a glimpse of a familiar man standing at the edge of the crowd. When Brady gave her a thumbs-up and a wink, Erin grinned back at her unconventional father-in-law.

No special Castlelough occasion could be complete without a *sean-nos* solo from Fergus, who, everyone would say later, was in fine form, his lyrical notes wheel-ing and soaring in the salt-tinged air like wild seabirds.

The ceremony concluded, Erin went over to gather up Shea, who was seated in the VIP stand with the rest of the family. Michael joined them, the Nikon around his neck making him look like the dashing photojour-nalist he'd once been. Photographer or farmer, tinker, tailor or candlestick maker, he'd always be dashing to her. And Erin would always be madly, deeply in love with him.

She wondered, as she had so many times in the past months, how it was that one person's life could be gifted with so many miracles.

"Something funny?" he asked as he idly skimmed a

hand through Shea's bright curls that were growing back in.

"I was just thinking how happy I was. And how much I love you."

"Believe me, darling, the feeling's mutual." He smiled down at her with his mouth and his eyes in a way that never failed to warm her heart. "So, would you be finished with your official duties?"

"All done." Erin understood the town's desire for a bit of pomp and ceremony, but she was looking forward to the day when the hospital would be built, and she could be working there, taking care of these people who had, in a short time, become so dear to her.

Even more appealing, she thought, as she watched the light in Michael's eyes darken with a familiar desire, was the idea of having his children in the planned intimate, cozy birthing center.

"Grand." He took Shea from her arms, put his daughter on his hip and slipped his other arm around his wife. "Then let's be going home."

Home. It was, Erin thought, as she made her way with her husband and daughter through the throng, a truly glorious word. Even now, months after their marriage, it still made her beam to think that after years spent traveling the globe, she'd finally found her own very special home with the forever love of her life.

Visit
❖ **Pocket Books** ❖
online at

....

www.SimonSays.com

....

Keep up on the latest new
releases from your favorite
authors, as well as author
appearances, news, chats,
special offers and more.

SIMON & SCHUSTER
A VIACOM COMPANY
www.SimonSays.com

Pocket
Books

2381-01